THE WARNING

Simon stood upon solid ground in the midst of billowing fog. A lone figure approached him from the distance, her long, full skirts flapping silently in the cold wind. He moved his right hand to rub his eyes and found to his distress that his hands were bound together at the wrist with heavy iron chain. He attempted to run, but his ankles were likewise shackled. He trembled with dread as the figure came forward, parting the fog before her like some demonic Moses.

"I can save thee," Gwendolyn said.

"G . . . Gwen? Is that you?" he stammered.

"There is yet time," she said. "I have given all I have, all I am, for thee. There is nothing for me without thee, my love. Nothing. Thou must live that thou mayest love me!"

Gwendolyn's face melted with a terrifying immediacy into a decaying death's head whose sole vestiges of humanity were the piercing green orbs which blazed from the naked eye sockets.

"But betray me, and I shall visit vengeance upon thee!"

CANDLEMAS EVE

by

JEFFREY SACKETT

BANTAM BOOKS
TORONTO · NEW YORK · LONDON · SYDNEY · AUCKLAND

CANDLEMAS EVE

A Bantam Book / May 1988

ACKNOWLEDGMENTS

"One Stage Before" by Al Stewart, copyright © 1976 Gwyneth
Music Ltd. All rights for U.S. and Canada controlled by Dick James
Music Inc. in care of PolyGram Music Publishing Companies, 810
Seventh Avenue, New York, New York, 10019. Used by permission.

"Be-Bop-A-Lula" by Gene Vincent and Tex Davis, copyright ©
1956 by Lowery Music Co., Inc., Atlanta, Ga. International
Copyright Secured. All Rights Reserved. Used by permission.

*"Pathfinder," "The Demon Lover," "Solstice Hymn," "Powers
Working," "Ballad of Abigail,"* and *"Candlemas Eve,"* by Jeffrey
Sackett. Copyright © 1987 by the author. Additional lyrics and
verses by Jeffrey Sackett, copyright © 1987 by the author.

"Thomas the Rhymer," "Shapechangers" (also known as *"The
Coal Black Smith"* and *"The Two Magicians"*), *"The Unquiet
Grave,"* and *"Pirate Chantey,"* all in the public domain.

"Roots of Oak" by Donovan Leitch. Copyright 1970 by Donovan
(Music) Ltd. International Copyright Secured. All Rights controlled
by Peer International Corporation. Used by permission.

ISBN 0-553-27068-0

Published simultaneously in the United States and Canada

PRINTED IN THE UNITED STATES OF AMERICA

KR   0 9 8 7 6 5 4 3 2

*This novel is dedicated to
my wife Paulette, the only
woman who ever truly bewitched me.*

Author's Note

Any reader interested in exploring the records of the events which transpired in Salem, Massachusetts, during the spring and summer of 1692 is urged to read Deodat Lawson's contemporary account, *A Brief and True Narrative of Witchcraft in Salem Village*, published in London in 1693 and available as a historical reprint in most large libraries. The original documents and records are housed in the county court archives in Essex County, Massachusetts. (Before you hop in your car and drive on over there, let me warn you that it is next to impossible to get permission to look at them.)

Any reader interested in other fiction regarding the events in Salem is urged, of course, to read or see Arthur Miller's classic drama, *The Crucible*. It was while teaching this play to high-school students that the idea for this novel first occurred to me. While I have taken pains to avoid being derivative, I nonetheless readily acknowledge my debt to this drama, even to the extent of accepting and perpetuating certain historical inaccuracies. I would like to make a special note of thanks to Marge Nelson, Joseph Granitto, and Norman Brust, who collectively hired me to teach at Kings Park High School. Had they not done so, I might never have taught Miller's plays.

Any reader interested in hearing old British folk songs arranged as rock and roll is urged to listen to any of the excellent records of the British rock group, Steeleye Span, in particular *Now We Are Six*.

Any reader who is offended by foul language, blasphemy, or sexual situations is urged to stop reading this book immediately. Please remember that the characters herein are not choirboys, and the situations herein are not Sunday school picnics. Any attempt to prettify modes of speech, patterns of behavior, or personalities would be unrealistic.

One more note:

If you happen to be a Satanist or serious witch, please do not read this book at all. It will offend you deeply, and I really do not need you people as enemies. I have enough problems at the moment.

J.S.

To understand witchcraft, we must descend into the darkness of the deepest oceans of the mind. In our efforts to avoid facing the realities of human evil, we have tamed the witch and made her comic, dressing her up in a peaked cap and setting her on a broom for the amusement of children at Hallowe'en. Thus made comic, she can easily be exorcised from our minds, and we can convince our children—and ourselves—that "there is no such thing as a witch." But there is, or at least there was. A phenomenon that for centuries gripped the minds of men from the most illiterate peasant to the most skilled philosopher or scientist, leading to torture and death for hundreds of thousands, is neither joke nor illusion.

—JEFFREY BURTON RUSSELL
Witchcraft in the Middle Ages

Blessed are all the simple emotions, be they dark or bright! It is the lurid intermixture of the two that produces the illuminating blaze of the infernal regions.

—NATHANIEL HAWTHORNE

And the Lord said unto Satan, Whence comest thou? And Satan answered the Lord and said, From going to and fro in the Earth.

—JOB 1:7

⟦ PROLOGUE ⟧
October 29

MARY WARREN SHIVERED slightly from both the cold and her own nervousness as she stood hidden in the darkness of the alleyway. She peered across the fog-shrouded street at the door of the tavern and heard the faint sounds of revelry and good cheer drift toward her, echoing from the cobblestones and then fading into the cold New England night. A hay wagon drawn by an old nag rolled noisily past her, and she moved back even farther into the darkness, grinning haughtily at the Puritan scowl which had been chiseled into the granite face of the old woman who drove the wagon. Mary's expression bespoke condescension and superiority, ridicule and dislike; and yet she withdrew farther into the alleyway. For most of her life she had lived in fear of such women, and the habitual shrinking back when in their presence asserted itself whenever she saw one of them.

"Old fool," she muttered. She stepped quietly forward to the edge of the alleyway and leaned out to watch the hay wagon move down the street. The loud rumbling of the wooden wheels on the cobblestones and the rhythmic clip-clop of the horse's hooves momentarily drowned out the sounds emanating from the tavern, and Mary neither saw nor heard the tavern door open as the two farmers left the inn and began to make their way home. By the time she noticed the two men ambling unsteadily down the street, they were already too far away for her to call out to them without attracting more attention to herself than she would wish. "Hell and damnation!" she muttered angrily. Mary pulled her shawl tight around her throat and returned her attention to the door of the tavern. It was just after midnight, and the town of Boston was covered by a blanket of darkness and fog so thick that Mary's eyes strained as she gazed across at the door. There were indeed certain areas of Boston which had street lights (actually little more than large candles in glass encasements), but this section of town, down by the wharves, remained unlighted. It was the opinion of the royal governor and the town magistracy that dock areas were breeding grounds for vice and corruption,

1

and they had no intention of encouraging nocturnal activitie by making them safer. The merchants and ship owners migh chafe under such decisions, but in the fall of the year 169: there was little they could do about it but grumble.

Mary started in anticipation as the tavern door opened and a portly, well-dressed middle-aged man walked out into the chilly night. He stood for a moment before the tavern and buttoned his long cloak. Mary walked out of the alleyway and moved to the edge of the street. "Good evening to you, good mister," she called out. "Why go you so early to your bed? The night is yet young."

The portly man peered myopically through the fog. "Who's there? Who speaks to me?"

She stepped into the street and ambled over to him, allowing her shawl to fall open and reveal her white throat. Her hips swayed as she walked, and she placed her hands upon them as she stopped a few feet away from the man. "My name is Mary," she said sweetly. "And how are you called, good mister?"

"What are you doing here alone at this time of night?" the man demanded, ignoring her question. "Why are you not home and in bed?"

"Truly, sir, 'tis home I'll be going very soon now," she said, moving slowly closer to the man. "But my bed, alas, is so cold and empty! It wants warming." She placed her hand softly upon the man's cheek. "Though my body is warm, very warm, yet my bed is too large for me to warm it alone."

The man grabbed her hand and thrust it away from him. "Have you no shame, girl?"

"Indeed, sir, I have shame. I have a flood of shame, I dwell in shame, I live for shame." She smiled and licked her lips. "Would you not take pleasure in shaming me with your flood?"

The portly man sputtered, dumbfounded. "Do you know who I am, girl?"

She leaned her head to one side. "I hope you are a man who will shame me."

"I am the Reverend Josiah Witherspoon! And you are a whore!"

"A minister?" she said calmly. "Then we have much in common, sir, for your livelihood depends upon sin, and my livelihood depends upon sin."

"You brazen—you—you—!" He grabbed her by the wrist and began dragging her down the street. "We'll see what the magistrate has to say to you, you little harlot!"

2

Mary clamped her teeth down hard upon his hand, and he released her with a cry of pain. She ran across the street and disappeared once again into the alleyway. The minister ran after her, his ample stomach bouncing in time to his gait, but he stopped before the alleyway and squinted his eyes in an attempt to see into the darkness. "Come out here, girl!" he commanded, but neither sound nor movement reached him from the blackness. "Come out here, I say!" He stepped back into the street. "Yes, yes, I understand. I am supposed to pursue you into the dark so your friends can rob and murder me. Well, I am not such a fool, harlot." He turned and began to stomp angrily away. As if his divine office occurred to him as an afterthought, he turned and called out, "God have mercy on you."

Mary Warren waited a long while, listening as his footsteps grew increasingly faint and then became inaudible. She stepped warily forward to the edge of the alleyway and looked down the street. She released a sigh of relief. "Damn all ministers," she muttered, "and damn all fat, ugly old men." She heard the clipping of wooden heels upon the cobblestones and drew back into the darkness. She waited nervously as the footsteps grew louder and closer. If the minister was returning with a magistrate, she could do nothing but run and hope that she was faster than they.

"Mary!" she heard a voice whisper. "Mary! Where are you?"

"Abby!" she said as she walked out into the street. "You frightened me! I thought you were a minister or a magistrate!"

Abigail Williams laughed. "A minister or a magistrate! By God, Mary Warren, you know me better than that!"

"Aye, but a footstep is a footstep in the darkness," she said. "I just approached a minister a moment ago, and he tried to bring me to the magistrate. I thought you might be one of them, coming back for me."

"Sorry." Abby shrugged.

"And why are you here?" Mary asked. "I thought we had agreed that you would go to the warehouses and I would stay by the wharves."

"Aye, but there is no one there! I wandered about for over two hours, and saw naught but rats."

"Did you wait by the taverns?"

"They are all closed, shut up as if it were Sunday! In truth, Mary, I'll not ply my trade there again. And it is getting late, and we need a man before morning."

"I know, I know. It has been a sparse night for me also,"

3

Mary sighed as she leaned against the wall of the alleyway. " had but three this whole evening, and none were rich."

"How much did you make?"

"Twelve shillings."

Abby sighed and brushed some dirt from her skirt. " 'Ti twelve shillings more than I've earned this night."

"Abby, look." Mary pointed at the tavern door and Abigail followed the direction of her finger. The door had been opened, and a husky young man was walking out into the street. His hair was long and full, pulled back into a ponytail and tied with a blue ribbon. Even at that distance and through the fog the girls could see the rich brocade upon his waistcoat and the slight glimmering sheen of the silk stockings which covered his calves. "He's perfect," Mary whispered. "Young, strong—"

"Perfect or not, he'll do," Abigail replied. She walked out into the street and drew her shawl from her head, allowing her rich black hair to fall freely about her shoulders. "Good evening to you, sir," she said cheerfully. " 'Tis a cold night, is it not?"

The young man turned in the direction of her voice and regarded her with amusement. "Aye, it is that."

Mary walked forward and stood beside Abigail. "My name is Mary, and this is my friend, Abby. We've been seeking all night some means of warmth, good sir. Can you help us?"

A confident smile spread over the young man's face as he looked at the two girls. The one who called herself Mary seemed twenty years old; the other girl, Abby, a few years older, but not more than twenty-five. Mary was thin but in a willowy fashion, not sickly or wiry like so many of these colonial farm girls. Her brown hair was cut short, but curled around her ears and neck. She had the plain honest face of a good Puritan, but it was soft and warm, not hard and cold. The other girl's hair was long and luxuriant, and her figure was full and curvaceous. Her large eyes glinted above high cheek-bones, and her full lips glistened in the moonlight. "Some means of warmth," he said. "What, shall I buy you rum or brandy?"

"Nay, sir, for we have drink of our own," Abigail replied. "The warmth we seek comes not from the cup."

"Are you from England?" Mary asked. "You speak not as we in New England speak."

"Yes, dear girl," the young man said, stepping onto the cobblestones and approaching the two girls. "I am from London. I am the Marquis of Stonehampton."

4

"A lord!" Abigail gushed. "I've never met a lord! Are you very, very rich?"

The Marquis laughed. "Rich enough, Abby, rich enough."

Mary placed her hands upon his arm and leaned slightly against him. "Then truly, sir, you will help two poor girls, will you not?"

"Help you in what way?" he asked. He was playing with them, enjoying the banter and the game. "Do you need lodgings?"

"Nay, sir, we have rooms not far from here."

"Yes, yes, I'm sure you do. Food, then. Are you hungry?"

"Aye, sir, we are," Abigail said, taking his other arm, "but it is not food for which we hunger."

"Well, then, how can I help you?" he laughed.

"If you please, sir," Mary said, "our bed is too large for the two of us, and we cannot together make it warm."

"Aye, sir," Abby chimed in, "there is always a cold spot in the middle between us, and it discomforts us both."

"What a pity," the Marquis said sympathetically. "You poor things!" He put one arm around Mary's waist and the other around Abigail's. "Show me where this bed is and I'll warm the center for you."

"You are kind, my lord," Abby smiled.

"And generous, I hope," Mary said sweetly.

"Ah, yes, my dear girls," he said as they began to walk down the street, "my generosity is renowned on two continents. In England too I have had the privilege of warming ladies' beds, and paid for the honor." He looked at Mary with condescending amusement. "And what does a gentleman pay for this honor in Boston?"

Mary and Abigail exchanged quick glances. "Three shillings?" Mary suggested.

"Each?" Abigail added hopefully.

"A modest fee for so great an honor," the Marquis laughed. The girls laughed as well and continued their coquettish conversation all the way to the old abandoned blacksmith shop which they had made their home. When the young Englishman saw the ramshackle structure, he frowned slightly. "And is this where you keep your bed, my dear girls? It has a very unpleasant appearance."

"We are but two poor girls without money," Mary said with mock sorrow, "and can afford no better."

"But it is pleasant within," Abigail added quickly, fearing that he might change his mind at the last moment. She took his hand and placed it upon her belly. "And so are we, my lord."

5

The Marquis smiled at her and laughed slightly. "Indeed I'm sure you are, my dears. Come, let us see what awaits, eh within." The girls giggled and pulled him forward, one on each arm. Abby lifted the outer latch of the abandoned shop, and they entered eagerly.

Mary Warren turned up the oil lamp which had been burning dimly upon the oak table which stood in the midst of the room, and the flame brightly illuminated the interior of the shop. She immediately turned down the lamp so that the light was less glaring and the old shop made more pleasing to the eye. But the flame still burned brightly enough for the Marquis to be able to view his surroundings with distaste, brightly enough for Mary and Abigail to see the distaste expressed clearly upon his face. "Pardon our poverty, my lord," Abigail hastened to say. "We make do as best we can, two poor girls shifting for ourselves in this cruel city."

"And yet our sheets are clean," Mary added, "and our mattress stuffed full with fresh straw."

"Fresh straw," he said with amusement. "How delightful! Feathers are just so uncomfortable!"

"Please, my lord, do not laugh at us," Mary said mournfully. "We are—"

"Yes, yes, I know," he said, not unkindly. "Just two poor girls getting on as best you can." They smiled up at him, and he allowed his gaze to drift lazily over the room. The unfinished wood which was the structure's major component element was dull and unreflective, and it lent an air of gloom to the starkness of the interior. A large mattress lay upon the floor in one corner, and a small table upon which stood a wooden cross rested against the far wall. But for the larger table upon which the oil lamp burned, there were no other furnishings. An old wooden trunk, which could hardly be called a piece of furniture, rested upon the floor next to the entrance. "How charming," the Marquis said blandly.

"'Twas not the charms of the house you've come to explore, my lord," Abigail said invitingly.

"Aye, good sir," Mary added. "Ignore the room." She tossed her shawl onto the floor and allowed her brown cloak to drop down about her feet. She deftly unbuttoned the simple green dress she wore and pulled it down, allowing it to fall upon the discarded cloak. She smiled sweetly at the Marquis. She had been naked beneath her dress.

The young Englishman returned her smile. "No wonder you were so cold, my dear Mary! Do you make it a custom to go about so unprotected?"

6

"Unprotected, but always prepared," she said softly. Mary stepped over the pile of clothes and walked over to the Marquis. She stood before him and snaked her arms up around his neck, pulling his mouth down to hers as she stood on tiptoe to reach up to him. He felt a familiar and delightful tingling in his organ as he allowed his hands to move over her muscular buttocks, her flat belly, her small, firm breasts.

Mary pushed him away gently and walked over to the mattress. She sat down upon it with a grace which surprised the young Englishman, and then removed her shoes and stockings. The Marquis turned to Abigail and asked, "And your charms, dear Abby? May I not explore them as well?"

"Indeed, my lord, indeed you may," she smiled. She removed her cloak and placed it upon the old wooden trunk. She wore a white blouse tucked into a gray skirt, and she unbuttoned and removed the skirt first. She then pulled the blouse over her head, revealing to the delighted Marquis her large breasts which seemed to spill over the half-corset which snugly embraced her waist. Her stockings came up to mid-thigh and were held up by two tightly tied red ribbons. She also wore no other undergarments. "And are my charms adequate for my lord's pleasure?" she asked.

"Adequate for more than one man, my dear," he laughed as he reached out and took one large breast in each hand. Abigail clasped her hands behind her head as he caressed her bosom, and she purred softly and swayed her hips back and forth.

The Marquis reached into his waistcoat pocket and drew forth a few coins. He tossed them onto the table and then said, "Come, my dears, attend me."

Mary rose from the mattress and joined Abigail in the process of removing the young Englishman's clothing. None of them spoke as the layers of silk and wool were removed, but the girls giggled slightly when his erect penis throbbed out as his trousers were pulled down. "In truth, my lord," Abby said, "'tis a fortunate thing that there are two of us!"

"Are all men from the old country such stallions, such bulls?" Mary asked. "The girth of your spear almost frightens me!" She dropped to her knees before him and took his penis into her mouth, allowing her saliva to mitigate the friction of her lips.

"Such kind words and actions!" the Marquis said, grinning. "I have been told that I am blessed with an unusual endowment."

"'Tis we who are blessed, good my lord," Abby said

7

gratefully as she knelt down beside Mary. They took turns sucking on his organ, stopping only briefly to kiss each other. Abby looked up at the Marquis. "Whom shall you take first, my lord, Mary or me?"

The young man's brow furrowed as he considered his decision. "Um . . . Mary, I think."

"Then allow me to prepare her, my lord," Abby smiled. She rose to her feet and took Mary's hand. Mary stood up and they went over to the mattress. Mary lay down upon her back and spread her legs wide apart as Abigail lay down in front of her and placed her face upon the velvety triangle between Mary's thighs. Mary moaned and quivered as Abigail's tongue insinuated itself into her vagina and flicked upon the hardening button of her clitoris. Mary began to massage her own breasts, pinching the nipples slightly, her eyes closed in an ecstasy so realistic that the Marquis could not tell if it was feigned or honest. All whores pretend enjoyment; this he knew. But seldom had he seen any who were so convincing.

"Mary is ready for you, my lord," Abigail said sweetly. The Marquis sat down upon the bed beside Mary and leaned down to kiss her. Her mouth was warm and wet, and she gently grasped his penis and began to rub it. He lay down upon her and she pulled her legs upward at the knees, opening herself to him. He placed the tip of his manhood against the cleft of her womb and drove it home. She gasped as his penis began to move in and out of her, as his mouth sought hers and his hands pushed her wrists back upon the mattress. She writhed beneath him as each stroke seemed to drive deeper and deeper into her.

Abigail lay down beside them and began to kiss Mary's lips gently. The Marquis leaned over as Abigail cupped her breasts and offered them to him, and he began to lick and then suck greedily upon her nipples, all the while continuing to slide in and out of Mary.

"Has my lord ever watched the horses and the cattle?" Abigail asked. "They take their females from behind."

"So they do, so they do." The Marquis grinned. "Shall we emulate them?"

Abigail seemed to blush slightly as the Marquis removed his organ from Mary and Mary moved backward into a sitting position, her legs still spread wide apart, the lips of her vagina glistening in the dim lamplight. Abigail moved in front of her and waited on her hands and knees as the Englishman mounted her, and then as he began to thrust in and out, she leaned down and began again to lick on Mary's opened tunnel.

"Such whores," he muttered, " . . . in Boston, of all places—"

"Oh, my lord!" Abigail gasped, "my lord, my lord! You are rending me!"

"Just a little time, my dearest Abby," he gasped. "Just a little time longer."

"But hold, my lord," Mary said, her voice seeming to quiver as if she were swooning. "Not yet, not yet. Give my mouth the pleasure of pleasing you."

The Marquis withdrew from Abigail and lay down upon the mattress as Mary slid down from her position against the wall. He moved into the center of the bed and Abigail lay down beside him, kissing him as he fondled her ample breasts. Mary took his penis into her mouth and began to move up and down rapidly, one hand embracing the shaft while the other gently massaged his testicles. "Oh, Mary!" he moaned. "You delightful little whore!"

Abigail Williams slid her hand beneath the mattress and grasped the hilt of the dagger.

"Oh, yes! Yes!" the Marquis cried as his manhood began to spurt its fluid into Mary's greedy mouth. "Yes! Yes!"

Abigail smiled at him as she deftly thrust the blade into his throat. He returned the smile for but a moment, and then confusion and panic mingled on his face as the pain registered and the hot purple blood began to gush forth from his severed artery. The Marquis attempted with pathetic futility to repress the sanguine flood with his trembling hands. The two women rose to their feet and looked down at him with amusement as his quivering body continued to eject its life's blood in a pulsing stream.

Abigail went to the table and took two pewter cups from its surface. She handed one to Mary Warren, who proceeded to spit the Marquis's semen into it. Abigail knelt down and caught some of the still-spurting blood in the other cup. They then turned their backs on the dying man, whose tremors grew less and less violent with every passing moment, whose bloody fountain seemed to grow weaker and weaker, who was soon lying still upon the blood-soaked mattress, his eyes staring madly, lifelessly at the ceiling.

Abigail and Mary knelt before the smaller of the two tables, the one upon which stood a simple wooden cross. Abigail pulled the cross out of the notch into which the base of the cross had been secured and turned it upside down. She then pushed the inverted cross back into the notch so that the small crossbeam rested a few inches above the table. Mary took the cup with the blood in it and poured the contents into the other cup. The blood and semen mingled as Mary slowly and carefully moved the cup around in a circular motion. She placed the cup upon the small table before the inverted cross and then nodded to Abigail.

Abigail and Mary knelt in silence for a few moments, and then Abigail chanted, "*Ave Satanas!*"

"*Ave Satanas!*" Mary responded.

"*Diabolus tecum.*"

"*Et cum spiritu tuo.*"

They began to chant in unison. "*Malo a nos libera sed tentationem in inducas nos ne et nostris debitoribus dimittimus nos et sicut nostra debita nobis dimitte et hodie nobis da quotidianum nostrum panem terra in et caelo in sicut tua voluntas fiat tuum regnum adveniat tuum nomen sanctificetur caelis in es qui noster pater.*"

Having spoken the Lord's Prayer backward as the ritual demanded, Abigail elevated the cup and said, "Hail, Satan, father of lies, fountainhead of evil, master of this world. We come before you in supplication, we come before you in worship and in awe."

Abigail sipped from the cup, her face a frozen mask of reverence. If she was at all repelled by the mixture, it did not show in her expression. She handed the cup to Mary.

Mary elevated the cup in turn. "Hail, Satan, ruler of hell, giver of power, lord of the flesh. We come before you in supplication, we come before you in worship and in awe." Mary sipped from the cup and then placed it upon the table.

The two women clasped their hands before them and inclined their heads, their eyes closing as their lips began to move in silent prayer. After a few moments, Abigail Williams looked up at the inverted cross and chanted, "All that I am, I offer to you."

Mary responded to the chant. "All that I am, I offer to you."

"Strike down mine enemies and confound their desires."

"All that I am, I offer to you."

"Reduce them to ashes and torment their flesh."

"All that I am, I offer to you."

"Burn them with sulfur and rend them with knives."

"All that I am, I offer to you."

"Grant thou my boon, thou master of hell."

"*Ave Satanas, gratia vacuus.*"

"Inflame thou my lusts, thou lord of the flies."

"*Ave Satanas, gratia vacuus.*"

"Praise to thee, Lucifer! Praise to thee, Lucifer!"

"*Ave Satanas, gratia vacuus.*"

"All hail Beelzebub, Mephistopheles hail!"

"*Ave Satanas, gratia vacuus.*"

"*Ave Satanas!*"

"*Ave Satanas!*"

They fell silent once again, their worship ceremony at an end. After a few moments Abigail rose to her feet and began to dress, and Mary watched her, an expression mingling love and pity upon her face. Then she too arose and proceeded to clothe herself. Mary glanced at the corpse which lay upon the blood-soaked mattress. "Where shall we lay him? Shall we burn him?"

Abigail shook her head. "No. No need. We'll bundle him in a blanket and leave him near the potter's field. Let the magistrates attend to him."

Mary reached down to fasten the buckles of her shoes. "What did you ask for, Abby?"

"Hmmm?" Abigail was tucking her blouse into her skirt.

"Did you ask for the same thing?"

Abigail Williams sighed. "Aye. Always the same thing."

Mary shook her head sadly. "Abby—" she began.

"I know, Mary Warren!" Abigail snapped. " 'Tis purposeless to repeat yourself."

"But he's dead, Abby! He's dead!"

"Aye, and who is master of the dead, and who can grant my prayer?"

Mary shook her head again. "Abby, 'tis foolishness."

Abigail spun angrily on her. "And are your prayers so wise and learned? Who are you to criticize my prayers!" Her anger was beginning to mingle with sorrow, and both were clearly visible on her face.

Mary walked over to her and took her hands gently in hers. "You know I love you more than a sister, Abby. You *know* that. I meant no unkindness."

Abigail sniffed back a tear and tried to smile, though her anger was far from quieted. "I know, Mary."

"I just don't wish to see you keep alive a flame which does naught but burn you. He's dead, Abby. John Proctor is dead. If his soul is in God's hands, God will not release him to you. If he is in Hell, will the Master release him to you? Has the Master *ever* released a soul firmly in his keeping?"

Abigail shrugged defensively. "I know not, and neither do you."

11

"You know as well as I, Abby. The prayer is futile. Why do you continue to ask?"

"Because I love him, Mary! I love him more than anything else in the world!"

"You *loved* him, Abby, you *loved* him! He's been dead for over six years. The hangings at Salem were over six years ago!"

"Six years or sixty, it makes no difference. I want my love back; I want John." Abigail gazed at the inverted cross. "And some day, somehow, the Dark Lord will give him to me."

The images of the two women seemed to freeze.

The stage director in the control booth waited for the audience to applaud. They did not.

The television screen went black. The house lights rose in the studio.

Turning to the studio audience, Percy Campbell said, "We've just been watching part of the soon-to-be-released film, *Satanists of Salem*, starring Laura MacDonald and Patricia Nelson, produced by one of today's guests, Mr. Simon Proctor. We'll be talking to Simon and our other guests after these messages."

I

ALL HALLOWS' EVE

For what is a man profited, if he shall gain
the whole world, and shall lose his own
soul?

—MATTHEW 16:26

⟦ CHAPTER ONE ⟧

October 29, continued

PERCY CAMPBELL ATTEMPTED to look serious as he gazed out over the packed studio, trying not visibly to revel in the popularity and success which his daily televised sensationalism continued to yield. The issue of witchcraft and devil worship in popular culture was a serious one, and it would be unseemly for him to appear as gleeful as he felt. He enjoyed pretending that he was a journalist and that his talk show had something to do with an exploration of contemporary issues, and so he had adopted a grim and rather disturbed expression as he waited for the director's signal.

When the director indicated to him that the taping had stopped, Campbell rose from the plush seat he was occupying behind the Formica desk on the right side of the stage and walked forward toward the audience. "Needless to say, we will not be broadcasting the entire film clip as you just saw it." A wave of nervous laughter rippled through the studio. "I figured that since we're going to be discussing some pretty serious issues on today's show, I owed it to you to make sure you knew exactly what we were talking about."

Campbell's face maintained its very concerned expression. "I apologize if any of you were offended by what you just saw. Rest assured, we'll edit out most of the sex and optically censor the rest of it. I do have a contract to live up to, after all." A brief smile and more nervous laughter. "I'm sure you know that I'd find myself unemployed and unemployable if we didn't clean up that film clip a good deal before this show airs on Thursday."

Campbell walked down the stage steps and stood silent for a moment. The boom mike did not follow him, for his words were not for the home audience. "I know that many of you are a little disgusted by what you just saw, but I warned you, didn't I?" A few more laughs joined mutters of agreement. "Okay, if the ushers would ask the folks out in the lobby to come back in?" He grinned at the audience. "I had to give you fair warning and a chance to leave during the film clip, or else I would have been lynched by now." A few more laughs.

14

Campbell could tell that the audience had been neither amused nor entertained by what they had just seen. Rather, they had watched it with the morbid fascination one exhibits upon seeing a serious traffic accident.

People began to enter the studio and soft bits of conversation reached the stage from the audience section. Campbell heard the words "revolting" and "disgusting" and "perverted," and he grinned. Can't say I haven't gotten the audience involved, he thought to himself. As the last of the people who had elected not to view the film clip found their seats, Campbell said, "Okay? Everybody ready?"

He resumed his place behind the desk on the stage and smiled at the audience. "One of the many advantages of taping shows in advance is that we can take fifteen minutes off during a three-minute commercial slot." A few desultory laughs. The stage director moved into Campbell's view and held out four fingers, then three, then two, then one, then pointed at the stage as the green lights in the studio turned to red.

"Welcome back to the *Percy Campbell Show*," he said into the camera. "Let me welcome my guests. . . ." He nodded to each of the people seated on the stage in turn. "Mrs. Barbara Wilkinson of the Concerned Parents' Alliance. . . ."

Mrs. Wilkinson smiled slightly and nodded a greeting in the direction of the camera, her rather plump face a bit shiny under the glare of the studio lights. Her hair was pulled back and tied into a rather severe bun, the streaks of gray standing out starkly against the fading, lackluster brown. The simple blue and white print dress she wore dropped its hem just below her knees, which were pressed together as if held in place by cement. She radiated propriety, primness, austerity, and an unforgiving, uncompromising mediocrity.

"Father Joseph Scotto, director of the Youth Services Division of the Archdiocese of New York. . . ."

The priest shot a curt nod at the camera, an almost impatient gesture of acknowledgment. He wore the traditional Roman collar and jet black suit, which made his bushy gray eyebrows and massively curled white hair all the more distinct by contrast. His thin lips were straight and hard amid the lines of his aged, craggy face, and seemed to threaten a scowl at any moment.

"Professor Ludwig Eisenmann of the anthropology and history departments of New York University. . . ."

The middle-aged Austrian grinned boyishly and said "Hello!" in a cheerful and eager manner. The small bow tie

15

with which he fiddled nervously accentuated the round and protuberant belly which obscured the buckle of his belt. H round, florid face and abundant brown hair combined with hi girth to present an image of robust if corpulent energy.

"Mr. Simon Proctor, well-known rock singer, self proclaimed warlock and Satanist, and the producer of the film we just saw. . . ."

Simon Proctor turned his steely eyes slowly toward the camera. He neither smiled, nodded, nor spoke. His jet black hair cascaded in long, luxuriant waves down about his neck and shoulders, forming a continuous, unbroken image of darkness as it merged with his black sports coat, his black turtlenecked sweater, and his black trousers which flared slightly outward at the tops of his black boots. Only the inverted silver crosses which dangled from his left ear and from the silver chain about his neck interrupted the blackness His face was thin and pale, resolving itself into a wispy black goatee. His cheeks were high and sunken, his eyes set deep beneath thin black eyebrows. He stared placidly into the camera.

Percy Campbell's ruddy, freckled face grinned happily at his guests as he said, "I'd like to thank you all for coming here today to share your views and concerns with us." The woman and the professor muttered thank-yous. The priest and the warlock sat immobile.

Campbell turned his face to the camera. "Most of us have heard in recent years about the sudden rash of rock music with Satanist and witchcraft themes. A recent congressional hearing dealt with the proposal from a parents' group that lyrics be rated, and some people have gone so far as to suggest outright censorship."

Campbell frowned slightly to emphasize the seriousness of the topic. "There have been crimes in many parts of the country, crimes committed by teenagers and even by pre-teens—murders, assaults, and mutilations—which some local police officials have suggested are connected with satanism and witchcraft. One such crime was committed in the town of Northport, Long Island, where Mrs. Wilkinson lives."

Campbell turned to his guests and said, "We expect to hear a variety of views from you today, and I hope we will be able to clear the air somewhat. I'd like to begin with a question for Mr. Proctor."

Simon Proctor nodded impassively.

Campbell tapped his pencil contemplatively upon his desk,

is brow furrowed in thought. Then he asked, "How did this witchcraft fad get started, anyway? What's its attraction for the kids? Why is there so much of it in recent rock and roll music?"

"Just a moment, Percy," Father Scotto broke in before Simon could utter a single word. The priest leaned forward, his bushy eyebrows knitting into a frown of outrage. "I wish to make it very clear to the audience and to you that I take the greatest exception to the showing of that film clip."

"So do I," Mrs. Wilkinson agreed. "I resent being misled into thinking that I'd be doing something to fight this sort of thing only to find myself on a program which is publicizing it."

"We want to stop the production of this kind of garbage, not be part of its publicity!" The elderly priest was flushed with anger.

"Wait a minute, here," Percy Campbell said quickly. "We want a frank and open discussion of this topic, and I felt obligated to give the audience—"

"You feel obligated to keep your ratings high, and you'll pander to whatever base instincts you must in order to do so."

Mrs. Wilkinson nodded. "It's disgraceful, Percy, simply disgraceful." The middle-aged historian sitting beside her chuckled with amusement, and she flashed her eyes at him angrily. "This is not a joke, Professor Eisenmann!"

"No, no, of course not," he agreed politely, nervously adjusting his bow tie.

"Folks, I'm sorry if there's been any misunderstanding of my motives, my purposes here," Campbell said earnestly. "I'm a parent, just like you are—" The priest raised his eyebrows. "—like most of you are, I mean, and I'm as concerned about the potential for danger in this fad as any other parent is. I think we should return to the topic and examine—"

"This *is* the topic!" Father Scotto said emphatically. "By giving publicity to this film, by putting this—person in the public eye"—he gestured contemptuously in the direction of Simon Proctor—"you are part of a system which both encourages and propagates this type of dangerous, antisocial perversity."

"The people who produce these things do so to make money, regardless of who gets hurt," Mrs. Wilkinson said. "You're showing that film clip for the same reason. I know you aren't a Satanist, and I'll wager that this person"—another gesture toward Simon—"isn't one either. But he's after a buck, and he'll do anything to get it, even destroy young lives and spread moral degeneration. And you are helping him do it. And I resent being made part of it."

17

Campbell seemed to wither under the verbal assault, and he moved instinctively to divert attention from himself. "Simon would you like to respond to any of this?"

Simon Proctor was sitting casually, his hands folded rathe primly in his lap. He reached up and slowly, almost languidly stroked the pointed tip of his goatee. Then, his voice projecting boredom and disinterest in its bass resonance, he said, "You asked me a moment ago how this 'fad' got started Let's clear up that point. Satanism is not a fad, like pink hair or platform shoes. It is a religion, like Buddhism or Catholicism." He looked pointedly at Father Scotto, who snorted his annoyance. "In fact, it's older than either of those religions, or any of the conventional religions." He nodded deferentially in the direction of Eisenmann. "I'm quite certain that the good Professor will bear me out in this. Satanism is really an improper, incorrect name for the faith. It's a system of worship and reverence for the forces of nature and the intelligence of the physical world, a system of thought and practice going back to the dawn of civilization."

"Are you seriously trying to say that sexual perversion and cold-blooded murder are forms of reverence for natural forces?!" Mrs. Wilkinson exclaimed. "That's the most ridiculous thing I've ever heard!"

Simon ignored her. "We give to the being which dominates the physical world the name 'Satan' because of a reaction against the hypocrisy and neurotic moralism of the Christians, but our Master has been known by many other names in many other lands throughout time."

"Oh, this is nonsense!" Father Scotto snapped. "And it's beside the point as well. We aren't here to allow this person to parade his money-making schemes around as if they were religions! We've come here to voice our concerns and to warn your viewers, Percy, about the violence and the perversity which this type of thing encourages."

"Precisely," Mrs. Wilkinson added, nodding emphatically. "This man isn't a Satanist at all, and the garbage he spews out isn't religion. He sees a way to make money, and he doesn't care how many poor children he destroys in the process." She harrumphed. "Why, he's no better than a pornographer!"

"Attacks upon my sincerity and my morality are nothing new to me," Simon said easily, languidly scratching his cheek. "In fact, they are common weapons in assaults upon all minority religious groups."

18

"Oh, this is absurd!" Father Scotto said. "We are not talking bout a religion! We are talking about a business!"

"Professor Eisenmann." Campbell turned to the portly cholar. "You've been pretty quiet during all this. How do you eact to Simon's claim that this is his religion, that he has a ight to practice it openly and freely?"

Eisenmann cleared his throat and again fussed with his bow ie. "Well, Percy, I am neither a parent nor a priest, so I don't ave too much to say about the, ah, moral or social issues nvolved."

"Oh, come now, Professor!" the priest said. "Surely you nust have a reaction to the sort of thing we just saw on the creen!"

"Oh, yes, certainly, of course I do. But I do not confuse a gut eaction with an opinion." He turned to Campbell and asked, "'Gut reaction' is the proper phrase, yes?"

"Yes, that's it." Campbell nodded.

"Ja, good." He turned back to Father Scotto. "Here in America a common idea is that all people must have an opinion on each subject, no matter how little he knows about it or how little he has to do with it. In Austria it is not so."

"Everyone knows right from wrong," Mrs. Wilkinson said angrily. "Almost everyone, anyway." She glanced at Simon, who smiled.

"Right and wrong are matters of opinion," Eisenmann said, "but historical fact and historical falsehood are not." He turned to Simon Proctor. "I'm sorry, Mr. Proctor, but your assertion that your religion is somehow connected to ancient nature worship or even medieval satanism is not tenable. Your film itself, from what I have seen of it here today, is filled with inaccuracies, distortions, and errors."

SHUT UP! Simon's thoughts screamed, but he held his tongue.

"What kind of errors are you referring to, Professor?" Campbell asked.

"Well, for example, the human sacrifice. Totally imaginary within the context of worship of the Devil."

"I beg your pardon, Professor," Simon said quickly. "As you well know, human sacrifice has been a part of religious ritual for thousands of years, since before—"

Eisenmann raised his hand to silence him. "No, no, you do not understand. When human sacrifice occurs in history, it occurs either as a regular practice in agricultural communities and is connected with the revitalization of the fields, or else it

19

is an aberration in times of great stress, such as the Puni[c] sacrifices at the time of the Roman siege of Carthage durin[g] the Third Punic War."

SHUT UP, GODDAMN IT! Simon's thoughts repeated[.] STOP IT!

"There were also fertility cults as well, of course. Th[e] connection between sexuality, birth, and death has long been [a] part of religious thought. But mixing human blood and seme[n] in a satanic parody of the Mass? Ridiculous. No tradition fo[r] that whatsoever."

"Uh-huh. Uh-huh." Campbell nodded. "So you're sayin[g] that there are no real Satanists nowadays, that Simon ha[s] concocted this whole thing?"

"No, I'm not saying that. If he believes in what he does, then I suppose we can call it a religion. What I am saying i[s] that what I have seen today has nothing to do with witchcraf[t] or satanism as it has been traditionally practiced and under-stood."

"You are a European, Professor, not an American," Simon pointed out defensively. "You are not familiar with the practices of the New England witches."

"Again, I'm sorry, Mr. Proctor, but that is incorrect. I have researched myth and ritual in all areas of the world, New England included. There is very little that you or anyone else can tell me about the events in your Salem during the late seventeenth century." He turned to Campbell. "You might have mentioned in introducing me that my academic speciali-zation is comparative religion."

"Oh, didn't I do that?" Campbell seemed surprised. "I'm terribly sorry, I thought I had."

"Well, no matter." He turned again to Simon. "New England or old England, it makes no difference. The inhabit-ants of Salem in 1692 were Europeans, English people, and their customs and traditions were European customs and traditions, and that would include whatever form of witchcraft they practiced." He paused. "If they truly did, any of them. That is still a hotly debated issue."

"Since the subject has come up," Campbell said, turning to Simon, "you have a personal connection with those trials, don't you, Simon?"

"Yes," he nodded gravely. "I am the direct lineal descendant of John Proctor, a warlock killed by the authorities in Salem. He was hanged in 1692. Even then, you see"—he glanced at Mrs. Wilkinson and Father Scotto—"we followers of the old ways were persecuted."

20

"Ah-h-h-h, Mr. Proctor," Eisenmann said, wagging his finger, "you're at it again!"

"Are you saying that this isn't true, Professor?" Campbell asked.

"About his ancestry?" Eisenmann shrugged. "I have no knowledge of that, of course. And there was a John Proctor hanged as a witch during the Salem trials. But he was definitely not a witch."

"Just a moment—!" Simon said.

"I'm sorry, sir, but if you are descended from John Proctor, then you are not descended from a practitioner of witchcraft, but from a victim of ignorance."

"I think I know my own family history better than you do!" Simon said heatedly.

Eisenmann shrugged. "Be that as it may"—he turned to the talk show host—"John Proctor was married to a woman named Elizabeth. Their maid was a girl named Mary Warren—"

"Like in the film?" Campbell asked.

"Yes. He had an affair with another girl of the village, Abigail Williams, whose name was also used in the film. Abigail denounced Elizabeth Proctor as a witch and coerced Mary into supporting her accusation, in the hopes of sending Mrs. Proctor to the gallows so that Abigail could have John all to herself. The scheme became all tangled up in the events of the day in Salem, and it was John Proctor who was hanged for witchcraft, not Elizabeth." He looked at Simon. "But John Proctor was most definitely not guilty of witchcraft."

YOU SON OF A BITCH, SHUT THE HELL UP! Simon thought.

"In addition, I would like to point out that the people of Salem, Massachusetts, were Puritan Calvinists, related to your current-day Congregationalists or Presbyterians. And yet in your film, Mr. Proctor, you have them conducting a satanic ritual which parodies the Roman Catholic Mass." He laughed heartily. "'*Ave Satanas, gratia vacuus*.'" He laughed again. "It's downright silly!"

I'VE GOT TWO MILLION DOLLARS INVESTED IN THIS FILM! I'M MORTGAGED TO THE HILT BECAUSE OF THIS FILM! SHUT UP, GODDAMN IT, SHUT UP!

"So you're saying that this film is not the historically based production which the advertisements say it is?" Campbell asked.

"Oh, well, somebody did a little research, to be sure." The

21

professor shrugged. "The rumors had it that Abigail William
did turn up later as a prostitute in Boston—not Mary Warre
though—and of course the connection with John Proctor
based in fact. But the impression I get is that the film is on
part history and five parts fantasy."

"In other words," Mrs. Wilkinson said with satisfaction, "it
entertainment!"

"In a word, yes," Eisenmann agreed.

"We can debate these matters of opinion all we want—
Simon began.

"They are not matters of opinion, Mr. Proctor; they ar
matters of fact. John Proctor was not a witch, the ritual a
portrayed in the film clip is not legitimate satanic ritual, an
witchcraft in seventeenth-century Salem is totally unrelated t
the nonsense in the film." Eisenmann's tone combined pom
posity with absolute certainty.

"Hold on!" Simon snapped, his agitation becoming eviden
"The rituals used in the film, as well as the rituals we use in ou
own worship, are taken from an ancient text, the *Caerimonia
Stupri Mortisque*, the Ceremonies of Debauchery and Death

"Ah, yes, the *Caerimoniae*," the professor nodded, smiling
"A collection of foolishness concocted by an early nineteent
century, self-proclaimed druid in Wales." He shook his head
"Sorry again, Mr. Proctor. Sheer fabrication."

"And seized upon in an attempt to lend legitimacy to what i
nothing more than an immoral and exploitative busines
endeavor!" Father Scotto said. "Religion indeed! Ha!"

"This all kind of puts your claims in a different light, doesn
it, Simon?" Campbell asked.

"Not at all," Simon Proctor muttered. "Opinion an
innuendo."

"Now, you're a bit different from the other so-called satani
rock singers, aren't you? I mean, they all treat witchcraft
astrology, all that stuff, they all treat it lightly, right? You're th
only one who says that your satanism is serious."

"I'm the only one whose satanism *is* serious," he huffed.

"And yet here we're being told that it's all hype, that it isn'
really satanism at all, that true witchcraft—"

"A moment," Eisenmann broke in. "I referred to tradition a
cultic practices commonly accepted as witchcraft."

"Okay," Campbell agreed, not seeing the difference. "—tha
what you do isn't witchcraft at all. If that's the case, then the
position of Father Scotto and Mrs. Wilkinson here is
strengthened somewhat, isn't it?"

Simon Proctor tried to think quickly. All he could concentrate on was diminishing box office receipts. "Well—ah—well, ow do you think Father Scotto would react to being told that e isn't really a Catholic? It isn't even worth refuting."

"That isn't much of a refutation," Eisenmann pointed out. "Simon, you also brought a film clip taken at your concert at ae Carrier Dome in Syracuse last June, didn't you?"

"Now wait a minute—!" Father Scotto began.

"No, no, I've seen this," Campbell said. "There's no sex or iolence in it. No more than in most rock concerts, anyway."

"Then there's too much," the priest grumbled. "If you're oing to continue to publicize these things, then I'm afraid I lust absent myself from this discussion."

"And I'll be going with him," Mrs. Wilkinson added.

Before Campbell could reply, Simon broke in by saying, "I ssume that these people are here under the same conditions s I am, receiving no fee because we are all trying to get a nessage across. Correct?"

"Well, sure," Campbell agreed.

"Do I not then have the right to the same opportunities for xpression—"

"Publicity, you mean!" Father Scotto snapped.

"Publicity, if you will," Simon continued. "Do I not have the ame rights as they have?"

"We aren't showing films!" Mrs. Wilkinson exclaimed.

"That, madam, is your own fault, not mine!"

"Perhaps we should break for a commercial and discuss this ssue a bit further before we resume," Campbell said in his best mediatory tone. To the camera he said, "We'll be back in a ew moments, ladies and gentlemen, after a word from our sponsor. . . ."

An hour later Simon Proctor was standing dejectedly on the corner of Fifty-third Street and Seventh Avenue, his arm outstretched in a thus far futile attempt to hail a cab. With his coat collar buttoned and his long hair tucked under his beret, he was not a distinct presence on the streets of Manhattan.

Son of a bitch tore me apart, he thought glumly. Made me look like a fool and a fraud on network television.

You are a fraud, his mind answered him. And if you lose your shirt on this goddamn movie, you'll be a fool as well.

Simon sighed and shook his head, then cursed under his breath as a cab sped by without seeing him.

Didn't even get to show the concert footage, with a concert tonight and half the tickets unsold. Shit!

"Mr. Proctor?" a voice said behind him.

He turned to find a diminutive young woman in a knee length leather coat standing there, leaning somewhat tentatively toward him. She gazed at him through thick glasses whose frames almost touched the bottom of her blond bangs. "May I ask you a few questions?"

"Who are you?"

She smiled nervously. "I'm Liza Goldman from *Rock 'Record* magazine?" Her tone said, Do you recognize the name? "I tried to catch up with you as you left the studio, but couldn't get through the crowds. I'd like to ask you a few things about the talk show."

Damn! he thought, but he said, "Proceed," in his most austere and sinister manner.

She took a small tape recorder from her coat pocket and switched it on. Holding it close to her mouth, she asked, "Your credentials as well as your sincerity were called into serious question today. Do you have any further comments to make on that subject?"

Simon thought for a moment as the young woman lifted the tape recorder to his face. "We followers of the old religion have always had to deal with prejudice and opposition. In this age of so-called religious tolerance, we have to deal with character assassination more frequently than outright physical attacks. Today was no different."

"Yes, but the point seems to be that you have been accused of not really being a follower of the 'old religion.' How do you respond to that?"

"It is an absurdity unworthy of a response."

"And the remarks made about the rituals your group practices, that they are not really witchcraft rituals?"

"Also unworthy of a response."

She nodded. "Okay. What about the film, *Satanists of Salem.* Any comments on the film?"

Simon glanced at the traffic on Seventh Avenue, hoping to see an unoccupied cab which might extricate him from this unwanted interview. He saw none. Sighing once again, he said, "I decided to make a historically based film dealing with my ancestor, the warlock John Proctor, and the people with whom he was involved during the Salem witch trials of the 1690s."

"Yes, yes, we know that, but what about the statements made on the show that your ancestor was not a practitioner of witchcraft?"

A passengerless cab drove by and responded to Simon's hail. "Excuse me," he said to the young woman as he climbed into the backseat.

"But Mr. Proctor . . . . ," she said, trying to press the tape recorder close to him and pulling back as he shut the door.

"Madison Square Garden," he said to the driver. Simon sat back as the cab moved out into the midtown traffic. He gazed blankly out into the maelstrom of humanity as it rushed past the window of the moving vehicle.

What a day, he thought dejectedly.

What a way to make a living.

⟦ CHAPTER TWO ⟧

October 29, continued

HARRY SCHROEDER CHEWED nervously upon his unlit cigar and glanced at his wristwatch for the seventh time in the past three minutes. He grabbed his stomach spasmodically as a brief wave of gas assaulted what he swore was the beginning of an ulcer, and he squinted into the cold wind as he looked down the seemingly endless expanse of city traffic. A black teenager pushing a garment rack nearly ran him over, and only the shrill "Heads up!" the boy shouted at him awakened him to the danger. Schroeder jumped back and shouted angry imprecations which, fortunately for the chubby middle-aged man, were blithely ignored.

Schroeder pulled a dingy gray handkerchief from the back pocket of his wrinkled trousers and wiped his face. He was sweating profusely, the cold wind notwithstanding. He was the kind of man who always perspired, who was forever physically uncomfortable no matter what his environment. He could bathe thrice daily and still seem unwashed. A freshly pressed suit would collapse into wrinkles the moment he put it on. A slight but perceptible aroma of the locker room seemed to follow him wherever he went, and he had both been aware of this fact and lived with it for so long that he no longer gave it any thought.

This was not the only reason for his wearing cheap suits. H was by nature a conservative, not in any political or socia sense, but rather in that he deplored waste and sympathize quite consciously with the ant rather than the grasshopper i the old fable. He had numerous clients in his manageria stable, but Simon Proctor had been his most lucrative fo many years. As the annual yield from Proctor's records an concerts began to diminish, slowly at first and then wit increasing rapidity over the past few years, Schroeder began to conserve. Why spend three hundred dollars for a suit from Lord and Taylor when one off the rack at Alexander's for fifty nine ninety-nine would do just as well?

Of course, he was not even beginning to approach penury. He was merely a cautious man. Simon Proctor had risked everything on the production of this film of his, and the next six months would tell if Proctor was at the beginning of a new and successful phase of his long, circuitous career, or if his recent efforts were merely the dying gasps of an incipient has-been.

Three years from now, Simon Proctor might have his own television special, or he might be a three-minute slot on a "Where Are They Now?" show.

Schroeder glanced again at his watch. Where the hell is he?

As if in answer to the unvoiced question, a taxi screeched to a halt at the curb in front of the forecourt of Madison Square Garden, and Simon Proctor climbed glumly out of the backseat. He tossed a few bills to the driver and turned to walk toward the massive entertainment complex. Harry Schroeder waddled over and intercepted him. "Simon! Simon!"

Proctor glanced angrily at him and kept walking. "Harry, if you weren't such a fat old fool I'd knock your teeth out."

Schroeder ignored the remark. "How'd the show go?"

Proctor spun on him. "Didn't I tell you to be sure to check out the other guests in advance?"

"Sure, of course. I did that, Simon. Why?"

"And what did you find out?" Proctor folded his arms and glared at Schroeder with impatient irritation.

"Well—" Schroeder thought for a moment, "there was some old priest pissed off about witchcraft and some lady from the PTA or something."

"And?" he demanded.

"That was it, Simon. Just those two."

"What about Eisenmann, the anthropology professor."

"Oh, yeah, him. What about him?"

"Yeah, Harry, what about him? Why the hell didn't you tell me about him?"

Schroeder shrugged in confusion. "I didn't see any need to. I mean, I figured he was just another guest for a later segment of the show, nothing to do with you."

Proctor closed his eyes as if imploring the powers that be to grant him patience. "Harry, what is anthropology?"

Schroeder shrugged again, somewhat defensively. "I dunno. Some kind of medical thing, isn't it?"

Proctor sighed. "Harry, you stupid son of a bitch!" He turned and began to walk toward the Garden, with Schroeder following behind him.

"Simon, what happened? What's wrong?" he panted.

"That guy was an expert on witchcraft and he made me look like a goddamned fool, that's what happened!" he spat.

"An expert on witchcraft! You're kidding!"

Proctor stopped suddenly and turned to Schroeder, his fists clenched at his sides and his face flushing. "Do I look like I'm kidding?" he demanded.

Schroeder gazed into the blazing eyes for a long moment. Then he averted his own eyes and muttered, "Gee, Simon, I'm sorry. I thought—"

"You're sorry!" Proctor shouted. "What damned difference does that make?! You're sorry!" He spat a guttural sound of contempt and turned again to walk on. "My whole goddamned career is riding on this stupid movie, every last cent I have is invested in it, my reputation is resting on the idea that it's a true story about real witches and real witchcraft, and I go on network television to have myself shown up as a fraud and a charlatan, to have the movie reduced to the level of a grade D slasher-porno flick, and you're sorry!"

Schroeder sighed dejectedly. "I'm sorry," he repeated.

"Oh, Harry, will you shut up?" Proctor entered Madison Square Garden by the main entrance and then walked left, down the long side corridors to the interior stage entrance. Schroeder followed him in silence all the way, huffing and puffing as he waddled in Proctor's wake.

Simon Proctor glanced at the stage from the right-hand wing before walking to the dressing room, but he did not take any time to inspect the stage preparations in any detail. I pay those goddamned roadies enough, he thought bitterly. Let them attend to it. He knew that the setup for his concert was rather complicated, what with the explosive devices and fog machines added to the customary light-show system, but he trusted the crew as much as he resented them.

27

"Lousy fifteen percent," he muttered under his breath.

"Wha'dja say, Simon?" Schroeder asked breathlessly.

"Fifteen percent," he repeated. "That's all I ever see of the proceeds from these goddamn concerts. After renting the hall, paying this fee and that fee, salaries for these assholes and those assholes, shelling out for overheads on all sides, all I ever see is fifteen lousy percent." He glared again at Schroeder. "And you get a cut of that."

Schroeder did not respond. He knew that Proctor was in a bad mood, and he had no intention of worsening it by pointing out that in a good year fifteen percent of concert proceeds was no mean fee. He followed Proctor into his dressing room and sat quietly in a chair a few feet away from the makeup table.

Proctor sat down and stared at himself in the mirror. He shook his head in disgust and then reached over for the jar of cold cream. He scooped a generous handful of the thick substance from the jar and began to slather it over his face. The green-tinged, clown white greasepaint of his customary warlock makeup began to dissolve beneath the cold cream, and as he rubbed it into his skin with one hand, he peeled off the mustache and goatee with the other. He winced slightly as the spirit gum caught on a stray whisker. He tossed the hairpiece onto the dressing table and then vigorously massaged his face with both hands for a few minutes. He reached over to a tissue dispenser and pulled out a few sheets. After carefully wiping the cold cream and greasepaint from his face, he went over to the sink and began to wash his face in hot, soapy water.

"Why bother, Simon?" Schroeder asked.

"Hmmm?" he grunted.

"Why bother taking off the makeup? You're just gonna have to put it back on in a couple of hours."

"It's obvious, Harry, that you've never worn makeup, never been married, never had sisters or daughters."

"Wha'dja mean?"

Proctor spit out some soapy water. "I put this makeup on early this morning. By the time of tonight's concert, it'd be half worn off and running anyway. If I don't put it on fresh tonight, I'll turn into the incredible melting man on stage."

"Oh." Schroeder nodded. "Well, that might be a good career move." He grinned at his attempt at levity. An angry glance from Proctor told him that the attempt was not appreciated, and he coughed nervously.

Proctor sat back down at the dressing table and lighted a cigarette. He inhaled and then blew the smoke out with a sigh as he gazed at himself in the mirror. Without the Mephistophelian makeup he was not the arresting, striking figure which his album covers presented to the public. He considered the sallow complexion, the weary eyes, the crow's-feet which radiated outward from them, the graying roots which were emerging from his scalp beneath the dyed black hair, and the hair itself, so long as to look absurd on a man in his midforties. A worn-out, washed-up old hippy, he thought morosely. Faded flower power.

"Look, Simon," Schroeder began gently, "it isn't as bad as you think it is. The movie is supposed to appeal to your fans. How many of them watch the Percy Campbell show?"

"Then why'd you book me on it?"

"Hey, publicity is publicity!"

"Yeah, and bad publicity is bad publicity." Proctor sat back wearily in his seat. "Besides, there was a reporter from *Rock 'n Record* magazine there. Tried to interview me after I left."

"You talk to him?"

"Her," Proctor said. "Briefly. But she heard the whole thing, and you can bet that their next issue's gonna carry a story about it. Let's face it," he sighed, "we're really screwed. Without my credibility, I'm just a painted clown up there."

"Simon, there are other singers who use all sorts of references to the Devil. It's all just entertainment."

"Of course it is, Harry," he spat, "don't you think I know that? But they make no pretense at being serious. My whole act is based on the idea that I'm for real, that I really practice witchcraft. Without that, I don't even have the saving grace of parody, of humor, of a put-on. I'm just a pretentious fraud." He shook his head again. "I'm ruined, Harry. This is it. I'll never be able to pay off the loans I took out against the film's proceeds. The other backers'll hound me for years."

"Oh, Simon, don't be such a goddamned pessimist!" Schroeder said, growing slightly annoyed. "The film hasn't even premiered yet. Okay, let's say it isn't a big money-maker. Let's say it's a complete flop! Don't you realize how much money there is to be made on video cassette sales? And after we cut out the sex and violence, we can rent it to TV stations."

Proctor laughed humorlessly. "Cut out the sex and violence and you'll have a fifteen-minute short."

"Yeah, well, I told you to tone that stuff down."

Proctor flashed an angry look at his manager. "Hey, look,

29

Harry, I don't need any I-told-you-sos, okay? Especially from you." He placed the cigarette between his lips and began to scratch his scalp. "I give you an easy little job that any jackass could do, ask you to check out the other guests on the show so I can be prepared for anything, and you mess it up."

"Okay, okay already," Schroeder muttered. "Look, the Campbell show isn't network, right? It's syndicated, and I don't think it's popular on the West Coast. It's on at eight in the morning or something. So even if the film bombs in New York, it might still go over big in California."

"Damn it, Harry, I'm not just talking about the goddamn movie!" Proctor shouted. "It's my whole career, don't you understand?"

"So let's say things get bad for you around here. So you move out to California. Why not, Simon? You've always been an East Coast act anyway, not too big on the other side of the country. Look, there's just as big a market for this witchcraft music out there as there is here—bigger, in fact."

"I won't move to California," Proctor said glumly. "I don't even like to spend time there."

"Why the hell not?"

"Because California's filled with crazy people, that's why."

"Oh, sure, and New York is sane city? Go spend a Saturday night in Washington Square Park, and then tell me about California!"

"I don't live in New York," he pointed out. "I live in New Hampshire."

"Okay, so you make your money in Los Angeles and San Francisco and you live in Oregon or Nevada. What's the big deal? Money from California isn't as good as money from New York?"

"They got people there who take all this Satanist crap seriously, Harry. I don't want to live in the middle of that."

"What am I hearing!" Schroeder exclaimed. "Your whole act is that you take it seriously yourself!"

"Yeah, but I don't!" Proctor turned to face him. "And the kids who listen to my records and come to my concerts don't take it seriously either. They just get a kick out of thinking that I do, and they pretend that they do, but it isn't serious, none of it."

"So maybe it's the same in California."

"Land of fruits and nuts? Don't make me laugh."

"Look, Simon—"

"Harry, will you shut up?!" Proctor yelled. "I'm in no mood

for this! What are you doing, trying to get me to move three thousand miles away before I turn into a losing proposition for you?"

This stung Harry Schroeder, and the hurt showed on his face. "Simon, that's not fair and you know it. I stuck by you for twenty years, didn't I? Who discovered you, singing retread protest songs in that basement in Brooklyn twenty years ago? I did. Who got you into the Village clubs, into Folk City, for Christ's sake! I did. Who got you your first record contract, and who kept getting you signed up with other record companies every time your contracts got canceled? I did." Schroeder turned away, his pursed lips quivering.

Proctor felt a twinge of guilt penetrate his anger. "Okay, okay, I'm sorry. I'm upset, that's all."

Schroeder condescended to be mollified. "Yeah, sure, I understand." He slapped Proctor lightly on the back. "Look, I'm going out to get some dinner. You wanna come?"

"No, I'm just gonna sit here and try to unwind. Hey, bring me back something, will you?"

"Sure. Whaddaya want?"

He shrugged. "Doesn't matter. Sandwich and a six-pack."

"Okeydokey," Schroeder said. "Lemme make sure I got some money with me. . . ." He fished around in the back pocket of his baggy trousers for a moment and then drew out his wallet. As he unfolded it, an envelope dropped out and landed on the floor. "What the—oh, yeah, right. Hey, Simon, this letter came for you today at my office. I almost forgot about it."

Proctor sighed and rubbed his eyes. "I thought you had somebody to take care of fan mail."

"Yeah, I do, but this isn't fan mail. I thought you might like to read it."

"Well, you were wrong. Toss it out."

"But you don't even know what's—"

"Okay, okay, so read it to me," he said irritably. He was in no mood to argue.

Schroeder shrugged and removed the letter from the envelope. "It's from Los Angeles."

"California," he muttered. "Great."

Schroeder cleared his throat. "It says, 'Dear Simon: You don't know us, but we know you. We've listened to your music for years now, and we think that you're one of the greatest talents around.'"

"Come on, Harry, will you?" Proctor said. "I don't need to hear any fan letters. They don't help pay the bills, you know?"

"This isn't exactly a fan letter," Schroeder said. "Listen: 'Because of your music we've become Satanists ourselves. We've been studying witchcraft for nearly a year now, and we feel that it is time for us to begin to spread the Satanist faith.'"

"Great," he repeated. "Missionaries. Wonderful. Just what I need."

"'But we are concerned about your songs,'" Schroeder continued reading. "'The more we have studied the black arts, the more we have come to suspect that you are not truly a member of an established coven. There are too many errors in your songs, too many inaccurate statements and misleading ideas. We have begun to suspect that you are not really a Satanist at all.'"

Simon Proctor laughed despite his depression. "This is a pisser, Harry, it really is. On TV today they called me a monster and a fraud, and my own fans are saying I'm either a fraud or a heretic! That's really wonderful, Harry. Thanks a lot for bringing me that letter. Really helps my mood."

"Shh," Schroeder said. "There's more."

"I can hardly wait," he muttered.

"'We will be able to visit you very soon. We feel that we can help you eliminate the problems in your presentation of the faith, and by doing so we believe that we can spread the message of satanism to an even greater number of people. We will see you soon after your New York City concert on the twenty-ninth.'" Schroeder looked up. "It's signed, 'Gwendolyn Jenkins and Adrienne Lupescu.'"

"Well," Proctor said, "I guess I'll have to beat a hasty retreat after the show tonight."

"Simon, I don't think they mean that they're coming to the concert. It sounds to me like they're gonna come to your house. That's why I brought you the letter. I figured you should know in advance."

"Yeah, thanks," he said, yawning. "If they show up at my doorstep, I'll give 'em an autographed photo and send them on their way."

"Good idea." Schroeder checked his wallet. "What did you say you wanted to eat?"

He repeated, "Doesn't matter. Sandwich and a six-pack."

"Okay," Schroeder said as he moved toward the door of the dressing room. "Just relax and take it easy. I'll be back soon."

"Yeah, yeah," Proctor grumbled. "See you later." Schroeder left the room, closing the door behind him.

Simon Proctor rose from the seat and walked slowly, heavily over to the sofa which rested against the far wall of the rather spacious dressing room. He fell backward onto it and threw his arm over his eyes. Might as well try to get a little rest, he thought. Got a two- or three-hour show to do tonight. All that hopping around on stage, all that gyrating. Was a time I had to worry about my fingers holding out . . . used to get one hell of a cramp in my left hand after a while, fretting that guitar, but it doesn't matter now. No problem. The bass, drums, lead, and keyboards are so loud and the music itself so deafening that no one can hear a simple old rhythm guitar anymore anyway.

Rest, he told himself. Sleep for an hour.

Five minutes passed before he hopped to his feet, annoyed at his inability to catch the few minutes of repose he felt he needed. Too keyed up, he thought. Too damned nervous. Too many pressures.

He sat down once again in front of the dressing table and stared blankly at his own reflection in the mirror. The old face was still there somewhere, underneath the worry lines, somewhere in back of the troubled eyes, resting somewhere beneath the lined brow, hiding somewhere behind the world-weary, jaded expression which varied only when it expressed apathy or panic.

Where did the years go? he thought. How the hell did I evolve into this ludicrous sideshow freak?

It had seemed so simple back in the early sixties, back in his teens, lining up with his friends at the record store down in Hanover, waiting for the latest release from Buddy Holly or Chuck Berry. Even in the timeless, unchanging mountain town of Bradford, New Hampshire, it had been possible to find other teenagers with whom to struggle through the process of learning simple guitar chords, simple chord progressions—E to A to B7 to E, G to C to D7 to G, C to F to G7 to C, and so on and so on through the nights of his adolescence. When he and his friend Jimmy decided that the day after high school graduation they would head south for New York, it had seemed that the world lay at their feet, just waiting for their raw, untempered talents to sweep them to wealth and fame.

Simon Proctor grinned, both happy with the memory and embarrassed at the presumption of his youth. Wealth and fame!

He spent three years hustling gigs anywhere and everywhere he could, playing for tips and beer, sometimes just for tips, sometimes just to play. And no matter what the current idiom, he adapted to it and adopted it as his own. When all the radios were playing old standards, white mountain music, and white interpretations of old black ballads, that is what Proctor played. "Freight Train, Freight Train," and "Man of Constant Sorrow," and "Five Hundred Miles." And when Bob Dylan moved folk music into the realm of social conscience, Simon Proctor followed suit, striking his guitar in angry denunciations of injustice and inequality, calling out with heartfelt sincerity for peace and brotherhood, asking how many roads a man must walk down and warning that the times were a'changing. Then when the Beatles went serious and Dylan went electric, Proctor hooked up with a few other musicians who had been pursuing the fragile illusion of success, forming a crude rock band which they named the Pentagons for no particular reason. His old friend Jimmy drifted into the group and then drifted out of it again before settling down as an insurance salesman in New Rochelle.

But things had gotten better after that. Gigs came their way more regularly, and Proctor had even begun to save some money, when the foolishness of competing egos caused the group to disintegrate, leaving Simon, now no longer a wide-eyed adolescent, once again hustling solo gigs in an increasingly quintet market.

It was Harry Schroeder who had heard him one night in a roach-infested Brooklyn club and had decided that this young man was to be grist for his impresarial mill. He got Proctor together with a few other musicians whom he represented and, using his limited contacts, helped them establish a small but growing reputation as an acid rock band in the New York metropolitan area.

It was around that time that he met Katharine, Proctor remembered. God, she was gorgeous! So much romance, so much love, so much intimacy, physical, emotional, spiritual, intellectual. So wonderful, until she took off one day with his bass player, leaving him filled with resentment and hurt, leaving him with Lucas, their six-month-old baby. Never did feel too fond of Lucas, he thought. Reminds me too much of his mother.

It seemed that everything went wrong at once. With the bass player gone and Proctor in a state of almost permanent self-sedation, the other band members soon went their own ways. Harry sent him to a health farm in Pennsylvania to dry out and get the drugs out of his system, and then attempted to build him up as a solo artist, but this time one with a rock band

34

to back him up. His talent was able once again to pull him through, and he made a nice living from performing—nothing opulent, but he was comfortable for the first time in many years. He even tried to rebuild the bridges he had burned years before between him and his father, Floyd, who still lived up in Bradford, retired on a civil-service pension. He spent an increasingly greater amount of time up at the old Proctor homestead, nestled in the mountains, leaving only when he had a concert tour or a recording session.

It was again Harry Schroeder who had managed to secure the recording contract—or rather, contracts. With each successive record label Proctor had managed to pull together one hit album, followed by a flop, followed by an album so bad no one bought it, followed by a canceled contract, followed by another signing with another label where the process was repeated. It was not very long before Proctor realized that he just did not have it in him to produce hit after hit after hit. But by the time he reached his late thirties, fame had become increasingly less important to him, financial security increasingly more so.

Especially since he had children to think about. It was before his first record was cut that he met Lucinda, a slightly plumpish but pleasingly round blonde with enormous blue eyes and sunshine in her smile. Their daughter Rowena was her mother's spitting image. When Lucinda died in that stupid, stupid traffic accident almost a decade ago, Simon Proctor had been so distraught that he even attempted suicide. It was his father Floyd who found him and rushed him to the hospital to have his stomach pumped.

Lucinda, he thought sadly. If only you'd lived I would probably never have gotten myself mixed up in this insanity.

The moment he met her something about her called to him as if he were being called home. She was so decidedly non-urban, no hint of pretense or sophistication, all purity and honesty and sweetness and practicality. Born and raised in Brooklyn, she nonetheless seemed hewn from New England oak. He took her to Bradford the weekend after they met, and married her the next week. Rowena was born the next year. And a few years after that, Lucinda was dead.

Do parents really bequeath their personalities to their kids? Proctor wondered. Or is it just that I've raised Lucas and Rowena so differently?

Lucas had been conceived on the road in the midst of the hurricane of music, drugs, booze, and sex which had formed the backdrop for his marriage to Katharine in that age of free love, free living, and free LSD. Lucas had grown up a scion of that age, typifying in himself everything negative in the heritage of the 1960s. But Rowena had never left Bradford, never been polluted by the degeneracy of the outside world. Simon Proctor had left the raising of Rowena to her grand-father Floyd. All he did was pay the bills, spend as much time with her as he could, and love her exceedingly. She was to him Lucinda incarnate, the image of her mother, and each time he saw her after a prolonged absence, each time she threw her arms around his neck, kissed him and called him "Daddy," he could barely restrain himself from weeping for love.

And Lucas? More of a younger brother than a son, an aimless, purposeless hedonist. A product of the very culture Simon Proctor had helped to create, the very culture the churches and the schools had been condemning for so many years.

Proctor shook his head to escape from his memories. He reached into his jacket pocket and took out a tobacco pouch. After pulling a thin square of rolling paper from the side compartment and pouring an appropriate amount of cleaned marijuana onto it, he proceeded to roll a perfect joint. One of my many skills, he thought. God knows I've rolled enough of them over the past quarter of a century.

He struck a match and held it to the tip of the thin, intoxicating cigarette. It's funny, he thought as he drew the smoke deep into his lungs. If Lucas were here I'd offer him a toke. If Rowena were here, I wouldn't even have lit it.

Maybe it was Rowena, in a weird and indirect way, who got me into this, he thought. It had not been long after her birth when first oblique, and then blatant, references to the Devil began to crop up in rock lyrics. Mick Jagger and the Stones had started it, almost innocently, and then other groups had begun openly to extol the virtues of the dark elements. Kinky sex and violence entered the rock world, and fortunes were being made from increasingly extreme efforts to outrage and offend.

And Simon Proctor had followed the trend once again, as he had so many times before, but now not an innocent youth in search of fame, not a would-be John Lennon or a Bob Dylan-to-be, not a part of a youth culture, not that wide-eyed kid who had hitchhiked from Bradford to Manhattan so many years ago. Now a grown man in his forties, with a twenty-year-old son and a sixteen-year-old daughter and an elderly father in failing health, a man with feelings of guilt over the son he had allowed to grow to young manhood as a bent and twisted bough, a man who wanted to give his baby, his lovely Rowena, everything she wanted, loving her all the more because she wanted so little; now a son who felt responsible for his ailing father, a son who paid the property tax and the fuel bills and the cost of repair and upkeep on the sprawling property in Bradford, New Hampshire; now a son who was beginning to see in the mirror, not the face of youth and opportunity and the future, but the watery eyes of his own father staring back at him from the reflection, a son knowing that it would someday be he, and not old Floyd, who would need care, care which he could never expect from Lucas, care which would be a burden he would never place upon Rowena's shoulders:

Now a man who realized that he had better make money while he could, that he had better save and invest what he could, that rock and roll singers have no pension plans, that money needed to be made *now*, saved *now*, invested *now*:

Now a cartoon figure who slopped his face with greasepaint and dressed like a monk onstage and sang of witchery and Satan and the black arts, because that's what the kids wanted, because that's what sold records, because that's what sold concert tickets:

Now a self-proclaimed warlock who sold himself as the leader of a totally imaginary, nonexistent cult, a man who realized that the only thing which would distinguish him from a dozen other singers who exploited this witchcraft nonsense was his claim to authenticity, his public avowal of his descent from John Proctor, which was true, who had been hanged for witchcraft in Salem in 1692, which was true, who had indeed been a warlock, which was false, just as his remote descendant Simon was a warlock, which was false:

Now a buffoon, sitting naked before the cameras while a pompous professor stripped away the mask to reveal, not the Phantom of the Opera, but Sammy Glick:

Now a tired, worn-out performer at the end of his tenure in the public eye, with everything he owned, even the roof over his father's head, held hostage to a film which had been held up to public ridicule before it even hit the theaters.

A man on the brink. A man on the edge.

A man at the end.

"Hiya, Simon," Harry Schroeder said cheerfully as he slammed the dressing room door and tossed a brown paper bag onto the dressing table. "Sorry I was so long, but I met Gladys

Duff in the deli. You remember Gladys? Lead singer with the Eldorados?"

Proctor started at the interruption and then gazed at Schroeder in surprise. "What time is it?"

"Seven o'clock."

Proctor shook his head. "Shit. I've been sitting here daydreaming for hours." He reached over and took the bag. "What did you get me?"

"Ham and cheese on rye, mayo and mustard, and some beer. Okay?"

Proctor unwrapped the sandwich and took a healthy bite from it. "Yeah, terrific," he muttered as he popped open a can of Schlitz. "So what's with Gladys? Was she eating in the deli?"

"No, working there," Schroeder said as he heaved his bulk into a seat. "Her husband Sonny ran off with somebody or other, and the group fell apart." Schroeder paused for a moment and studied Proctor's face carefully. "You okay?"

"Yeah, yeah, fine," he said, taking a swig from the beer can. "Just wish I could still play 'Be-bop-a-lula.'"

"Huh?"

"Remember what one of the Beatles said, McCartney I think, or maybe Lennon? He said that when they started out they weren't looking to be multimillionaires or world-famous celebrities, or anything like that. He said they were just a bunch of kids who wanted to chase girls, drink beer, and play 'Be-bop-a-lula.'" Proctor sighed and took another drink. "That's how I'm feeling, Harry. I wish I could go back to when I just wanted to play 'Be-bop-a-lula.'"

Schroeder smiled sympathetically. "Regrets over passed youth and lost innocence, right?"

"Yeah, something like that."

"Well, join the club. If everybody who ever wanted to live his life over again had the chance to do it, there'd never have been a generation of people after the first one."

Proctor laughed. "Harry, you're a philosopher!"

Schroeder laughed in turn. "Yeah, I'm a philosopher like you're a witch."

Proctor swallowed a bite of sandwich. "How are the box office sales? Any better?"

"No," Schroeder replied, shaking his head, "still the same. But don't worry, we'll do okay. We'll see some profit tonight." He yawned. "Looks like snow outside."

"In late October? It never snows in New York City in late October."

38

"Yeah, I know, but it still looks it. Feels it, too. I got a wet chill in my bones."

"Comes from not washing that suit since 1968." He finished the sandwich and threw the wrapping paper into the wastebasket. "It isn't going to snow." He gazed once again at his reflection in the mirror. "I look like shit," he muttered.

"If it snows, a lot of people won't show up tonight," Schroeder said, not hearing him.

"Get off it, will you?" Proctor snapped. "It won't snow." He studied his aging face more closely. And where, he wondered, are the snows of yesteryear?

The house lights did not dim: they were instantaneously extinguished. The babble of excitement in the audience rose like a sudden wave and then dropped immediately into a silence pregnant with anticipatory glee.

"DISCIPLES!" a voice boomed over the amplification system. "THE MASTER APPROACHES! ALL HAIL SIMON, BELOVED OF LUCIFER, PRINCE OF THE DARK POWERS!"

Six explosions onstage filled the front of the concert hall with billows of white smoke, colored red and green and yellow by the flashing lights. Simon Proctor, warlock, emerged from one of the pillars of smoke, his white face gleaming in the spotlight, the flowing sleeves, train, and cowl of his black monk's robe fluttering in the wind generated by the offstage fan which also dissipated the smoke, revealing the band in similar attire.

Proctor raised his arms in a gesture of salutation. "Hail Satan!" he cried.

"Hail Satan!" ten thousand sixteen-year-olds boomed back with laughter and excitement.

A girl in a tight black leotard strode onstage to a barrage of catcalls from the pimply lotharios in the audience, and handed Proctor his guitar. He slung the strap over his shoulder and struck the opening chord to his song "Pathfinder." The band came in on cue, and the audience cheered to the sound of the familiar music. The cheering redoubled when Proctor began to sing the lyrics, and the spectators began to clap along with the rhythm.

"Can't you hear that old north wind beating the sky,
    Beating the sky, beating the sky,
With a grip in your gut and the fear in your eye,
    Waitin' on the Judgment Day.

39

Wind gonna come, gonna blow out your light,
  Blow out your light, blow out your light,
Find you a'dyin' on a cold winter night,
  And then it's gonna blow you away."

The lead guitar riff screeched out of the amp between
verses, tearing deafeningly through the eardrums of the
audience, who cried out for more.

"Near the sign by the crossroad, the Devil he smile,
  Devil he smile, Devil he smile,
You been travelin' toward him for many a mile,
  Without even a soul to save.
One road leads to your lover's room,
  Your lover's room, your lover's room,
Other road leads to a cold, hollow tomb,
  Where Death's gonna dance on your grave."

My God, what garbage! Proctor thought as the keyboards
trilled shrilly into their showcase. He stood immobile as a
statue during the first part of the show, leaving the bouncing
about and gyrating for the second half. Just as well tonight, he
thought as his hands moved mechanically through the chord
progression: Am–G–F–Am, F–Am–E. Right now I couldn't
muster up the energy to square dance.

The opening number ended amid the requisite cacophony
from the instruments, well matched by the din arising from
the audience. He allowed the cheering to continue for a few
moments and then raised his hands upward, lifting his eyes
and looking as ecstatic as he could. "AVE SATANAS!" he cried.

"AVE SATANAS!" the audience responded.

Simon Proctor lowered his gaze and looked out over the
throng who sat, cheering loudly, before him. "Whom do you
serve?" he asked in a loud voice.

"Satan!" they cried, laughing and clapping.

"Who is the master of the earth?" he asked.

"Satan!" was the rejoinder.

"Who is the master of the delights of the flesh?"

"Satan!"

"Do you dedicate yourselves to his service?"

"Yes!" and "Hail Satan!" they cried.

"Do you swear to plumb the depths of sin?"

"Yes!"

"Do you swear to taste the pleasures of the forbidden fruit?"

40

"Yes!" "Yes!"

"Then I welcome you, my children, into the house of Satan!"

The audience went wild, screaming and cheering and throwing things at the stage and at each other. It was to all appearances a successful beginning to a concert packed with devoted fans; but from his vantage point on the stage, Proctor could clearly see the empty seats generously interspersed among the occupied ones around the hall. The front seats, the most expensive seats, were filled. But there was no way of knowing if their occupants had actually purchased front row seats or had merely moved down to fill up the empty spaces.

Proctor tried to look impassive and sinister. Then he raised his hand imperiously to command silence. The cheering settled. He strove to lower his already bass voice and said into the microphone, "We'd like to do a song for you written by an old friend of mine named Donovan. I first heard him sing it as we drifted on a raft upon the moat of his castle in the mountain fastness of Wales."

The audience cheered afresh as the band struck up the tune. The fact that he had never met the old folksinger Donovan Leitch was irrelevant to Simon Proctor. He had paid the necessary fee for the use of the song, and besides, none of these kids had ever heard of Donovan anyway. He came from a past era, when songs had melodies and lyrics had atmosphere.

"Shadow of cloud fall, and with it a chill.
  High o'er the heather, hawk hover o'er the hill.
Just begun is my journey, and Danu's my name.
  I am the juggler of fortune and fame.
Let me not hear facts, figures and logic,
  Fain would I hear lore, legend and magic. . . ."

"Fain," Proctor thought to himself. How many songs use words like "fain" nowadays? How many kids know what "fain" means?

"Feathers of raven, slithers of coal,
  Armor of silver in the mackerel shoal.
Sun in the west, 'tis ruby blood-red.
  Travellers a-weary, so weary, do make their bed.
Let me not hear facts, figures and logic,
  Fain would I hear lore, legend and magic. . . ."

The concert dragged on into the night, and by its end Simon Proctor was gelatinous with fatigue, drenched with sweat, bleary-eyed, and sore. I'm too old for this, he thought as he sat down again in the seat before the mirror in his dressing room and massaged the aching muscles in his legs. How the hell does Jagger go on doing it, year after year?

Harry Schroeder leaned his head into the room and asked, "Simon? Can I come in?"

"Since when do you ask," Proctor replied. Then, in a more friendly tone, "Yeah, sure, Harry, come on in." He began for a second time that day to remove the makeup. "Well, give me the bad news."

"What bad news?"

"How much did we lose tonight!"

"Oh, Simon, don't be stupid. We made a nice little profit tonight, just like always."

"How little?"

"Well, we still have to pay the band . . . and the Garden people insisted on extra security at our own expense . . . and—"

"Come on, Harry, cut the shit. What do I end up with?"

"Well—and I'm approximating now, you understand—somewhere between two and three grand."

Simon Proctor threw the towel with which he was daubing his face down with disgust. "Damn!"

"Hey, come on, Simon. A lot of people would be ecstatic over that much money for one night's work!"

"Sure, but not if they only work one night every month, not if their asses are in the bank's shotgun sights over a movie that's a flop before it even opens, not if their record sales are off and their concerts play to half-empty halls!" He rose to his feet and began to pace around the room. "I have to do something, Harry, but I don't know what to do!" He turned his eyes desperately to his manager. "What can I do, Harry? Tell me, please, what can I do?! I'm drowning, Harry, I'm drowning!"

Schroeder spoke with a forcefulness of which even he thought himself incapable. "Goddamn it, Simon, cut it out! You have a bad day on a talk show and your concert doesn't sell out, and you're ready to lie down and die. What the hell's the matter with you? You act like you got a terminal disease or something. Jesus!"

"All right, Harry, all right. I don't need a fucking lecture, okay?" Proctor sat back down at the dressing table and returned to his task. Schroeder sat down in the same chair he had occupied earlier that day and watched in silence as Simon Proctor removed his makeup.

Schroeder remained seated, remained silent, as Proctor showered and dressed. At last he asked, "You staying in town tonight?"

"What the hell for?" Proctor asked. He was buttoning an old, faded work shirt which had obviously been worn and cherished through many years, a shirt which he had tucked into dungarees which could be similarly described. He sat down and slipped his feet into a pair of old, battered boots. "I got a month before the tour promoting the movie. Why the hell should I stay here tonight?"

"It's late, Simon, and you look bushed. Why don't you stay at my place and head up to Bradford tomorrow?"

"Because I hate it here," he snapped. "I have to go home, Harry. I don't think I could sleep anywhere else tonight, not after today. I have to get back to Bradford, back to the mountains. I have to sleep in my own bed, breathe country air." Then, as an afterthought, he added, "Thanks anyway."

Schroeder shrugged. "Sure, okay. Come on, I'll walk you to your car."

The two men trudged quietly from the dressing room to the corridor to the elevator which carried them downward to the subterranean parking lot beneath Madison Square Garden, the lot reserved for VIPs. Simon Proctor climbed into the front seat of his 1972 Toyota (wish I could get one of those new ones with all that computerized stuff in it, he thought glumly) and turned to Schroeder. "Harry, I should apologize for my behavior. I'm in a crappy mood, and I took it out on you. I'm sorry."

Schroeder smiled. "Forget it, Simon. I've taken worse than this from bigger bastards than you."

Proctor laughed and then started his engine. He threw Schroeder a parting wave as he backed out of the parking space and then drove away toward the exit ramp. Schroeder watched him sadly, followed the red taillights until they disappeared around the bend of the ramp. "Poor son of a bitch," he muttered.

You're finished, Simon, he thought. I'll never say it to your face, but it's all over for you. When that show hits the air on Thursday, you'll be a laughingstock. People will go to see the movie out of curiosity, maybe, and then it'll die. It'll close in a week; the video cassettes, if they get released at all, will sit on the shelves of the video rental stores and gather dust, and your records'll end up in the ninety-nine-cent rack at Times Square Stores.

Harry Schroeder shook his head. "Poor son of a bitch," he repeated. He turned and walked slowly back toward the elevator.

A few moments later, Simon Proctor was speeding along the Major Deegan Expressway, heading north toward New Hampshire. The fluorescent street lights whizzed by him, and he wove in and out of traffic in his haste to be quit of the city. He drummed absentmindedly on the steering wheel as he drove.

"Be-bop-a-lula, she's my baby . . . ," he sang quietly.

The green road sign with the white letters which stretched over the Major Deegan Expressway warned him that he had better bear to the left, lest he return to Manhattan via the Bronx.

"Be-bop-a-lula, I don't mean maybe. . . ."

An Elmhurst Dairy truck honked its horn angrily as Proctor sped ahead of it and then moved in front of it a bit too quickly so as to be able to move from the service road onto the expressway proper.

"Be-bop-a-lula, she's-a my baby. . . ."

He settled back in his seat as he pushed down on the accelerator and sent the car into a speed well in excess of the speed limit. It didn't matter. Getting close to the Westchester border. New York City highway patrol are on the other side, waiting for drivers coming in from Westchester, who don't drop down from fifty-five miles per hour to fifty.

"Be-bop-a-lula, I don-a mean-a maybe. . . ."

Soon the Cross County Mall sped by on his right and he was zipping through Westchester, heading for the turnoff to the New England Thruway.

"Be-bop-a-lula, she-he-he's my baby doll my baby doll my baby doll. . . ."

Simon Proctor drove off into the silent, moonlit New England night.

{ CHAPTER THREE }
October 30

EREMY SLOAN WORSHIPED Simon Proctor. Perhaps it was for his reason that he had become best friends with Simon's son Lucas; but the affection Jeremy felt for Simon's daughter Rowena would have developed no matter who her father was.

Like so many teenage boys, Jeremy had a tendency to idolize rock stars, even stars on the downward slope of the mountain of success as Simon was. And like many teenage boys, Jeremy also felt a thrill of vicarious and totally innocent wickedness in the companionship of an inveterate rebel like Lucas. Jeremy had never committed a crime more heinous than refusing to go to his uncle's church on Sunday morning; but in Lucas's company, he felt quite the misfit, and he relished the feeling.

Jeremy's thoughts were filled with images of Rowena's face and form as he stood with Lucas and Karyn just off the road on Route 25, watching Lucas attempting to flag down a passing pickup. He had met Lucas and Karyn in Greenwich Village two nights before, as they had arranged over the phone the previous week. The three of them had been in the audience for Simon's concert last night, and had had every expectation of riding back up to Bradford with him the next day. But none of them had thought to let him know that they were in Manhattan, and they were quite annoyed to learn that he had driven home directly after the show.

Thus it was that they stood, uncomfortable and tired at the end of a long day of hitchhiking. Their last ride had dropped them off at the juncture of Route 25 and Interstate 93, leaving them to cover the remaining twenty miles to Bradford with some other friendly motorist. This was no easy task, nor had many drivers who passed by them deigned to stop and pick them up. The frantic warnings issued to the American public by the Traffic Safety Council about the dangers of hitchhiking had been ignored by Lucas, Karyn, and Jeremy, but most of the people who drove past them on the road had apparently taken the caveat to heart. The six-hour drive had thus far taken them close to ten hours, with nearly five hours spent in standing on the roadside with outstretched thumbs.

The drivers who ignored them could hardly be faulted for so doing. The image struck by the three young people was not one to inspire confidence or sympathy. Lucas and Jeremy were both tall, muscular young men clad in denim jackets and denim pants, and both stood arrogantly with one thumb hanging from a belt loop and one knee slightly cocked as they stood in dusty, battered motorcycle boots. Or rather, Lucas stood thus, and Jeremy emulated him. Lucas had brown hair, and Jeremy's hair was a darker shade approaching black, but both had hair which cascaded down their backs in greasy, matted strands. Lucas's finely chiseled features and bright hazel eyes contrasted strongly with the dark, lupine cast of Jeremy's countenance, and anyone seeing them together would be led to assume that Jeremy was the greater danger. This was exactly opposite of truth, of course; but it nonetheless discouraged drivers from stopping and picking them up.

Karyn Johannson was another matter altogether. Had she been hitching on her own, she would have had no difficulty in getting rides. Whether she would have reached her destination in one piece, alive and unraped, is another matter. She was a strikingly attractive young woman, stimulating rather than beautiful, though a pale complexion which spoke more of long nights than of delicacy, and eyes which had seen too much in their nineteen short years, foretold an incipient aging which would in the not too distant future destroy the attractiveness she now possessed. Her red hair was long and layered, embracing her face with stark points and cascading down her back. Her full figure was made fuller by the child which had for four months been growing in her womb, Lucas's child, the tie with which she hoped to bind him. Her light brown eyes seemed forever half-closed. Whether this was intentional or natural, an attempt to project a bedroom sexuality or an attempt to hide their bloodshot cast, no one could tell. It certainly never occurred to Lucas to wonder about it.

"Hey! Fuck you, asshole!" Lucas shouted at the car which had just sped by them. "Son of a bitch!"

Karyn rubbed her eyes and yawned. "Take it easy, babe. We'll get a ride sooner or later. We're almost home anyway."

"Yeah, but we ain't home yet," he grumbled. "Leave it to my fuckin' old man to cut out early. Shit! If we'd'a known, we'd'a been home last night!"

"No use crying over spilt milk," Jeremy said quietly.

46

"Huh? Whatcha say?" Lucas turned to him.

"Nothing. I mean, it doesn't help any to get all angry and upset. Karyn's right. We'll be home soon, so take it easy."

"Ahhh," Lucas muttered. Another car approached them and Lucas extended his right hand, thumb up. The car drove by without slowing down. "Hey! Fuck you, asshole!" Lucas shouted once again. He glanced over at Jeremy, who was clutching to his chest a small rectangular object wrapped in brown paper. "Whatcha been totin' around, anyway? You pick up some porn down in Manhattan?"

Jeremy laughed uneasily. "No, nothing like that."

"Well, what is it then? You been holdin' it like it was made outta gold or something."

"It's a present."

Lucas smiled maliciously. "For Roweeeeena?" he simpered.

"No," Jeremy grinned. "It's for your dad."

This took Lucas aback. "My dad! No kidding?"

"No kidding."

"What is it?"

It was now Jeremy's turn to adopt an air of superior indifference. "It's for your dad."

"Hey, come on, Sloan, whatcha got?"

Jeremy shrugged. "You'll find out when I give it to your dad."

The sound of an approaching car caused Lucas to forget the response he was formulating, and he turned and squinted down the road. He did not take his eyes from the vehicle in the distance as he said, "Hey, Karyn, com'ere."

She was not distant from him, but she moved closer. "What, babe?"

"Flash this guy some tit."

"What?!"

"Come on, come on, flash your tits at him. Maybe he'll stop."

"Maybe it's a woman," she huffed. "Why don't you flash her your dick?"

Lucas refused to respond as if she were joking. "Damn it, Karyn, I don't wanna spend the whole goddamn day on this fuckin' roadside! Will you give me some help, for Christ's sake?"

She laughed disparagingly. "How? By getting us all chucked in jail? I swear, Lukie, sometimes you are so stupid!"

"Uh—" Jeremy said tentatively as he peered down the road

47

at the approaching automobile, "I don't think we're gonna need any extra help, Lucas."

Lucas followed his gaze and stared at the auto as it chugged with slow deliberation toward them, and he grinned as it began to slow and drift over to the side of the road. "Hey, mint!" he said. "Who is it?" He glanced over at Jeremy. "You recognize 'em?"

"You don't?" Jeremy asked. "It's your granddad and my uncle. Shit, Lucas, who else has a car that old still on the road?"

Lucas's eyes widened as the car came within clear view. Then he spat. "Fuckin' shit!"

"Hey, a ride's a ride," Karyn counseled. Responding without thinking to years of social conditioning, she drew a brush from her tattered leather shoulder bag and swept it through her hair, even though there was neither any need nor any possibility of her making a good impression upon old Floyd Proctor. "It's a damn good thing I didn't do what you wanted me to do."

"Huh? What? Oh—oh, yeah, I guess so," Lucas muttered. He and his grandfather were not the best of friends, and the prospect of being trapped in a car with the old man and the old minister, Jeremy's uncle, had disgruntled him instantly.

The old Dodge slowed to a stop a few yards away from them, and Jeremy walked over to it smiling. He opened the back door and climbed in, saying, "Hiya, Uncle Fred, Mr. Proctor. Gee, it's lucky for us that—"

"Where have you been, boy?" his uncle, the Reverend Frederick Wilkes, thundered, glaring at him from beneath enormous brows.

"I went to New York, Uncle Fred. I left you a note. Didn't you read my note?" Jeremy seemed to sink into the seat as he spoke.

"Oh, certainly, of course I got your 'note'!" the old man replied angrily. "And I suppose leaving a few words on a scrap of paper tossed onto the kitchen table is supposed to be sufficient nowadays, taking the place of a conversation?"

Before Jeremy could respond, Karyn slid beside him onto the seat and smiled broadly at the two old men in the front. "Hello, Mr. Proctor, Reverend Wilkes. Thanks so much for stopping for us." Lucas entered the car right after her and sat, silent and morose, neither offering nor receiving any acknowledgment from his grandfather or Jeremy's uncle.

Nor did either of them respond to Karyn's salutation. His

48

fiery eyes fixed on Jeremy, Reverend Wilkes continued his reprimand. "I remember a time when a young fellow wouldn't think of lighting off for days on end without discussing it with his parents. Now, I know I'm not your father, Jeremy—"

Oh, Lord! Jeremy thought dejectedly.

"—but when your Momma died she gave you over to my care, and the Lord knows I've cared for you as a father ever since. I will not have you flout my authority at every turn the way you do. I simply will not stand for it!"

"Jesus, Uncle Fred, I only—"

"Do *not* blaspheme, young man!"

"—went to New York to see Simon's concert with Lucas and Karyn. I mean, good grief! I'm not a ten-year-old, you know!"

Reverend Wilkes glanced momentarily at the other two occupants of the back seat, as Floyd Proctor slowly drove the car back onto the roadway and began the short drive to Bradford. "I have told you time and time again that I do *not* want you to have anything to do with that blasphemous nonsense! You know full well that if you had told me about this beforehand, I would have forbidden you to go!"

Jeremy grinned sheepishly. "That's why I left you a note, Uncle Fred."

"And don't take that tone of . . ." He stopped and studied Karyn for a moment. "You pregnant, girl?"

She blushed. "Uh, yes. Yes I am, Reverend."

He looked at Lucas. "You going to marry this girl, Lucas?"

Lucas did not reply, choosing instead to stare out the window at the rows of pine trees which were drifting slowly by. Karyn answered hastily, "Oh, maybe we will, maybe we won't. We haven't decided yet. But we'll be together like for good, you know?" She smiled sweetly at the old man.

Wilkes turned to Floyd. "You know 'bout this, Floyd?"

Floyd Proctor nodded his head slowly. "Yup. Didn't say nothin' 'bout it, though. Just another thing for me to be ashamed of." He rolled down the window and spat a wad of tobacco juice. "One damn thing after another. Thank God my Bessie ain't alive to see all of this. My son hoppin' around on a stage like some damned fairy, talkin' all that Devil garbage, my grandson nothin' but a low-life bum, his girlfriend nothin' but a—" He stopped, being from a generation of men who did not disparage women to their faces, regardless of the low esteem in which the woman in question might be held. "Thank God for Rowena, that's all I can say."

"Amen to that," Wilkes nodded.

"She's worth twice of all three of you put together," Floyd said bitterly, his eyes fixed on the road before him and his hands grasping the steering wheel so tightly that his knuckles were white against the corroded metal.

"I agree," Jeremy said. "She's a dynamite chick."

Reverend Wilkes shot him an angry glance. "You just remember that she isn't some floozy from New York. You keep your hands off that girl." The implicit contrast between Rowena and Karyn was not lost on the latter, and she flushed slightly.

"Hey, look, I really like Rowena, Uncle Fred, I really do!" Jeremy said earnestly.

"Yes, I know you do, and you just keep your hands to yourself!" He turned to face the front of the car and gazed out the window as fixedly as Floyd. "Generation of vipers," he muttered. "Generation of vipers."

They drove along in silence, the uneasy atmosphere hanging over them like a cloud. Karyn made a few attempts at conversation, but a few desultory grunts were all she could elicit, and she soon ceased her efforts. They all sat in uncomfortable silence as the car chugged slowly into town.

Bradford, New Hampshire, was well on the way to becoming a ghost town. Resting serenely in the river valley which separates New Hampshire from Vermont, thirty miles north of the Dartmouth College town of Hanover, far inland from the coastal city of Portsmouth, removed by distance and mentality from any hint of industry, trade, or tourism, Bradford seemed to lack any economic or demographic raison d'être. It was surrounded by farms—dairy farms, corn farms, truck farms, subsistence farms—worked by simple, rugged people, none of whom had any need of the small town, all of whom were in closer proximity to other towns in other directions. It was the presence of the river which had engendered the construction of a mill on its banks in the 1680s by Thomas Bradford, grandnephew of the great William Bradford who had chronicled the voyage of the *Mayflower*, and the town had grown around the mill almost coincidentally.

Bradford had become a small, settled community by the early 1700s. Today there were telephone poles, paved streets, a gasoline station, and an occasional television antenna thrusting up into the gray October sky, but if one could ignore these modern innovations one could feel very much as if it were still 1700 in Bradford. The town had changed very little in the nearly three hundred years since Elizabeth Proctor, having

50

resolved with typical Yankee stubbornness to put the horrible events in Salem behind her, had remarried and moved here from Massachusetts with her new husband and the two children she had borne her late husband John. The large white house which she and her new husband had built in the hopes of becoming innkeepers was still referred to by the locals as the Old Proctor Place, even though her new married name had been Robbins. She had lived and died in that house, and successive generations of Proctors had followed suit, eking out bare livings as innkeepers, supplementing their incomes as best they could by working the small farm, little more than a large garden really, which stretched out behind the inn away from the town's street. Not the town's main street, but the town's street. It had but one.

And that one Bradford street was a slice of the old colonial world preserved for an age which could neither understand nor appreciate it. If a visitor, more than likely a misdirected motorist, were to turn from the highway and drive into Bradford, the first sight which would greet him would be the grubby old gas station which had been built in, and unrepaired since, the days of the Great Depression. It was the town's sole acknowledgment of the twentieth century, for from that point on the observer would be moving into the colonial past. A few simple white wooden homes lined the street, and the large grange hall, painted red as a barn, rose up in their midst. Beyond that were a few more houses and then a fork in the road. The left hand of the fork, which sloped suddenly downward, would carry the visitor to the old wooden bridge beside the ruins of the old mill and thence across the river toward Piermont, Vermont. The right hand of the fork moved rapidly into the center of Bradford, and just as rapidly out of town completely.

Just beyond the point of the fork on the right-hand side of the street stood the old Proctor home, a large but still uncomplicated building of red brick and whitewashed pine, two stories high and girdled by an ample lawn. In the midst of the lawn stood a gnarled old oak tree, its twisted branches and sloping trunk seeming to bend under the weight of the centuries. Directly across the street was a smaller building, the downstairs of which had been a combination of post office, general store, and barber shop back in the days when there were still enough people living in Bradford to warrant such things, the upstairs of which served as the parsonage for the church.

The church itself, entitled simply the Bradford Congregationalist Church, stood removed from the parsonage by a broad, tree-enclustered field, with a similar expanse of land on its far side which separated it from the few remaining houses on the outskirts of town. The church was indistinguishable from a thousand other such buildings in New England, with its single spire reaching high into the sky, resolving itself into a weather vane in deference to the Puritan abhorrence of symbols, with its line of high, square-bottomed, round-topped windows flanking each side, with its sturdy, broad oak doors contrasting starkly with the gleaming white wood of the rest of the building.

The old cemetery faced the old church from across the street, and the weather-beaten stones of granite and marble and rotted limestone and decaying wood testified to the continuance of families, for the names Bradford and Proctor and Sloan and Robbins and Wilkes abounded. Beyond the church and the cemetery stood a few more houses, and then there was nothing but a narrow road stretching off into the dense New Hampshire forest.

It was an old town, a dying town. Reverend Wilkes still held his Sunday service for the half dozen old folks who attended, and Jeremy still kept the church clean and cared for at his uncle's command; the Proctors still lived in the old inn; and a few of the old houses were still inhabited; but people had been moving away from Bradford for a generation. There was little there to hold them.

Floyd Proctor pulled into the dirt driveway beside the old inn which had been his family's homestead for the past three centuries. He switched off the ignition and said sarcastically to Lucas, "It's pert' near four o'clock. Your father should be awake by now." To Wilkes he said, "Been asleep all day. It's tirin' bein' a fool."

As they all climbed out of the automobile, Wilkes began to walk across the street toward the parsonage, saying to Jeremy, "You come home right now, boy. I got a few things I'd like to say to you in private."

Spare me, Jeremy thought, but he said, "I'll be home soon, Uncle Fred. I want to see Rowena first."

His uncle glowered at him. "You remember what I said to you, boy!"

"Yes, Uncle Fred." God, what a pain in the ass! Jeremy walked around the corner of the house and, as he had hoped, found Rowena Proctor sitting on the old wooden bench

52

beneath the gnarled old tree on the side lawn. He smiled as he approached her, astounded as always at her loveliness, aware as always of the quickening of his heartbeat in her presence.

Rowena did not see him at first. She was sitting with a book in her lap, absentmindedly stroking her calico cat, Pistopheles. She had named the cat Pistopheles as a way of expressing her dislike of her father's satanism act, but the pun on the name Mephistopheles was lost on everyone. Rowena was the only member of her family who had ever paid any attention in school, and was thus the only one who had ever read *Faust*.

She had become a good student almost by default. The reputations of her father and brother had preceded her, and from the time of her childhood onward she had found herself largely friendless, as the parents in the other towns which supported the county schools forbade their children to associate with her. Her brother had been expelled from high school for selling drugs, and was generally known to have gotten at least two girls pregnant. Neither charge had been proven, of course, and the police and courts were never involved; but schools need less proof as a prelude to action than do the civil authorities, and Lucas was promptly expelled. It did not bother him in the least.

And her father's exploits were of course known to all. Rock stars were all junkies, everyone knew that; and Simon was a devil-worshiper to boot. Rowena came from bad stock, bad seed, the locals assumed, and she was ostracized. She had gone out on dates, of course. Her long, white blond hair, crystal blue eyes, flawless skin, and fetching figure had turned more than one head in high school; but she had been asked out only by boys who had assumed that, as Simon Proctor's daughter, she would be easy, which she was not. Only Jeremy had treated her with respect and genuine affection, and for this reason more than any other, she had fallen in love with him with that passion which only uncritical and unreasoning adolescence can experience. Their love was pure, joyful, unsullied. It made Lucas and Karyn sick.

Rowena looked up from her book and saw Jeremy approach. She flushed with happiness and rose to meet him. "Hi," she said. "I'm glad you're back." Pistopheles regarded them both indifferently.

"Yeah, me too," he said, grinning. "I missed you. Wish you'da come with me." He leaned down and kissed her lightly on the lips. She returned his kiss. It was a nervous, uneasy, unfamiliar gesture for them both. His appearance was one of worldliness and a jaded hedonism, but it was a facade, and Rowena knew it. He was as shy and inexperienced as she in affairs of the heart, and his attempts to give an impression to the contrary deceived no one who knew him. It had taken him over a year to work up the courage to kiss her in the first place, and he still felt that she was letting him get away with something.

"I wish you had stayed here with me," she replied. "I can't stand my dad's concerts. It would have been nice if you could just have stayed here, without Lukie or Karyn." She eyed the brown package he was holding. "What's that?" Is it for me? she thought hopefully.

"Oh, I bought this in Manhattan for your father."

"For Daddy? That's nice." She was disappointed.

Jeremy reached into his pocket. "And I bought this for you, Row." He handed her a small square box, feeling delight as her eyes went wide and her smile broadened.

Rowena tore open the wrapping paper and flipped up the hinged top of the box. It contained crescent moon earrings, golden with two ruby inlays on each. It was not really gold, and the rubies were glass, but that was of no consequence. "Oh, Jeremy, they're lovely!" she gushed. She rose up on tiptoe and kissed him again on the lips, thrilled by her own audacity.

"Oh, shit, ain't that just so fuckin' sweet?"

She blushed at the sound of her brother's voice and nervously distanced herself slightly from Jeremy. "Lucas." She nodded, an acknowledgment of his presence more than a greeting. "Hi, Karyn."

"Hiya, kid," Karyn replied pleasantly. She had nothing against Rowena, though she found her virginal propriety a bit irritating.

"Hey, where's the old man?" Lucas asked.

"Daddy or Gramps?"

"Dad," he replied. "I just got a lift from Gramps. It was lots of fun, let me tell you!"

"Daddy's still asleep," Rowena said, picking her schoolbooks up from the bench. "He got in real late last night, and he's still resting up." Her movement startled the cat, who jumped to the ground.

"Aw, poor guy!" Lucas dripped. "Son of a bitch didn't even wait around long enough for us to find him and we had to hitch all the way back up here." Pistopheles began to rub her neck against his leg.

"Did he know you were there?" she asked.

"No, we were gonna surprise him." He pushed the cat roughly away.

Rowena sniffed impatiently. "Well, what did you expect, Lucas? If Daddy'd known you were in New York, he would have waited for you. I mean, good grief! He's not a mind reader!"

"Maybe he is," Lucas grinned maliciously. "Warlocks have lots of powers."

This irritated Rowena, which is of course why he said it. "Stop it, Lucas! I mean it!" she added over his snickering. "Daddy's just an entertainer, and you know it!"

Lucas turned to the house and cupped his hands around his mouth. "HEY, DAD!" he shouted. "WAKE UP! JEREMY'S GOT A PRESENT FOR YOU!"

"Lucas, cut it out!" Rowena commanded. "If he's still sleeping, leave him alone."

Simon Proctor, bleary-eyed and disheveled, opened his bedroom window and looked down at the three young people. "Good morning," he said, feigning cheer.

"It's late afternoon, Daddy," Rowena called up to him. "I'm sorry we woke you up."

"Come on down, Dad," Lucas said. "Jeremy's got something for you, and I'm tired of wonderin' what it is."

"Yeah, yeah, okay," Simon mumbled. "Hold on. I'll be down in a minute." He disappeared back into his bedroom, shutting the window behind him.

Karyn walked over to the bench and sat down, yawning. "Jesus, what a day!"

Rowena sat down beside her. "How are you feeling?"

"Oh, I'm okay." She grinned, patting her belly. "Little bastard's gettin' bigger."

Lucas took out a cigarette and lighted it. "I still don't know why you don't get an abortion. I mean, shit, neither of us wanted this to happen."

"I don't want another abortion," she countered. "This time I want the kid."

He shrugged. "Up to you. Just don't start thinkin' about you and me startin' to play Ma and Pa on the farm or nothin'."

Karyn glanced at Rowena and grinned as if to say "We shall see." Rowena returned her smile. I have to get along with this bimbo, she thought. She's probably going to be my sister-in-law.

Simon Proctor opened the side door of the old inn and

55

walked briskly over to them. He held open his arms an[d]
Rowena rushed into them. He hugged her to him tightly,
lifting her from the ground and swinging her back and forth
few times. "Hello, baby. I'm sorry I wasn't up to take you t[o]
school this morning."

"That's okay, Daddy," Rowena said, hugging him back. "[I]
knew you needed sleep, so I didn't want to wake you up."

He released her and extended his hand to his son. "Lucas[.]
Where were you last night? I got in about four in the mornin[g]
and you weren't home."

"No, Dad, I was in Manhattan. We went to your concert las[t]
night."

"You're kidding! Why didn't you—" Then he realized that h[e]
had fled from the concert as if from a plague. "Oh, shit! How
did you get back?"

"We hitched."

"Oh, shit!" he repeated. "I'm sorry, kids. You should have le[t]
me know you were there. I would have waited for you."

"Hey, no problem," Lucas said casually. "We got here okay.
No big deal." He looked over at Jeremy. "Well?"

Jeremy Sloan walked forward. "Hiya, Simon," he said,
grinning and extending his hand. "I got a present for you."

"Well, isn't that nice!" Simon Proctor said, shaking the
proffered hand. "You shouldn't have done this, Jeremy. You
can't afford it." He took the rectangular object which Jeremy
held out to him, and as he began to unwrap it he said, "Hello,
Karyn. How are you doing?"

"Just fine, Mr. Proctor, just fine," she replied. She and Lucas
had been with each other for nearly two years, but Simon
Proctor still made her a bit uneasy. The fact that he was a
famous rock singer had impressed her from the start, and she
was still uncertain how much of his satanism image was a show
and how much was rooted in reality. Lucas, Jeremy, and
Rowena had all told her that the whole thing was an act, but
she had her doubts. He was just so *convincing* when she saw
him on stage, as she had frequently over the past two years.

Simon finished unwrapping the package and stood silently
for a moment, examining its contents. In his hands he held a
very old book, bound with soft leather. He opened it gently,
fearing that its age might cause him to damage it. He gazed at
the cover page and his eyes widened. "Jeremy, where did you
get this?"

"A book store in Greenwich Village," he said proudly. "The
guy there didn't even know what it was, so he didn't charge me

a whole lot for it. I figured you'd like to have it. Maybe you can use it in your show or something."

"What is it, Dad?" Lucas asked, looking over his father's shoulder at the book.

"It's an old copy of the *Caerimoniae Stupri Mortisque*," Simon replied. "The old book of witchcraft that I've used for some of my bits. Used it for the film, also." And had it ridiculed by that son of a bitch professor on television too, he thought glumly. What had he called it? A collection of foolishness concocted by an early nineteenth-century, self-proclaimed druid in Wales, wasn't it? The words, indeed the entire talk show, seemed burned upon Simon's memory. But what he said to Jeremy was, "Well, thanks an awful lot. This is a beautiful gift."

Jeremy flushed, pleased at Simon's gratitude. He wanted very much to ingratiate himself, for Simon was at once his musical hero, his best friend's father and, Jeremy dared to hope, perhaps someday his father-in-law as well. "I'm glad you like it," he said, smiling.

"Lemme see it, Dad," Lucas said.

"Here," Simon handed it to him. "Be careful with it It's very old and fragile."

"I think it's a first edition," Jeremy said. "A first printed edition, I mean. I know that there were probably handwritten ones that go back centuries and centuries, back to the Middle Ages."

"Sure, sure there were," Simon lied. Nineteenth-century foolishness—

"Hey, listen to this!" Lucas said excitedly. "There's a preface by"—he squinted at the handwritten signature—"Dr. William Price—"

"He was a druid," Simon said authoritatively. "Early nineteenth century." Damn!

"Yeah?" Lucas said. "Well, listen. 'Herein are set forth the ceremonies and spells whereby the powers of the underworld can be tamed and brought to use by those who devote themselves to the old religion. But be warned, reader! This is not a game, nor is it a responsibility to be taken lightly. With this book can the dead be raised, the souls brought forth from the Pit, the demons enslaved and the powers of the world be confounded. Woe to him who thinks not piously upon these dread secrets.'" He looked up. "This is great! Dad, you gotta use this in your act!"

"Yeah, yeah, sure," Simon said. Another few months and I

57

might not have an act, he thought. I might not even have this house!

"Impious garbage!" a voice boomed from behind them. They all turned to see Reverend Wilkes hobbling across the lawn in their direction. "Blasphemous nonsense! I heard that, I heard that, boy, and it isn't 'great' at all! It's dangerous, damnable nonsense!"

Simon sighed. I don't need this right now, he thought. "It's all in fun, Reverend. It isn't serious."

"It *is* serious!" Wilkes shouted. "You are leading young people to damnation, Simon Proctor! You are acting as an agent of Satan, and there are many souls being lost to God because of you!"

Simon Proctor took the book from his son and closed it. "Listen, Reverend, don't take this all so seriously. Really! Nobody else takes it seriously!"

"No? Well, God takes it seriously!" His visage darkened. "And whether you know it or not, Satan takes it seriously!"

"Oh, please," Simon said tiredly. "Please."

"Do not beg me, young man," Wilkes said. "I beg *you*! I beg *you*! Stop this dangerous, blasphemous impiety. It is not a joke, Simon, it is not just show business. You will feel the wrath of God for this, I warn you!" He looked at his nephew. "Jeremy, come home this instant!"

"Yeah, yeah, okay, Uncle Fred. I'll be right there." Jeremy turned to Rowena. "Can I come over later on, after supper?"

"Sure," she said happily. "I have to study for a biology test. You can help me."

He laughed. "Gee, Row, I don't remember too much about that stuff. I think I got a D in bio when I was in high school."

"Jeremy!" his uncle shouted. "This instant!"

"Okay, okay, okay!" To Rowena, "I'll see you later." He followed his uncle as he crossed the street back to the parsonage.

"Studying for a test," Lucas nodded approvingly. "You're a real fun date, Rowena."

"Oh, shut up, Lucas!" she snapped.

Lucas sat down on the bench beside Karyn. "Babe, I got a math test tomorrow. Can you help me with my homework tonight?" he simpered. She poked him in the ribs and whispered, "Shhh! Be nice!"

Rowena repressed her annoyance and turned to her father. "Are you hungry, Daddy?"

He smiled lovingly at her. "I could eat a horse."

"Okay." She grinned. "I'll go get supper started." She began to walk toward the door.

Karyn got uneasily to her feet and said, "Hold on, Row. I'll give you a hand." She followed Rowena into the house, leaving Simon and Lucas alone on the lawn.

Simon pulled his shirt collar closed. "Getting chilly out here."

Lucas nodded. "Yeah. Probably gonna snow."

"Yeah." Simon shifted his weight from foot to foot nervously. He and his son were not comfortable in each other's presence. There had been too little closeness between them for too many years. "It's kind of early for snow, though."

"Yeah, kinda early." He lighted another cigarette.

Simon nodded. "So. You and Karyn going to get married?"

Lucas grimaced. "No. What the hell for?"

Simon shrugged, not really wanting to pursue the topic, not feeling that he had any right to comment on his son's life because he had had so little to do with it. "Just curious."

"Well," Lucas said, dragging on the cigarette. "I'm gonna go in and take a nap. I'll see you later."

"Yeah. See you later." He watched as his son ambled into the old house. He waited a few moments before following him in, and he passed those few moments by examining the old book he held. "Foolishness," he muttered, ". . . concocted . . ." He shook his head. "Shit!" Then he entered the house, slamming the door loudly behind him.

A cold wind whistled through the bare branches of the old oak. The sky grew gray and filled with dark clouds.

⟦ CHAPTER FOUR ⟧
October 31

AND THE SNOWS came early that year to Bradford, New Hampshire. Just after dusk the first few flakes of white drifted lazily down from the colorless sky and crowned the few remaining blades of brown and withered grass with baby's-breath spots of crystal. There was a stillness in the midst of the snowfall, as if the wind had for some reason ceased its circuit, as if it had elected to exempt the first few delicate flakes from its ruthless buffeting. Soon the snow was falling heavily, covering the little country town with its first winter blanket months before winter, adorning it and clothing it, making it as white as a wedding gown. Or a shroud.

Simon Proctor sat behind the old mahogany desk in the study beside the library on the first floor of the old Proctor Inn, staring morosely out at the thick white clouds which were enveloping the old oak. Nature mirroring mood, he reflected.

Simon looked back down at the pile of bills which rested upon the stained ink blotter on the surface of the desk, and he sighed. I can handle this month, he thought, maybe next month. Land tax, heating oil, insurance, phone, credit card bills—all marginally manageable. But the month after that the loans would start to fall due, the loans he had contracted to finance the film, the loans against which he had used his house and future earnings as collateral.

He sat back in his swivel chair and looked once again out the window. "So I have three months," he muttered. Three months in which to make enough money to extricate himself from his situation, three months in which to solve an unsolvable problem. One month of repose before beginning the concert tour to publicize the film.

Sighing once again, Simon reached into his breast pocket and drew out a cigarette. Lighting it, he shook his head. Impossible, he thought. "Never do it," he muttered. I can't sell out a concert hall anymore, record sales are down, nobody's going to go to see that stupid, stupid film. I'll be lucky if I break even on the concert tour itself. And then . . .

And then . . . ?

Bankruptcy, perhaps? Homelessness? That's a possibility. Shame, despair, nervous collapse, suicide . . . all possibilities.

He exhaled a long fume of smoke. "Shit," he muttered.

Floyd Proctor pushed open the creaking old door and walked into the study. "Simon, I want to talk to you."

Simon glanced up at him quickly and then returned his attention to the bills. "Not now, Pop. I'm busy."

Floyd seated himself beside the desk. "Don't look busy to me. You never look busy to me."

He tossed the pen he held down onto the desk angrily. "Goddamn it, Pop, not now, okay? Just leave me alone, will you?"

Floyd leaned forward. "Can't do that, sonny, because I

never get left alone, and neither does Row. We have to live with the crap you peddle every day of the week, week after week, month after month, year after year. Did you know that I ain't got no friends left 'round here? None worth speakin' of, anyway, 'ceptin' Fred Wilkes. Poor Row ain't got one friend in this whole damn world 'ceptin' young Jeremy, and I ain't too happy 'bout that friendship."

Simon pretended to busy himself with the bills. "Jeremy seems like a nice kid."

"Yeah," the old man nodded, "seems so. But he spends too much time with Lucas, and that's bound to corrupt him. Now, Lucas is a lost cause. Never gonna be nothin' but a bum, just like his father." Simon bristled, but Floyd went on as if he had not noticed. "But Rowena still has some decency in her, and I don't want to see it ruined. She's all I got left to show for my life."

Simon threw the pen down again, more forcefully. It bounced off the desk top and clattered against the window pane. "For Christ's sake, Pop, will you leave me be?!"

"Nope," the old man said stubbornly. "You're gonna hear me out, Simon."

"You always say the same goddamn things! What's the point of listening? What's the point of your saying them?"

"The point is that you *don't* listen, and I'm gonna keep right on saying the same things until you do!"

Simon gazed at the wizened old face which stared back at him, and he felt a twinge of guilt mixed with unwilling affection. Old Floyd had worked hard all his life, and each crease in the ancient face seemed to be a battle scar from life's wars. Each hair which had fallen from the now bald head seemed to have departed from the strain of labor and worry, not a small part of which had been provided by Simon.

Floyd had worked multiple jobs for decades, running a small general store, running the old inn which was as unprofitable in this century as it had been over the past two, farming the small plot of land out back until arthritis barred him from it, working as the town's postmaster for forty years until the government retired both him and the town's status as a postal district, merging it with the postal zone of Carltonville, twenty miles away. At least he got a federal pension from his efforts. Were it not for that, Floyd would have been totally dependent upon his son, and that would have killed him.

It still might, Simon thought, if he ever finds out that he made a mistake signing the house over to me, if he ever learns that I may very well have lost the family home. Simon forced himself to speak gently. "Look, Pop, don't take things so seriously, okay? Row's going to be fine and Lucas is going to straighten out too, you just wait and see."

Floyd shook his head. "The boy ain't never gonna straighten out as long as you keep on twistin' him. And Lord knows how many other troubled kids you been twistin' with that disgustin' garbage of yours."

"Damn it, Pop—!"

"You just listen to me, sonny." Floyd stood up and leaned forward over the desk, resting his swollen, arthritic knuckles upon it. "What you been doin' is wrong, it's just plain wrong! You're shamin' me, Simon, and you're shamin' your daughter, and you're shamin' the memory of your mother. Why, there never lived a more God-fearin' woman than my Bessie. She took you to church regular, tried to raise you up like a good Christian boy." He stood up straight. "And look at you! Just look at you! Prancin' around like some goddamned idiot, talkin' about the Devil, makin' dirty movies, wearing all that damn faggy makeup, wearing *earrings*, for Christ's sake!"

Simon leapt to his feet. "Pop, will you just shut up and get the hell out of here?! I don't need this aggravation!"

"Don't you talk to me that way, boy! Why, I got a good mind to slap your face!"

Simon took his father's arm firmly in his hand and pulled him roughly toward the door of the study. "I'm busy, goddamn it!" he shouted as he pushed his father out into the hallway. He slammed the door and locked it. Simon Proctor sat back down at the desk and tried to concentrate on the bills, tried to ignore the furious pounding of his father's fists upon the locked door. Floyd's angry knocking from behind him was matched by the heavy thudding of the snow-drenched wind upon the window before him.

Stereo, he thought absently.

The wind blew the snow around Bradford in frenzied tornadic circles, assaulting the branches of the naked trees and weighing them down with piles of frozen whiteness. House lights were dimly visible through the thick snowfall, oases of warmth and calm in the midst of the relentless attack of nature. The weather vane atop the old church spun madly about, testifying mutely to the fact that the wind seemed to be blowing in from all directions at once.

The wind hurled snow against the windows of the parsonage across the street from the Proctor Inn, and Jeremy Sloan watched it quietly, enchanted by its pristine, awesome beauty as well as seeking to avoid having to listen to his uncle. The spoon which he held in his right hand moved lazily through the steaming bowl which rested on the table before him. He stirred his supper absentmindedly.

Reverend Wilkes looked up at him. "Jeremy!"

He was startled momentarily. "Hmm? Yeah, Uncle Fred?"

Wilkes gestured impatiently at the bowl. "Eat your stew."

"Okay, okay."

"Food is a gift of God. It's a sin to waste it."

"Okay, okay!" he repeated, taking a spoonful of broth and vegetables and slopping them into his mouth. "I'm eating it, okay?"

Wilkes returned his attention to his own bowl of stew. They ate in silence for a few moments. Then he said, "I want you to fix the lectern tomorrow."

"What's wrong with it?" Jeremy was struggling to find a piece of meat somewhere in the thick brown stew. He could not.

"Steps are loose." Wilkes blew on his spoon of broth to cool it off. "Don't want to fall down when I preach this Sunday."

Jeremy nodded. "Okay. I'll check 'em out in the morning."

A few more moments of silence. "Spoke to Jed Rutherford, over in Piermont yesterday. Says he needs a few new hands at the lumber mill. If you get there early Monday, I'm sure he'll take you on."

Jeremy sighed. "Uncle Fred, I really don't want to work in no lumber mill."

"I know, I know," Wilkes said with disgust. "You want to spend your life playing games with that Lucas Proctor. Well, everybody's gotta do something with their lives, Jeremy. You're out of high school, not going to college. Gotta get a job. Lumber mill's as good as anything. An honest dollar's an honest dollar."

Jeremy didn't want to argue about it. He returned his attention to his meal, as did his uncle. Jeremy reached across the table for the plate piled high with sliced whole wheat bread. His uncle glared at him. "You got a tongue, boy?"

Sighing, Jeremy withdrew his hand. "Please pass the bread."

Nodding with satisfaction, Wilkes pushed the plate nearer to his nephew. "You been behaving yourself with that little girl?"

"Huh?"

"You heard me, boy. You been behaving yourself with the Proctor girl?"

Jeremy blushed. "Cut it out, will you, Uncle Fred?"

Wilkes's eyes blazed at him. He seemed the embodiment of Mosaic wrath, an Old Testament prophet with large, bushy brows and a craggy face, an enormous head bristling with wild white hair atop a thin, stooped, almost delicate body. "You answer me, boy!" he demanded.

"Of course I've been behaving myself with Rowena," he said angrily, angry at his uncle for asking so personal a question, angry at himself for not having the backbone to refuse to answer it. "I like Rowena, I like her a lot."

Wilkes studied Jeremy's face suspiciously. "You do anything to hurt that little girl, and I'll whip you to within an inch of your life."

Jeremy sighed. "Yes, Uncle Fred."

Wilkes nodded, satisfied. They both returned to their meal. After a few minutes of silence, Wilkes said, "You come to church Sunday."

"Yes, Uncle Fred." Jeremy sounded resigned, depressed.

"I know there aren't many people left in the congregation. I know it's a small church, always has been. But that doesn't mean that folks who're still here can't go when the services are held."

"Yes, Uncle Fred."

Wilkes nodded. "See if you can bring that poor girl with you, the one that Lucas Proctor has got into trouble."

Why argue the absurdity of the idea? Jeremy thought. "Yes, Uncle Fred."

"Most disgraceful thing I ever heard of in my whole life. Poor girl's not even old enough to be out on her own, let alone having a baby, let alone that miscreant's baby."

"Yes, Uncle Fred."

He looked up at Jeremy. "And I don't like you spending so much time with that Lucas Proctor."

"Yes, Uncle Fred."

"Now, I know that he's Floyd's grandson, and Floyd and I go back more years than either of us cares to remember, but he's just no good, that boy, no darn good."

"Yes, Uncle Fred." Jeremy was staring out the window at the snow.

"Probably takes after that strumpet Simon used to be married to. Bad blood, most likely. Always comes out."

"Yes, Uncle Fred."

Wilkes paused. "You listening to me, boy?"

"Yes, Uncle Fred."

"What did I just say?"

"Yes, Uncle—what?"

Wilkes threw his spoon down angrily. "Consternation, Jeremy Sloan! You give me your attention when I'm speaking to you."

"Yeah, I'm sorry, Uncle Fred. What were you saying?"

Wilkes resumed his tirade and Jeremy looked directly at him, not hearing a word. Every now and then he would glance out the window at the Proctor home across the road, looking for some sign of Rowena, a shadow against the curtain perhaps, or a visible movement in the lighted window of her bedroom. The snow was falling more heavily now than before, almost obscuring the house lights across the way.

The snow seemed to rush down Bradford's street, striking the old monument to the town's Civil War dead, whipping around the barren flag pole in front of the Grange hall, blanketing the buildings and making even the dirty old gas station look clean and new. The wind threw the snow in all directions as it howled and whistled through the moonless night.

Rowena Proctor sat by her window, watching the storm. A good night to be home, she thought. A good night to be inside. But a bad night to be reading this book.

She looked down at the dog-eared volume which she had taken from the school library the day before, the old copy of Deodat Lawson's *A Brief and True History of Witchcraft at Salem Village*. She had intended to do her social studies term paper on the War of the Roses, but her teacher, attempting to be helpful, suggested that she might be able to distance herself from her father's reputation by reporting objectively and critically on the events in seventeenth-century Salem. She had not decided as yet, but she had taken the book out anyway.

It's so hard to believe that anybody actually took all of this seriously back then, she thought as she allowed her eyes to drift over the yellowing pages. This book had first been published in London shortly after the trials in Salem, and the reprint which the school library had in its stacks seemed almost as old. Such utter foolishness! she thought as she read about the beginning of the hysteria.

In the beginning of the evening I went to give Mr. Parris a visit. When I was there, his kinswoman, Abigail Williams, had a grievous Fit; she was at first hurryed with

Violence to and fro in the room (though Goodwife Ingersol endeavoured to hold her), sometimes makeing as if she woulde fly, stretching her arms as high as she could, and crying, "Whish! Whish! Whish!" several times; Presently she said there was Goody Nurse and said "Do you not see her? Why there she stands!" And then she did scream and cry and then she did laugh and clap and then she said Goody Nurse offered her The Book, but she was resolved she would not take it, saying Often, "I wont, I wont, take it, I do not know what Book it is: I am sure it is none of God's Book, it is the Divels Book, for ought I know." After that she run to the Fire, and begun to throw fire brands about the house; and run against the Back, as if she would run up the Chimney, and, as they say, she had attempted to go into the Fire in other Fits.

It's almost funny, Rowena thought. Some girl with a mental problem starts going crazy, and people end up being hanged for witchcraft. "How could they believe that?" she wondered aloud. She paged through the old book, and her eyes were caught by the sight of her own family name.

And Goodman John Proctor testified that he had beaten Mary Warren out of some of her Fits, and threatened to burn her out of them by firey tongs, and he said that she grew calm when he threatened her, so that this be no True witchcraft, but the sillynesse of a silly girl. Then Mary Warren took a Fit at his words, and he said "If you are afflicted, I wish you were more afflicted," and she said, "Master what makes you say so?" and Proctor said, "Because you go to bring out innocent persons." And Mary Warren answered, "That cannot be so."

Rowena flipped a few pages ahead, looking for further references to her ancestor. Such a superstitious period, she thought. People actually believed in witches and magic and all that. "Incredible," she muttered. She noticed her family name again and read further.

And on April 11th of 1692 Mary Warren was accused in Court of signing the Divel's Book. And she said, "I look up to God and take it to be a Great Mercy of God," and Judge Hathorne said "What, do you take it to be a great mercy to afflict others?" And then came into Court Abigail

Williams and Mercy Lewis and Elizabeth Parris and the other afflicted girls, and Mary Warren fell into a Fit and she cryed out "God have mercy on me." And then came into Court Goodwife Corey and John Proctor and his Goodwife Elizabeth, and Mary Warren began to confess, saying it were sillynesse. But then Abigail Williams fell into a Fit, and so did the girls, and Mary Warren continued a good space in a fit so that she did neither see nor hear nor speak. Afterward she started up and said, "I will speak," and cried out, "Oh, I am sorry for it, I am sorry for it," and wringed her hands, and fell a little while into a Fit again, and then came to speak, but immediately her teeth were set. And then she fell into a violent Fit and cried out "Oh Lord help me, Oh Lord help me!" And then afterward cried again "I will tell, I will tell" and then fell into a dead Fit again. And afterward cried "I will tell, They did It, They did It!" and then fell into a violent Fit again. After a little recovery she cried "I will tell, They brought me to It" and then fell into a Fit again, after which fits continuing she was ordered to be had out of Court.

She flipped ahead a few more pages and then stopped again to read when she saw her name.

John Proctor and his Wife being in prison, the Sheriff came to his House and seized all the Goods, Provisions and Cattle that he could come at, and sold some of the Cattle at half price, and killed others and put them up for the West Indyes; threw out the beer out of a Barrel, and carried away the Barrel; emptied a Pot of Broath and took away the Pot, and left nothing in the House for the support of the Children; Proctor earnestly requested Mr. Noyes to pray with him and for him, but it was wholly denied, because he would not own himself to be a Witch.

"Barbarians!" Rowena muttered. "Barbarians!" They wouldn't even let a minister pray with him! They wouldn't even leave food for his children, with both their parents in prison. She knew that Elizabeth Proctor eventually was released from prison—otherwise she would not be alive to read this book, not be living in the small New Hampshire town of Bradford to which Elizabeth eventually moved—but she was horrified at the idea of a group of lonely, frightened children being robbed and starved while their parents languished in prison, charged with witchcraft, of all things! "Incredible," she repeated aloud. She turned a few more pages, looking for her name.

On August 19th were executed in Salem Village George Burroughs, John Willard, John Proctor, Martha Carrier and George Jacobs, a very great Number of Spectators being present. Mr. Cotton Mather was there, Mr. Sims, Hale, Chiever, &ct. All of the condemned prisoners said they were Innocent. Mr. Mather said they died by a Righteous Sentence. Mr. Proctor by his Speech, Prayer, protestation of his Innocence, did much move unthinking persons, which occasions their speaking hardly concerning his being executed. So were all executed by hanging except Proctor's Wife, who pleaded Pregnancy, and so was spared until she be delivered. After this a little While and Salem became becalmed, but much was said harshly against the accusers. And Mr. Parris was denied his pulpit and left the Village. Mercy Lewis was soon wed to Samuel Hale, and Abigail Williams and Mary Warren went to the Citty of Boston.

So the number of persons accused of Witchcraft in Salem was Fifty-Seven; and the number declared Guilty of Witchcraft was Thirty-Two; and the number hanged for Witchcraft was Nineteen. And that be an End to this Doleful Episode.

The wind smote the window with a sudden ferocity, and Rowena started slightly as the snow assaulted the glass. "What a night!" she said aloud. And it's only October! She glanced over at her clock. Well, it'll be November in three more hours, so I guess it isn't too unusual.

She closed the book and left it lying upon her desk. She rose and walked over to her bed, allowing herself to fall down upon it, thinking about the Salem trials, about her father and brother, about Jeremy Sloan, all of her thoughts mixing with each other in her mind. Been a long day, she thought. Must be why I'm so sleepy. Maybe I should turn in. Maybe I should.

Rowena was sound asleep in moments, sinking into her dreams before even removing her clothes and putting on a nightgown, unaware of the growing violence of the blizzard as it cast its frozen burden again and again at the windowpane, not hearing the mournful howl of the wind, free of the oppressive gloom of the early winter storm.

Two rooms down from her, Karyn Johannson was watching eagerly as Lucas Proctor stuffed a small, ornate metal pipe full with hashish. They too had been reading, but while Rowena had been studying historical records, Lucas and Karyn had been reading the old copy of the *Caerimoniae Stupri Mortisque* which Jeremy had purchased in Manhattan, and which Simon had left in the library downstairs. The book was propped open in Lucas's lap, and he was running his eyes over line after line as he filled the pipe in a slow and leisurely fashion. "Come on, babe, hurry up!" Karyn said peevishly.

"Huh?" Lucas asked.

"I wanna get loose. Hurry up with the dope."

"Oh, yeah, yeah, right. Sorry." He tamped the powdery hashish down with his forefinger and then placed the pipe between his teeth. He turned to Karyn. "Ooo a-ha att?"

"What?"

He took the pipe from his mouth. "You got a match?"

"Oh, sure. Hold on." She reached down for the purse which lay beside the bed on the floor and rummaged around in it for a moment before drawing forth a lighter. "Here you go, babe."

"Thanks," he muttered. Lucas returned the pipe to his mouth and held the flame over the bowl. Soon curls of pungent smoke began to rise from the pipe as he passed it over to Karyn. He had drawn the intoxicating smoke deep into his lungs, and his eyes watered slightly as he struggled to hold the smoke in. He finally exhaled just as Karyn, having taken a greedy draft herself, passed the pipe back to him. He took another long drag and then said, "You know, we ought to try this stuff."

"What stuff?" she asked dreamily as the effects of the hashish began to make themselves felt.

"The spells and ceremonies in this book. It'd be a pisser if they worked."

"Yeah, it would," she replied, not the slightest bit interested.

Lucas thought hard for a moment as he sucked on the pipe. "It's nearly Halloween, isn't it? I mean, in a day or two?"

"It is Halloween, babe," she yawned. "Today's the thirty-first."

"Today? Right now? No shit?"

"No shit. Why? What difference does it make?"

Lucas considered this for a moment. Then he said, "Look, let's get Jeremy and break into the old church and do some witchcraft. What do you say?"

Karyn laughed. "Are you serious, Lukie? Have you looked out the window lately? It's a goddamn blizzard out there!"

"So what? The church is just up the street." He hopped up onto his knees and bounced on the bed. "Come on, Karyn, it'd be fun! Maybe we could conjure up a demon or bring back the dead or see the Devil or something!"

She continued laughing. "Oh, Lucas, don't be so stupid. Nobody wants to go out on a night like this!"

"Well, I do," he huffed. "Shit. It's fuckin' Halloween, for Christ's sake! We gotta do somethin'."

She reached over with a languid motion and began to massage his crotch. "Okay. Let's do something."

"No, no, that's not what I meant."

"Look, baby, we're only gonna be able to screw for a few more weeks. I'm getting too big, and pretty soon it's gonna get too damn awkward. Don't you want to make the most of it while we can?"

"Well . . ." Lucas was weakening.

"Come on, baby," she whispered, taking his hand and placing it upon her full breasts. "Warm me up."

Lucas grinned at her and then, tightening his grasp upon her right breast, kissed her lustfully. "Okay, you win," he said softly. "But later on, afterward, we're gonna do some spells."

"Sure, honey, sure," she whispered. "Anything you say." She slid down from her sitting position to lie upon her back. Lucas rolled over onto her.

And the snows blew and the wind whipped and the small town of Bradford rested in frozen silence beneath the white pall. The snows covered the roofs and hid the streets and buried the ground. The snows fell upon the church and the Grange hall and the old inn and the parsonage. The snows covered the old cemetery, covered the tombstones, covered the graves, as if seeking further to bury the dead, as if seeking to erect a barrier against their emergence, as if seeking to keep them safely entombed.

And elsewhere, in the ultimate elsewhere, in the eternal nowhere, in the eternal nowhen, a blind, deaf, faceless, formless thing writhed in bitter agony upon the surface of a burning lake.

[CHAPTER FIVE]
Eternity

PAIN.

Relentless, unending, excruciating, tearing, searing, rending pain.

The thing crawled across an insubstantial, groundless, bottomless surface of acrid, sulfurous liquid. It had no eyes, it had no ears, it had no skin, no nerve endings, no vocal cords. And yet somehow it could see the billows of red and yellow as the pit vomited forth wave after wave of invisible fire. Somehow it could hear the inaudible screams, the shrieks, the wails, which assaulted it from every direction. Somehow it could feel the flesh which it did not possess sizzle upon the charred bones it lacked, feel the water boil within its absent eyes, feel the very blood which did not course through the illusory veins bubble and steam. Somehow it could feel the stabbing agony rip and rip and rip through its fleshless form, tear it asunder, burn and burn and burn. Somehow in its mute agony it screamed and cried and wept and begged and pleaded and prayed.

Pain.

Relentless, unending, excruciating, tearing, searing, rending pain.

It raised what would have been its head, turned what would have been its eyes, and gazed blindly upon the ice white epicenter of energy which spewed out bolts of bitter agony. It opened what would have been its mouth and croaked what would have been a question.

When? it asked. When?

A wave of soundless, inhuman laughter washed over it, pressing it down into the boiling liquid upon which it floated. The pain grew suddenly more intense, more profound. It always grew more intense and more profound. It never lessened, it never abated. It always grew worse.

It floated in timeless misery upon the burning lake.

Another form approached it unknowingly. The other form was as insubstantial and as agonized as itself, and they became dimly aware of each other in the midst of their misery.

71

You, said the thing.

You, said the other.

It hurts, said the thing.

Hurts, said the other, and was gone.

There were no days, no minutes, no seconds. Time passed timelessly, without years, without decades, without centuries. Time had no reality. The only reality was pain.

The thing was blindly aware of other tortured forms floating by, other voiceless screams, other cries, other pleas for pity. It had no nostrils with which to smell the burning flesh, but it smelled the burning flesh nevertheless.

When? it begged. When? it wept. When? When? And the thing braced itself for the inevitable onslaught of inhuman laughter from the epicenter of misery.

But the laughter did not come. There was a silence uncommon for the soundless torture chamber, and a sudden, subtle lessening of the pain.

When? a voice echoed. Do you ask when you will be released, when you will walk again upon the earth?

Yes, the thing wept. Yes. When?

Do you know who you were? the voice asked. Do you remember who you were?

No,' the thing wept. All it knew was pain.

Do you remember why you hope for release? the voice asked.

No, the thing wept.

You must remember, the voice said. You must remember and understand.

The thing felt itself slowly and inexplicably rising from the boiling surface. It looked down with the eyes it did not have and saw the invisible flames receding from it as it rose slowly and smoothly from the blistering heat into the very gradually increasing cool. Its absent eyes saw the other rising also from the agony into the numbness, from the black into the red into the blue, from the nowhere into the somewhere, from the nowhen into the now.

You, said the thing.

You, said the other. Is it time?

It is time, said the voice. Remember who you were. Remember your lives. Remember and understand.

Memory began very, very slowly to emerge from the dead minds so long dulled by agony and misery and terror and sorrow. They remembered the smell of evergreen trees and the sound of snow crunching beneath leather boots. They remembered the cold wind and wintry silence of New England in November of 1691.

Yes, said the things. Yes. . . . Yes. . . .

. . . Mary Warren pulled her scarf tightly around her neck as she walked down the narrow, pitted country road which led from Salem Village to the farms northwest of the town. It was bitterly cold, but the sky was clear enough and it was early in the day, so she had no fears for her safety or survival. It was clearly not going to snow today, and she would be back home at the Corey farm long before dusk. The Indians also posed no problem, not anymore, not since the skirmishes and the massacres four years ago. Her parents had been among the whites murdered by the savages, and the townspeople visited a horrible vengeance upon the red men, burning their villages, killing the men, enslaving the women and children. It was their own fault, the sturdy Puritans reasoned, for refusing to behave in a civilized manner.

So Mary Warren was not afraid to walk alone down the snow-covered path toward the Proctor farm, carrying the pumpkin pie which Martha Corey in a burst of infrequent and uncharacteristic charity had baked for Goodwife Proctor. She had borne her husband John his second child just last summer, and it had been a hard delivery. Though Elizabeth Proctor had steeled herself to her labor and her tasks, she was weakened and still ailing, and the women of the area expressed their concern by sending her and her family pies and stews, prepared and ready for eating, so as to spare her the labor of cooking more than necessary.

This was not charity, nor did it reflect unkindly upon Goodman John Proctor as a provider. He was a skilled hunter and a willing laborer in the stoney New England fields, and he housed and fed and sheltered and cared for his own as well as any man in Salem; but Salem in 1691 was still basically a frontier community, and each family felt dependent upon every other family, felt responsible for every other family. They helped each other out of a feeling which combined self-interest with Christian obligation, and when food was sent to the weak and frail Elizabeth, it was with full knowledge that when her health returned, as all prayed that it would, she would be baking pies and simmering stews for other ailing wives in the town and on the surrounding farms.

Mary whistled as she sped over the snow with quick, small

steps. It was a beautiful day, cold but still, without the bitter, biting wind so common in Massachusetts once the snows came. She looked forward to seeing Goodman and Goodwife Proctor, and she looked forward even more to spending some time with their serving girl, her friend Abby Williams. Mary saw most of her friends—Betty Parris, Mercy Lewis, Suzannah Wolcott—in church on Sunday, but the Proctors rarely went to Reverend Parris's services, and so rarely brought Abigail with them. Abby could walk the distance, Mary well knew; but Abby never really cared enough about church to make that kind of effort.

Mary turned off the road and walked toward the simple log cabin which stood at the foot of a broad expanse of white snow-covered fields which was the Proctor farm. An inviting stream of smoke drifted lazily up from the chimney into the quiet, windless sky, and Mary smiled, hoping that Goodwife Proctor would offer her a cup of tea. Almost everyone drank the tea harvested in the Indias, and that was good enough for Mary, but Goodwife Proctor had managed somehow to get tea grown in the Japans, which was green and rich and much more pleasurable. She probably bought it from that smuggler, Thomas McCollough, but it tasted good, no matter what its source.

She knocked softly on the front door of the cabin and called out, "Goody Proctor? Goody Proctor? 'Tis I, Mary Warren." She heard a sound of motion within, and a few moments later the door swung open and Elizabeth Proctor smiled at her. "Good morrow, Goody Proctor," she said happily.

"Hello, Mary," the older woman said. "Come in out of the cold." She ushered Mary into the large central room of the cabin and pushed the door shut behind them. "I fear I'll not be in good health until spring, and it portends a cold winter."

"Aye," said Mary, unwrapping her scarf and removing her cloak. "'Tis but November and already three snowfalls." She held out the small burlap bag she had been carrying. "Goody Corey asked me to bring you this pie."

"Why, bless Martha!" she said, taking the bag. "She's a good woman, no matter what anyone says."

"She's been very good to me, that's a fact," Mary agreed, "taking me in and giving me work and a roof and meals after my parents died."

"Would you like some tea, Mary? I have a kettle a-boil over the fire." She took the pie out of the bag and set it on the oaken table, clicking her tongue appreciatively.

"Aye, I would like that very much, Goody Proctor!" she smiled.

"Fine. Mary, go and fetch Abigail. If you and I are having tea, she should join us. She should be out in the barn, tending to the livestock."

"Certainly, Goody Proctor," Mary said. "I haven't seen Abby in weeks. I was hoping she'd be free for a little while today." She threw her cloak back on, leaving the scarf on the peg beside the door. She walked quickly back out into the cold, making certain to close the door behind her, and then walked around the house toward the small barn which rested in the snow some hundred yards away.

She pushed open the barn door and was about to call out for Abigail, but her mouth froze open and her words remained unuttered as she beheld the sight in front of her. Abigail Williams was lying upon her back in the hay, her skirts thrown up and her feet flailing wildly in the air. John Proctor, his trousers pulled down to his ankles, was lying between her legs, thrusting into her mercilessly. My God! Mary thought. He's raping her!

"Oh, John," Abigail panted, running her hands over his back and through his hair, "John, John!"

Mary backed up as quietly as she could and went back outside. She pulled the door shut, hoping that she had not been heard. It was not forced, she thought as she turned back toward the house. He isn't taking her against her will. She is giving herself to him. Poor Goody Proctor! How terrible! How awful!

How delightfully wicked! She could hardly wait to get Abigail alone and talk to her about it. They had no secrets from each other, and this was the most exciting topic of conversation Mary could think of since the Cheever boy got Magdalene Smith in the family way last autumn.

Abigail and Goodman Proctor! Mary thought wonderingly. How exciting! She went back to the Proctor cabin and said, "I cannot find her, Goody Proctor. Perhaps she is on an errand for Goodman Proctor."

"Perhaps," Elizabeth said innocently. "Here, sit down, child. Let me get you your tea. . . ."

. . . Yes, said the thing. . . . I remember. . . . February . . . 1692. . . .

. . . Tituba was an Indian, though neither she nor her husband Jon nor her owner, Reverend Parris, knew her tribe.

She had been enslaved so long ago that she had never known any other life, even though her mother had tried to teach her the ways of her people. She had failed in the attempt, and Tituba had been sold to the Parris family long before her lessons could take serious root. Tituba was then told by her owners that she was now a Calvinist Protestant, and she dutifully pretended to be one; but her religion was actually a curious eclectic amalgam of native Indian religion, European superstition, and English Puritanism. She had heard from her mother about the spirits of the forests and the spirits of the groves, about the casting of spells and the brewing of secret herbs, about the bright forces which bless and the dark forces which injure. Reverend Parris had told her long ago that such things were of the Devil, and she naturally believed him. It would never have occurred to her to doubt him. It would also never have occurred to her to stop reverencing the powers of nature about which she had heard so much on her mother's knee. If, as Reverend Parris said, she was in reality worshiping the Devil, that was fine with Tituba. What, after all, is in a name?

Her adherence to an eccentric and personal variant of the "old religion" was an open secret in Salem Village, and though it was a clear violation of the laws of the colony, it was ignored because she was an Indian, and thus presumably incapable of knowing any better. This did not mean she could practice her spells openly; it meant merely that she was left alone to practice them in private. Were the truth to be known, many local people had come to her from time to time for special favors, special assistance, for help in guarding against miscarriage or ensuring fertility, for protection from consumption or influenza, for love potions, for curses against enemies. One woman, Goodwife Anne Putnam, had even asked Tituba to conjure up the spirits of her dead children in an attempt to learn why they had all, but for the eldest, died before reaching full childhood. Tituba's activities were both common knowledge and totally secret, common knowledge because everyone knew everything about everyone else in a community as small as Salem, and secret because such acts of conjuring, which perforce involved calling upon the power of the Devil, were punishable by death.

It was then no surprise to Tituba when Abigail Williams and her friends came to her one day in the winter of 1692 to ask for her help in casting both a spell and a curse. She had no objection to either, for what the white people did to each other was of no interest to her, not after all the things which they had done to her people, to the red people of the forests.

The girls met Tituba in the appointed place in the forest at the appointed time, and she stood beside the small cauldron which bubbled atop the impromptu wood fire and watched them approach. Abigail Williams, her green eyes flashing eagerly, led the group, followed by Suzannah Wolcott, the fattest, most abrasive girl in the village; by Betty Parris, the minister's daughter and Abigail's cousin, small, almost child-like, but headstrong and willful, and an endless source of trouble to her nurse Tituba; Mercy Lewis, a slender girl of great dignity and aloof demeanor; and bringing up the rear, a girl who had not come to see Tituba before, who had not been with Abigail and the others when the subject of the spell and the curse was first broached. Mary Warren trailed behind the other girls, having invited herself along when Abigail told her what was afoot.

Though she regarded the other girls as her friends, and Abigail as her best friend, in truth Mary was something of an outsider whose presence was only tolerated by the other girls, and often just barely that. Mercy had a hearty dislike of her for her timid ways, her inbred obsequiousness, her eagerness to please. Betty and Suzannah played merciless pranks on her, and only Abigail seemed to treat her with a modicum of friendliness. Inasmuch as Abigail was the natural leader of the little adolescent band, being the prettiest, the brightest, the most glib and the most popular, the other girls extended to Mary a strained tolerance for Abigail's sake. Mary worshiped Abigail. She was everything Mary wished she were, and could never be.

"Girls, you be comin' late," Tituba scolded them. "Much to do, much to do. You got the frog and the salamander?"

They had given Mary the task of finding and catching the two amphibians, and she held out the small jar which housed them. "Here they are, ma'am," she said.

"Don't call her 'ma'am,'" Betty Parris said testily. "She's my uncle's slave, not my mother!"

"Give it here, child," Tituba said, taking the jar from Mary's hand. "Now listen to me, all of you. What we be doin' is a hangin' thing. Any of you talk to the reverend, we in trouble deep."

"We know that, Tituba," Abigail said. "Don't worry. We aren't going to tell anybody anything."

"Of course not!" Mercy said emphatically.

"Good. Now here be what we're doin'. I makes the potion in the pot, and you all dances around the pot while I says the spells. Then we takes the potion and you gives it to Goodman Proctor to drink. He drink it, he fall in love with you. Then you waits two days, then you takes the potion and you sprinkles it on Goody Proctor. All her life then go out of her and go into the potion, and she die." Tituba pulled the string which held the leather cap in place around the mouth of the bottle and removed it. She dropped the frog and the salaman-der into the boiling water and then reached into her pocket. She drew forth a small pouch and after opening it poured some unidentified brown powder into the water as well. "Now, girls, you takes off your clothes and you dances around the pot."

"Take off our clothes!" Mercy said. "Tituba, it's freezing cold out here!"

"Aye," Betty said. "We'll catch our death of cold!"

"'Tis February!" Suzannah added.

"Hush," Abigail said. "We'll not need to dance for long, and 'tis necessary for the spell, isn't it, Tituba?" The old Indian nodded. "Well, then, we must do it."

"Well, I'll not be first," Mercy huffed.

"We're not all as immodest as you, Abigail Williams," Betty said pointedly.

Abigail ignored the remark. She turned to Mary Warren. "Mary, you and I shall be first, together. Agreed?"

Mary's joy at being singled out for Abigail's special trust easily outweighed her reluctance to undress in the presence of the others, and she began to remove her clothes. Her skin rose in bumps from the cold air, and she shivered, but Abigail was disrobing calmly and so Mary strove to appear as nonchalant. The other girls followed suit unwillingly, and soon all were prancing about in the snow, naked but for their shoes, the speed of their movement made all the greater by the terrible cold. They ran around the cauldron as Tituba chanted in her native tongue, a tongue which even she could not identify.

Mary did not remember which of her friends she heard scream first, but Betty Parris was the first to fall down on the cold, snowy ground and sink into terrified unconsciousness as Reverend Parris came bursting through the woods toward them, screaming and threatening and waving his fists. My God! Mary thought. We've been seen, we're discovered! She joined the other girls in grabbing her clothes and throwing them on, cowering beneath Parris's cane as it rained blows

78

down upon all of them. "Miscreants!" he cried. "Generation of vipers!"

"It wasn't us, it was her, it was Tituba," Abigail cried. "She made us do it, she sent the Devil on us and made us do it!"

"It was Tituba, it was Tituba!" Mary agreed quickly.

"No!" Tituba cried. "No, Mister Parris, not me, not poor old Tituba! It was the Devil, he force me, he force me!"

"It was Tituba!" the girls all cried. "She cast a spell on us and made us dance, she made us do it!"

The cane rained its blows down upon them. Then Reverend Parris stopped and looked at the terrified faces. "Abigail," he snapped at his niece, "clothe your cousin. You girls, get to your homes and stay there. Tituba . . . ," he walked toward her menacingly, "I want you to go with me to see Marshal Cheever."

"Not the marshal, Mister Parris, I didn't do nuthin' wrong, I swear I didn't," she babbled. "It was the Devil, the Devil took over my body, the Devil, Mister Parris, not poor old Tituba!"

"So you conjured up the Devil?!" His eyes went wide with shock and disgust.

"No, no, Mister Parris, not me, it wasn't me, somebody sent the Devil on me, somebody else!"

He leaned forward and bore his eyes into hers. "Who?"

Tituba's terrified mind cast about desperately for a name, any name, someone to blame, someone else, anyone else. "Martha Corey, Martha Corey, it was Martha Corey! I seen her with the Devil, she come to me with the Devil!"

Parris grabbed Tituba roughly by the wrist. "Well, we'll see what Goodwife Corey has to say about it!" He began to drag her back toward the town. The girls followed, trembling, Abigail and Mary helping the only semi-conscious Betty Parris.

The madness had begun its descent upon Salem. . . .

. . . Yes, the thing said. . . . The madness. . . . March. . . . March 1692. . . .

. . . The two months during which Mary Warren had worked as a serving maid in the Proctor household had been pleasant ones for no one. When John Proctor's Puritan sensibilities had compelled him to confess his adultery to his wife, Elizabeth had reacted with wounded pride, forgiveness she felt obligated to give but did not truly feel, and, of course, a demand for Abigail Williams's dismissal from their service. Mary had taken

Abigail's place and had thus entered a household of strained conversations, long silences, infrequent but bitterly explosive arguments, and an unspoken suspicion on the part of Elizabeth that a serving maid, any serving maid, even one as shy and retiring as Mary, was a potential threat to the sanctity of her marriage bed.

Abigail had not helped, of course, seeming rather irrationally to hold a grudge against Mary for having replaced her; but inasmuch as Mary was now her only link to John, she repressed her resentment and questioned Mary closely whenever she saw her. It had been one month now since Reverend Parris had discovered the girls dancing naked in the woods, and what little respite Mary enjoyed from the tension in the Proctor home whenever she went into the village was now replaced by fear and anxiety. Tituba had denounced Martha Corey as a witch, and Martha Corey had sealed her own fate by replying to the charge with blasphemous invective. When four weeks ago Abigail, Mary, Mercy, Betty, and Suzannah had been brought in for questioning and examination, the girls were so frightened and so on edge that the latter three began to have convulsions. The examiner, Judge Corwin, voiced his opinion that the three girls were obviously the victims of someone else's witchcraft, and this led Abigail and Mary, after a quick exchange of glances, to imitate them. The five girls had thus become the chief denouncers for what was rapidly becoming a standing court for witchcraft charges, and the list of those accused grew longer with each passing day. Each accused in turn accused another, and the five girls would go into convulsions at appropriate moments, thus damning the accused persons with their dramatic evidence. At times Mary felt that she was in reality possessed by a power which she could not control, and the "fits," as the court called them, which had begun in the forest out of fear on the part of Betty Parris, which had occurred spontaneously in court on the part of Betty, Mercy, and Suzannah, which were imitated in defensive pretense by Mary and Abigail, were becoming uncontrollable by any of them. Fear mingled with guilt, and both mixed with an exhilarating sensation of power to half persuade the girls that what they were saying, what they knew to be lies, was truth.

Mary, so accustomed to taking orders and being scolded and walking about in fear of the disapproval of others, found herself growing slightly arrogant. Thus it was that when she returned to the Proctor home from court that day, she sauntered in breezily and tossed her cloak onto the peg beside the door with an aloof aplomb. John Proctor, sitting at the table, brooding over his mug of hot rum, looked up at her and glowered. "What do you mean draggin' yourself in here this time of day, girl?" he demanded.

"Please, do not harry me, John," she said wearily. "I have been all day testifying in court." She made to walk by him to the ladder which led to the loft alcove where she slept.

Proctor grabbed her by the arm as she passed and yanked her down to her knees. "What did you call me, girl?" He squeezed her arm tightly.

She gulped. "I—I meant, Mr. Proctor—" she stammered.

"John, unhand the girl," Elizabeth Proctor said as she entered from the same door through which Mary had just come. "'Tis true, the girl has been all day before the judges." Elizabeth looked tired and worn, and John, ever deferential, ever guilty for his sin against her, released Mary's arm.

"'Tis her disrespect which angered me," he muttered. He took a swig of rum. "And as for her court, 'tis a pack of salivatin' wolves, if I be asked."

"Now, John," Elizabeth said in a voice of perfunctory warning.

"'Tis true, Liz, and you know it as well as I," John Proctor responded. "Martha Corey's accused by an addle-brained old slave, and what happens the next week but her husband Giles is denounced as a witch by Henry Duke, who lost a lawsuit to Giles last year. Rebecca Nurse has nine living children and eighteen living grandchildren, and she is denounced as a witch by Anne Putnam, whose children all have died. There is envy workin' here, envy and greed and spitefulness." He nodded his head in agreement with himself and took another swig of the hot spiced rum.

"One—one cannot argue with signs, sir," Mary said tentatively. The hysterical convulsions in which she had indulged herself so frequently recently threatened to rise up in her as she spoke. She had become so adept at bringing them on that the slightest upset, the most trivial emotional surge, served as a catalyst sufficient to bring them on. She trembled. "The Devil is loose in Salem Village. We are serving God's holy purpose in calling out the names of Satan's servants."

"You are, are you?" Proctor spat. "You're a silly girl with a head too big for her brain, that's what you are, and you're making mischief in the town, is all."

"'Tis—'tis—untrue," Mary stammered. "'Tis the Devil, 'tis

the power of the—of the—Devil. . . ." Mary's limbs began to shake uncontrollably.

Elizabeth watched her, horrified, as white froth began to drip from her mouth. "John," she whispered urgently, " 'tis a fit, and here in our house! If anyone were to see! . . ."

John Proctor rose to his feet and walked over to Mary. He watched her intently as she began to jabber, as her head began to whip madly back and forth. He smiled with amusement and then struck her hard across the face. Her convulsion ceased immediately, and she stood looking at him stupidly. He laughed. "The Devil must be a weakling, Liz," he said to his wife. "The ministers must have lied to us. A slap in the face tames him." He sat back down at the table.

Elizabeth rushed over to the confused girl and put her arm around her shoulder. "John!" she said. "You should not beat the child!"

"I didn't beat her, and she isn't a child," he muttered. "Listen to me, woman. There is something loose in Salem, I'll agree with that, but 'tis not the Devil. 'Tis spitefulness and envy and greed. If you or I had enemies, I'd expect us both to be hauled before the judges!"

A moment later Marshal Cheever came to the Proctor home and arrested Elizabeth. She had been denounced as a witch by Abigail Williams. . . .

. . . Yes . . . yes . . . I remember, said the thing.
. . . I remember. . . . I remember, said the other.

They seemed to circle around a shaft of cool air as they rose from the nowhere into the somewhere, from oblivion into existence, from eternity into time. They heard laughter, very soft and very gentle but retaining some element of malevolence and hatred.

Prepare, the laughing voice whispered. The hour is nigh.

Waves of cool healing swept over the formless things as they began to perceive faint glimmers of light penetrating the eternal darkness.

You, said the thing.
You, said the other.

The light grew stronger, the healing coolness seeped into them and gave them strength, and gave them form.

"Abigail," the thing whispered.

"Mary," echoed the other.

They continued to rise toward the light.

⟦ CHAPTER SIX ⟧

October 31, continued: All Hallows' Eve

THE SOUND OF PEBBLES striking her window was able after a few minutes to rouse Rowena Proctor from her slumber. She sat up in bed groggily, taking a moment to get her bearings, and then heard once again the brittle sound of the small stones against the cold glass. She went over to the window, thinking at first that the snow had turned to hail, but then realizing with excited pleasure that Jeremy Sloan was standing on the snowy ground beneath her bedroom, tossing handful after handful of pebbles up at the window. How romantic! she thought gleefully as she smiled down at him. He motioned for her to open the window, and she proceeded to push it up against the frozen track, straining against the tight fit.

When she at last had the window sufficiently opened, she leaned out into the snowy wind and said in a loud whisper, "Jeremy! What on earth are you doing out there!"

"Can you come out, Row? Right now?"

"Shhh!" she cautioned. "Don't wake Grampa. Come out and do what?" She was struggling to repress an eager smile, and bit her lower lip slightly.

"You'll find out when you come out. Hurry up! I'm freezing out here!" He began to rock back and forth from one foot to the other as if to illustrate his point.

"Okay, okay. Hold on a minute. I'll be right down." She shut the window and rushed over to her dressing table. She gave her long blond hair a quick brush, applied a thin trace of eyeliner and a few strokes of eye shadow, and then grabbed a parka from her closet. As she pulled the parka on with one hand she gave herself a quick spray of cologne with the other.

Rowena closed her bedroom door slowly and softly and proceeded to descend the stairs on tiptoe, wincing each time the old boards creaked, hoping that her grandfather was too soundly sleeping to be easily awakened. It never occurred to her to worry about waking her father or brother.

She walked carefully through the dark hallways of the old inn and then unlocked the front door as quietly as possible.

She opened it slowly and then slipped out into the snowy night.

Jeremy was waiting for her just outside the door, and both of them made bold by the surreptitiousness of their actions, they laughed quietly and embraced. It was the first time Jeremy had held her in his arms, and his heart leapt with delight even though bundles of clothes separated them. She reached up and gave him a quick kiss. "Jeremy, what are you doing out here?" she asked with a laugh.

"Shhh, shhh, come on," he replied and wrapped his arm around her waist to lead her off into the storm. "Lucas and Karyn are waiting for us at the church."

Her romantic expectations began immediately to sour. "Lucas and Karyn! I don't understand."

"Lucas realized that tonight is Halloween," Jeremy explained as he pulled his jacket collar tight against the cold wind. "He wants to try to conjure up a ghost or something."

Rowena stopped walking on the spot. "Wait a minute, Jeremy. I don't want anything to do with that kind of thing."

Jeremy was thrown off balance by the abruptness of her stop and he slipped on a patch of icy pavement, falling on his rump with an audible thump. "Jesus!"

"Oh, Jeremy!" she said, filled with sudden concern. "Are you all right? Oh, I'm sorry!" She fell to one knee beside him and grasped him by the hand.

He started to laugh at his own clumsiness, and she soon joined him. After a few moments he said, "Look, Row, it's just for fun. You know Lucas. He's always doing something outrageous, just for fun."

She shook her head, less emphatically than she might have wished. "I don't like all that stuff, honestly I don't." He jumped to his feet and helped her to hers, and she continued, "Listen. I've been doing some reading about the whole witchcraft thing—you know, back in Salem, three hundred years ago. It was horrible, all those poor innocent people being killed like that."

Jeremy was confused. "Yeah, I've heard about it. So what? I mean, like you say, it was three hundred years ago."

"Well—I mean—" She seemed to be groping for the words. "I mean, let's say Lucas wanted to dress up like Nazis and parade around and stuff like that, just for fun, you know? It wouldn't be serious, it wouldn't really mean anything, but I still wouldn't want to do it. I mean, the Nazis killed millions of people, innocent people, so pretending to be Nazis wouldn't be very funny." She seemed frustrated by her inarticulation. "Do you know what I mean?"

Jeremy shook his head. "No, I don't, Row. Look, the Nazis were real. The witches—well, they all claimed to be innocent, right?"

She shook her head vigorously. "You don't understand what I'm trying to say." She paused for a moment, shivering slightly as the cold, snowy wind whipped through her hair. "Hey, can we go inside and talk? I'm freezing out here."

"Let's walk toward the church." He took her arm once again.

"Jeremy . . . ," she said, her tone one of warning.

"Look, Row, you don't have to take part in it, you don't have to participate. Hell, maybe I won't even stay. But we have to go and tell Lucas anyway, and you want to go inside somewhere, so let's just go to the church." He smiled at her, almost paternalistically. "Okay?"

She nodded slowly, reluctantly. "Well, okay, I guess."

"Great," he said happily, placing his arm around her waist. They walked slowly and carefully through the drifting snow on Bradford's street. Though he did not mention it, Jeremy could feel an aching bruise emerging on his hip from the fall he had taken a few moments before. He tried to ignore it as he said, "Okay, go on. Tell me again what you were trying to say."

Her smooth brow furrowed. "Well, you know that me and Lukie are descended from—"

"From one of the witches," he finished for her. "Yeah, everybody knows that. Your dad makes a big deal out of it."

She stopped again, less abruptly this time, but resolutely. "No, Jeremy, no! That's the whole point. My ancestor John was *not* a witch or a warlock or whatever the heck it is you call a man who does that stuff. He was framed, maybe, by a nutty girl who had a crush on him—"

"Abigail Williams?" he asked.

"Yeah, that was her. Or maybe she was just a lunatic who accused lots of innocent people, and he got caught up in the whole craziness. I don't know for sure. I've just started reading about it all."

"Wow, Row, I didn't know you were interested—"

"I'm *not*," she said quickly. "I hate the whole thing, really. I'm just doing some research for a report."

"Oh, like for school?" He tried gently to impel her forward in the direction of the church, but she either did not notice or ignored the slight pressure on her waist.

"Yeah, for social studies class. But that's beside the point."

"So what's the point?" He exerted a bit of forward pressure again, and she began to move slowly.

"The point is that my ancestor John died—I mean, they wouldn't even let him have a minister pray with him!—I mean—" She stopped again and faced him. "He was an innocent man, Jeremy, an innocent man, not a Satanist. And he died rather than confess to a crime he hadn't committed, just like the other poor people who were executed—no, not executed, murdered, murdered in Salem. For me to take part in some sick devil worship thing—" she shrugged, embarrassed at her own words, but meaning them anyway, "it's just disrespectful, you know? I mean, for me to treat this whole thing like a game when John Proctor was killed because of it—" She shook her head angrily. "I don't know what I'm trying to say. I just can't express myself too well, I guess."

Jeremy reached over and stroked her hair affectionately. "I understand what you're saying, Row. But, hell, your dad makes his living out of this stuff, doesn't he? I mean, if he doesn't mind it, why should you?"

"It isn't the same thing, Jeremy," she said firmly. "Daddy has a responsibility for me and Grampa and even Lucas, sort of. He does what he feels he has to do, to make money, you know?"

"Yeah, yeah, I know. But it's all a joke, Row. It isn't anything to take seriously. People back in the old days believed in Satan. We don't, not nowadays."

"Do you believe in God?" she asked quietly.

The question made him a bit nervous. "Well—I guess so, sort of—in a way, I guess so, yeah," he stammered.

"Okay, so if you believe in God, how can you not believe in the Devil? It's like up without down, isn't it? Or like right without left?"

He shrugged. Such metaphysical contemplations were not among Jeremy's customary preoccupations. "Okay, I guess so. So you think that there really is a Satan?" His tone warned of incipient ridicule.

She sidestepped it. "I don't know, really. I just don't think that any of this stuff is funny, and I don't think it's a good way to pass the time. . . . Listen, Jeremy," she said, stopping once again. "I don't want to make you mad at me or anything, but I'm just not comfortable with this witchcraft stuff. I'm really not."

He nodded. "Yeah, I understand. Well, look, we don't have to take part in it or anything. We can just sit there and watch, okay?"

This was less of a concession than she might have wanted, but it was a compromise. She nodded unhappily. "Okay. We can just watch."

"Great. Great. Come on. Let's hurry up. My toes are getting numb." He pulled her more quickly along the icy street toward the church. She matched his pace, unwillingly, but equally unwilling to annoy him. She looked up at his dark, striking face as they walked along. He's so damn *cute,* she thought.

Bradford was such a small town and its sole street so short that Jeremy and Rowena reached the church in a few minutes. Rowena, trying to make conversation, nervous and ill at ease, gestured at the framed placard which stood on the snow-covered lawn in front of the church and asked, "When is your uncle going to change that?"

"Huh?" Jeremy asked as he guided her away from the front door toward the rear entrance. "Change what?"

"The sign that says, 'Services at eight and ten o'clock.' There hasn't been more than one service here on Sunday for as long as I can remember."

"Oh, I don't know," Jeremy replied, not really caring. "There isn't much of a congregation left here for the old man. Why bother to change the sign when the half dozen old men and women who attend his services all come at eight anyway?"

"That's too bad," she said sincerely. "It's such a pretty old church, and your uncle's such a good preacher."

Jeremy laughed grimly. "Yeah, I'm sure he is, but all he ever does is preach, day in and day out, all the time. It's really a drag to have to live with, you know?"

"Yeah, I guess so," she said. Why am I doing this? she asked herself. Why didn't he ask me out to go to a movie or go have a hamburger or something? Conjuring up ghosts. Good grief! What she said was, "Still, it's kind of sad to see an old church die off like this."

He shrugged as he opened the rear door. "There was some kind of merger or something, 'bout ten years ago. All the Congregationalists around here joined with some other denominations and formed—I don't know, the United Church of Christianity, or something like that. Most of the folks in town go to the church over in Piermont on Sunday. Uncle Fred should've retired when that happened, but he just wouldn't give up his church." Jeremy pushed open the door at the rear of the old wooden building. It creaked loudly, but he did not seem to notice. "I guess he and this church kinda got left out in the cold when all that happened. But he doesn't care. I swear, I think he'd be willing to preach to a row of empty pews."

He held the door open for her and she entered. "I guess he's just real dedicated," she said.

He shrugged as he closed the door behind them. "If that's what you want to call it. Pigheaded, more likely."

A sudden wave of warmth enveloped Rowena, and she smiled with relief. "Hey, that's better."

"What's better?"

"It's so warm in here. What did you do, turn on the heat?"

"Yeah. Lucas came and woke me up about an hour ago, and we came over here first. The boiler was on anyway. I just turned it up." He unbuttoned his jacket. "Yeah, it's nice in here now. Come on." He took her by the hand and led her up the stairs, through the small office and the choir rehearsal room, and then through the door which led to the steps behind the lectern in front of the pews.

The old church, which had always been so comforting and ethereal in its austere sanctity when Rowena went there for Sunday services, had now a totally different atmosphere. The clean white of the interior was clouded by darkness, and the few candles which had been lighted did not dispel the gloom. As they walked past the lectern Rowena saw Lucas and Karyn sitting in the front pew. She was holding a candle unsteadily in her right hand, giving Lucas sufficient light by which to read the book which was held open in his hands.

Lucas looked up nervously when he heard them approach, and he grinned, relieved that it was they and not some other less-welcome visitor. "Holy shit!" he exclaimed. "I didn't think she'd come, Sloan. What'dya do, promise to marry her or somethin'?"

Jeremy coughed and Rowena said, "Oh, shut up, Lucas! That's not funny." She glanced at Karyn. "Hi," she said glumly.

"Hiya, kid," Karyn replied thickly, her head wobbling slightly as she spoke. Great, Rowena thought. Stoned as usual. Drunk too, probably. Rowena's supposition was verified when Karyn lifted a bottle of bourbon in her direction and asked, "Want a slug?"

She shook her head. "No. I don't drink."

Karyn nodded stupidly. "We got some hash. You wanna get high?"

"She doesn't smoke dope either," Lucas answered for her. "She also doesn't fuck. A real fun date."

"Lucas—" Rowena began, a threat in her voice.

"Okay, okay, I'm sorry," Lucas cut her off. "Really. I'm sorry. Come on, Sis, sit down. You too, Jeremy. This is gonna be fun."

Rowena walked to the pew and sat down. "You know, Karyn, you really shouldn't be drinking or smoking. Not when you're pregnant."

Karyn nodded her head and shrugged. "Yeah, I know. It's a bitch, isn't it?" Her attitude seemed to be that such things were beyond her control.

"Okay, now listen up," Lucas said as Jeremy sat down beside Rowena. "This is what we're gonna do—"

"*We* are going to sit here and watch," Rowena said firmly. "I've already told Jeremy that I don't like this sort of thing. I'll watch what you do, but I won't participate in it."

Lucas glared at her. "Jesus, Row! We haven't even started yet and you're already fuckin' everything up!"

"I don't care," she snapped.

"Come on, come on, don't argue," Jeremy interposed. "This is all in fun, right? Let's just have fun. If Row doesn't want to take part in it she doesn't have to, right, Karyn?"

Karyn turned her eyes toward him and looked at him blearily. "Huh?" she asked.

"Don't ask her to make any decisions," Lucas chuckled. "When she gets this high she can't even remember her own name half the time."

"I can so!" she huffed, and then giggled for no apparent reason.

"Okay, you wanna sit there and be a drag like usual, okay with me," Lucas said. Rowena did not deign to reply, so he continued. "Now, I've already turned the cross upside down. . . ."

Rowena turned her attention quickly to the front of the church, and was infuriated to see the wooden cross atop the communion table removed from its holder and rested, cross end down, against the wall behind it. "Jeremy!" she said angrily. "You can't let him do that! Not here in church!"

"Relax, Row," he said soothingly. "I take that cross out all the time, to polish it for Uncle Fred. Hey, it's just a piece of wood, right?"

"No, it isn't just a piece of wood," she said. "It's a symbol of God's love."

"Hey, Row, why don't you just get the fuck out of here?" her brother asked impatiently. "Why don't you just go the fuck home!"

"Come on, Lucas, calm down, will you?" Jeremy asked. Then to Rowena, he said, "Listen. It's just a piece of wood, okay? I'll put it back right when we're done. Honest I will." He took her hand and looked earnestly into her eyes. "It's all a game, Row. It's just for fun. Don't take it so seriously. Okay?"

I wish you weren't so cute, she thought glumly. "Okay. But I still don't like it."

"Let's get going, hey?" Lucas asked. "It's getting close to midnight."

"Okay, okay, go on," Jeremy said.

"So, we got the cross upside down. We got candles lit, and we got enough people—"

"I'm not—" Rowena began.

"Yeah, yeah, I know, I know!" Lucas snapped. "Will you just shut up, for Christ's sake?" Rowena tightened her lips and was silent. Lucas continued. "Now, what we have to do is all take off our clothes—"

"That's it! That's all!" Rowena leapt to her feet and began to walk toward the door of the church.

"Wait a minute, Row, that's locked," Jeremy said quickly as he followed after her.

"How the hell did I ever end up with a sister like this?" Lucas asked. "What an asshole!"

Rowena spun back upon him. "Listen, Lucas, I'm the one who has had to suffer because of you, you know!"

"Oh, bullshit!" he spat. "Just because you're a prudey little goodie-two-shoes—"

"I am not a goodie-two-shoes," she shouted, stamping her foot and looking adorable in her wrath. "I'm just not a jerk like you!"

"What have you got to hide, anyway?" Lucas asked maliciously. "You ashamed of your body?"

"Don't try to be clever, Lucas!" Rowena said angrily. "You aren't smart enough."

"Well, damn it, either go home or join in or at least sit down and shut up, will you?"

"I am not taking off my clothes!" she said emphatically. "And neither is Karyn. Right, Karyn?" She looked to the other girl.

"Welllll," Karyn said with an evil twinkle in her bloodshot eyes, "I don't know about that . . . ," and she began to giggle uncontrollably.

"Oh, jeeze!" Rowena said, her voice filled with irritation.

"Look," Jeremy said, "how about we compromise?"

"I've already compromised just by being here!" Rowena answered.

"Listen, Row, you've worn bikinis on the beach down in Portsmouth, right? Well, just undress down to your underwear. That's just like a bikini." To Lucas, "And it'd still be okay for the ritual. I mean, you don't have to be totally naked, right?"

Lucas sniffed. "I don't know. I guess it'd still work."

"Still work!" Rowena's eyes went wide. "Still work! Don't tell me you honestly believe you're going to accomplish something here!"

Lucas shrugged. "Beats me. Maybe. Worth a try, isn't it?"

She turned to Jeremy. "This is nuts! This is crazy!"

He shook his head. "No, it's a game, that's all. Come on, Row, play along, okay? Please?"

She sat back down in the pew and folded her hands across her chest. "Absolutely not!" Then, as if on an impulse, she kicked off her shoes. "There. I've taken off some clothes. And that is *it*!" She glared at Jeremy and Lucas defiantly.

"Life of the party, Row," Lucas muttered, "a real shit load of fun. At least just shut up and don't bother me, okay?" He did not wait for an answer. "Well, then, after *most* of us get undressed, we read the invocation. Then we debauch the altar, and then we offer the sacrifice—"

"What sacrifice?" Rowena asked. "You're not going to kill some poor little animal—!"

"No, no, nothing like that. Just shut up and listen, will you?" Lucas snarled. "Then we say the spell to raise the dead. And then we wait and see."

"Wait and see what, honey?" Karyn asked thickly.

"Wait and see if we've raised any dead people, what else?"

Rowena shook her head. "Lucas, you are the stupidest person I've ever met in my entire life!"

He refused to be insulted. "Yeah, but I'm fun." Karyn giggled. "Okay," Lucas said, "let's get going. Ready, set, strip!" He began gleefully to disrobe Karyn. She continued to giggle.

Jeremy and Rowena averted their eyes from each other as he began to disrobe. Now that he was actually undressing in Rowena's presence, Jeremy found himself a bit less enthusiastic about the situation. She looked at the walls, the ceiling, the floor, anywhere and everywhere but at him. She was red with embarrassment. It figures, she thought glumly. Other girls' boyfriends take them skiing, take them to dances. Mine takes me to an old church to conjure up ghosts. Great, just great.

Jeremy finished undressing and he uttered a silent prayer that he would not get an erection. He need not have worried. He was so tense and so cold, the heat in the building notwithstanding, that his genitals had shriveled. When he noticed this fact he became beset by a new worry: that Rowena would look at him and think him inadequate. It did not occur to him that she would not have cared, would not look, and had no basis for comparison anyway.

As it was, they both became so fascinated at the spectacle of Lucas and Karyn that they paid no attention to each other. Lucas was eagerly tossing his own clothes in all directions as Karyn, already naked, leaned against the lectern and watched with drunken amusement. Her long reddish-brown hair fell loosely down around her shoulders and chest, and she swept it behind her with her hands to reveal her swollen belly and pendulous breasts. Lucas grinned at her as he removed his last remaining sock. His penis was erect, bobbing up and down as if it were a fifth member of their circle, eager to begin the game.

"Okay," Lucas said. "Come here, Jeremy. We have to stand in a circle to begin." Jeremy coughed nervously as he rose to his feet and walked forward, awkwardly trying to shield the front of his body from Rowena's line of sight. She was not looking at him anyway. She was staring at Karyn, astounded by the other girl's boldness and lack of modesty. Lucas positioned Jeremy to his right and Karyn on his left, saying, "You both have to read along with me. Hold it. Get a couple of candles." They did as they were bidden. "Okay. You hold the candles and I'll hold the book."

Karyn squinted her eyes as she looked over the page. "I can't understand a word of this," she said.

"It ain't English," Lucas explained. "It's some magic language or something."

"It's Latin," Jeremy pointed out tactfully.

"Yeah, yeah, that's it. It's Latin. It don't matter if we know what we're sayin' or not, so long as we say the right words."

Karyn shrugged. "Okay by me, babe."

Lucas looked back and forth from Jeremy to Karyn. "We ready?" he asked.

"Sure," Jeremy replied. Karyn nodded, giggling again.

"Okay. There's some English stuff in here too, but that don't mean we can skip the Latin shit. We gotta do the whole thing and do it right." He shot a glance at Rowena. "And just be quiet, Sis, okay?" No response. "Okay?!"

"Yes, okay," she said morosely. "Just get it over with."

Lucas took a deep breath. "Okay. Here we go." He cleared his throat. The flickering candles and the howling wind outside sent chills up his spine. *This is so goddamn creepy,* he thought. *This is mint!* "*Ave Satanas!*" he intoned darkly.

"*Ave Satanas!*" Jeremy and Karyn responded.

"*Diabolus vobiscum.*"

"*Et cum spiritu tuo.*"

He looked up. "We read this part together." He and Jeremy began to read the reversed Lord's Prayer. Karyn struggled to keep up with them.

"*Malo a nos libera sed tentationem in inducas nos ne et nostris debitoribus dimittimus nos et sicut nostra debita nobis dimitte et hodie nobis da quotidianum nostrum panem terra in et caelo in sicut tua voluntas fiat tuum regnum adveniat tuum nomen sanctificetur caelis in es qui noster pater.*"

"*Ave Satanas!*" Lucas repeated.

"*Ave Satanas!*" Jeremy and Karyn responded again.

"*Diabolus vobiscum.*"

"*Et cum spiritu tuo.*"

Lucas took Karyn by the hand. "Come on. We gotta debauch the altar."

"We gotta do what?" she asked. Her tongue seemed to be sticking to her mouth and the room was spinning slightly. She was very, very drunk.

"Debauch the altar. We gotta fuck on the altar." Lucas heard the mutter of disgust from the pew, but he ignored it. "Come on, Karyn." He pulled her forward to the communion table (this being a Congregationalist church, there was no altar per se) and said, "Get up on it, on your hands and knees."

"Uh, Lucas," Jeremy said, "I don't think that old table will hold your weight." *This is so embarrassing!* he thought.

"Don't worry about it," Lucas replied. "Seems sturdy enough." Karyn knelt upon the table, and Lucas hopped up onto it behind her. The table did indeed seem sturdy as Lucas mounted her from the rear. Karyn blushed and giggled as Lucas began to thrust in and out of her, but her giggles turned to a cry of alarm as the left front leg of the communion table snapped and sent them both sprawling onto the floor beside the lectern.

"Shit!" Lucas said. "Goddamn it!"

"Oh, great, that's just great!" Jeremy said angrily. "How the hell am I supposed to explain this to my uncle?"

"Serves you all right," Rowena muttered, her eyes still averted from the scene before her.

"Well," Lucas began slowly as he surveyed the damage. "I guess the ritual's still good. I guess we did enough on the table."

"The ritual!" Jeremy exclaimed. "The hell with the ritual! How am I supposed to explain this to my uncle?"

Lucas ambled over to the table leg and picked it up to examine it. "No big deal. It just popped out of its socket. We can glue it back in later. See? Nothin's snapped or broken. Your uncle'll never know."

This seemed to calm Jeremy down a bit. "I guess not," he said as he too examined the table leg. "But, wait. What if it comes loose again and falls off?"

"Then nobody'll know it was your fault, right? Besides, how often do you think people fuck on this table, anyway?" Lucas dismissed Jeremy's worries with a wave of his hand. "Come on, let's get back to it." He picked the book up from off the floor and ran his eyes down the page. "Let's see . . . let's see . . . okay, yeah, here we are. Now we offer some prayers. Get back in the circle. Come on, Karyn."

"Yes, thank you very much, Lucas, no I didn't get hurt, yes I'm fine, thank you very much!" Karyn snapped.

Lucas grinned at her sheepishly. "I'm sorry, babe. Are you all right?"

She sniffed, wounded by his indifference. "Fine," she muttered.

"Good. Okay, back in the circle." He held the book open, waiting for them to position the candles so that they could read along. "Everybody ready?"

Jeremy and Karyn muttered their assent. They both seemed to have lost the mood.

"Come on, you two, loosen up! You gotta get into the spirit of this, you know?" He thought for a moment and then walked over to the spot where he had tossed his jacket a few minutes before. Reaching into the pocket, he pulled out the hashish pipe. "There's still some dope in here. Let's do a bowl, okay? Then we can get on with the prayers, okay?"

This suggestion seemed to brighten Karyn immediately. "Yeah, yeah, good idea."

"Terrific," Lucas said. "Jeremy, gimme that candle for a minute. You take the book." Lucas tilted the candle to the left and after placing the pipe between his teeth tilted it to the right. He drew on the pipe and the candle flame dipped into the bowl, lighting the powdery lump of hashish. Lucas drew some smoke into his lungs and then passed the pipe to Karyn, who followed suit. She handed it to Jeremy, who took a perfunctory drag and exhaled it almost immediately. He was aware of Rowena glowering at him. *This isn't working out at all like I thought it would,* he thought unhappily.

"Ahhh, that's better," Lucas said contentedly. "Ain't it, babe?" Karyn purred an assent. "Okay. I'll read the prayers. You two read the parts with an 'R' next to them. Ready?"

Jeremy and Karyn nodded. "Ready," Jeremy said quietly.

Lucas cleared his throat and began reading. "Hail Satan, father of lies, fountainhead of evil, master of this world. We come before you in supplication, we come before you in worship and in awe."

"Hail Satan, father of lies," Jeremy and Karyn responded.

"Hail Satan, ruler of hell, giver of power, lord of the flesh. We come before you in supplication, we come before you in worship and in awe."

"Hail Satan, ruler of hell."

"All that I am, I offer to you."

"All that I am, I offer to you."

"Strike down mine enemies and confound their desires."

"Shouldn't it be 'my enemies'?" Karyn asked.

"Damn it, Karyn, read the goddamn line, will you?" Lucas said.

She shrugged. "Okay, okay." Jeremy joined her in the response. "All that I am, I offer to you."

"Reduce them to ashes and torment their flesh."

"All that I am, I offer to you."

"Burn them with sulfur and rend them with knives."

"All that I am, I offer to you."

"Grant thou my boon, thou master of hell."

"*Ave Satanas, gratia vacuus.*"

"What does 'gratia—'?" Karyn began.

"Shhh," Jeremy said.

"Inflame thou my lusts, thou lord of the flies."

"*Ave Satanas, gratia vacuus.*"

"Praise to thee, Lucifer, praise to thee, Lucifer."

"*Ave Satanas, gratia vacuus.*"

"All hail Beelzebub, Mephistopheles hail."

"*Ave Satanas, gratia vacuus.*"

"*Ave Satanas!*"

"*Ave Satanas!*"

"This is so fuckin' weird!" Lucas cackled gleefully. "Isn't this great?"

"Really great," Rowena muttered from her place in the pew. "Worshiping the Devil. Really great."

"Oh, shut up, Row," he said. "Don't mess up the mood." He turned to Jeremy and Karyn. "Okay, now for the sacrifice. We need two ingredients: blood and semen."

"Oh, my God, Lucas!" Rowena said. "That's disgusting!"

"Hey," he said innocently, "I didn't make up this shit. It's all right here in the book."

"She's right, babe," Karyn added. "It *is* disgusting."

"Oh, shit, Karyn! Don't fag off on me!"

"I didn't say it bothered me," she shrugged. "I just said that it's disgusting."

"Well, we gotta do it," he said, the irritation clear in his voice. "I'll give the semen, and Jeremy, you give the blood."

"What do you mean, I'll give the blood?" Jeremy asked. "Why don't you give the blood!"

"Okay with me, I'll give the blood and you give the semen"—he jerked his thumb in the direction of Rowena—"if you can get the Virgin Mary over there to blow you or jerk you off."

"That's it! I've had enough of this!" Rowena said, jumping to her feet and reaching for her shoes. Tears began to flow from her eyes.

"Wait a minute, Row," Jeremy said quickly. "He was just kidding. You were just kidding, weren't you, Lucas?"

"Hey, you can't get semen by wishing for it!" Lucas replied simply. He found Rowena so annoying at almost all times that the prospect of her departure did not upset him in the least. He had been irritated by Jeremy's insistence that she attend in the first place.

Rowena pulled on her shoes, hurriedly tying the laces, and was putting on her jacket when Jeremy took her arm. "Wait, Row, please."

"Wait for what?" she demanded. "God, Jeremy, look at you! Look at what you're doing!" She wiped away a tear as Jeremy, made aware of his nudity, covered his pubic region with his hands. "I thought you were a nice boy, but you're just as big a jerk as Lucas!" She finished pulling on her parka and then ran weeping toward the exit beside the lectern.

"Rowena, wait a minute, wait a minute," Jeremy said desperately. "Let me get dressed. I'll walk you home."

"Don't bother!" she spat, and slammed the door behind her.

Jeremy stood there, his eyes fixed on the closed door, waves of depression washing over him. Lucas walked over to him and slapped him on the back. "Good riddance, I say. Come on,

96

Jeremy, don't let it get you down. You'll be friends again tomorrow. She's just like real sheltered, you know?"

"Yeah," he sighed. "I guess so. But why'd you have to say what you said? She was sitting there quiet, not interfering. Why'd you have to go out of your way to get her upset?"

He shrugged. "Sorry. Besides, what I said was true. One of us gives the blood and one of us gives the semen, and if you want to be the one who gives the semen, you ain't getting it out by havin' my girlfriend give you a hand." He laughed at his unintentional pubescent humor. "Give you a hand! Ha! Get it?"

"Good one, babe," Karyn said tiredly. "Real funny."

"Come on, come on, let's get back to the ritual. I wanna see if we can call up some ghosts or something."

"Yeah, yeah," Jeremy muttered. "Okay. What do we do next?"

"Well," he turned and grinned at Karyn, "you gotta make me come, babe."

"You got a hand," she said with irritation. "Make yourself come."

"Hey, come on, Karyn. Jesus! You two are getting to be a couple of real pains in the ass! Come on, now. Let's do this right."

"Oh, all right, all right," she grumbled. "But you're gettin' a hand job, not a blow job. I got a fever sore."

"Okay, whatever. Where's that cup?"

"What cup?" Jeremy asked.

"I brought a coffee cup with us for this part of—ah, there it is," he said, walking to the end of the pew. "I couldn't see it in the candlelight." He picked it up and handed it to Karyn. "We'll catch the stuff in this."

She examined it. "'World's Greatest Grandfather,'" she read. "Real demonic, Lukie."

"Hey, a cup's a cup." He sat back onto the pew, his legs spread wide. "Okay, woman." He grinned. "Get to work."

Karyn laughed despite herself. "You're such a cretin sometimes, honest to God." She knelt down in front of him, holding the cup in her left hand. She began to massage his penis with her right.

"Feelin' good, babe." He smiled. "You had a lotta practice doing—ouch!" She had squeezed his member hard as a way of keeping him in line."

"Behave," she said, grinning.

A few moments passed. "A little dry there, babe," Lucas

said seriously. "Maybe you should—I mean, just a little—I mean—"

Karyn giggled and bent over, enveloping his penis in her mouth, running her tongue around its tip and then taking it deep into her throat. A contented sigh escaped from Lucas as he began to ejaculate freely. Karyn pulled back and placed the cup in front of his spurting penis, catching a few drops of semen. Most of it missed the cup, but she scooped a bit more up from the floor with her finger and wiped it off on the lip of the vessel.

Lucas put his hands behind his head and slouched down in the pew. "Okay, Sloan. I done my bit. Your turn."

"Thanks a lot," Jeremy mumbled. "How do I do this?"

"Just prick your finger—you got a penknife, right? on your key chain, right?—and put a few drops of blood into the cup."

Sighing, Jeremy went over to the place on the pew where he had deposited his clothes earlier, and rummaged around for his keys. Finding them, he opened the small penknife and walked back over to Lucas and Karyn. "Okay," he said. "Here goes."

Karyn held the cup out, and he reached his left hand out over it. Wincing in advance against the coming discomfort, he stabbed his left thumb with the knife, and drops of blood began to ooze from the small wound. He allowed the blood to drip into the cup and then put his thumb into his mouth. "Shit," he muttered. "Lots of fun, Lucas."

"Look on the bright side, Sloan. If we were gonna do this right, we woulda had to kill you." He cackled malevolently. "Okay, Karyn, mix it all up."

She handed him the cup. "You mix it up. I've done my bit too."

"Okay, okay," he replied testily. "Jesus, what a couple of drags you guys are." He swirled his forefinger around in the cup. "There ain't much in here."

"That's tough," Jeremy said, still sucking on his thumb. "That's all the blood you get."

"It'll have to do, I guess. Okay, now we all drink from it and say—"

"No way, man," Karyn said emphatically. "I ain't drinking blood."

"No, and I ain't no queer," Jeremy added with equal conviction. "I ain't drinking nothing that came out of your dick."

"Oh, for Christ's sake!" Lucas whined. "What's with you two? This is the ritual, damn it!"

"Well, do it yourself," Karyn said. "And hurry up. I'm getting sleepy."

Sighing with exasperation, Lucas returned to his position before the broken communion table and looked for the proper place in the book. "Karyn, will you at least hold the fuckin' cup for me for a minute?"

"Okay, okay," she said wearily, moving to his side. She took the cup from him and stood there as he leafed through the book.

"Ah, here it is. Okay." He cleared his throat and began to read. "I offer this sacrifice to you, lord of the dark powers. I offer you the blood and the seed. I offer you my soul in the next world and my services in this world, if you will but grant my boon."

"What's a b—" Karyn began.

"Shhh!" Lucas silenced her. He ran his finger along the inside of the cup and then licked it clean. "I partake of the unholy sacrifice, O master of the infernal regions, and present you with my supplication. Upon my soul's damnation do I beg it."

The last few words seemed to sober the three young people. There was a frightening solemnity to the words which caused Karyn's heart to beat a bit faster and caused Jeremy to feel himself perspiring. Lucas cleared his throat. "Release to me the souls of the dead which are in your keeping. Release to me the souls of your servants which are in your keeping. Release to me the souls of the damned which are in your keeping. This I beg you, master of hell. Give their souls to me now, and my soul is yours for eternity. *Ave Satanas! Ave Satanas!*

He fell silent. They waited. The only sound was that of the howling wind and their own agitated breathing. A few minutes passed.

Lucas sighed with disappointment. "Nothin's happening."

Karyn laughed. "Well, what did you expect? Some corpse to come trotting into the church?"

"Wait a minute," Jeremy said. "Wait a minute. . . . Listen. Do you hear that?"

They listened. "I don't hear anything," Karyn said.

"No, neither do I," Jeremy agreed. "The wind has stopped."

Lucas and Karyn listened more carefully. It was true. The wind, which had been whipping through the small town for hours, casting bundles of snow against the windows and the homes, had suddenly ceased. The silence was profound and unnerving.

"Creepy," Karyn whispered.

"Yeah," Lucas agreed. "Real creepy."

As if propelled by a sudden explosion, a ferocious gust of wind thrust open the front door of the church and assaulted them with an almost vicious power. The candles were immediately extinguished, and a cold, biting winter wind wrapped the three naked people in its icy tendrils. "Shit!" Lucas shouted. "Where the hell are our clothes! I'm gonna freeze to death like this!" He began to grope about in the darkness.

"Oh, Lukie, don't be such a—" Karyn began, and then screamed. "LUCAS! LUCAS! SOMETHING'S CLAWING AT MY HEAD!" She screamed again as a pair of wings beat the air around her ears and sharp talons scraped against her scalp. "IT'S A BAT! IT'S A BAT! LUCAS!"

Lucas and Jeremy collided with each other in the darkness in their attempts to get to Karyn. "Sloan, turn on some lights in here, will you?"

"But my uncle might see—" Jeremy began.

"Fuck your uncle! Turn on some fuckin' lights!" In the blackness Lucas could hear Jeremy's footsteps as he rushed to the rear of the church, and then Lucas's screams mingled with Karyn's as wings began to beat near his eyes and he felt a claw rip through his forehead. "JESUS CHRIST!" he shouted. "MY HEAD IS BLEEDING! SLOAN! SLOAN! HURRY UP!" And he screamed again.

The lights of the church interior switched on, and Lucas was startled at the blood which was dripping from his forehead onto his hands. "Shit! Shit!" he said. "What the hell . . . ?"

"Look. Up there," Jeremy said, pointing at the rafters. "It isn't bats. It's a couple of birds."

Karyn and Lucas followed the direction of his finger. Two large black birds sat serenely upon one of the rafters beneath the roof of the church. "What are they?" Karyn asked. "Crows?"

"One of them is," Jeremy answered. "I think the other one's a raven."

"Well, what the fuck are they doing here?" Lucas asked bitterly. "Aren't they supposed to fly south or something?"

"Yeah," Jeremy nodded. "These two are probably lost or late or—I don't know. I ain't no bird-watcher."

"But why did they attack us?" Karyn asked, beginning to weep.

"The wind probably blew them in when it blew the door open, and they panicked."

100

"They ain't the only ones," Lucas said bitterly. "Look at me. Shit!"

"Oh, honey!" Karyn said, noticing for the first time Lucas's state. "My God, are you all right?"

"What do you mean, am I all right!" he shouted. "I'm bleeding, for Christ's sake! My fuckin' head's ripped open!"

"Let me see," Jeremy said calmly. If he was less adventurous than Lucas, he was also less easily flustered by emergencies. "It ain't too bad," he said as he examined the cut. "The bird just grazed you."

"Just grazed me!" Lucas exclaimed. "Are you nuts?! Look at all this blood!"

Jeremy shook his head. "It isn't a deep wound, it's just long. I'll bet it won't even leave a scar. You ought to clean it up, though."

"Do I need rabies shots?" Lucas asked in a panicky voice. "Do birds carry rabies?"

"No," Jeremy replied. "Only mammals. But you should clean it out right away, before it gets a chance to get infected."

"Yeah," Karyn agreed as she began to collect her clothing. "Let's get the hell out of here. This is one night I'd like to end right now." She began to dress.

"Well," Lucas muttered as he daubed his head with the handkerchief he had pulled from the pants which he was holding, "until those birds freaked out it wasn't bad. It was kinda fun, wasn't it?"

"Yeah," said Jeremy, recalling Rowena's face as she ran out of the church, "lots of fun." He looked around for his clothes and found them where he had left them. He began to put them on.

"Come on, honey, let's go home," Karyn said after pulling on her boots. "We gotta get that cut fixed up."

"Yeah, yeah." He turned to Jeremy. "You need any help here?"

Jeremy shook his head. "No. I'm just gonna leave everything like it is, open door and busted communion table and everything."

"But your uncle—"

"The wind blew the door open, shattered that old lock. He'll just think the wind knocked the table over also, busted it up."

Lucas nodded. "Makes sense. Listen, I'll come over tomorrow and help you repair it."

"No need, no need," Jeremy said. "Thanks anyway. Just needs some glue."

"Lukie, let's go!" Karyn demanded.

"Okay, okay. You comin', Jeremy?"

"Yeah. Just let me turn off the lights. Gather up the candles and that cup. Don't forget your father's book."

"No, no, I won't," Lucas replied as he walked about, picking things up from the floor and the pew. "Hey, won't Dad get a kick out of this when we tell him about it?"

"Lucas!" Karyn snapped. "You will *not* mention this episode to your father!"

"He won't care, Karyn. He'll think it's all kinda funny, what with the wind and the birds and everything—"

"Lucas!" she repeated threateningly. "You *will not* tell your father what we did here tonight! I have to look the man in the face, you know. Just because I go along with the nutty things you think up all the time doesn't mean that I want to broadcast it all over the place!"

"All right, all right! Jesus!" he said, quite disgruntled. "First Row brings her wet blanket in here, then you two start gettin' to be drags, then those fuckin' birds mess everything up, and now we can't even tell anybody about all of it." He sniffed. "Well, my night's ruined!"

"Poor Lukie!" Karyn and Jeremy said in unison as they walked out the front door of the church.

"Ah, fuck you guys," he muttered.

Before walking away from the church back out into the still-heavy snowfall, Jeremy cast a last look up at the rafters of the church. He reached over to the light switch on the wall beside the door and turned on the lights in the entrance way. These afforded illumination sufficient for him to see the two birds still perched upon the rafters. They stared at him impassively as he looked up at them. "Dumb birds," he said softly, and laughed. "Scared the hell out of us." He switched off the light and left.

The birds remained seated upon the rafters in the darkness of the now deserted church. After a few moments the raven began to preen itself. The crow continued to stare at the door.

⟦ CHAPTER SEVEN ⟧

November 1

THE EARLY MORNING fog had descended upon the river valley shortly before three, and the automobile which had already been moving cautiously along the narrow, winding country roads moved even more slowly as the visibility became increasingly poor. The chubby, freckle-faced young woman who was driving muttered under her breath with annoyance. Her companion, a skinny, acne-scarred woman of about the same age, turned to her and said, "What?"

"Hmmm?" was the reply.

"What did you say?"

"I said 'Goddamn fog.' That what I said," she spat.

"Oh," the other woman replied. They drove along in silence through the dim half-light of the empty hours between darkness and dawn, the first woman straining her eyes to pierce through the dense mist, the second woman biting her nails nervously and drumming her fingers on the dashboard. "How much longer?" the second woman asked.

"I don't know. An hour, maybe. I'm not certain where we are."

"Would have been quicker if we'd taken the highway instead of these little—"

"I know that," the first woman said irritably. "It just looked shorter on the map. How was I supposed to know that we'd be driving on these winding mountain roads? And I couldn't very well have predicted the fog, either."

They fell silent again for a few moments. Then the second woman asked, "Do you think he'll be expecting us?"

"He should be," the first woman replied. "We sent him a letter."

"How do you think he feels about having us try to—"

"How the hell should I know?" the first woman interrupted. "We'll find out when we . . ." She stopped speaking and slowed the car.

"What's wrong?"

"Nothing." She shook her head. "It just seems . . . look up there, in the middle of the road. You see anything up there?"

"No," she replied, squinting. "Just fog and the yellow line."

"Look along the line. Up ahead. Is that people?"

The second woman paused. "Yeah," she said dubiously. "Yeah, I think so. Maybe."

Two black shadows seemed to be standing in the midst of the swirling fog, visible dimly in the inadequate headlamps of the car which now crawled toward them at a snail's pace. When the car was no more than six feet from the two figures, the first woman stopped the car and leaned out the window. "Hey, assholes! You wanna get out of the way?"

One of the two figures approached slowly, seeming to float gracefully through the mist. The driver glared at her angrily, but then became uneasy as the figure drew close to the window. The black cloak which the figure wore was wrapped around it from head to foot, with only the sparkling green eyes visible through the narrow slit formed by the folds of the black fabric. "Come," said the deep, rich, melodious female voice. The second figure remained motionless in the center of the road.

"Come!" echoed the driver. "Are you kidding? Get the hell out of the way!"

"You serve the Dark One," the melodious voice said. "You must come."

"Listen, asshole," the driver said, "you tell your friend there to get out of the way, or I'm gonna drive right over her." As she spoke, her companion nervously locked the doors of the car and made certain that her window was rolled up tightly.

The figure leaned over and gazed into the driver's eyes. The woman behind the wheel grew suddenly weak as the green fire of the figure's gaze burned into her. "Come," the figure repeated.

"L-listen," the woman said shakily, "we're g-going to see Simon Proctor. We're—"

"I know whither you go, and why," the figure said. "You go not of your own volition. You go unknowing to serve the Dark One."

"Are—are you a friend of Proctor's?" the second woman asked.

The figure laughed softly, a laugh without humor, a cold, frightening laugh. "Aye, I am a friend of the Proctors'. An old, old friend." She paused, and the laughter ceased. "You must come."

"Come where?" asked the driver, shaking as the green eyes bore deeper into her.

"To serve the Dark One," the figure replied. "Come!"

The driver reached forward spasmodically and switched off the engine. Not knowing why she was doing so, she opened the door and stepped out into the night fog. "Get back in here this instant!" her companion said. "What do you think you're doing?"

The green eyes turned on her and gazed at her, and the second woman felt her limbs grow weak and her heart begin to beat fast with fear. "Okay," she muttered. "Okay, okay—just—just—"

"Come," the black-cloaked figure repeated in the same soft, patient, but unrelenting voice. The second woman opened the door of the car and followed her companion into the swirling fog. "Come," the figure repeated yet again, and then began to move slowly from the road off into the woods which bounded it. The two women followed the figure, and the other shadow which had until then stood motionless before the car followed behind them.

In silence they walked deep into the woods until they came to a small clearing in the midst of which burned a smoky fire of twigs and sticks. "Sit," said the cloaked figure.

The two women looked around at the snow-covered ground. "Sit on what?" the second woman asked.

"Sit," the figure repeated. After looking discontentedly at each other for a moment, the two women sat down upon the snow. In a matter of seconds the moist cold began to seep through their clothes. The figure turned to her counterpart and said, "I shall dream and you shall summon."

"You shall dream and I shall summon," the other agreed quietly.

The two figures sat down in front of the fire and began to chant softly in a language unknown to the two bemused, nervous women. The chant went on for a long while, and then there was silence but for the crackling of the dying fire. A sound from deep in the black forest startled the two women, and they looked around them uneasily. A third black-cloaked figure emerged from the darkness and asked, "Who has released me?" It was a man's voice, old and tremulous.

"I," said the second figure.

"To what end?" the third figure asked.

"You know," the second figure replied.

The third figure nodded. "Aye, I ken, I ken. Know that I am Thomas of old Elcebourne, hight the Rhymer. I shall teach you what I may."

"I know," said the second figure.

"How long am I free of the pit?"

"You are free at the Master's pleasure," the second figure replied, "as are we."

The third figure looked around him. "And what is here? What do these others?"

"She sends forth her spirit," the second figure said, nodding in the direction of her companion. "These others serve in ways they know not."

"As did we all," the third figure said sadly.

"As did we all," the second figure agreed.

The third figure remained standing as silence descended once again upon the small company. One of the women began to ask a question, but a peremptory "Shhh!" from the second figure silenced her, and she and her friend sat, cold and shivering, upon the snow in the dark wintry silence.

An hour passed, and the fire died out. The two women huddled together for warmth. Each tried to rise at one time or another throughout the dim dawn hours, but neither could get her legs to move. At last the first figure snapped its head up and said, " 'Tis done. The seed is planted."

"All is well?" the second figure asked.

"All is as I had hoped," the first figure replied. She glanced over at the third figure, which still stood at the edge of the woods. "The Rhymer," she said, a statement, not a question.

"Aye," the third figure replied.

The first figure rose to its feet and moved slowly over to the two seated women. "Whom do you serve?" she asked.

"Satan," the women replied in unison, their teeth chattering and their limbs numb with the cold.

"Then know that he has chosen you to perform a service," the first figure said as she walked around and took a position behind the two women. "Be joyful in his service."

The two women looked at each other in confusion, and then both turned their heads upward so as to be able to see the shadowy figure which was addressing them. The figure reached up and grasped the edge of the black cape which was wrapped about its head. With a rapid yet graceful motion it whipped the cape around and discarded it. The two women screamed, for the piercing green eyes which had so over-powered them were set into the sockets of a decaying skull.

The women rolled over onto their hands and knees, still screaming, trying to force their numb limbs to move, trying to crawl away from the grinning monstrosity which gazed down upon them. The creature reached beneath its cloak and drew forth a dagger. It leapt upon the back of one of the women and grabbed her by the hair, pulling her head upward and forcing her to gaze into its eyes. And then it placed the edge of the dagger against the left side of the woman's throat and drew it across to the right. The blood from the severed neck spurted onto the white ground. The creature then jumped onto the other woman and, rolling her over onto her back, plunged the dagger into her chest.

The creature rose to its feet and faced the other two figures. "We must begin," it said.

"We have begun," the second figure said softly, a hint of sadness in its voice.

"Give me heed," said the third figure, "and mark well my words. . . ."

Simon Proctor awakened in a cold sweat. He bolted upright in his bed and his eyes darted frantically around the room. His muscles were tense and his body was shaking. Then he seemed to relax, and he wiped his brow with his hand.

"Holy shit, what a dream!" he said aloud, softly.

Simon grabbed the small clock from the night table beside the bed and looked at the illuminated dial. Four-thirty in the morning. He glanced over at the window, at the snowfall and the few dim rays of the incipient sunrise. A wave of tension struck him and he reached over to the lamp on the night table. He turned on the light, and became immediately calmed by the familiar surroundings.

"What a dream!" he repeated. He turned off the light and lay back down, but a sudden impulse warned him against going back to sleep. "Think I'll make some coffee," he said to himself. "Have a drink, maybe."

He turned the light back on and fumbled with his toes for the slippers beneath the bed. He had been sleeping in his underpants, as was his custom, and he pulled on an old pair of dungarees before leaving his bedroom to go down to the kitchen.

He walked down the second floor hallway of the old colonial inn and stopped in front of the door to Rowena's room. He pushed it open as quietly as he could manage and peered inside. He was able to see the sleeping form dimly in the dark, quiet room, and satisfied that his daughter was sleeping soundly, he pulled the door softly shut and continued on down the hall. He did not stop before Lucas's door—he has Karyn in there after all; don't want to intrude—and then began to descend the stairs.

Simon turned on the kitchen light and walked over to the coffee pot. Pulling off the lid, he could see that it had not been washed since the previous morning. The prospect of doing dishes soured him on the idea of having coffee, so he instead took a bottle of brandy from the cupboard above the sink and poured himself a generous glass. He sat down at the kitchen table and poured some of the fiery liquid down his throat.

"What are you doin' up this time of night, boy?" his father's voice demanded. Floyd was standing in the doorway, his bent and shriveled body clad in an old-fashioned, long nightshirt. He was probably the last man in the United States who still wore a nightcap.

"I couldn't sleep," Simon explained.

"I see," Floyd said as he sat down at the table beside his son. "You couldn't sleep, so you decided to have a drink."

"No, Pop, I decided to have a drink because I want a drink," Simon snapped. "I couldn't sleep because I had a bad dream."

"I don't wonder," Floyd harrumphed. "If I did what you do for a living, I'd have bad dreams too."

Simon rubbed his eyes. "Pop, go back to sleep, will you? I don't feel like company right now."

"Yeah, especially when the company is me, right?" The old man's lower lip trembled slightly as he spoke.

Simon felt a sudden pang of guilt. Even through his own problems, he still felt for the old man, felt sorry that he had been such a source of unhappiness to him. "I didn't mean that, Pop," he said gently. "I'm just worried. I have money problems, business problems."

Floyd nodded, happy for the opportunity to speak to Simon in a fatherly manner. "Business troubles work out, as long as you're willing to work hard and not waste money. Whatever the problem is, boy, you'll come out of it all right." He seemed to be warming to his topic. "Why, I remember, back in nineteen and twenty-two, your mother and I—this was before your Uncle Jason lost the farm over in Fairleigh, remember that?—no, no, you weren't born yet . . ."

Simon smiled and nodded, making the appropriate responses each time the old man raised his eyebrows inquisitively at him, not really listening to a word he was saying. He had heard the story about the failed general store and the near foreclosure on the house a hundred times, but it made the old man happy to repeat it, so Simon smiled, nodded, pretended to listen. You're a relic, Pop, he thought as he watched him. Pop, your heart's in the right place, but you're from a different century. You don't understand the world of high finance . . . not that I'm very good at it myself. If I were, I wouldn't be in this fix right now. Working hard and being honest and meaning well doesn't mean a damn thing in this world.

You couldn't begin to understand what I've done, what a risk I took, how badly I'm going to land when I hit bottom, how great is the chance that I'm going to drag you all down with me.

" . . . so we just tightened our belts and saw it through," his father said. "You can do it too, boy. You got to get into some other line of work, though. There ain't no future in that damn crazy music of yours."

"I know, Pop. I know," he said affectionately. "We'll see what happens, okay?"

Floyd nodded, happy with what sounded to him like a gesture of agreement. "What was your dream, boy?"

Simon shook his head. "Nothing worth talking about. Just a bad dream."

"What was it about?"

He shrugged and sipped from his glass of brandy. "About a woman, mostly."

"About a woman? And you call it a bad dream?" The old man laughed heartily, and his laughter infected his son, who joined in it. "Hell, boy, I've had my share of dreams 'bout women, but ain't one of 'em been bad!"

"Well," Simon laughed, "this one was."

"Well," Floyd said gently, "maybe you oughta thinka gettin' married again. It's been too long since you've had a woman—I mean a woman regular, a wife, not those—well, those women you hang 'round with when you're out there grindin' out that garbage you call music. Lord knows, I try to ignore that caterwaulin' when your son plays it 'round here . . . and by the way, you got to do somethin' about Lucas. . . ."

Well, so much for this month's five minutes of good relations with Pop, Simon thought. As before he merely smiled and nodded and uttered perfunctory grunts of assent, and ignored his father's words completely.

That was the damnedest dream, he thought again as he nodded and smiled. That woman with the large, feline eyes and that hair . . . what was it? brown? black? . . . I can't remember . . . and her voice, that soft, seductive voice. . . .

But what was so frightening? he asked himself. I never seem to be able to remember my dreams. They're crystal clear when I wake up, and then I lose them. It seems that she was trying to take me somewhere, somewhere I didn't want to go, somewhere frightening, horrible, and I couldn't get away from her.

Simon shook his head and sipped again from his brandy, nodding and grunting automatically as old Floyd continued his rambling invective. Somewhere in the back of his mind, another memory from the dream was struggling to assert itself, struggling to bring itself forward to his consciousness before sinking forever into oblivion. Then for a moment he remembered a peculiarity in the dream; it was most definitely he who was in the dream with the woman. But she had not called him by his name, she had not called him Simon.

She had called him John.

II

WITCH'S SABBATH

Ye are like unto whited sepulchres, which
indeed appear beautiful outward, but are within full of dead men's bones and all uncleanness.

—MATTHEW 23:27

⟨ CHAPTER EIGHT ⟩

November 16

It had taken Jeremy Sloan over two weeks to muster up sufficient courage to go over to the Proctor home and make an attempt at mending his relations with Rowena. He had watched from his bedroom window as she left for school each morning during the week, watched and strained his ears to listen as she and her grandfather exchanged cheerful pleasantries as they climbed into the old Dodge each school day. He had spent each evening sitting in the back of Saunder's Bar over in Fairleigh, drinking with Lucas and Karyn, irritating Lucas with his constant questions about Rowena. Has she said anything about me? Is she still angry at me? Have you spoken to her about what happened? Has my name come up in conversation?

It was Lucas who finally had said to him, "Look, Sloan, the chick ain't gonna come crawlin' to you, you know. You wanna get back in the goods with her? Go over and talk to her. Don't keep botherin' me. I never talk to her anyway."

Thus it was that Jeremy approached the Proctor home, eager and uneasy, hopeful and pessimistic, on that clear, cold morning in mid-November. He had shaved, bathed, polished his boots, put on a clean shirt, and done all the other magical rituals to which young men turn in faith when having dealings with young women.

He cleared his throat and then knocked on the front door. It seemed an eternity before he heard footsteps approaching from within. The door swung open and old Floyd stood for a moment, staring at Jeremy as if trying to place his face. Then the old man smiled broadly and said, "Oh, Jeremy. Hello, young fella. Come in, come in."

"Good mornin', Mr. Proctor," Jeremy said cheerfully. He felt reassured by Floyd's friendly greeting. It meant that Rowena had not been speaking ill of him to her grandfather. "Is Rowena home?"

"Sure she is, sure she is. Go on into the sittin' room. I'll go get her." Jeremy went into the sitting room, but did not sit. He paced nervously back and forth. He reached down and scratched Pistopheles behind the ears, and the cat closed her eyes and purred. She looked up at Jeremy inscrutably as he resumed his pacing, and then she sauntered over to the sofa and hopped up onto it. Pistopheles began to lick her paws and wipe them over her face with a casual deliberation, oblivious to Jeremy's presence.

Jeremy turned when he heard light footsteps descending the stairs. Rowena skipped down, and Jeremy's heart melted at the sight of her. She was wearing a fuzzy, oversized green sweater which hung down to just above her bare knees. Her white blond hair was pulled back into a ponytail, and her clear blue eyes appraised him quizzically. "Hello, Jeremy," she said. "What do you want?"

She spoke in a tone cold enough to freeze lava, and Jeremy walked toward her hesitantly, realizing that he had not given much thought to precisely what words to use. He stammered, stuttered, started to speak and then stopped, started again and then stopped again. At last he just spread his hands out at his sides and said, "I'm sorry, Row. Please forgive me."

She sniffed, refusing to be so easily mollified. "You had a lot of nerve getting me mixed up in something like that, when I trusted you and everything."

He nodded with sincerity. "I know. I'm sorry. Please forgive me."

She looked him up and down quickly and tried to keep the smile she felt emerging from breaking into the austerity of her expression. He polished those ratty old boots, she thought. Isn't that sweet? What she said was, "You know I don't like that sort of stuff. You weren't being very thoughtful."

He nodded again. "You're right, I wasn't being thoughtful at all. I'm sorry. Please forgive me." A slight twinkle in her eyes told him that she was weakening. Impulsively he added, "I love you, Row."

She had not expected that, and it took her aback. Her mouth fell open and she stared at him for a moment. "What did you say?" she asked.

He sighed and shrugged. "I love you. I can't stand the idea of you being mad at me. It's driving me nuts."

Her look of wonder dissolved into one of happiness, and she cried, "Oh, Jeremy!" and ran to his arms, throwing her own around his neck and pressing her lips to his. His tongue insinuated itself into her mouth and she accepted it willingly, eagerly. Then he hugged her tightly against him and she rested her head against his chest, and they stood there in silence. At

113

last she looked up into his dark, soft eyes and whispered, "I love you too." And they kissed again.

Jeremy felt like weeping for joy, but he sniffed back whatever tears threatened to emerge. He smiled impishly. "Does that mean you forgive me?"

"I'll let it go this time," she laughed, and hugged him.

They did not hear Simon Proctor as he stumbled down the stairs, scratching his rumpled hair and yawning. He saw them hugging and kissing in the foyer, and for a moment his eyes saw but did not register. Then a surge of paternal jealousy rose in him and he said in a shocked and angry tone, "What the hell's going on here?"

Startled, Rowena jumped back. "Daddy!" she said, exhaling heavily. "You scared the heck out of me!"

"What the hell's going on here?" he repeated.

Rowena and Jeremy stood in confused and uneasy silence for a few moments. Then she said, "I was kissing Jeremy."

Simon did not know what to say or how to respond. Somewhere in the back of his mind he knew that he was slipping into the role of the possessive, overprotective father, but his annoyance quickly overrode all other considerations. "Well—well, *don't!*" he said at last, and walked toward the kitchen.

They watched him leave, and Jeremy's hand reached over to take hers. She turned to him and said, "Daddy's just being grouchy. Don't worry about it. You know that he likes you."

"Yeah, sure," he replied uncertainly. "And I like him."

"I've never really had a boyfriend before, and he's never seen me kiss anybody. It must be a shock to him. He'll get over it." She smiled and kissed him again. He closed his eyes and returned the kiss, but opened them again when he felt a sudden tensing of her mouth, as if she were distracted. He saw that she was looking past him, out the picture window. "I wonder who that is?" she asked. As he followed her gaze, he saw the cat Pistopheles leap onto the window sill and arch her back, hissing angrily at something outside.

The window looked out from the eastern side of the old inn, giving an unobstructed view of Bradford's sole street as it stretched out past the Grange hall and wound its way up toward the mountains. Jeremy squinted in an attempt to bring into focus the distant figures to whom Rowena had referred. "You got good eyes," he said with a soft laugh. "I can hardly see them."

"It's funny, isn't it, for them to walk right in the middle of the road like that?" she asked. "I mean, shouldn't they stay off to the side?"

"Yeah, sure, I guess so," Jeremy nodded, not really caring. "Not much traffic on this road, though."

"No, I guess not," she replied. She continued to stare out at the distant, moving figures. "Aren't they dressed funny?"

"Jesus, Row," he laughed. "How can you see so far? I can't even tell how many people there are out there, and you're talking about how they're dressed! Good Lord!"

"I always eat my carrots." She grinned. "Just watch, you'll be able to see them in a minute. They're coming in this direction."

Jeremy watched and waited patiently as the figures drew near. It was a misty morning, and the fog further obstructed his vision, but in a few moments he was able to see the two people more clearly, two dots of black against the white world outside. As they came closer, he could see that both wore black cloaks whose hoods had been secured about their heads. They walked with rapid, small steps, and this led him to assume that they were women. "Dressed like Friar Tuck," he muttered.

"Huh?" she asked.

"Remember Friar Tuck from the old Robin Hood movies? They look like that, with those hoods and all."

"Oh, yes, I know what you mean." She watched as the two people came to the center of the road directly in front of her house. They stopped walking and stood there for a moment, speaking to each other quietly. Or rather, one of them, the taller of the two, was speaking to the other, punctuating her discourse with hand gestures as the slightly shorter person listened and nodded. Rowena could not see their faces because they had their backs to the window, so she studied what she could about them. Their coats were not all that similar to monk's robes as they had appeared to be from a distance. They were simple, unadorned woolen cloaks with attached hoods. Rowena's brow furrowed slightly as she appraised the suitcases which the two people were carrying, realizing after a moment that the shape of the cases precluded the likelihood of their being luggage of any sort. The taller of the two people carried a case which was triangular, and the case carried by the shorter person was oblong and rounded at the ends.

"I wonder what they're doing?" Jeremy muttered.

"God, I hope they aren't a couple of Daddy's fans," Rowena said with concern. "I hate it when those people show up here."

Jeremy was not particularly concerned with the identity of

the strangers who were standing out in the snow. He stroked Rowena's hair absently and asked, "It goes with the business, doesn't it? Fans showing up once in a while, I mean."

"Sure it does"—she nodded, watching the conversing figures with apprehension—"and I've always hated it. Don't forget, Jeremy, Daddy's music appeals to a particular type of people. Nutty people, weird people."

"Hey!" he laughed. "I like Simon's music! Am I nutty or weird?"

She returned his laughter and leaned forward to kiss him lightly on the lips. "Of course not. But you're the exception that proves the rule."

"Okay, I'll accept that." He grinned. "Anyway, Simon's fans don't seem to come around here much. I've never seen any of 'em."

"That's because they don't come to your house," she replied. "Just last month a kid came here and threatened to burn down the house if I didn't let him in."

"Are you kidding?!"

"Nope," she said. "I called the cops and they came and got him. But still, it happened. That's why I get nervous whenever people I don't know show up in town. It seems—" She stopped speaking and looked back out the window. "Hey! Where did they go?"

"Maybe they went on their way," he suggested. The sudden, insistent knocking on the door told them that his suggestion was incorrect.

"Oh, great," Rowena muttered as she rose from her seat and went to the front door. She moved to open it, but decided at the last moment to be cautious. She opened the peephole and looked out. "Yes?"

Rowena saw a pale white face of exquisite beauty gazing back at her with striking emerald green eyes. "Is this the home of Simon Proctor?" the woman asked. Her voice was deep and rich, like thick, sweet liquid.

"Yes it is," Rowena answered. "What do you want?" Her tone was wary.

"Fetch your master, girl. Tell him we have come far to see him."

The woman's manner was imperious, and her choice of words annoyed Rowena. "He's my father," she said pointedly. "Who wants to see him?"

The woman laughed. "Two cold, wet, weary travelers."

Rowena waited in vain for further identification. She was

116

tempted to slam shut the peephole and ignore the people standing outside, but she could not bring herself to be so rude. Reluctantly, she pulled the door open to admit the unexpected guests. The two women entered and pulled the hoods back from their heads.

The first woman, the one with whom Rowena had spoken, looked at her coolly, a hint of a smile on the corners of her mouth. "I meant no offense at calling him your master, girl," she said. "But please fetch him."

Rowena began to make a remark about strangers giving orders in someone else's house, but the steady gaze of those green eyes unnerved her and the comment died unspoken. "Wait a moment, please." She walked quickly toward the kitchen.

The women walked into the center of the foyer, and the second woman looked over at Jeremy, who was still sitting upon the sofa in the adjacent sitting room. She smiled slightly and nodded a greeting. He returned both the smile and the nod, and then she turned away from him, ignoring him completely. Pistopheles hissed at her and then ran off.

A long minute passed before Simon Proctor walked out of the kitchen and down the hallway toward the foyer. The women watched him approach, motionless and silent. He came up to them and said, "I'm Simon Proctor. What can I do for you?" He seemed to be annoyed at having been disturbed during breakfast.

The first woman said, "My name is Gwendolyn Jenkins. This is my sister in the faith, Adrienne Lupescu." She paused. "We are witches, Mr. Proctor. And you are a fraud."

"Oh, Lord!" he sighed, remembering the letter they had sent him.

"I have not come here to remonstrate with you," the woman said. "I have come to give you the opportunity to join with us, to help us spread the gospel of Satan, to become a true warlock."

Simon rubbed his eyes wearily. "Look, sweetheart—"

"Please, Mr. Proctor," the woman named Gwendolyn interrupted, "all we ask is a half hour of your time. If what we say pleases you, we will stay longer. If not, we will depart and come not back again."

Come not back again? Simon thought. Is she trying to sound weird or something? If she is, she isn't succeeding. She just sounds silly. He said, "Miss Jenkins, I'm a rock and roll singer.

This witchcraft-satanism stuff is just an act, that's all, nothing but an act. Now if you'll excuse—"

"Aye, an act it is, a pretense," Gwendolyn said. "And fraud yields no profit after a time."

"Huh?"

"I know you, Simon Proctor, I know you better than you know yourself. I know that you seek wealth, and yet have it not. Well," she said confidently, "I am come to bring you wealth, more wealth than you can imagine. We shall join you in your theaters, we shall bring witchcraft, true witchcraft, to the young people of this land, and they shall yield up their wealth to you, for you shall be real in their eyes, and no charlatan."

"What do you mean, you know me?" he huffed. "I've never met you before."

"Nor we you," Gwendolyn replied. "But I know you notwithstanding. The world is filled with men such as you, who wish for what they cannot have, who have what they do not want, who dream of things beyond their grasp." She moved closer to him, and her eyes penetrated his. There was something about this woman, something about her *presence*, which Simon found disquieting. "But hear me well, Simon Proctor. You can have that which you desire. You can fulfill your dreams and build a world for yourself in any shape you wish. Satan can do this for you, through us."

Great, Simon thought. Just what I need at eight o'clock in the morning. A couple of crazy people standing in my foyer. "Miss, I'm sorry, but I'm not a Satanist, and I don't think that your preaching would go over very well at my concerts. Now if—"

"Preaching!" the woman exclaimed. "What am I, a minister? I speak not of preaching, but of song, of dance. You are a maker of music, are you not?"

"Yes, but—"

"Fine. Then we shall join you in the making of music, and we shall draw people to our Master with melody and with the beauty of words."

Simon smiled despite himself. "You are a musician? What do you play?"

"Will you hear us?" she demanded.

Simon glanced over at Rowena, giving her a look of weary resignation. She winked at him. Turning back to Gwendolyn, he said, "Sure, why not. Give us a tune." He walked into the sitting room and took a seat in the overstuffed armchair beside the sofa.

The women followed him in. Each was carrying an oddly shaped case by a wooden handle, and they rested their burdens on the floor. They silently unbuttoned their long cloaks and removed them, tossing them casually onto the floor in the corner. Rowena jumped to her feet to retrieve them and carried them to the hallway to hang them in the closet. The second woman smiled at her as she walked back in to the sitting room. "Thank you," she said very softly.

"You're welcome," Rowena responded, doing her best not to sound too friendly. Witches! she thought glumly. Wonderful!

She looked over at her father and found him enraptured by the woman with whom he had been speaking. Rowena had noticed the extreme beauty of her face at once, but now, without the cloak, the woman was even more stunning. Her hair was black, straight, shiny, falling without a ripple from her perfectly shaped head down to the small of her back. Her skin was like white marble, which accentuated the ruby redness of her full lips and the piercing green of her catlike eyes. She was tall, almost as tall as Simon, with a high waist and a voluptuous figure. When she leaned over to unlock the clasp of her case Rowena noticed the brightly painted red fingernails which looked long and sharp, and when the woman spoke Rowena noticed for the second time the aristocratic features of her face, the delicate pointed nose, the slightly cleft chin, the high, thin cheekbones.

"I have some skill on the harp, the native instrument of my country," Gwendolyn said as she drew a simple wooden instrument with twenty-five gut strings from the black carrying case.

"Your country?" Simon asked. "Where are you from?"

"I was born in Llechtenich, a small town in Wales," she replied. "My friend Adrienne plays the lute."

Simon glanced at the other woman, who had removed a lute from the case she had been carrying and was attending to its tuning. He gave her no more than a glance, for she was as unimpressive as the other woman was striking. Both were attired in long black skirts and simple, gauzy peasant blouses, but whereas her clothing served only to make Gwendolyn even more stimulating, it made Adrienne appear a bit dowdy. Her hair was a nondescript brown, cut to shoulder length but otherwise unstyled, falling in indifferent waves. She was almost boyishly thin and appeared very unhealthy. Her face was broad and plain, unflattered by makeup of any sort, and her complexion, which at first glance was as white as Gwendolyn's, was in reality merely pallid.

"Have you heard of the old singer of songs, Thomas the Rhymer?" Adrienne asked Simon. It was the first time she had spoken, and her voice was timorous and high.

"No, I don't think so," Simon replied.

"He was a minstrel of the old times," she explained softly, "centuries ago."

"I've heard of him," Rowena said. "We read about him in English class. He lived in Scotland in the Middle Ages, right?"

"Aye," Adrienne said, smiling at her. "Here is a song of Thomas the Rhymer."

"Hold," Gwendolyn muttered as she tuned her harp. For a few moments the women plucked their strings and turned their pegs to bring the two instruments into tune with each other. Then Gwendolyn looked at Simon and said, "Here be Thomas's song of demons and witchery." She had seated herself upon the floor.

She began to pluck the bass strings of her harp with her thumb, setting up an infectious rhythm, and a melody soon began to emerge from the treble strings which she plucked with her fingers. She held the harp upon her lap, cradling it with her left arm while playing it with her right. Adrienne remained standing, the lute suspended from a leather strap around her neck. Gwendolyn played through what seemed to be an introductory bit of music, and then Adrienne joined in with a contrapuntal harmonic melody upon the lute. The sound was hypnotic and unusual, and both women's eyes closed as each became enraptured by her own music. They then began to sing, Gwendolyn's low, rich voice combining with Adrienne's wavering soprano to produce an enchanting harmony.

"When cold blew the North Wind and bleak was the sky,
    when earth was enveloped in winter shade,
when spirits ephemeral hoverèd high,
    and winter ghosts haunted the water,
Through land of the Saxon and land of the Celt
    full weary and worn my way I made.
I came to a river where winter did melt
    from the warmth of the druid's daughter."

The words seemed to flow like an ancient paean from votive lips, transporting Simon, Rowena, and Jeremy to another time, another age. They sat openmouthed and enchanted by the sheer beauty and artistry of the two women.

"Her name was callèd Evangeline.
  Her eyes were as blue as the Scandian Sea,
Her hair was of texture so ruddy and fine
  That sunsets prostrated before her.
Her father, a druid, a sorcerer dread,
  So lovèd this child of wizardry
That skillfully kept he her soul from the dead
  That earth might forever adore her.

But over her brooded a demon so foul
  That only her smile could hold him still,
Her demon lover Ra'igma'oul,
  A spawn of the pit's bloody nation.
His eyes were as red as the fires of hell,
  His hands were beclawed for to tear and kill.
But demon or no, he lovèd her well,
  And kissed her feet with adoration.

I met her by a mountain stream
  As she did bathe in morning dew.
I found her part woman, part spirit, part dream,
  An angel to hover above me.
Cast down at her feet I told her so slow
  That my heart was her prisoner fast and true.
She knelt down beside me and whisperèd low
  That then and forever she'd love me."

Adrienne proceeded to play a lilting musical interlude upon
the lute as Gwendolyn swayed slightly to and fro. Simon
looked over at Rowena and gave her a look which indicated
that he was impressed by the singers and the song.

"The demon was wroth and he prayed to the Powers
  Which dwell in the clouds upon days of storm.
He called out unto them for many long hours
  When voices he heard calling to his soul.
'Ra'igma'oul,' the voices did say,
  'Blow thou but three blasts upon shepherd's horn
And Evangeline will wither away,
  Be lost to the universe temporal.'

The demon foul, red eyes aflame,
  Did creep up to where m'love did lay,
And softly calling out her name
  Prepared to sound the death-horn.
Evangeline looked up at him
121

And screamed as he sounded the fatal tone.
Her form, it shrank and waxèd thin
     And then faded into the dewy morn."

It was now Gwendolyn's turn to play an interlude. Adrienne maintained a melodic rhythm as Gwendolyn's harp spun out a wildly sensuous rill of rapidly ascending and descending notes. She opened her eyes and gazed at Simon, her white teeth slowly revealed by the lascivious smile which spread over her face. Simon tried to return her unwavering gaze, but found himself growing nervous and slightly dizzy, and he looked away. Gwendolyn emitted a short, low laugh and then returned her attention to the harp. Adrienne joined her voice to Gwendolyn's once more as they began the final verse of the song.

"And so during summer when grasses are green,
     When forest sprites dance upon rock and bough,
When spirits and serpents of mystical mien
     Abound in the budding world fair and fine,
The sound of lamenting will often arise
     And waft on the wind to the lands around,
The hater and lover, the demon and I,
     Bemoaning the loss of Evangeline."

A few final rills ran delicately upon the strings of the harp and the lute, and then descended to a minor key resolution. As the final echoes of the strings faded and died, Gwendolyn turned to Simon and said, "That is not preaching, is it, Mr. Proctor?"

Simon laughed. "No, I'll say it isn't. That was a lovely piece. Who did you say wrote that?"

"Thomas the Rhymer," Adrienne said.

"Thomas the Rhymer," Simon repeated. "I must make a point of looking him up in the library. I'll bet there are lots of songs of his which I can use."

"Aye, but you'll not find that song in a book," Gwendolyn said. "It is known to us and to us alone. It has never seen the printed page or the handwritten paper."

Simon furrowed his brow. "What are you talking about? How do you know the song if it isn't written down anywhere?"

"He taught it to us," Adrienne said.

"Who taught it to you?"

"Thomas the Rhymer," she explained innocently.

Simon paused before replying. At last he said, "Yeah, sure. Thomas the Rhymer." He stood to his feet. "Well, ladies, thanks for the entertainment, but I really don't think that this would work out for either of us."

Gwendolyn Jenkins raised her fine black eyebrows in surprise. "Our song does not please you?"

"Oh, yes, very much," Simon said honestly. "It was beautiful. Very beautiful. In fact, it's much better than most of the stuff we grind out in the music business nowadays. It has the same kind of atmosphere—you know, mystical lyrics, antique melody—that Jethro Tull used to do about ten years ago, and Donovan did ten years before that."

"Well, then!" she said with satisfaction.

"So don't be offended when I say it just wouldn't work. Really, it is a beautiful song. You should be proud of it." He laughed. "I wish I'd written it, fifteen years ago."

"We did not write it," Adrienne said. "It—"

"Yeah, yeah, I know. Thomas the Rhymer," he interrupted, repressing a laugh. "Anyway, the music I use in my act is a lot louder and more driving than that. Like I said, I'm a rock singer. That was a folk song."

"Simon," Jeremy offered tentatively, "didn't the Byrds do some of Dylan's folk songs with rock music?"

Simon Proctor shot him an irritated glance. "Shut up, Jeremy."

"Listen, Mr. Proctor," Gwendolyn said. "Music is music, and dance is dance. I know nothing of your music or this rock and roll. But I know that songs which last for centuries do so because they pluck the harp strings of the soul and speak to needs buried deep within the human breast."

Woman has a way with words, Simon thought.

"Tell me this," she continued. "When you make your music, is the theater filled? Are there yet spaces which remain empty?"

"Oh, a few, sometimes," he lied, not wishing to discuss the incipient collapse of his business with a total stranger. "It's quite common for a few seats to remain open at a concert. But that—"

"So. You attract the spectators, and yet a little space remains. What ill is done by allowing Adrienne and I to fill those empty spaces?"

"Well—" he began uncertainly.

"We seek no payment, ask for no reward. If we can enlarge the number of spectators, then all is well. And if it be not so, then all is as it was before, and you have lost nothing."

He paused before speaking. "What do you mean, you don't want to be paid? Everybody wants to be paid for what they do."

"We do not," Gwendolyn said emphatically. "We seek to make your representation of our religion accurate and true. Such rewards as we receive will come from our Master, not from you."

Wait a minute . . . wait a minute, Simon thought. What's the harm? It won't cost me anything. It might help me out. It couldn't hurt. I can't be in much worse of a position than I already am. No payment? No salary? No percentage of the take? I like those terms. . . .

"Wait a minute," he said aloud. "Let me think about this." Gwendolyn and Adrienne stood silently, expectantly. Rowena studied her father's face, trying to discern his thoughts.

It'd make for good PR, he thought. Real witches, from Wales. I can see the posters now! If we can get their songs rearranged, put them to a rock setting . . . not heavy metal, sort of the old folk-rock sound . . . dress them up in some sort of sexy outfit . . . it just might work. . . . It just might work. . . .

"Okay," he said at last. "Here's what I'll do. We'll give it a try—"

"Splendid!" Gwendolyn exclaimed. Adrienne remained mute.

"Hold it," he cautioned. "We'll give it a try in one concert, just one. I'm starting a concert tour in about two weeks. We're going to have to get together with my band and do some rehearsing, get your songs—you do have other songs, don't you?"

Gwendolyn smiled triumphantly. "Hundreds," she replied.

"Great. Get your songs arranged for rock, get you some costumes—" he was growing feverish with anticipation, "it might go. It might sell. But no commitments, you understand, beyond this one concert. No contracts signed or anything."

Gwendolyn laughed. "When I was but a girl I signed the Devil's book. I have signed nothing since, nor shall I."

"Yeah, sure, fine," Simon said carefully as Rowena rolled her eyes heavenward. "Well, good. Great. Row, why don't you get a couple of the rooms ready for—give me your names again?"

"Gwendolyn Jenkins," she said, "and my friend is Adrienne Lupescu."

"Right. Both from Wales."

"No, sir," Adrienne said softly. "I am from Romania."

Simon was disappointed. "Oh, yeah? That's too bad. There's

124

something mystical about Wales that Romania just doesn't have. Unless, of course—" he paused. "Where in Romania?"

"I was born in the village of Bloisci, near the town of Cluj."

He shook his head. "That doesn't mean anything to me. I mean, what is the region called where you come from?"

"The region? Transylvania," she answered simply.

Simon smiled at her. "That's what I was hoping you'd say. Wales is great, but you can't get more mystical than Transylvania. I'm thinking in terms of publicity—if this all works out, you understand." He turned to his daughter. "Row, fix up a couple of rooms for our guests, will you?"

As she rose to her feet, Rowena sighed and shook her head. "Grampa isn't gonna like this," she muttered.

"Just go with my daughter," Simon said. "Where are your bags?"

"We have none," Gwendolyn said, "but for our instruments."

"Okay, fine," he said, feeling for all the world like a motel owner who had just admitted two suspicious guests. "Just follow Rowena. I have some calls to make."

Jeremy got to his feet. "I can put off washing the church windows for an hour or so. You need some help, Row?"

"No, she doesn't," Simon said pointedly.

Rowena cast a disparaging look of strained tolerance in her father's direction and said, "Go wash the windows, Jeremy. I'll see you later."

"Okay," he replied. "I'll come over after supper."

She smiled. "Great." She disappeared up the stairs, Gwendolyn and Adrienne following behind her.

Jeremy stood nervously in the sitting room. Simon appraised him coldly. "Jeremy, don't misunderstand me. I think you're a nice kid, and I like you. But you and Rowena . . ." He shook his head.

"Shit, Simon, I'd never do anything to hurt her!" he said, wanting desperately to avoid the conversation which he knew was beginning.

"I know that," he said gently, but with a hard edge to his voice. "But I think that Rowena is too young to have a boyfriend."

"Too young!" Jeremy exclaimed. "She's nearly seventeen!"

"She's only sixteen," Simon pointed out obstinately. "Look, if you two are friends, that's just fine with me. But I don't want any of this huggy-kissy stuff, you understand?"

"Jesus!" he said with disbelief. "You're starting to sound like my uncle!"

"Jeremy . . . ," Simon said darkly, a hint of warning in his voice.

"Okay, okay!" he said quickly. "God!" He left the room in a huff and then left the house, closing the front door loudly behind him. Simon watched him leave, frowned, and then walked over to the telephone.

As Rowena led Gwendolyn and Adrienne down the corridor which led to the guest rooms, Karyn ambled out of the room which she shared with Lucas. Lucas was right behind her, and both of them looked exhausted and worn out, though Rowena knew full well that it was not from any legitimate expenditure of energy. They each rubbed their bloodshot eyes and scratched their scalps through matted hair, yawning loudly. Karyn looked blearily at Rowena. "Hiya, kid," she muttered.

"Good morning," she replied. "Uh, Karyn and Lucas, these are our guests for the next day or two. This is Gwendolyn, and this is Adrienne."

Adrienne nodded deferentially. "My pleasure to greet you." Gwendolyn said nothing.

"They may be joining Daddy's act," Rowena said.

This seemed to awaken some spark of interest in Lucas. "Oh yeah? What do you do, sing?"

"Aye," Gwendolyn replied, "and make music. We are also witches."

Lucas gazed at her uncomprehendingly for a moment. "Say what?"

Rowena sighed. "Gwendolyn and Adrienne say that they are witches, real witches. Daddy thinks that maybe they can draw bigger crowds to his shows." Rowena's opinion of the whole thing was clearly expressed in her tone of voice.

Lucas nodded, impressed. "No shit! That's mint!"

Gwendolyn cocked her head slightly. "You be Proctor's son?"

"Yeah," Lucas yawned. "I be." He gestured over at Karyn with a movement of his thumb. "This be my woman."

Karyn shot him an angry glance and then smiled at Gwendolyn. "Please pardon Lucas. He's an asshole." She extended her hand and added, "Nice to meetcha."

Gwendolyn regarded her proffered hand quizzically for a moment and then shook it awkwardly. She ran her eyes up and down Karyn's body and then observed, "You are with child."

Patting her belly, Karyn grinned. "Yup."

"And when will it be delivered?"

"Not sure," she replied. "Sometime in February, I think."

Gwendolyn thrust her hand into a deep pocket on the side of

126

her long black skirt and fished around for a moment. "Have you a chain, a necklace?"

"Sure," Karyn said, pulling forth the chain which had been hidden by the wrinkled collar of her soiled shirt. It was a cheap imitation gold chain with a plastic shark's tooth on the end.

Gwendolyn took a small amulet from her pocket and handed it to Karyn. "Here," she said. "Place this upon the chain and wear it until you are delivered of your child."

Karyn took it from her hand and examined it. "It's pretty," she said, not quite truthfully. The amulet was a plain square ornament with a noticeable seam and a small catch on one side. "Is it a locket? Does it open?"

"Aye, but do not open it," Gwendolyn said quickly, "lest the contents spill out."

"What's in it?"

"Dried dog's blood and a powder made from the grindings of the testicles of a bull."

"Oh," Karyn said, not knowing quite how to react. "That's, uh, very interesting."

"It will insure a manchild," Gwendolyn explained.

"Hey, come on, huh?" Lucas whined. "That's disgusting. I feel sick enough without hearing shit like that!"

Gwendolyn laughed. "You have, I think, sucked too freely upon Bacchus' teat, young mister."

Lucas stared at her blankly. "Huh?"

"I can be of help, perhaps. Many were the times I helped my father recover from a night of revelry."

"Yeah?" Lucas said. "How?"

"A drink which I can prepare for you," she explained, "which will lessen the effects of the grape and clear your mind."

"No kidding?" he asked. "What's in the drink?"

She thought for a moment. "Some dried cattle dung and the legs of a dozen spiders."

Lucas looked at her for a few moments as he began to turn a pale green. Then he placed both hands over his mouth and began to run down the corridor to the bathroom. Karyn shot Gwendolyn an irritated glance and then followed him.

Rowena was trying to stifle her laughter as she said, "Come on. Your rooms are this way." She walked before them down the corridor, saying, "This place used to be an inn, so we have lots of bedrooms." She opened the door to one of the unused rooms. It had a slightly musty smell. "I guess I'd better change the sheets."

127

" 'Tis a goodly house, and a fair room," Adrienne said politely.

"Thanks," Rowena replied. "Hold on. I'll go get some fresh linen."

A moment after Rowena left the room, Gwendolyn turned to Adrienne and said, "Did you see? Did you see? 'Tis the same!"

She shrugged. " 'Tis similar. There is a semblance, but—"

"Tosh! 'Tis the same countenance, the same visage!"

"It has been a long while, a long, long while. How can you be so certain?"

"Some things one can never forget."

Adrienne shook her head. "Even if he looks the same, he is not the same man. This is folly!"

Gwendolyn turned on her angrily, her green eyes blazing. Adrienne shrank back from her as she said, "Speak not to me of folly! 'Twas your folly which killed him, your folly which ruined me!"

"I—I meant no—"

"You are here, are you not? You breathe and live, do you not? Is this folly?!" She heard Rowena returning, and silenced her companion with a stern, angry glance.

Rowena walked back in, weighed down with piles of linen and wool. "I'll make up the beds in a moment. Just let me leave half of this stuff here, and then I'll show you the other room."

"By your leave, miss, I'll not trouble you," Adrienne said, still shaking from Gwendolyn's anger. "I can make ready the beds."

"Oh, I wouldn't hear of it," Rowena responded, pleased by the courteous offer. "I know my duties as a hostess." She noticed a slight movement off to the side, and turned to see her grandfather leaning his bald head into the room quizzically. "Oh, Grampa, this is Gwendolyn Jenkins and Adrienne Lupescu." He nodded to them and they nodded back. "They're gonna be staying with us for a couple of days. They're joining Daddy's act."

Floyd Proctor did not smile. "Oh, really?" he said noncommittally.

"It will be a good done by each for each," Gwendolyn said.

"That's nice," he said evenly, and began to walk toward the stairs.

Rowena shrugged, blushing slightly. "He probably doesn't like you."

"He does not know us!" Adrienne observed.

"That doesn't matter," Rowena explained. "If you're involved in Daddy's business, Grampa doesn't like you." She shrugged again. "Just try to stay out of his way. It's only for a couple of days, after all."

Floyd descended the stairs and began to wander from room to room, looking for his son. He found him at last in the first room he should have checked, the sitting room near the base of the stairs. He walked in to hear Simon saying into the phone, "That's right, Harry. Just one concert, just to test the waters, but we're gonna need some rehearsing. Can you get the boys together by, say, Tuesday? . . . Yeah, yeah, I know everybody's on a break, but this might . . . Right, a buck's a buck. . . . Okay. . . . Okay. . . . See you Tuesday in Tom's basement. . . . Right. Okay, take care." He hung up the phone. "Gotta call Mark—"

"Who are those women, boy?" Floyd demanded.

"Just a new act I'm gonna use, Pop, that's all," he said. "They're just staying here for a couple of days, and then we're going down to Manhattan."

"They do the same crap you do?" his father asked. "That devil crap?"

"Stop it, Pop, will you?" he said curtly. "I'm busy."

"I don't like strangers staying under my roof without my permission! I don't like that one bit!"

Leave me be, Simon thought, and maybe you can stay under your own roof for a few more years. "Just be tolerant," he said. "They won't hurt anything."

Floyd snorted his displeasure as he turned and walked away. Simon watched him leave and then walked over to the picture window and gazed out at the snow-covered street. "Might work," he said softly to himself. "Can't tell until you try." A fresh approach is a good idea, he thought. They sure do have lovely voices. I hope they can handle rock and roll. I'm pretty sure Gwendolyn can—her voice is strong—but I'm not sure about Adrienne. Voice seems a little too delicate. But we'll see. We'll see.

He left the sitting room and went to the closet beside the front door to get his coat. If I'm driving back to Manhattan day after tomorrow, he thought, I'd better get that muffler attended to. Don't want to make a long drive like that with my tailpipe dragging on the ground.

He donned his scarf and coat absentmindedly, lost in deep thought. He did not turn around to see the green eyes staring

129

intently at him from the top of the stairs as he walked out the front door.

Gwendolyn Jenkins stared after Simon as he closed the door behind him. She sat down softly upon the top step and folded her arms around her knees. Her nostrils flared slightly with some unspoken excitement and her eyes grew wide with some as yet unrealized vision. Adrienne came up quietly from behind and sat down beside her. She cleared her throat and whispered, " 'Tis not he, in truth. You know that. 'Tis not as promised."

Gwendolyn smiled. "Is it not?"

"Nay," Adrienne replied soberly. "You know 'tis not."

"But he will serve," she laughed. "He will serve as well. If I shall not have the one, then I shall have the other."

"But you know not if he will love you," Adrienne said. "Perhaps 'twill be as before, perhaps—"

"He will love me," Gwendolyn said evenly, turning her cold eyes upon her friend. "He must love me. 'Tis predestined."

Adrienne shrank back slightly from the withering stare. "But what if—"

"Oh, hush up!" Gwendolyn snapped. "He will love me. And if he does not . . ." Her jaw clenched as she turned away from her friend. "If he does not, then there is another prayer which shall be answered."

They sat in silence for a few moments longer, and then Gwendolyn rose to her feet. Adrienne followed suit immediately, and they both turned to walk back toward the rooms which Rowena had prepared for them. They passed Pistopheles in the hallway, and the calico cat pressed herself against the wall as they walked by. She ruffled the fur on her back and emitted a threatening hiss.

Gwendolyn smiled casually at the animal as she passed. There was no hint of humor or amusement in her smile. "Do you remember Goliath?" she asked her friend.

"Hmm? Who?"

"Goliath, Giles Corey's cat. The one that scratched me?"

Adrienne sighed, remembering both the cat and what her friend had done to it. "Aye, I remember Goliath."

"I have always hated cats," Gwendolyn muttered, and continued on toward her room.

{ CHAPTER NINE }
November 16, continued

SIMON PROCTOR STRUCK a match and brought the flame close to the tip of the perfectly rolled marijuana cigarette which dangled from his lips. He rarely smoked pot up here in Bradford, realizing that it would upset his daughter and infuriate his father, but now, late in the evening with everyone in the house securely tucked into bed, he felt entitled to a brief respite from his tension and his worries. He had spent the day on the phone, speaking to the musicians in his band, speaking to his agent, to his road manager, his lighting team, his lawyer, his accountant, and his depression was at this point over-whelming.

He inhaled deeply and allowed the drug-soaked smoke to sink into his lungs. After a few moments of holding his breath, he exhaled and expelled a billow of sweet fumes into the darkness of his bedroom. The rays of moonlight danced silently upon the smoke.

Day after tomorrow, he thought. Hit the road before seven, get to New York around noon, if there's no traffic. Got to rehearse. Got to rehearse. See if these girls are any good with the band. Simon inhaled again, and then lay pensively, drumming his left hand on the night table. Hate to leave here, he thought. So calm, so relaxing. Wish I could just stay here all the time, never have to go on tour, never have to see the inside of a recording studio. Well, he laughed grimly to himself, you may get your wish. If the movie flops, if the tour doesn't sell out, if the creditors drop down on you like vultures, you'll find yourself with all the spare time you want. Of course, it won't be spent in this house. You won't own this house anymore, or the acreage stretching out back. You'll have to get a job pumping gas or working in a warehouse or something. Rent a place for you and Row and the old man. Let Lucas take care of himself.

"God," he muttered. "Why the hell didn't I incorporate? At least then my house wouldn't be up for grabs."

Come on, come on, he told himself angrily. Things aren't as bad as all that. All you have to do is break even on the film, and everything will be all right. Look at all the crap kids shell out money to go and see nowadays. Enough of 'em will go to see your film to let it break even. And maybe the tour will go all right too. Never can tell. You can still draw a crowd, still fill a stadium. Hell, Madison Square Garden was just too big a place, that's all. Got to be a few empty seats in a place that big. Got to be. Got to be.

No, there doesn't, the other side of his mind replied. And things are exactly as bad as you think they are. You're mortgaged up to your neck and your career is petering out. Just look at you! You're so far gone and so desperate that you're hoping that a couple of crazy broads are going to be able to bail you out! Clutching at straws, clutching at straws.

"Hey," he said aloud, as if trying to attract his own attention, "I'm getting stoned to try to forget all this shit, right?" Take it easy. Calm down. Forget it all. Just forget it all.

A gentle knocking on his bedroom door disturbed his thoughts. Ah, shit, he said to himself. "Yeah? Who's there?"

"Gwendolyn," came the reply. "I smelled a fire as of burning wood, but can find no fireplace in use."

"A fire! Wait . . ." Then he realized that she had smelled the pungent aroma of his marijuana. "Hold on a minute." He rose from his bed and, after stubbing the joint out into the ashtray, walked over to the door. As he opened it he said, "Nothing to worry about. I was just blowing some weed."

"Just blowing—what? Weeds?" she asked in confusion. "You were burning weeds in the house?"

"Shhh! Not so loud. You'll wake everybody up."

"Oh, I'm sorry. I did not mean to speak so loudly. But I do not understand."

"I was smoking pot." No response. "You know, pot. Marijuana, grass. You know?"

She shrugged slightly. Though it was as dark in the hallway as in his bedroom, he could see the moonlight which was reflecting from his wall mirror glisten upon her black hair as she moved her head. "I know what grass is, of course. But—"

"Jesus, don't tell me you've never smoked pot!" He laughed. "What kind of rock singer do you expect to be?!"

A low throaty laugh floated toward him from the darkness. "I shall be whatever you want me to be, Simon Proctor."

There was something about her laugh which caused him to smile, something sensuous and earthy. His smile could be heard in his voice as he replied, "You know, it's awfully hard to believe that a witch in the United States has never smoked pot. Are you sure you aren't putting me on?"

"Pretend that I am pretending, if you like," she said softly in the darkness. "What is this weed you burn indoors?"

Simon hesitated for a moment and then said, "Come on in for a minute." He pulled the already opened door farther open, and he half saw and half heard Gwendolyn glide into the dark room. "Hold on a minute. I'll get the light." He walked over to the night table, stubbed his toe on the bed post, muttered an imprecation, and switched on the small, dim lamp beside the bed. He was wearing his dungarees and no shirt, and he said, "Pardon my appearance. I was getting ready to . . ."

He stopped in midsentence as he turned to face her. She was standing before him in a sheer white negligee which dipped at the bodice, revealing the unencumbered and unsupported cleavage of her ample breasts. "I found this nightgown among some old clothes in your basement earlier today. I had nothing to wear for sleeping, so I borrowed it and washed it. I hope you do not mind."

"No, uh, no, I don't mind." He allowed his eyes to drift lazily up and down her voluptuous form, not noticing the slight grin on her face. The nightgown had belonged to his first wife, who was a smaller woman than Gwendolyn, and the garment did not fit in any practical sense of the term. But from the standpoint of erotic effect, it was perfectly tailored. The thin cloth clung tightly to her bosom and hips and thighs. Her dark nipples thrust out against the tight fabric, seeming to pinch the cloth inward as they hardened under his gaze, and a dark triangle was clearly visible through the nightgown just below her high waist.

"Does it flatter me?" she asked innocently.

"Yes, ah, yes, it, ah, it looks quite nice." He coughed. "Would you like to get high?"

She laughed. "I cannot fly in this shape, Simon Proctor."

"No, no, I mean would you like to smoke some dope?"

"That is the burning weed?" she asked. "Ah, I think I understand. It is like tobacco, is it not?"

He felt his sexual excitement die down and his irritation begin to reassert itself. "Look, don't play around with me, Gwen. You wanna get stoned or not?"

She seemed to tense suddenly, and her eyes, which had been soft and wide a moment before, assumed a sudden air of wariness. "What do you mean?"

"Look, for Christ's sake, do you or do you not want to get

high?" As he spoke he picked up the small plastic bag with the marijuana in it and held it up for her to see.

She regarded it and him with continued uncertainty, and then allowed a smile to break from the corners of her mouth. "'Tis like unto tobacco, I think. I will indulge."

"Delightful," he said humorlessly. He gestured toward a wooden chair which stood beside the bed and said "Have a seat" as he sat down upon the bed and began to roll another joint. Gwendolyn walked slowly over and sat down on the bed beside him. She allowed their bare arms to touch slightly. To Simon her skin seemed appealingly warm, and her scent was very stimulating. "I like your perfume," he said. "What kind is it?"

"I wear no perfume. 'Tis me you smell."

He laughed as he poured some powdery flakes into the paper he held cupped in his palm. "Yeah, sure. Essence of Gwendolyn, right?"

She giggled. "If you like."

He rolled up the paper and licked it side, front, and back. Taking a match from the table he lighted the tip of the cigarette, inhaled from it, and then handed it to Gwendolyn. She looked at it quizzically for a moment and then imitated his actions. She had no sooner inhaled the smoke than she began to cough violently, dropping the smoldering joint onto the floor. Simon retrieved it and placed it into the ashtray before saying, "I guess you don't smoke too much, huh."

"I—ugh—ugh—I never—" She continued to cough.

"Hey, I'm sorry, Gwen," he said. "I didn't know you were new to this. I should have warned you. It can be a little rough."

"A little rough!" she coughed. "Like swallowing coals it is!"

"Wait a minute. Here." He reached over to the night table and took the half-empty can of beer which he had been drinking earlier, and which was now warm and flat, and handed it to her. "Take a swig of this. It'll help."

Gwendolyn took the beer can and poured the liquid down her throat. "Aye, 'tis better somewhat." She turned to him, a look of confusion on her face. "Why in the Devil's name do you do that to yourself?"

"Do what?"

"Smoke that horrible plant!"

"Oh," he laughed, "come on. I'm sure you've known people who smoke pot."

She shook her head emphatically. "No, never. My father

used to smoke tobacco in a pipe, but neither he nor any other man I ever knew coughed like this." And she coughed again as if to illustrate her point.

"Well, you don't get the same effects from tobacco as you get from pot, so I guess it's just a question of being willing to pay the price for the pleasure."

"Pleasure!" she exclaimed. "What possible pleasure—!"

"Hold it, here, here, take another drag, but slowly this time, just a little bit." He held the still-smoldering joint out to her, and she took it from him cautiously. "Take a few more small drags and you'll see what I mean. You'll get stoned."

She did not place the joint between her lips, but rather appraised him with furrowed brow. "And yet again you use this term. What do you mean by it?"

"Mean by what?"

"Being stoned."

"Stoned? Well—well, like, getting high. You know, intoxicated."

Her eyes went wide. "As with rum or brandy?"

He smiled. "Different. Better."

"Indeed." She looked at the joint with renewed interest and then took a few small puffs on it. She inhaled the smoke, seemed about to choke, but managed to repress the urge to cough. Simon took the joint from her and dragged on it again, after which he handed it back to her and the process was repeated.

They sat in silence for a few moments. Gwendolyn was staring blankly out at the half-moon which floated among the dark clouds. Simon was staring at her breasts. Gwendolyn began suddenly to giggle uncontrollably. "What's so funny?" he asked, smiling.

"Oh, I don't know. Nothing," she said, calming down. Then she began to giggle again, louder and more forcefully.

"Shhh, shhh!" he cautioned.

"Shhh, shhh!" she repeated and began to giggle again. It was an infectious laugh, and Simon found himself beginning to laugh along with her. "Shhh," he repeated. "We'll wake the whole house."

"Sorry, sorry," she said, trying to stop laughing and failing in the attempt. At last she managed to calm down a bit, though an occasional chuckle interrupted her words. "I feel so light and silly."

"Yeah, that's the general idea," he smiled. They sat in silence for a few moments. Then he said, in an attempt to make conversation, "Well, are you excited about the day after tomorrow?"

"Hmmm?" she asked languidly. "What is to happen then?"

"Meeting the band, rehearsing your numbers. You know."

"Oh, that. Not really. It will be a simple thing. We will do well, you will grow wealthy, and my Master will bless me."

"Yeah, right." I hope to hell you're right, he thought. "You're pretty calm about it. If I were you, I'd be real excited."

She shrugged and then smiled slightly. "Such petty prospects do not excite me. But you excite me, Simon Proctor. You make me mad with longing." She leaned toward him and pressed her mouth against his. She took one of his hands and pressed it palm first against her breasts, moving it around on top of them with a strong circular motion. Simon followed his first instinct and thrust his tongue into her mouth forcefully as he grabbed one of her breasts tightly in his hand, but then disengaged himself from her. "No, wait a minute."

"Why?" she asked with concern. "Do I not please you?"

He laughed at the foolishness of the question. "Are you kidding! I can barely keep my hands off you! But, listen, if we're going to have a professional relationship, we should think twice about getting involved with each other. I mean—"

Gwendolyn giggled. "Such a foolish man! What has tomorrow to do with tonight? And what has tonight to do with yesterday?"

"Huh?"

Gwendolyn stood up and faced him. He was sitting on the edge of the bed, gazing upward at her. Slowly she lifted the nightgown up around her waist and stepped with one foot off to the right, so that though standing, her legs were spread and her pink cleft revealed. She then knelt on the bed, placing one knee on either side of him, wrapping her arms around his neck, squeezing him with her thighs. "I have longed to have you take me, Simon Proctor. I have longed to feel your hands upon my body." She bent down and kissed him passionately, her fingernails raking his back, pressing her vaginal lips against the coarse denim bulge beneath his belly. "What has tomorrow to do with it, or next week, or next month, or next year?" She pulled the thin straps of the negligee from her shoulders, allowing her breasts practically to pour out into his face. "I want you to impale me, to pierce me, to fill me with your seed."

Simon was filled with a lust unknown to him for many years. There had been groupies by the hundreds, female bodies available to him wherever he went for whatever he wanted, and he had grown accustomed to masturbating within those bodies while dreaming of his dead wife, but not until this moment, not since Lucinda's death over a decade ago, had he felt this aching need, this overwhelming impulse to take, to possess.

He grabbed her roughly by the shoulders and spun her over onto her back upon the bed. As he unzipped his dungarees and pulled them down, Gwendolyn spread her legs wide apart and caressed her inner thighs with her long white fingers. Simon fell down upon her without preliminaries, but none seemed to be needed. She was wet and open, and his erect member slid easily into her tight warmth.

He began to thrust in and out of her, grunting and muttering wordless expressions of joy. Gwendolyn's back was arched and her eyes were closed, but small, almost pained gasps broke from her throat. She alternately hugged him to her tightly and dug her nails into his back, trembling and shuddering with ecstasy and pleasure. He grabbed her by the wrists and pressed her arms back over her head, pinning her to the bed as he threw himself into her harder and deeper, feeling her large breasts sliding beneath his sweaty chest, as her thighs crushed him between them. With a quick motion he released her wrists and reached back with each arm, hooking his elbows behind her knees and pulling them forward toward her head, bending her already opened body upward and even more open, spreading her nether lips even wider apart, thrusting deeper and deeper into her. A cry escaped from her lips—a cry of pleasure or of pain, he knew not, he cared not. He bore down upon her madly, pounding his flesh against her flesh with ever increasing passion, passion at that moment indistinguishable from violence, a study in possession and need. He did not stop to wonder who was in fact being possessed by whom.

At last the almost painful ecstasy rose in his member, and he began to spurt into her, to flood her, to drench her interior with his fluids. It seemed an endless torrent which he spewed into her, and when finally the river was dammed he fell forward upon her, spent and exhausted, dizzy and breathless. She lay limp beneath him, panting and quivering, her trembling hands gently stroking his head.

They lay there motionless for what seemed a long while, an eternity, silent and weak. At last he rolled over onto his side, extracting his already-shriveling organ from her sopping passage, and then breathed deeply, allowing the exhalation to pass long and loud from his mouth. "Good grief!" he muttered.

"Hmmm?" she asked softly, rolling over and placing her head upon his trembling chest. "What did you say, my love?"

"I just said—I just said—" he stopped. "I don't know what I just said."

She laughed softly, a deep, rich laugh. "I hope it was kind, whatever it was."

He draped his arm over her shoulder and gently moved his hand up and down her side. "I'm sure it was. I'm sure . . ."

They lay still, silent. The low moan of the wind as it whistled through the naked branches of the trees outside the window, and the slow and steady breathing of the two people, were the only sounds. Soon Gwendolyn could hear Simon's breathing lapse into a slight snore. She smiled and hugged him. "Dear, sweet man," she whispered. "Sleep and dream, sleep and dream. . . ."

The hours passed, and the motionless silence of night pervaded the Proctor home. In the rear bedroom, old Floyd Proctor snored heartily, the tassle of his nightcap lying across his face and tickling his nose. The shot glass and bottle of rum stood, both empty, upon the table beside his bed. The Proctors had been makers of rum for three hundred years, and old Floyd, who heartily disapproved of drinking to excess, nonetheless maintained the old custom of taking a healthy draft of rum before retiring. The custom went back to the old days of the triangle trade, when New England traders bartered West African slaves for New Indies molasses, the prime ingredient of the rum they brewed and both drank and sold to the Indians and the few hardy adventurers who braved the dangers of the trans-Appalachian West.

He had been taking a drink of rum each night before retiring for the last seventy years, since he was a boy. And though he never altered the amount, the passage of time and the inevitable weakening of the human body had significantly reduced his capacity. He thus slept soundly, so soundly that the passion which had transpired a short time before in another bedroom on the same floor went unnoticed. Old Floyd slept peacefully, his jagged snores drowning out the clock which ticked upon the night table.

Next door, Lucas Proctor and Karyn Johannson slept the deep but unrefreshing sleep of utter intoxication. Lucas resolved almost daily not to mix his drinks, but this resolve was invariably made as he knelt slumped over a toilet bowl early in the morning. He broke his resolution nightly, as soon as he returned to a relatively normal condition. He regarded himself as an inveterate partier, but he was in reality little more than an alcoholic and drug addict. His sleep was drug induced and imparted neither regeneration nor true repose.

Karyn lay beside him, insensate from yet another night of overindulgence in bourbon, brandy, and hashish. She slept with apparent soundness, but her sleep was mere sedation, albeit self-administered. In the dead sleep into which they had both fallen, neither had heard anything from the bedroom down the hall.

Next door to them, Rowena Proctor tossed about her bed in the grip of a tense insomnia. She had not slept, she had not drunk, and she had heard everything. She had smelled the pungent odor of marijuana, had heard the soft voices of her father and Gwendolyn Jenkins, heard the laughter, the creaking bedsprings, the cries and the moans.

Damn her! she thought. Daddy, how could you!

The Proctor home was silent with both sleep and watch-fulness. For reasons known best to herself, Adrienne Lupescu was weeping quietly into her pillow. Rowena Proctor had buried her head beneath her covers, hoping to keep out any further unwanted sounds. Lucas, Karyn, and old Floyd were sound asleep.

And as the moon began to set, Gwendolyn Jenkins gazed down at the sleeping face of Simon Proctor, her green eyes glowing in the darkness with an inhuman ferocity. She whispered a prayer to the Dark Lord, and sent her spirit out upon Simon. And he began to dream.

Simon felt himself moving, but the feeling was not connected to any truly discernible motion. He sensed himself falling, and yet was standing upright, watching as indistinct forms floated by him. They moved from below to above, thus giving him the impression that he was descending, whither he knew not.

He sensed at last that he was standing upon solid ground in the midst of billowing fog. He saw a lone figure approaching him from the distance, her long, full skirts flapping silently in the cold wind. He moved his right hand toward his face to rub his eyes, and found to his distress that his hands were bound together at the wrists with heavy iron chains. He attempted to run, but his ankles were likewise shackled. He trembled with dread as the figure came into view, parting the fog before her like some demonic Moses.

"I can save thee," Gwendolyn Jenkins said. "Do thou but

denounce her as we all have, and bind thyself to me, and thou shalt not hang."

"G-Gwen? Gwendolyn? Is that you?" he stammered.

"There is yet time," she said, her voice a monotone devoid of expression. "I have given all I have, all I am, for thee. I ask but this little thing in return."

"I—" he began, and then was startled to hear a voice which was not his own issue forth from his trembling lips. "I'll not compound my sin with lies and betrayal," he heard the voice say. "Get thee gone from me, harlot! Get thee gone from me! Leave me to die in God's grace!"

"There is no grace for thee, or for me," Gwendolyn said in the same even tone. "There is nothing for me without thee, my love, nothing. Thou must live, that thou mayest love me!"

"I love thee not!" he heard the voice scream and felt his throat tear with the vehemence of the cry.

"'Tis not true," Gwendolyn replied softly. "Thou art my love, my dearest love, thou art my all. Do but denounce her, and thou shalt live. Do but love me, and thou shalt be as a prince among the rabble." Simon felt his heart leap into his mouth as Gwendolyn's face melted with a terrifying immediacy into a decaying death's-head whose sole vestiges of humanity were the insane green orbs which blazed from the naked eye sockets. "But betray me, lie to me, abuse me, deceive me, and I shall visit a vengeance upon thee which will make thee beg for the hangman's noose!"

Simon Proctor jumped up in his bed and screamed. When Gwendolyn reached out to soothe him, he jumped from the bed and slammed himself loudly against the wall. He stumbled over to the doorway and switched on the overhead light.

All was as it should have been. His bedroom was the same as always. Gwendolyn was sitting up in the bed, the covers pulled up to her neck, her black hair tousled, her green eyes given a ruddy cast by the shock of suddenly interrupted sleep. "What is wrong?" she asked.

Feeling suddenly very foolish, Simon said, "Nothing. A bad dream, that's all." He smiled sheepishly. "It's nothing, really. Just a silly dream."

Gwendolyn lay back down and placed her left arm behind her head with a slow, languid motion. "And of what did you dream?"

"Not worth talking about," he said as he climbed back into bed. "Just nonsense."

"Was I in the dream?" she asked, smiling impishly.

He laughed. "Yeah, but you wouldn't be flattered by it." He laughed again, and she joined in his laughter.

"I do not like that at all, Simon Proctor," she said, her smile telling him that she was not the least bit offended. "Perhaps you are afraid of me."

"Maybe, a little," he said, returning her smile. "You really are quite an extraordinary woman."

"And you," she said, rolling over and placing her head upon his chest, "are an extraordinary man."

"Hey," he laughed, trying to preserve levity and avoid a conversational turn toward seriousness, "you already got the job, right? No need for the flattery."

She raised herself up upon one elbow and gazed into his eyes. When she spoke, her voice was serious and earnest. "Know this one thing, Simon Proctor, that I am as steady as the North Star, and that I will uphold you in many things. You can rely upon me as though I were of your own flesh, for you are my beloved and the sole lord of my person. My soul belongs to the Dark One, but in all else I am yours, and will be faithful to your wants and your needs and your desires, even unto death!"

There was an intensity about her words which unnerved him, and he attempted to dismiss her protestation of devotion with a gentle skepticism. "Gwen, come on! You and I have just met, for Christ's sake!"

"Nay, 'tis not so," she said breathlessly as she moved her face closer to his and brought her lips near to his mouth, "for I have known you and loved you for centuries—"

The kiss which seemed inevitable was interrupted by a loud knocking on the door of the bedroom. "Daddy?" Rowena sobbed. "Daddy? Are you awake? Daddy?"

"Hold on a minute, Row," he said as he grabbed his dungarees and pulled them on. "Hold on." The tone of his daughter's voice upset him. She was not a crybaby, never had been. There had to be a good reason for her to be crying, and that fact frightened Simon.

He flung the door open wide and then stood dumbly as he beheld the pathetic scene which presented itself to him. Rowena, her nightgown tattered and torn, stood weeping before him, cradling her cat Pistopheles in her arms. "I tried to pick her up, and she just went crazy, Daddy, she just went crazy!" she wept. "What's wrong with her?"

Simon looked down at the trembling animal, looked at the open, frothing mouth and the panicky, shuddering, extended

141

claws, and he thought for a moment that the cat had contracted rabies. Then he looked at the filmy and expressionless, wide and terrified eyes.

The cat was blind.

⟦ CHAPTER TEN ⟧
November 18

"TOM'S BASEMENT," as Simon had referred to his customary rehearsal hall when speaking on the phone a few days before, was not the subterranean vault of a building, as the name might suggest. It was a rock club of some repute on the Lower East Side of Manhattan, and it had come by its name in an honest, if somewhat fanciful, manner. The small group of musicians with whom Simon Proctor had been associated for the past ten years had seen their fortunes rise and fall with his. Good musicians all, they nonetheless lacked as individuals the stage presence, composition skills, and imagination with which Simon had risen to the heights from which he seemed about to fall precipitously. All watched with suicidal fascination as their careers and incomes seemed to be teetering beside his upon the brink.

All but Tom Mahoney, the bass player, who alone of the band had the common sense to save and invest money rather than spend it. It was he who had purchased a failing disco five years before and had managed in that short time to transform it into a popular night spot for devotees of heavy-metal rock. He continued to function as Simon's bassist, but he was frequently heard to comment that when they finally went bust, he at least would have his club to fall back on. Mark Siegal, the drummer, rejoined that, considering Tom's prodigious intake of alcohol and drugs, he would more likely need something to fall into. Inspired by the quip, lead guitarist Carl Strube produced a crudely fashioned but effective drawing of Tom stumbling down a flight of steps into a dark cellar, and thus the nickname "Tom's basement" was born.

Whenever they were preparing for a tour, Simon and the band used the large, reverberative dance floor as their rehearsal site. The club did not open to the public until eight in the evening, and until then it was regarded as Simon's preserve, Tom's ownership notwithstanding.

Tom Mahoney leaned his tall, lanky form against the piano, tuning his bass to the keyboard as Larry Herricks, a fine pianist with an atrocious singing voice, plunked apathetically upon the appropriate keys. Herricks scratched a pimple beneath his scraggly black beard, yawned, and said, "Where the hell are they, anyway?"

Mahoney brushed back the graying blond lock of hair which was constantly slipping down over his eyes and grinned at Herricks from his boyish face. "Relax, Larry. It isn't even one o'clock. It's gotta be a six-hour drive from that old house of his."

"Yeah," Herricks grumbled, "but he was supposed to be here at noon. I got better things to do than fart around here waiting for him to show up."

Mahoney, eternally cheerful, and thus a source of irritation to all who knew him, shrugged. "Maybe he hit traffic. Don't worry about it. He'll be here soon enough. Hey, you want a beer?"

Herricks yawned again. "Sure. Why not."

As Mahoney swung the bass guitar strap over his head and placed the instrument carefully into a standing holder, the door of the club swung open and Carl Strube and Mark Siegal entered noisily, laughing over a shared and doubtless inconsequential joke. Strube's jet black skin was glistening with sweat, and he wiped his face with a handkerchief and said, "Tommy boy, you gotta do something about your thermostat!"

"Why? What's the matter with it?" Mahoney asked.

"It's colder than a witch's tit out there, and it's like an oven as soon as you walk into this building. Shit, I started sweating out there in the hallway before I could even get my scarf off!"

"Sorry," Mahoney shrugged, not caring in the slightest.

"Hey, watch that witch's tit stuff," Mark Siegal warned. "Simon told me on the phone that these chicks he's bringing with him say they're witches, real witches." Siegal unbuttoned his raggedy old sheepskin coat and pulled it off, tossing it unceremoniously onto a nearby chair. "I don't know if they're serious or not, but let's kind of be polite, okay?"

Strube punched him good-naturedly, but forcefully, in the arm. "Aw, Markie doesn't want to hurt nobody's feelings."

"I just know how to behave around women, that's all," he said.

"Yeah, right. That's why you never have any!"

"Yeah, yeah, fine," Herricks grumbled, "but where the hell

143

is Simon?" He snorted back some phlegm which, he claimed, had been inhabiting his sinuses since 1969. "I mean, shit! We gotta go out on another fuckin' tour in a couple of weeks, I gotta tell my old lady to amuse herself while I go out to rehearse—God knows who's plowin' my furrow right now— I didn't plan to see fuckin' twelve noon for another two weeks, and here I am, sitting here with my finger up my ass, listening to this Boy Scout tune his fuckin' bass!" He snorted again and then rubbed his nose. "I'm, like, really pissed off, you know?"

"Ah, Larry," Mark Siegal said sadly, "I have never ceased to be impressed by your articulation and vocabulary."

Herricks harrumphed. "Hey, listen to NYJew over here."

Ethnic slurs from Herricks were not good-natured, and Siegal bristled. "That's NYU, asshole! Don't get bitchy just 'cause you couldn't read well enough to graduate from high school!"

"Ahhh, fuck you," Herricks muttered.

"Don't get your hopes up," Siegal rejoined.

Mahoney ambled back from behind the bar with a six-pack of Old Bohemian beer in his hand. "Anyone want a brew?" he asked, smiling.

"Yeah, sure," Herricks muttered. Mahoney tossed a can toward him and he appraised it disgruntledly. "Warm Old Bohemian!" he spat. "Hey, thanks a lot, Tom! What does this shit cost you, a buck a six-pack? Where's the Heineken, the Miller, the Beck's, that British ale you're always pushing?"

"Old Peculiar Ale?" Mahoney asked innocently.

"Yeah, that shit. Old Bohemian! Christ, this stuff tastes like hippopotamus piss!"

Siegal turned to Strube with a grin. "Didn't know Larry drinks hippopotamus piss, did you?"

Strube gazed at Herricks appraisingly. "Don't surprise me none."

"Ahhh, fuck you guys," Herricks muttered as he pulled back the pop-top and poured the amber liquid into his mouth. "A brew's a brew."

Strube, Mahoney, and Siegal smiled despite themselves. The four of them had shared the road with each other and Simon for the past decade, and they knew each other well. It would have been impossible for any four men to share the same cramped quarters, to drop their heads upon each other's shoulders in rumbling, screeching buses in the early hours of the morning, to drink from the same bottles of warm beer, to share the same women on occasion, without a spirit of camaraderie to develop. The fact that Herricks was an anti-

Semite who disliked blacks and Irish Pollyannas did not keep the Irish bass player, the Negro lead guitarist, and the Jewish drummer from feeling a bond with the perpetually curmudgeonly piano player. And, were the truth forever unspoken by the latter to be known, the feeling was reciprocated.

"What time is it?" Herricks muttered morosely.

Mahoney glanced at his watch. " 'Bout quarter after one."

"Well removed from the witching hour," Gwendolyn Jenkins said as she breezed into the room ahead of Adrienne Lupescu and Simon Proctor, "but 'tis as good a time for conjuring as any."

Strube, Herricks, Mahoney, and Siegal spun their heads around at the sound of the unexpected female voice and then gazed at her in the silent, portentous manner exhibited universally by males when confronted by striking females. Gwendolyn had taken the time to purchase—or rather, Simon's plastic money had purchased—a few items of clothing less concealing and austere than those which she had worn when she first approached the door of the Proctor home in Bradford. She wore skintight dungarees which hugged her long legs and curvaceous hips, both of which were accenuated by the high-heeled boots which reached to midcalf before bending over in soft leather folds upon the top of the boot. She wore a dark green leotard above the wide leather belt which circled her waist, and the bra which she had condescended to don thrust her large breasts impertinently outward. She gazed at the members of the band with eyes wide with amusement, as if her ability to excite them sexually was known, understood, evaluated, and dismissed as irrelevant.

Simon Proctor entered the room immediately after her, and Adrienne Lupescu, looking nerve-wracked and ill at ease, followed hesitantly behind him. "Hiya, guys," Simon said. "Sorry we're a little late. We hit some traffic, and we wanted to stop and pick up a few things." He was carrying his guitar in an old, faded case, and he placed it gently down upon the floor. "These are the two girls I told Mark about on the phone. This is Gwendolyn, and this is Adrienne."

"Good day to you, sirs," Gwendolyn said casually. Adrienne smiled weakly and nodded.

"This blond Adonis over here is Tom, our bass player," Simon said with a gesture to Mahoney. "This scrawny little runt—"

"Hey, thanks, Simon, thanks a lot!"

"—is our drummer, Mark. That's Larry at the piano, and

Carl over here plays lead." He grinned at Gwendolyn. "Lead is a bit beyond me, I'm afraid. I'm mostly rhythm."

Mark Siegal came forward and smiled. "Hi. Nice to meet you. Simon tells me you have a whole collection of old songs about witchcraft that'll go good with the act."

"Witchcraft, and other things," Gwendolyn replied, smiling a bit coldly at the short, sallow-skinned man. "We sing songs of mystical events and old times."

"I think maybe we can adapt some of them to rock," Simon explained to the others. "You see, Gwen and Adrienne here are practicing witches, I mean, real witches, you know? The PR value of that alone is tremendous, if you think about it."

"Real witches," Herricks grumbled. "Give me a break."

"You believe not in the dark powers?" Gwendolyn asked haughtily. "Are you all like Simon, mere charlatans?"

"No, honey," Herricks replied, "we're all like Simon, musicians trying to make a buck."

"Come on, now, Larry," Carl said. "You gotta believe in witches."

Herricks looked with irritation at the black man. "Yeah? Why?"

"'Cause there must have been somebody somewhere with magic powers who turned you into such an idiot."

"No," Siegal said matter-of-factly. "It's natural."

"Hey, fuck you guys," Herricks muttered.

"Enough, enough," Simon said. "Listen up. I want you to hear a few of their songs and play around with them a bit, rock 'em up a little. Then we'll start working on some sort of vocal arrangement for the girls."

"How many of their songs have you heard?" Carl asked.

"Only one"—he ignored Herricks's groan—"but it was really terrific. Tom, I left their instruments in the trunk of the car. Go get 'em, would you?" He pulled his key ring from his pocket and tossed it to the blond bassman, who went out toward the main entrance.

"I assume that we'll be dealing with folk songs, right?" Carl asked.

"Basically, yes," Simon replied. "But I figure, hell, if the Byrds could make a best-selling rock single out of Seeger's 'Turn, Turn, Turn,' we should be able to make some good stuff out of these songs of theirs."

"Simon," Herricks said, "I ain't had nothin' to do with folk music or anything even near it for nearly fifteen years."

"Yeah, right. Who has? Nobody. I know I sure as hell haven't. But I honestly think it's worth a try." Simon paused as

Tom Mahoney entered, carrying the lute in one hand and the harp in the other. "Thanks, Tom."

"Excuse me—Gwendolyn, is it?—but is there an Irish harp in this case?"

"Nay, 'tis a Welsh harp," she replied.

"But they're pretty much the same thing, aren't they?"

She shrugged. "I know not, having never seen an Irish harp."

He placed the cases down beside Simon's guitar. "My mother used to play the Irish harp, when I was a little kid. I always loved it."

"Well, I hope you'll be finding this as pleasing," she smiled.

He smiled back, liking her enormously. "I'm sure I will."

Herricks snorted. "Fuckin' Sunday school around here. Any more good manners and I'm gonna puke!"

"Well, that'll refresh things," Siegal said.

"Ah, fuck you," Herricks grumbled.

Siegal deadpanned to Strube. "His brilliant retort has stung me into silence."

Gwendolyn knelt down beside her instrument and opened the case. Adrienne sprang to emulate her with a startled overaction, as if she had eagerly been awaiting a cue. The two women took their instruments from the cases and proceeded to tune them to one another.

Mahoney grinned. "Hey, it's just like my mom's!"

" 'Tis not surprising, Tom," Gwendolyn said. "The Welsh and the Irish are kindred races, united by a common dislike of the English rulers."

"Yeah, but at least Ireland is rid of the Brits, except in the north."

She paused for a moment. "Indeed," she said noncommittally.

"Play that one you played the other day," Simon said eagerly, "the one about the druid's daughter." He grabbed a warm beer from the piano top and sat down in one of the folding chairs which Tom Mahoney had placed at random around the large room.

"Nay, Simon," Adrienne said softly, "but we shall sing another, by your leave."

"Well, sure," Simon said. "Play anything you want."

"Have you heard of shapechangers?" Gwendolyn asked.

"Shapechangers?" He thought for a moment. "You mean like werewolves, stuff like that?"

"Werewolves are shapechangers," Adrienne agreed.

"An example of one," Gwendolyn said. "To become a wolf or

147

a bird or a cat, 'tis all the same to a shapechanger." She plucked a few mellow chords on the harp, and Adrienne echoed them on the lute. "Here is an old song about two shapechangers." She cleared her throat and then began to pick out a sprightly Celtic air, again echoed harmonically by Adrienne's lute. They began to sing, their voices bouncing around the delightful melody.

> "She danced into the meadow, as white as any milk,
> And he ran into the meadow, as black as China silk.
> Alack-a-day, the girl did say, you coal black smith.
>> Heed well my warning song.
> You never shall have the maidenhead
>> Which I have kept so long.
>> I'd rather die a maid.
> Ah but then, he said, you'll be buried all in your grave.
> 'Tis better than loving a musty, dusty, crusty, fusty
>> Coal black smith.
>> A virgin I will die."

The melody was light and breezy, and a brief interlude between the opening verse, which soon proved to be a chorus, and the next vocal section was so infectiously pretty that even Herricks began to tap his foot to the rhythm.

> "She became a duck, a duck upon the lake.
> She thought that she was safe until
>> The smith became a drake.
> She became a rose a-growing in the wood,
> And he became a bumblebee and
>> Stung her where she stood.
> She became a fish a-swimming in the brook,
> And he became a wiggly worm and
>> Catched her with his hook.
> Alack-a-day, alack-a-day, you coal black smith.
>> Heed well my warning song.
> You never shall have the maidenhead
>> Which I have kept so long.
>> I'd rather die a maid.
> Ah but then, he said, you'll be buried all in your grave.
> 'Tis better than loving a musty, dusty, crusty, fusty
>> Coal black smith.
>> A virgin I will die."

They began to play another dancing interlude, and Mark Siegal leaned close to Simon and said, "It's beautiful, honest to God it is. But it doesn't sound like material for rock and roll to me."

"I don't agree," Tom Mahoney said. He was standing behind Mark and Simon and had overheard the whispered comment. "The melody's great. All we gotta do is syncopate it and buzz up the interludes."

"Shhh," Simon said. "Let them finish."

"She became a nun, a nun all dressed in black,
And he became a hermit monk and
   Prayed her to come back.
She became a star, a star up in the night,
And he became a looking glass and
   Kept her in his sight.
She became a tree, a withered tree and grim,
And he became a furry bat and
   Lighted on her limb.
Alack-a-day, alack-a-day, you coal black smith.
   Heed well my warning song.
You never shall have the maidenhead
   Which I have kept so long.
   I'd rather die a maid.
Ah but then, he said, you'll be buried all in your grave.
'Tis better than loving a musty, dusty, crusty, fusty
   Coal black smith.
   A virgin I will die."

Another musical interlude, but the bright major chords slipped into dark minors, and the bright and sprightly melody assumed a gradually dark and mournful aspect. And then they concluded the song.

"She became a corpse, a corpse all in the land.
And he became the coffin wood and
   Held her in his hand.
She became the dust and mingled with the ground.
And he became the moldy clay and
   Smothered her all around.
She became a soul when the kirk did ring its bell,
And he became Belzebub and
   Dragged her down to hell.
Alack-a-day, alack-a-day, you fair young maid,

Who would not be my wife.
The flames will burn the maidenhead
    You guarded all your life.
    You're welcome to your pride.
Is it better then to find yourself Satan's bride,
Than to love a musty, dusty, crusty, fusty
    Coal black smith?
    A virgin did you die."

The lute and the harp descended sadly to the final resolving note, and as its last echoes faded, Adrienne looked at the musicians hopefully and asked, "Did it please you?"

"Great, really great," Herricks said with an uncustomary and, to his associates, totally unexpected enthusiasm. "Did you write that?"

Gwendolyn laughed. "Oh, no! 'Tis an old, old song!"

"Well, I loved it." He turned to Adrienne. "You got a real pretty voice, real pretty." She blushed full red and turned away from his friendly yet penetrating gaze.

"Well, what do you think?" Simon asked. "What can we do with it?"

"Change the rhythm," Tom Mahoney suggested. "It's in four-four time. Change the verses to three-four, and we can do a riff between verses in five-eight."

"Five-eight!" Herricks exclaimed, suddenly reverting to his usual personality. "What am I, fuckin' Dave Brubeck or something?"

"It's not hard, Larry," Carl Strube interjected. "The Beatles did 'All You Need Is Love' in seven-eight."

"So what?" he grumbled. "I'm not John Lennon either."

"That's for sure," Siegal muttered.

"Wait a minute, wait a minute," Simon Proctor said. "Before we get into detailed suggestions, are we agreed that it can be done?"

"Absolutely," Mahoney said, grabbing his bass guitar and slinging the strap over his shoulder.

"Yeah, sure," Larry Herricks said, "but none of that twelve-seventeenths shit."

"I think the whole idea is kind of exciting," Carl Strube said. "No offense, Simon, but I really think we need some fresh ideas, and if these ladies have more old songs as good as that one, it'll really give the act a boost."

"Which it needs," Simon agreed. "No offense taken, Carl. I know we're in trouble, and I know you know it." He turned to Mark Siegal. "What do you think, Markie?"

Siegal walked over to the drum set which stood far removed from the piano and the other instruments. He plopped himself down upon the cushioned stool and took into his hands the two drum sticks which were resting in the elastic strap on the side of the bass drum. He looked up at Simon. "I have my doubts, man, I really do. I don't know if we can make rock out of this stuff, and even if we do, I don't know if it's gonna go over with the kids." He turned quickly to Gwendolyn and Adrienne. The former gazed at him imperiously, the latter averted her eyes. "Don't get me wrong, girls. I really liked what I just heard. It was beautiful, really beautiful. But as for turning it into rock and roll"—he shook his head—"I don't know. I just don't know."

Simon smiled warmly at his old friend. He and Mark Siegal had known each other for well over fifteen years, and he knew that Siegal was an eternal pessimist. "So why are you sitting at your drums?" he asked, grinning.

Siegal returned the grin and shrugged. "Nothing ventured, nothing gained," he said.

"Look before you leap," Mahoney countered.

"Faint heart ne'er won fair maiden," Simon pointed out.

"A bird in the hand is worth two in the bush," Strube added.

"Comedians," Herricks muttered as he rubbed his eyes.

The rest of the afternoon was devoted to the attempt to transform a centuries-old song from the mountains of Wales into a rock song which would be grist for the contemporary teenage mill, and by four o'clock the results were generally satisfactory to all. Both Gwendolyn and Adrienne seemed to take to the new musical idiom with an enthusiasm and verve which both surprised and pleased Simon Proctor. As the seven musicians went through their final, perfected interpretation of the old song, Gwendolyn began to dance during the musical interludes between the verses, executing a bump and grind made all the more stimulating by its essential innocence. She leapt and strutted around the room, flailing her long black hair against the microphones and the musicians, laughing and uttering unintelligible words of approval, encouragement, and happiness. She seemed a bizarre mixture of uninhibited pagan and base wild beast, and as Simon Proctor watched the drops of sweat glisten upon her white throat, as he saw her hips sway in opposition to her breasts, as he looked into the wild, mad, heathen eyes, he felt an excitement and a desire so intense that he found it almost uncontrollable.

He was not alone in his reaction. Larry Herricks pounded

upon his piano keys with his customary consummate skill, but his eyes were glued to the woman who danced before him with such sensual abandon. Mahoney, Siegal, and Strube were all equally fixated upon the wildly gyrating form, and the sexual energy she imparted seemed to drive them to even greater musical exertions. In any rehearsal session, musicians who play primarily by instinct take musical chances, musical risks, which often produce an effective result, and as often fail; but each chance taken by the band at that moment succeeded, each risk was worth taking, each attempt worked.

The song as they had now arranged it exploded into its cacophonous denouement, and as the last deafening chords and shattering cymbal cries faded, they all stood up and cheered. Gwendolyn, trembling and drenched with perspiration, threw herself into Simon's arms and kissed him passionately upon the mouth. He felt an urge to tear her clothes from her body and take her right there on the floor in the midst of all the others. He strove to restrain himself from so doing, but felt himself weakening as the sultry green eyes gazed lustfully into his own, as he saw the tip of the pink tongue dart slightly outward and touch the full, red lips. He fought to retain his sense of time and place, and would have lost his struggle had not Harry Schroeder's voice broken into his thoughts with a glaring and totally demanding incongruity.

"Hey, Simon, hiya. Hiya, boys," Schroeder boomed as he waddled into the room. "That sounded terrific, fantastic, really great!" Everyone knew that his enthusiasm was feigned, for Harry Schroeder rarely took pleasure from any music more contemporary than that of Glenn Miller, but they all grinned at him appreciatively.

"Harry!" Simon exclaimed. "What are you doing—oh, yeah, right. You said that you'd drop by."

"Sounds really good, Simon, honest it does. I think you're on to something here." He looked at the two women and then returned his attention to Simon expectantly.

Simon picked up on the unspoken request. "Harry Schroeder, my manager, this is Gwendolyn Jenkins and Adrienne Lupescu."

"Howahya." He smiled. "Was that one of your songs?"

"Not ours," Gwendolyn said. "An old song which we sing." She took Simon's arm impetuously and held it tight. "But it has never seemed so exciting a song as now."

"Well, I think it's gonna go over good," Schroeder nodded. "Uh, Simon, you got a minute?"

"Yeah, sure, Harry." He gently removed Gwendolyn's hand from his arm. "Excuse me for a minute. I'll be right back." He and Schroeder walked out of the room and stood in the corridor which led to the entrance way. "What's up, Harry?"

"A few things," he said easily. "That was really pretty, that song you guys were doing."

Simon laughed. "Thanks, but I know you hated it."

"No, no, really!"

"Sure," he smiled, unconvinced. "That Gwen is really something, isn't she? She's gonna have those kids going crazy, especially the boys."

"Yeah, yeah," Schroeder nodded. He paused and then said, "You sure this is a good idea?"

"Having them join the act? Sure I do. It's worth a try, anyway, isn't it?"

He shook his head. "I don't know. I mean, they aren't people trying to make a buck playing Wizard of Oz, you know what I mean? They think they're honest-to-God witches, right? That sounds to me like they're nuts."

"Don't worry about it," he said. "So what's up?"

"Oh, yeah. I got a call from Percy Campbell this morning. He wants you back on the show."

"He does, does he?" Simon became immediately wary. "Me and who else?"

"That professor—what's his name—Eisenmann—?"

"Forget it," he said emphatically. "Absolutely not. No way, man!"

"Hold it a minute, Simon. I don't think you should just reject the invitation without—"

Simon pulled a cigarette from his pocket and lighted it angrily, throwing the match away with an irritated snap of his wrist. "Listen, Harry, the last time . . ." He turned as he heard the door behind him open, and smiled despite his annoyance when Gwendolyn leaned in from behind it. "Hiya, Gwen. I'll be in in a minute."

"Very well, Simon," she said deferentially. She remained where she was, listening.

"The last time I went on that damned show," he resumed, "I was made a fool of by that fat bastard. There's no way I'm gonna let myself be put in that position again. Forget it, Harry. Call Campbell and tell him to forget it!"

"Hold it. Listen for a minute, will you?" Schroeder said heatedly. "He got a lot of mail about that show. This whole popular witchcraft thing has a big audience, I guess. He wants

153

to do another show, have a debate between you and that professor—"

"Sure, sure, so his ratings go up, that Eisenmann jerk gets some brownie points at his college, and I end up looking like an asshole again. Forget it!"

"Simon—" Harry began.

"I do not understand," Gwendolyn broke in. "Who is this man who has held you up to ridicule?" Her voice was angry, protective.

"Oh, it's nothing, Gwen. It doesn't matter."

"It matters to me," she said firmly. "Mr. Schroeder, please explain this all to me." Her tone allowed no refusal.

"Well," Schroeder sighed, "Simon here was on a talk show a few weeks ago, and there was a college professor on it with him, and they started arguing about witchcraft, and Simon thinks that he ended up looking bad."

"I ended up looking like a goddamned fool!" he shouted.

"It wasn't that bad," Schroeder lied. "Anyway, the guy who runs the show wants him back on to debate with the professor. I think it'd be a great way to get free publicity—"

"Publicity with who?" Simon spat. "Teenage kids don't watch Percy Campbell, for Christ's sake! You should never have booked me on that show in the first place!"

"Simon—" Schroeder said tiredly.

"No, listen, I'm not kidding, Harry. Forget it!"

"How did this man offend you?" Gwendolyn asked levelly, though her jaw seemed to be clenching.

Simon did not reply, so Schroeder said, "He said that Simon wasn't really a warlock."

At this, Gwendolyn began to laugh. "Indeed! This man is most perceptive, for in truth you are not!"

"Hey!" Simon snapped. "I don't need—"

She walked over to him and wrapped her arms around his waist. "Hush, dear man, I am not the enemy. I am an ally, and a more reliable ally has no man ever known." She turned to Schroeder. "Would it be helpful to us to meet again with this man? Will there be others there to hear?"

Schroeder paused, uncertain of her meaning. "Of course there will. I mean, it's a TV show!"

She looked up at Simon. "Then we must meet with him. Remember, Simon Proctor, my goal is the service of the Dark Master. I shall go with you, for this man cannot tell me that I am not a witch!"

Simon looked at her doubtfully. "You? You'll go on the show with me? You'll debate this guy?"

She laughed and shook her head. "I debate no one. I shall proclaim myself to be what I am, and if this man casts doubts upon my word, I shall cast a spell upon his body and he shall be destroyed."

Schroeder and Proctor stared at her dumbly for a long moment. Then as if with one voice, they said, "What?!"

"I have done so many times in the past," she replied easily. "The essence of the service of the lord of this world is power, and it is in exchange for power that we serve him. I have the power to kill and the power to heal. If this man you speak of offends me, I shall cast a spell upon him, and he shall die."

Schroeder walked over to Gwendolyn and took her arm gently, speaking to her as one would to a distraught child. "Listen, sweetheart, I'm glad that you have powers like this, but I don't think—"

"Great!" Simon said loudly. "Great! That's *great*! That's fantastic! That's *fantastic*!!!"

Schroeder looked at him in confusion. "What are you talking about? That's the craziest idea I've ever—"

"No, no, Harry, you're not thinking this through," Simon said with excitement. "Think of the PR we can get out of this! She can cast a spell on somebody on syndicated television! Everybody will be talking about it! It's never been done!"

"Of course it's never been done! It's never been done because it can't be done, because it's stupid!"

"Take care, now," Gwendolyn said darkly.

Schroeder looked at her. "I didn't mean anything, honey, honest I didn't." To Simon, "What's gonna happen when she casts a spell on this Eisenmann guy and nothing happens to him? Then it'll be just like you felt before. You'll look silly."

"No, no, no! Don't you see? It won't matter one damned bit when nothing happens to him! People will be curious to see if there's any effect, and that'll get us in the papers, on the local news shows—people will be talking about it. . . . By the time anyone really makes a point of the fact that he's okay, we'll already have the PR for the tour and the movie! Hey, Harry, you know the way the press works. Reporters are all whores. They'll print anything that'll sell papers, say anything on the tube that'll draw an audience."

"Simon, Simon," Schroeder said with exasperation. "Nobody's gonna take it seriously if she casts—"

"Harry, you're missing the point!" he said heatedly. "It doesn't matter if anybody takes it seriously! It'll be good PR, *real* good PR! I mean, shit, who takes my act seriously anyway? The whole thing is just camp, right?"

Schroeder nodded reluctantly, unwilling to be persuaded. "Yeah. I guess so."

"So we both go on the Campbell show, I argue with the guy, she casts a spell on him—" he glanced over at Gwendolyn, "one that you'll say will take a while to work right?"—he turned again to Schroeder—"and the local news people will eat it up!"

"More than likely, they'll ignore it," Schroeder said.

"Okay, so if they ignore it, we haven't lost anything, right?"

Schroeder frowned. "Wait a minute, wait a minute. Are you trying to talk me into booking you on the show? I mean, what the hell just happened here? I told *you* that I thought it—"

"It doesn't matter, it doesn't matter," Simon said quickly. "Just book us both on the show. Make sure it's both of us, not just me."

Schroeder shrugged. "Okay, okay. Anything you say." He shook his head and muttered, "I thought I had to convince *you*!"

Simon turned and grabbed Gwendolyn by the waist. He lifted her up in front of him and spun around a few times. "Great idea, honey, great idea!"

She smiled down at him from her elevated position, but her smile was strained. "Such a doubter, Simon Proctor! And if I cast a spell upon this man and he dies? Then what will you say?"

Simon laughed. "Babe, if you cast a spell on somebody and he dies, I'll say anything you want me to say!"

She laughed freely as he put her down on her feet. "I shall hold you to your words, sweet man," she said.

Simon turned to Schroeder. "What time is it, Harry?"

He glanced at his watch. "'Bout twenty after four."

"Tom's gotta start setting up for tonight in an hour or so," Simon said. "I'd like us to get going on at least one more song before we have to quit." He turned to Gwendolyn. "You two got another one, a less complicated one than the shapechanger song?"

Gwendolyn began to reply, but stopped as she inclined her ear toward the closed door behind her. "I believe that Adrienne is singing a song for your friends right now. Perhaps this one?"

Simon listened hard. The gentle, tinny resonances of the lute were dimly audible through the closed door. "Let's go back inside," he suggested.

He opened the door softly and held it as Gwendolyn and Schroeder entered the large room. Adrienne was sitting on a

156

folding chair, her yellow lute resting upon her knee. Her fingers ran easily over the strings as she sang.

"True Thomas lay on yon grassy bank,
    And he beheld a lady gay,
A lady that was brisk and bold,
    Come riding o'er the fernie brae.
True Thomas he took off his hat,
    And bowed him low down to his knee.
'All hail thou mighty Queen of Heaven,
    For your like on earth I never did see.'
'Oh no, oh no, true Thomas,' she says,
    'That name does not belong to me.
I am the queen of fair Elfinland,
    And I am come here to visit thee.'"

Adrienne drifted off into a brief interlude upon the lute, and Gwendolyn leaned over to Simon and whispered, "'Tis a song of Thomas the Rhymer. He was a poet and a great prophet. 'Tis said that he was kidnapped by the queen of the elves and dwelt seven years in Elfinland, whence he returned with his gift of prophecy. 'Tis of this the song tells."

Simon repressed a smile, remembering that this old poet, dead these seven hundred years, was the one who Gwendolyn and Adrienne claimed had taught them a song. He looked at Adrienne whose head was inclined slightly to the right as she plucked delicately upon her lute. Herricks, Strube, Siegal, and Mahoney were sitting in a circle around her, as if they were worshipers at the feet of a divinity. They hung open-mouthed on every word and every note.

"She turned about her milk white steed
    And Thomas leapt up from below.
And aye whene'er her bridle rang
    The steed flew swifter than the driven snow.
'Come and go,
    Come along with me,
Thomas the Rhymer. . . .'"

Simon smiled, pleased at the archaic melody and the tremulous voice which intoned the ancient words of the old British ballad. Casting a spell on that son of a bitch, that fat kraut. That's great, he thought, great! Might compensate for the last time, might be good for the tour, might be a help to the

157

film. Doesn't matter if she ends up looking stupid. It'll make money, maybe. Can't hurt. Can't hurt.

"'O see ye not yon narrow road,
    So thick beset with thorns and briars?
That is the path of righteousness,
    Though after it none enquires.
And see ye not yon braid braid road,
    That lies across yon lily leven?
That is the path of wickedness,
    Though some call it the road to heaven.
And see you not that bonny road
    Which winds about the fernie brae?
That is the road to Elfinland,
    Where you and I this night maun gae.
Come and go,
    Come along with me,
Thomas the Rhymer. . . .'"

Gwendolyn Jenkins looked at the rapt face of Simon Proctor, and she smiled, a smile filled with love and devotion. Sweet man, she mused silently. Sweet, sweet man. How like unto him you are. How like unto him.

She stepped quietly back from him and withdrew to the door of the large room in which the band had been rehearsing. She leaned her back upon the door and hummed softly to herself, ignoring the lovely music which Adrienne was spinning.

"'But Thomas, you must hold your tongue,
    Whatever you may hear or see,
For if a word you chance to speak,
    Never go you back to your country.'
Thomas got a cloak of the elfin cloth,
    And a pair of shoes of velvet green,
And until seven years were gone
    Thomas on earth was never seen.
'Come and go,
    Come along with me,
Thomas the Rhymer.
    Come and go,
Come along with me,
    Thomas the Rhymer. . . .'"

Adrienne Lupescu repeated the final supplication over and over, her thin body swaying to the rhythm of the melody, her eyes closed and her brow lined with intensity. Simon Proctor stood and watched and listened, absorbed in the sound and the subtle presence of the retiring girl. Gwendolyn was watching him from her position near the door. She was smiling warmly and humming to herself. Then, as Adrienne moved into the final chords of her song, Gwendolyn began to sing softly to herself, her muted melody unheard by most of the others present.

"Fair was Lizzie Proctor,
  Dark was Abigail.
Both they loved the same man,
  And both they loved him well,
  Both they loved him well,
In heaven and in hell. . . ."

Adrienne had to concentrate on the strings of her lute, to be able to conclude the song properly. But she had heard the soft melody drifting toward her from the rear of the room. She recognized the song.

She shuddered.

⟦ CHAPTER ELEVEN ⟧

November 23

ROWENA PROCTOR GAZED distractedly out of the window of the Trailways bus, the fingernails of her right hand making little circles on the top of Jeremy Sloan's left knee. She glanced quickly at the back of the seat in front of her. Karyn's disheveled red hair was hanging down on one side of the head rest, and Lucas's matted, stringy brown hair was mingling with it slightly as he leaned upon her shoulder, sound asleep. Jeremy sat quietly beside her, a bit groggy from the early start they had made that morning. He yawned.

Rowena did not want to be on this bus, did not want to be riding down to New York City, did not want to be part of the studio audience of the Percy Campbell show. But when Simon had called to remind Floyd to call the repairman about the water heater and had mentioned in an offhand manner that he was going back on the talk show, Lucas, who had been listening in on another phone, broke in to demand tickets. When Simon promised to have four tickets waiting at the gate, Rowena alone felt no excitement at the prospect. Lucas derived a vicarious pleasure from his father's notoriety; Jeremy admired Simon and was eager to take advantage of any opportunity of seeing him in action in full warlock regalia; Karyn was grateful for anything which would get her out of Bradford for a day or two.

But Rowena would have much preferred to remain in the little country town. She disliked large cities, she disliked long bus rides, she disliked her father's witchcraft act, and she heartily disliked Gwendolyn Jenkins. I just know she's going to be there with him, Rowena thought morosely, I just know it. God, how I hate that woman!

There were many reasons for Rowena's dislike of Gwendolyn. The imperious, abusive attitude she displayed toward poor Adrienne, the easy way she had around men, the haughtiness, the arrogance, the witchery. The real cause of Rowena's dislike, the root Electral cause, was known to her, of course; but she repressed it, telling herself that her father's dalliances were none of her business. But it bothered her. It bothered her deeply.

"Isn't this exciting, Row?" Jeremy asked.

"Yeah," she muttered. "I can hardly wait to get there." I can hardly wait to get home, she thought. It was only the prospect of time spent with Jeremy which had prompted her to devote Tuesday of her Thanksgiving week off from school to this expedition; and she would rather have spent the time sitting in front of the fireplace with Jeremy, reading, talking, cuddling. But Jeremy had been determined to go, and Rowena had no wish to sit around the old house all alone all day. Floyd was going to spend the day in Piermont, and her poor little cat had been put to sleep, so the house would have been oppressively empty had she remained at home. And yet, to have to see that—that—

"That bitch," she muttered.

"Huh?" Jeremy said. "You say some—"

"No, Jeremy, no," she snapped, and then regretted it. "I'm sorry, I'm really sorry. I'm just a little cranky today. Just ignore me."

He smiled at her and then leaned over and kissed her lightly on the lips. "The last thing I intend to do is ignore you," he said in a soft voice.

She returned his smile without conviction, took his hand and squeezed it, and then released it quickly, turning once again to gaze out the window. Jeremy stared at her for a few moments, puzzled by her attitude, and then leaned his head back upon the head rest and closed his eyes. Probably getting her period, he thought, following the age-old custom of men in ascribing to the lunar cycle female moods which they did not understand. Such an explanation has always been generally satisfactory and usually wrong. This instance was no exception.

The New England Thruway sped by outside the window, and Rowena watched with growing apprehension as the hours passed and the green and rocky environment of New England gradually changed until it became the sooty, broken face of the Bronx. God, she thought, I hope he doesn't introduce me and Lucas on that show! What would I say, what would I do? I should have stayed home. Why didn't I stay home? I hate this, I *hate* it!

A short time later the bus pulled into the Port Authority Bus Terminal on Eighth Avenue and Forty-second Street, and the passengers shuffled out of the front door of the vehicle. Most of the people on the bus had suitcases and other types of luggage which had been stored in the compartment beneath the seating area, but the four young people from Bradford had, in Rowena and Jeremy's case, only backpacks and, in Lucas and Karyn's case, no luggage whatsoever, so the four proceeded to walk immediately away while the others milled about, waiting for their bags.

Lucas, both more familiar and more comfortable with Manhattan than either Jeremy or Rowena, led them all out of the Port Authority onto Eighth Avenue, pulling Karyn with him, his arm around her waist though he was a step ahead of her. "Hey, slow down, man!" she said testily. "I can't walk that fast." She placed one hand upon her swollen belly as if to illustrate her point.

"Sorry, babe," he said. "I'm just, like, anxious to get there, you know?"

"Eager," Rowena muttered.

"Huh?"

"Eager, not anxious," she said coldly, obviously ill at ease and discontented. "'Anxious' means nervous, worried. You mean that you're eager."

Lucas stared at her with irritation. "Holy shit! Rowena's like a werewolf, 'cept when the moon rises she turns into an English teacher!"

"Oh, Lucas," she muttered. I want to be home in Bradford, she thought. I hate this, I just *hate* this!

"Come on, you two, play nice," Karyn said. "Where do we have to go from here? Where are we, by the way?"

"Eighth and Forty-second," Lucas said. "We gotta go over to Sixth and then up to Fifty-third."

"Oh," Karyn nodded. "You gonna hail a cab?"

"A cab! What do you think, I'm rich or something?" He laughed derisively. "It's only thirteen blocks from here to—"

"Thirteen blocks!" Karyn exclaimed. "Are you out of your mind? I'm pregnant, for Christ's sake! I ain't walkin' no thirteen blocks!"

"Hey, do you know what a cab costs in New York City? It's like a hundred dollars for the first ten feet or somethin'. We ain't taking no cab!"

He pulled on her to impel her forward, but she planted her feet upon the pavement with a mulelike obstinacy. "Goddamn it, Lucas! I am *not* walking thirteen blocks!"

"Hey, Lucas, come on," Jeremy said soothingly. "Let's just take a cab. If we run short of money, you can always grub some off your dad."

He laughed. "My dad! Are you kidding?! He's probably gonna grub off me pretty soon!"

"Okay, okay, so I'll pay for the cab, all right?" Jeremy said. The implication was clear: You cheap bastard, making your pregnant woman walk!

Lucas grimaced, recognizing defeat when it struck him in the face. "Okay, okay, we'll take a fuckin' cab. Jesus!" He grabbed Karyn roughly by the arm and dragged her from the Port Authority entrance toward the corner and began waving wildly at the taxis which drifted by. He became rapidly annoyed at their reluctance to stop for him, not aware that his appearance did not inspire the drivers with confidence. Lucas presented his customary scruffy, unwashed, outcast form to the passing cabs, and he was consequently ignored. "Shit!" he muttered. "It's gonna be time for the show pretty soon."

"Well, let's take a bus or something," Karyn said.

"Yeah, yeah, right. We gotta walk over to Seventh Avenue to get a bus uptown—wait a minute, wait a minute. Which avenues go uptown and which ones go downtown? I always forget that."

Karyn sighed. "Lukie, sometimes you are such an asshole! The even avenues go uptown and the odd avenues go downtown, except for the ones east of Fifth Avenue. Everybody knows that!"

I didn't know that, Jeremy thought. Rowena did not care.

"Okay, so we take an Eighth Avenue bus and then walk east two blocks." He turned to Jeremy and asked sarcastically, "I mean, if you think poor Karyn can make it two blocks on foot."

Jeremy looked down, intimidated. "Come on, Lucas, cut it out."

"Yeah, right," he snorted, satisfied that he had scored a point. "Let's go to the bus stop." He pulled Karyn behind him as he strode across Eighth Avenue toward the bus stop. Rowena and Jeremy followed them, each looking nervously at the multitude of automobiles, trucks, and taxis which sped to and fro seemingly from all directions. God, how I *hate* this! Rowena thought.

They stopped walking near a metal pole upon which at one time a sign proclaiming the spot to be a bus stop had once hung. It had long since been removed, or stolen, or had dropped off into the gutter to be swept up and discarded. But the yellow paint had not yet totally faded from the curb, and this, coupled with the queue of people who stood numbly along the yellow line, still testified to the fact that buses did in fact stop there.

As they waited for a bus to arrive, Rowena gazed around with undisguised distaste. There were so-called adult bookstores and pornography emporia everywhere she looked. She turned away from the broad expanse of Eighth Avenue in an attempt to shield herself from the offensive vista, and found that she was standing in front of a large theater which dwarfed the other sex shops in size and audacity. A large flashing neon sign proclaimed Girls, Girls, Girls to any and all onlookers, advertised Live Sex Show, One-on-One Booths, and Peep Show—25¢. She snorted her disgust and turned to Jeremy, saying, "Isn't this the most dis—"

Jeremy was gazing at a large poster of a presumably well-known star of pornographic films who was appearing live at the theater. His eyes were wide and his jaw hung open with fascination. Rowena grew suddenly incensed, and she punched him hard in the stomach.

"Ouch!" he said. "What did you do that for?!"

"Because you deserved it!" she said without further explanation. She turned away from him in a huff. He stood staring at her in confusion, trying to decide what to say just as the bus pulled up.

They mounted the steep steps into the bus—another bus! Rowena thought glumly—and sat, all of them silent, as the bus gasped and hissed and rumbled up Eighth Avenue. Karyn was angry at Lucas, Lucas was angry at Karyn and Jeremy, Rowena was angry at Jeremy, and Jeremy was totally confused. They were not a happy group.

It was a short ride from Forty-second Street up to Fifty-third, and they left the bus on the corner of that street and Eighth Avenue. "This way," Lucas said disgruntledly, and proceeded to drag Karyn and lead Rowena and Jeremy down Fifty-third Street toward the Avenue of the Americas, which the locals and everyone else familiar with the city still called Sixth Avenue. They walked the two long blocks quickly—more quickly than Karyn would have liked, in fact—and soon arrived at the studio in which the Percy Campbell show was taped for subsequent broadcast over the syndicated networks of local stations.

Lucas pushed open the doors, which swung back with a velvety *swoosh*, and preceded the others into the theater lobby. There was a desk in the corner of the large high-ceilinged room, and he walked over to it. An attractive young woman sat behind the desk, examining some papers. Lucas coughed so as to attract her attention, and she looked up at him with a quizzical austerity and said, "Yes? May I help you?"

"Yeah," Lucas said. "We're here to see the Percy Campbell show. There are supposed to be—"

"I'm sorry, sir," the girl interrupted in a peremptory manner, "but there are no more tickets available for today's taping."

"Yeah, yeah, right, I know," he said, "but there are supposed to be some—"

"If you would like, you can put your names on our list, and we will send you tickets for the next available show."

"Hey, listen to me, will you?" Lucas said heatedly. "There are supposed to be some tickets waiting for me."

The girl raised her eyebrows skeptically. "And your name, sir?"

"Lucas Proctor. My father is on the show today."

The girl looked at him blankly for a brief moment, and then her face dissolved into a pubescent smile of unsullied adulation. "You're Simon's son?! Oh, wow! I *love* your father, I mean I just *love* him!"

Lucas grinned. "Hey, great, that's great. Uh, you got the tickets my dad said he'd get for us?"

"Oh, sure, sure, absolutely!" The girl fished about in the

drawer of the desk and drew out an envelope which she handed to Lucas. "I'm really sorry. I didn't know who you were."

Lucas grinned sheepishly, basking in the worshipful gaze. "Skip it," he said magnanimously.

He walked away from the desk and moved toward the row of doors which led to the theater seats, with Karyn, Rowena, and Jeremy following in his arrogant wake. The girl jumped up from behind the desk and rushed over to Lucas, saying "Do you think maybe you can get me in to meet your father? I mean, like, I've been a fan of his for, like, years and years!"

Lucas smiled at her and glanced sideways at Karyn, who was already waiting impatiently at the door to the auditorium. He leaned forward toward the girl and softly whispered, "What's your name?"

"Nancy," she breathed. "Nancy Kaufmann."

"Okay, Nancy Kaufmann," he said, grinning. "Give me your phone number and I'll see what I can do."

"Oh, sure!" she said and rushed back to the desk in search of paper and pen.

Karyn lumbered over to Lucas and asked, "What's the problem?"

"Oh, uh, nothing, babe, nothing. She's, uh, she's just, uh—"

The girl returned to Lucas, scribbling on a small notepad as she moved. "Here it is," she said. She tore off the sheet of paper.

Karyn glared at Lucas. "And what's this all about?"

"Nothing, babe, nothing," he said quickly as he stuffed the slip of paper into his pocket. "Come on, we'll miss the opening of the show." He hustled her into the auditorium, tossing the four tickets to the usher as he passed through the door. Rowena and Jeremy followed behind them nervously.

They made their way down the aisle which stretched from the doorway nearly to the studio stage, and found to their chagrin that there appeared to be no empty seats close to the stage. The tickets were admission tickets, not reserved seat tickets, and they had arrived so close to show time that the best seats in the house were already occupied. An usher stood complacently against the right wall, staring off into space. In a well-lighted studio without reserved seats, there was precious little for an usher to do.

Lucas walked over to him and said, "Excuse me?"

The usher started, as if awakened from some private reverie. He gazed impassively at Lucas.

"Excuse me," Lucas repeated, hoping to elicit some response from the usher.

"Yes?" the usher said impassively. He was a self-important, middle-aged man who apparently strove to make the most of his meager prerogatives.

"I'm Lucas Proctor. My dad—Simon? Simon Proctor?—is on the show today. He told me that Mr. Campbell had reserved four front-row seats for me and my sister and our friends."

The usher seemed to collapse into obsequious solicitude. "Oh, yes, of course, certainly, certainly, certainly. Wait just one moment please." He scurried away from them and began whispering feverishly to the people who were sitting in the front seats. A few long moments passed, and then four obviously annoyed people rose from the front row and began to make their way reluctantly to the rear of the studio. The usher returned to Lucas and the others and said, "Your seats are available, Mr. Proctor." He looked at Karyn. "Miss Proctor."

Karyn swung a lazy thumb at Rowena, who tiredly raised her hand halfway. "That's me," she muttered.

"Oh, oh, I *am* sorry, Miss Proctor. This way, please!"

He led them to the front row and smiled at them insipidly as they took their seats, Rowena taking the first seat and pulling Jeremy behind her by the hand, followed by Karyn and Lucas. As they settled into their seats Lucas said, "I guess Dad's doin' okay. We've gotten pretty good treatment."

Rowena sniffed. "If Rickie the Magic Pixie were on the show, and his kids Trixie and Mixie showed up, they'd get good seats too."

Lucas glanced at her with annoyance. "You know, Row, it doesn't matter where we are or what we're doin', you're always a royal pain in the ass."

Rowena was in the mood neither for a debate nor their customary exchange of insults. "Lukie, just shut up, will you?" She sank down into the uncomfortable seat and folded her arms across her chest, determined neither to be pleasant nor to enjoy herself.

About ten minutes passed and then the houselights dimmed very slightly. It was the practice of the Campbell show to maintain an atmosphere of audience presence even when the audience was not actually participating in the day's presentation, so the houselights were never completely dimmed.

A technician wearing a set of headphones, which were to all appearances connected to nothing, strode onto the stage. He

166

reached up and grabbed the boom mike which hovered above him and, after tapping it to make certain that it was working, he spoke into it and said, "Ladies and gentlemen . . . ladies and gentlemen . . . your attention please. . . ."

The general buzzing in the studio fell almost immediately into an attentive silence.

"The show's gonna start in a moment or two. I'd like to direct your attenion to the audience response screens, which are on either side of the stage. . . ." He gestured to his left and his right with clipboard-encumbered hands. "This show is taped and will be shown in three days, but it is still a live show."

Say what? Rowena thought.

"Sometimes we need to enhance the audience's response with taped laughter or applause, but we like it to be as real and honest as possible. So please respond appropriately when the monitors say applaud or laugh or cheer. Okay?"

There was a murmur of assent from the audience, and the man with the headphones smiled and walked off the stage. There was a bustling sound of activity and preparation among the stagehands, and then a voice from the glass-encased control booth which was set, elevated, into the left wall of the studio said, "Roll tape. Recording. Cue music in five, four, three, two . . ."

The bouncing melody of "You Are My Sunshine," Percy Campbell's theme song, broke from the speakers, and Campbell himself walked purposefully onto the stage, smiling at the audience and waving. His ruddy, freckled face beamed out at the applauding spectators, and he came to a stop in the middle of the stage and stood humbly, allowing the waves of admiration to wash over him. He moved his eyes over the audience from left to right, a puckish grin alternating upon his face with a businesslike frown. At last he raised his hands, saying, "Thank you, thank you," and the audience quieted down.

"Hello, everybody," he said. "Welcome to our show. We're going to be trying something a little different today. Instead of our usual assortment of panelists discussing an issue, we're going to have only two—oh, er, I mean three."

He rubbed his hands together thoughtfully. "A few weeks ago we did a show on the use of witchcraft and satanism in rock and roll and in the movies, and talked about the effects this all may be having upon our young people. Well, you people at home seemed to find that topic interesting, judging by the mail we received, so we've decided to reopen the question once again, to present it once more for your consideration."

He stepped forward, close to the edge of the stage. The

hovering boom mike followed him. "Two of today's guests were members of that panel we had on the show a few weeks ago. Dr. Ludwig Eisenmann is Professor of Anthropology and History at New York University. Professor Eisenmann is a scholar of international repute, and is a specialist in the area of comparative religion. He is an authority on the practice and history of witchcraft."

Campbell paused for a moment. "Our other returning guest is Mr. Simon Proctor, well-known rock singer and composer. Mr. Proctor is also by his own admission a practicing warlock. Our other guest is Miss Gwendolyn Jenkins—"

Oh, great, Rowena thought.

"—a new member of Simon's band. Miss Jenkins is also a practicing witch. We'll be talking to all three of these people in a moment."

He stepped back slightly, more toward the center of the stage, until his back was against the closed curtain. "But first, we have an unexpected treat. Simon and his band will be beginning a concert tour in a few days, and they are going to perform one of their new numbers for us. Ladies and gentlemen, let us welcome Simon Proctor and his band, Witch's Sabbath."

The audience reaction screen began to flash Applause over and over, and the audience did what it was told. But this collection of housewives and retirees seemed to stir impatiently in their seats, not at all pleased at having to sit through a few minutes of what they believed would doubtless be blaring rock music. Only Jeremy and Lucas clapped loudly and with enthusiasm. Karyn gave her applause perfunctorily. Rowena sat motionless, her arms still folded across her chest. I hope he doesn't point me out, she thought as she sank lower into her seat. I'll die, I'll just *die*!

The curtain parted and the band began to play music which, to everyone's pleased surprise, was not at all discordant. Neither was it of earsplitting intensity, though the rhythm was somewhat eccentric. Rowena surveyed the people on the stage, noting their costumes and makeup. Her father wore his customary Merlin outfit, monk's robe, false goatee, white-face coloring. She had met her father's band on numerous occasions, and she looked from one to the other with a modicum of interest. Mark Siegal, dressed in green and brown clothing, the sleeves of his shirt billowing as he pounded upon the drums, looked for all the world like a pirate. Tom Mahoney was made up to look elfin, with tight green leotards and sprigs of holly in his blond hair. He has the face of an elf, Rowena thought. Kind of cute. Mahoney thumped away happily on the bass.

Carl Strube's erratic, buzzing lead guitar was establishing the melody of whatever it was they were about to play. The black man accentuated his coloring by dressing in stark white, even to the white bows which lay at the end of each twisting dreadlock which fell from his head down about his back and shoulders. Larry Herricks, typically, refused to wear a costume at all, dressing instead the way he always dressed and thus presenting yet another unique visual image. He wore a fringed buckskin coat which appeared not to have been cleaned for at least a decade. His dungarees were covered with patches, and his boots scruffy and wrinkled. He wore a faded old headband to keep the hair from falling into his eyes as he ran his fingers over the piano keys. Beads of perspiration dripped from his forehead and ran down his nose and cheeks to be trapped in his bushy beard.

Rowena looked at Adrienne Lupescu and thought, Doesn't she look pretty! I guess they got costumes for the girls too.

Adrienne stood off to one side, delicately fingering her lute. A contact microphone had been taped to the instrument so that it could be amplified and thus heard along with the other louder instruments. She was dressed as a fairy princess in a long, flowing white gown with a simple blue sash around her waist. The long white sleeves hung down to her knees, and her plain brown hair, which had been styled into a bowl cut reminiscent of Joan of Arc, was adorned with a garland of white flowers and green leaves. She looked delicate, frail, vulnerable, ethereal—lovelier than Rowena had thought it possible for Adrienne to look.

Gwendolyn Jenkins, on the other hand, looked the consummate whore. She wore a jet black dress which hugged her torso tightly from bodice to belly and then erupted into streams of tatters and jagged points at the extremities, after the fashion so popular with contemporary British punks. The neckline plunged down practically to her navel, and the rounded contours of her breasts were clearly visible beneath the ragged, carefully tattered fabric. The long hemline was likewise cut into jagged points, though one side was slit almost up to the hip so that as she moved the fishnet stocking which encased her shapely leg was in constant view. Her hair, still long and blue black, had been layered so as to frame her face with soft, wispy points. Her shoes with winklepicker toes and stiletto heels were bound to her calves by strips of leather.

169

As the music played, Simon said into the standing microphone, "This is an ancient tale of shapechangers, magicians who can change their shapes at will." He was strumming the rhythm guitar easily, and he stepped back as Gwendolyn took his place at the microphone. She began to sing, joined by a motionless Adrienne off to the side in front of another standing microphone.

"She danced into the meadow, as white as any milk,
And he ran into the meadow, as black as China silk.
Alack-a-day, alack-a-day, you coal black smith.
Heed well my warning song. . . ."

They proceeded to play through the song which the two women had first presented to the others a few days before, and the work, effort, practice, and imagination which the band had put into their rendition showed clearly. Simon joined the women for each chorus, his resonant bass voice blending perfectly with Adrienne's soprano and Gwendolyn's alto. In the musical breaks between verses Gwendolyn would dance about the stage, swirling and twirling her long black hair and long black skirt shamelessly. As before when first she had danced to this song, she seemed a joyous beast, a frenzied pagan. She radiated animal lust. She exuded sexuality.

The band drove the song home to its conclusion, and the audience responded enthusiastically, some of them pleased that the music was not just the raucous noise they had expected, and others, the older men in particular, responding to Gwendolyn's performance. As the last note sounded and the last cymbal clashed, loud applause drowned out the fading music, and the band acknowledged the audience's reaction. Simon bowed slightly, Adrienne executed an awkward curtsy, Mahoney, Siegal, and Strube nodded. Herricks ignored everyone as he pulled out and lighted a cigarette despite the clearly visible No Smoking sign. Gwendolyn stood haughtily, her balled fists resting upon her hips, her feet placed arrogantly wide apart, her chest heaving from her exertions, the sweat upon her face, throat, and bosom glistening beneath the studio lights. She stared out at the audience.

Percy Campbell walked onto the stage, clapping his hands and mouthing congratulatory phrases to Simon, who nodded his thanks without allowing a smile to break onto his face. They *loved* it! he thought to himself gleefully. Even if the kids don't, this may be a whole new market! Fantastic!

"Simon Proctor and his band, Witch's Sabbath, ladies and

gentlemen," Campbell said. "We'll be right back to talk to Simon, Gwendolyn, and Professor Eisenmann in a moment. Please don't go 'way." He waited for the engineers to signal that taping had been halted before turning to Simon and saying, "Hey, that was great. That's a lot different from the stuff you usually do, isn't it? I mean, my kids have some of your records, and none of them sound like that!"

Simon allowed himself a laugh. "That's Gwen's influence, and Adrienne's. They have a vast repertoire of old songs about magic and wizardry. We've been at work all week adapting them for rock instruments."

"Well, it sounds to me like a good departure for you. Let's get over to the dais and get ready for the rest of the show." His eyes twinkled. "Think you're ready to take on the professor?"

Simon smiled. "I think so," he said darkly. He took Gwendolyn by the arm and led her to the seats which stood beside the desk on the raised platform off to the left of center stage. The stage crew worked quickly at dismantling the instruments and moving them off, and when this had been accomplished the dais, which was on rollers, was pushed over to the center of the stage. Simon grinned at Gwendolyn as they rode the few yards. "You did great, Gwen, unbelievably great!"

She smiled at him warmly. "I am pleased that I have pleased you. I seek to do naught else." She looked around the dais. "Where is the bag I brought with me?"

"Backstage," he said. "I made sure the prop men know to bring it out here before the talking starts. Hey, what's in that bag, anyway? Props for the spell?"

"Materials for the spell, yes," she said softly. As she was speaking a member of the stage crew walked over and handed her the very bag she had been discussing. It was a plain leather purse, about a foot long, caught together at the top by a strip of thin rope. She took it from him without comment or thanks, and placed it at her feet. She and Simon sat quietly, waiting for Campbell to return with Eisenmann.

After a few minutes Percy Campbell came back into view, leading Ludwig Eisenmann toward the dais. The middle-aged Austrian once again wore a silly little bow tie, and once again fiddled with it nervously. Seeing him, Simon experienced a knot involuntarily growing in his stomach. As the chubby little man walked up the two steps onto the dais and heaved his girth into one of the chairs, Simon began to have second thoughts. I hope this wasn't a mistake, he thought. I hope we get the kind of PR out of this that we need.

171

Simon was distracted by hands waving at him from the audience, and he looked out to see Lucas standing up and flailing his arms back and forth. "Hey, Dad!" he shouted. "Hey!"

Simon smiled at his son and returned the wave. He saw Karyn sitting beside him, and he saw Jeremy Sloan as well. Where's Row? he wondered. Didn't she—? Then he saw the top of a blond head just barely visible above an opened program magazine which the station distributed to studio audiences. Rowena seemed to be hiding behind it.

Simon was about to make an attempt at getting Rowena's attention when Campbell sat down behind his desk and said, "Professor Eisenmann, you of course remember Mr. Proctor, don't you?"

Eisenmann smiled his little-boy grin and extended his hand to Simon. "Of course, of course."

Simon shook his hand quickly and coldly and then released it without a word. Son of a bitch, he thought to himself.

"And this is Miss Gwendolyn Jenkins," Campbell said. "Professor Ludwig Eisenmann."

"Charmed, miss," Eisenmann said, nodding politely. He did not extend his hand to her, which was wise, for she would not have taken it. "That was a very interesting interpretation of that song."

"Oh?" she asked easily. "Are you familiar with the tale of the shapechangers?"

"Yes, oh, yes," he said. "It originated in the steppe region of what is now Soviet Central Asia some two thousand years ago. In its original form it dealt with a woman who could change into a deer and a man who could change into a wolf. Of course," he added, "it has undergone quite a few—"

"Ah, Professor," Campbell said, "that sounds very interesting, but maybe you should wait until we start taping again so you can share the information with the audience."

"Oh, of course, certainly," Eisenmann giggled.

"Jake?" Campbell called out. "We're ready when you are."

A pause, and then a voice from the control booth said, "Tape on, cue music in five, four, three, two . . ."

"You Are My Sunshine" began playing once again, and as it was faded out by the audio control technician, Percy Campbell smiled into the camera and said, "Welcome back to the Percy Campbell show. My guests today are Professor Ludwig Eisenmann, Mr. Simon Proctor, and Miss Gwendolyn Jenkins." Each of them nodded in turn at their host. "Professor," he said, turning to Eisenmann with a serious and interested look on his face, "just before, you were beginning to tell us something about the song which Simon and his band just played. Would you mind beginning again, for the benefit of the home audience?"

"Certainly," he said and cleared his throat. "I was saying that the song about the shapechangers—more commonly entitled 'Two Magicians,' by the way—originated in what is now Soviet Central Asia about two thousand years ago, and dealt with a deer-woman and a wolf-man. It underwent many, many changes over the centuries, of course, and exists today in many forms in many different countries. The song we just heard—very pretty, by the way, very nicely performed—is a Celtic variant. In India the story involves the god Krishna as the man capable of assuming a variety of shapes, and the woman has become seven women who are cow-women."

"Interesting, interesting," Campbell nodded. To Gwendolyn he said, "I suppose that you learned this song as a child in—Wales, isn't it? You're from Wales?"

"That is correct," she said calmly. "Yes, 'tis an old song of my land."

"And of many other lands as well," Eisenmann pointed out.

She shrugged. "Of that I know nothing. But the shapechangers of Wales have always been spoken of and sung of. We have many of them, still dwelling in the hills where the old tongue is still spoken."

There was a titter of amusement from various parts of the audience when she said this, and Eisenmann laughed slightly. "Of course, there are no such things as shapechangers."

"Nay, but there are," she said firmly.

"I think this'll lead us into our topic," Campbell broke in. "Professor, you said the last time you were here that Mr. Proctor and the other entertainers who popularize witchcraft and satanism were—" he turned to Simon, "pardon, Simon," and then resumed, "—that they were not really Satanists."

"Not exactly," Eisenmann said. "Whether Mr. Proctor and his friends happen to be devil worshipers or not, I do not know. But the *practices* in his film and, from what I understand, in his stage show are purely imagination without any connection with witchcraft as it was practiced."

"And I still maintain that this is a matter of opinion," Simon said heatedly. This was starting to become depressingly familiar. Gwendolyn patted his hand reassuringly and smiled at him. She was calm, unruffled, confident, much more at ease than he.

"Mr. Proctor, I do not wish to re-cover old ground here," Eisenmann said, "but surely you must admit—"

"Hold," Gwendolyn said firmly. "Let us not waste words on trifles. May I ask you a question, Professor?"

Eisenmann shrugged. "Uh, yes, well, certainly you may."

"Thank you," she said. She crossed her legs as she spoke, and the long, curvaceous limb distracted Eisenmann from her voice for a moment. As she spoke to him she fixed her eyes unblinkingly upon his as if to master him, and he found himself looking down frequently so as to avoid the penetrating stare. Unfortunately, when he did this he found himself looking at her chest, and thus becoming further discomfited. "Allow me to ask you if you believe in witches."

"Oh, of course I do," he said quickly, and then added, "if by that you mean people who practice witchcraft."

She was puzzled. "'Tis one and the same, is it not?"

"Yes, but I wish to make this very clear. There are indeed people who believe that they have magical powers, and these people are called witches. But that does not mean, of course, that they actually do have such powers. Such beliefs are holdovers from a different age, an age of credulity and ignorance, superstition and fear. Such beliefs are atavisms, like, oh, like a tail on a newborn baby."

"I see," she said easily. "And so when I say to you that I am a witch, and that my master, the Devil, has given me powers in exchange for my worship, you say this is untrue?"

Eisenmann laughed. "Miss Jenkins, I do not wish to offend you, but of course it is untrue! You seem to expect people to hold unscientific beliefs in a scientific age!" He leaned forward and said earnestly, "Listen to me, miss. Beliefs in magic and sorcery and devils and demons and all of that arose in human civilization because people in prescientific societies could not understand the processes of nature, could not manipulate nature as we can today by the uses of technology—which is, of course, merely applied science—and they thus sought for explanations of things which they could not understand. This is the origin of the belief in supernatural powers."

"Hmmm." She smiled, pretending to consider his point. "And so there have never been true magicians or true wizards or witches? The tales are untrue that are told of Merlin, and Thomas the Rhymer, and old Tam Lin?"

"Well, of course, there was a thirteenth-century Scottish poet named Thomas the Rhymer, but the nonsense about him running off with the queen of the elves?—Untrue, of course. As for Merlin, merely a late medieval addition to the Arthurian legends, without basis in fact. And Tam Lin is just an old story." He paused for a moment, and then added, "Of course, there were people like the alchemists and the astrologers who, without realizing it, were beginning to discover some natural laws back in the Dark Ages. Such people may have been popularly regarded as sorcerers, may even have thought of themselves as sorcerers. But that was because of the time, not because of any magical powers." He laughed and turned to the audience. "For example, I'm sure that most of us here today know how to drive an automobile. But imagine what would be the reaction in, say, ninth-century Ireland if an automobile came driving down the road." Laughter from the audience. "You see? This is where superstition begins, with people trying to explain things which they do not understand."

"Do you believe in God?" Gwendolyn asked.

"I believe that there is a creative intelligence to the universe," Eisenmann replied, "but I am not wed to any particular religious perspective. I believe that all of man's faiths hold elements of truth which point beyond to an even greater truth which we as yet cannot understand."

"But how then can you believe in God and not believe in the Devil?" she asked. "And if you believe that God has power to answer prayer, how can you not believe that Satan has power to answer prayer?"

He giggled nervously. "Excuse me, miss, but I think you are deliberately misunderstanding me. I do *not* believe in the orthodox Jewish, Christian, Moslem idea of the heavenly patriarch. I am much more attracted to the Hindu or Buddhist concept of deity as universal mind. I do not believe in prayer, to anyone or anything!"

She nodded understandingly. "I see, I see. So you are saying that my belief in Satan differs not from someone else's belief in Christ, correct? Both are mere superstitions, correct?"

Eisenmann coughed uneasily, and Simon thought, Good, Gwen, good! Get him to equate satanism with Christianity, and we've scored a point against him!

But before Eisenmann could reply, Gwendolyn said, "But enough. 'Tis of no importance."

NO, Simon shouted inwardly, NO! LET HIM ANSWER THE QUESTION!

"I merely wish to make certain that you are quite secure in your beliefs," she went on. "You are absolutely certain that there are no such things as real magical powers? The spells which are cast upon people by witches, these too are superstitions?"

"Well," Eisenmann said, grateful for a change of subject, "if you believe that you have powers, and I believe that you have powers, and you then cast a spell on me, the spell might work in that I convince myself that it is working." Eisenmann fiddled with his bow tie and turned to Percy Campbell. "For example, the Australian aborigines believe that you can sing a man to death by pointing a hollow tube at him and singing a death song through the tube. There is at least one recorded, documented instance of this actually happening, but of course it was the man's belief that he could be killed in this manner which caused him to die."

Gwendolyn smiled. "And you, of course, hold no such belief."

"Of course not!" he laughed.

"So that were I to cast a spell upon you, it would be without effect?"

Eisenmann laughed again. "Really, Miss Jenkins. I am quite certain that so attractive a young woman as yourself can cast many effective spells upon members of the male sex." A few laughs from the audience.

Gwendolyn nodded her appreciation at the compliment and then said, "I am quite serious, good sir. Are your convictions so firmly founded that you could be subjected to a spell, a death spell, say, and not be made nervous by it?"

"Of course," he replied jovially. "I have no superstitions."

She leaned back in her seat. "Then let us conduct an experiment, Professor Eisenmann, right here and right now. I shall cast a spell upon you, and we shall see what happens. Is this agreeable to you? And to you, Mr. Campbell?"

Percy Campbell was attempting to repress a grin. What a great segment this is gonna make! he was thinking. "It's fine with me, if it's okay with you, Professor."

Eisenmann smiled and waved his hand as if to dispel any doubt. "Feel free to do your worst, Miss Jenkins."

The time element, Simon was thinking. Don't forget to say that the spell will take a while to work. As Gwendolyn reached down for the black leather bag and seemed to have forgotten this important point, Simon decided to remind her obliquely. "The spell you shall cast, my dear," he intoned ominously. "How long will it take before the effects become evident?"

She looked up at him with amusement as she opened the bag. She knew exactly why he had asked that, and she knew exactly what he expected her to say. "The effects," she said, grinning at him, "will be immediate."

Simon stared at her numbly, unable to believe what he had

176

just heard. "What did—? I mean, the effects—the effects will take a few—"

She stood up. "The effects will be immediate, my dear Simon." She turned from his astounded and infuriated face and said to Campbell, "May I use your desk, Mr. Campbell? And may I ask that the lamps be dimmed?"

"Oh, yes, certainly," Percy Campbell said, standing and moving away from his desk. "Jake, you wanna cut the houselights?" he called out.

I don't believe this, Rowena thought glumly as she watched the woman on the stage begin to draw materials out of the leather bag. Did Daddy know she was gonna do something this stupid? Good grief!

Jeremy leaned over and whispered, "Isn't this wild?"

"This is sick," she whispered back. "That woman is nuts! At least Daddy knows that all of this stuff is just make-believe." She shook her head. "She's crazy!"

Gwendolyn Jenkins took a small candle from the bag and placed it upon the desk top. Then she took a small vial of thick, brown liquid and set it beside the candle. She looked at Simon and said, "A flame, please?"

Simon rose from his seat and took a pack of matches from his pocket. He struck a match and as he applied it to the wick he leaned close to Gwendolyn and whispered, so low that the boom mike could not pick it up, "What the hell do you think you're doing?!"

"Hush, my love," she said calmly. "Sit, and behold." He had no choice but to resume his seat and hope that he was not watching the beginning of the end of his career. I *knew* I shouldn't have come back on this show, he thought. I just knew it! Whatever possessed me to think that I could make up for the last time this way? Simon sighed and shook his head.

Gwendolyn continued her preparations. The houselights dimmed but did not go fully dark. This was apparently sufficient for Gwendolyn's purposes, for she made no comment on it. She took a small, vicious-looking dagger from the bag, and then a small cloth doll. She turned to Eisenmann and said, "May I please have an article of your clothing? A handkerchief, perhaps, or your tie?"

Eisenmann laughed once more and began to untie the bow about his neck. "Really, Miss Jenkins—!"

"This will not take long, good sir," she said amicably. He handed her his tie, and she wrapped it around the torso of the cloth doll. She looked out at the audience and began to speak. There was total silence in the studio. The flickering candle flame sent shadows dancing upon her white face, and the flame reflected as pinpoints of light in each of her green eyes.

"This is a simple poppet," she said quietly, holding the doll aloft and then placing it down upon the desk. "And in this vial is a potion made according to ancient ritual and laws. I shall drink a portion of the liquid, sprinkle a few drops on the good professor, and pour the rest upon the poppet. This will create a mystical bond among the three of us, and after the appropriate words have been spoken, what is done to the poppet will in fact be done to the man."

"It's like voodoo, right?" Campbell asked. He had seated himself beside Simon in the chair which Gwendolyn had vacated.

"It is witchcraft," she replied simply. "I know it by no other name." She uncorked the vial.

"It is known technically as sympathetic magic," Eisenmann said. "The belief was that powers could be bent to the will of the practitioner by transference of action from a symbol to an object."

"Oh," Campbell said, not understanding what he had just heard.

Gwendolyn said, "Shhh!" sternly. There was silence on the stage. She lifted the vial upward as if in parody of the elevation of the elements in a Christian sacrament, and then sipped delicately of the liquid. She brought the vial down to the level of her waist, and tipped it slightly. A small amount of the thick brown potion oozed out into her palm, and then she placed the vial down upon the desk. She dipped her fingers into the liquid by clenching her fist once or twice, and then turned and tossed a few droplets at Eisenmann. He blinked as one of the drops struck his cheek, and he wiped it off with his hand. He brought his hand to his nose and sniffed at it, grimacing. The smell was putrid, vile.

Gwendolyn took the small bottle and poured the remaining liquid over the small cloth doll which lay upon the desk. Then she took the dagger in one hand, placing the vial down upon the desk top with the other, and raised her arms high above her head. She looked up at the ceiling and stood as if frozen for a few moments. Then she began to pray.

"Hear me, *Satanas!* Hear me! Hear me, Master of the world, hear me! Hear me, lord of the flies, hear me! Hear me, father of lies, hear me!" The silence in the studio was so profound that even her increasingly rapid and labored breathing was clearly audible. "I am come to bring death, *Satanas*, hear my prayer! I am come to destroy, my Master, hear my prayer! I am come to visit destruction upon the sons of men in accordance with thy commandment, thou harbinger of death! Hear my prayer! Hear my prayer!" A slight chuckle escaped from Eisenmann's lips, but she either ignored it or was too deeply involved in her prayer to hear it. "Give me the power to slay without touching! Give me the power to kill without touching! Give me the power to destroy without touching! I am thine instrument, open to thee! Flow thou through my limbs and visit death upon mine enemy!" She stood for a long moment as immobile as a statue, and then moved her arms together above her head and grasped the dagger with both hands. She seemed to freeze once more. Then with all of her might she brought the dagger down and plunged it into the doll.

Eisenmann screamed.

Gwendolyn held the doll down with one hand while pulling out the dagger with the other, and then plunged it once more into the center of the cloth form.

Eisenmann jumped from his seat and began to clutch madly at his chest, screaming and stumbling off the dais, falling upon his back in the center of the stage, his body wracked with tremors.

Gwendolyn continued to stab the doll, over and over again.

Percy Campbell leapt to his feet and ran over to Eisenmann, who was staring in shock at the ceiling as his blue tongue began to protrude from his quivering mouth. "Get the lights!" Campbell shouted. "Get a doctor! Hurry!" He pulled open Eisenmann's shirt and then just knelt there, not knowing what he was doing, not knowing what to do.

The dagger plunged downward into the doll, again and again.

People in the audience began to scream as the realization struck them that this was not an act, not a skit, not a rehearsed falsity. People began to rise to their feet, some to come down to the stage, others to flee from the studio. Rowena Proctor sat in the front row, staring in dumb shock at the sight before her. Jeremy was speaking to her, but she did not hear a word that he said. She was staring at the poor man lying upon his back, staring at the look of utter bewilderment on the face of her father, staring at the insane green eyes which seemed to be blazing with delight and fury.

"I—I think he's dead," Percy Campbell stammered as people from the audience and the studio crew encircled him and Eisenmann. "I can't find—I can't find a pulse. I think he's dead!"

A sudden stunned silence descended upon the studio. The people stood and looked impotently on as Campbell muttered, "This can't be happening! This can't be happening!"

They turned as they heard Gwendolyn's low, throaty laugh start very softly and then quickly build to a frenzied pitch. Her eyes were wide and mad, and her laughter overwhelming and dreadful. She raised her arms above her and began to cry out. "AVE SATANAS! AVE SATANAS! AVE SATANAS!"

] CHAPTER TWELVE [

November 23, continued

"DAMN IT, LUKIE, will you stop pacing like that?" Karyn snapped. "You're driving me nuts!"

Lucas Proctor sat down on the edge of the motel bed and started biting his nails. "I wish Dad'd get here. I'm dying to find out what's happening."

"What's happening!" Karyn exclaimed. "They're probably both under arrest, that's what's happening!" She shook her head in amazement. "Did you see that? I mean, my God! That guy is lying there dead, and she's screaming like a goddamn maniac!"

"It was an accident," he muttered. "You can't kill people with spells. That's all bullshit. The cops have gotta realize that."

"Oh, it's all bullshit? This coming from a guy who tried to bring back the spirits of the dead last Halloween?"

"I was just fuckin' around, babe, you know that," he said. "I never really thought that anything was gonna happen." He sighed. "Jeeze, I hope Dad's okay."

Karyn looked over at him and felt suddenly very sorry for him, and regretful that she had been snapping at him all day. She was lying on the far side of the large motel bed, and she slid over and gave him a hug. "He'll be okay, Lukie, honest he will. Don't worry about him. He didn't do anything, really. It's Gwendolyn who's up the creek without—"

She stopped speaking when she heard the sound of voices and footsteps coming down the motel corridor toward the room. Lucas jumped up and ran to the door, throwing it open anxiously and looking out. "Hey, it's Row and Jeremy!" he said happily as he walked out into the corridor. "Where's Dad, Row? What's going on?"

Rowena pushed past him and went into the motel room. "He's down at the police station. He told us to wait for him here."

"How'd you get here?" Lucas asked. The rooms which Simon had reserved for his children, their friends (one each for Rowena and Jeremy, of course), and the two women and himself were in a motel on Northern Boulevard in Queens, quite distant from the mid-Manhattan police precinct where he and Gwendolyn, followed anxiously by Rowena and Jeremy, had been taken after the death of Ludwig Eisenmann. Lucas had an almost pathological fear of police stations, a result no doubt of the drugs he always carried with him, so he and Karyn had gone straight to the motel by subway, and there waited anxiously for the others to return. Lucas knew that Rowena hated the subways and steadfastly refused to ride them on those rare occasions when she was in New York, and this fact had prompted his question.

"Mr. Schroeder drove us over," she said. "He was going home to—I don't know, someplace, and he said he would be passing by here anyway, so he dropped us off."

"So?" Lucas asked.

"So what?"

"So what's going on at the police station?"

Rowena just shook her head and sat down on the edge of the bed. As she pulled off her shoes and began to massage her tired feet, Jeremy removed his jacket and said, "They're interrogating all of them—the band, Adrienne—all of them."

"Yeah," Rowena said. "Adrienne is in bad shape. They had to call in a doctor to give her a shot and calm her down. I have never seen an anxiety attack like that before. I thought she was going to have a stroke or something."

"No shit!" Karyn said. "The poor thing. But it's understandable. I mean, seeing that guy die like that."

Rowena shook her head. "That wasn't it at all. She was acting just like always—you know, quiet, withdrawn, like that. But when Simon told her that they had to go with the cops to be questioned, she went nuts! She started screaming and crying, she fell on the floor in a panic and they had to drag her out into the police car. I mean it, Karyn, I've never seen anything like it in my life."

Lucas shrugged. "Makes sense to me."

"Yes, I'm sure it does," Rowena said bitterly, "but Adrienne isn't a walking drug store like you are!"

181

"Yeah, yeah," he said impatiently. "But what about Dad? What's gonna happen?"

She lay back upon the bed, exhausted from the ordeal. "I don't know, I don't know," she sighed. "I think they're doing an autopsy on the professor right now." She shook her head. "God, I hope that damned nut didn't poison him or anything!"

"Maybe there was something in that stuff she splashed him with," Jeremy suggested.

"Couldn't have been," Karyn countered. "She drank some of it, remember?"

"How do we know she drank anything?" Jeremy asked. "Just because she put that little bottle to her lips? That don't mean nothing."

Karyn considered this. "I never thought of that," she said slowly. "Jesus, that'd be horrible!"

"That'd be Murder One!" Lucas said. "And nobody'd believe Dad if he says he didn't know about it!" His face grew panicky.

"Oh, come on, cut it out," Rowena said irritably. "Daddy didn't do anything. He's not gonna get charged with anything." She spoke forcefully and with conviction, but her trembling lip and the tears which were beginning to collect in her eyes belied her words.

Karyn saw through her confidence and she put her hand on Rowena's shoulder. "You're right, kid." She smiled. "Everything's gonna work out okay."

There was silence for a few moments, and then Jeremy said, "Hey, there's a Burger King down the street. Why don't I go get us some food?"

"Good idea, good idea," Karyn said. Anything to distract Lukie and Row. "Why don't we all go out and get something?"

"I don't want to go out again," Rowena said wearily.

"Yeah, and I want to wait here in case Dad comes back," Lucas added. "You and Jeremy go get some burgers and fries and like that, okay?"

Karyn sighed, but not wishing to annoy Lucas, she said, "Yeah, sure. Let's go, Jeremy. Row, you want anything in particular?"

"Yes," she muttered sleepily. "I want a time machine. I want to go back to yesterday."

Karyn slid to the side of the bed and got up to don her coat. "We'll be right back. Don't go away, okay?"

"Yeah, yeah, sure," Lucas said. "Hurry up, though, okay?"

"Sure. We'll be right back." Jeremy opened the door and she preceded him out of the room. When they were safely distant from the door Jeremy said, "Karyn, this is without doubt the most bizarre thing I've ever heard of."

She laughed grimly. "It's crazy, it's really crazy. Did you see the look on Gwendolyn's face when Campbell said that the guy was dead? My God, she looked like a raving maniac!"

"How close are you to Simon?"

They walked out of the lobby and into the cold wind which was whipping down Northern Boulevard. "What do you mean?"

"Well, I mean, can you talk to him? Do you have a close relationship with him?"

She shrugged. "Not really. I don't even know if he likes me. I mean, shit, he doesn't even really like Lukie!"

"Hm," Jeremy said. "That's too bad."

Karyn looked at him quizzically. "Why? I don't understand what you're trying to say."

"Listen," Jeremy said seriously, "somebody's gotta get Simon away from that crazy chick! I mean, he's stuck on her, it's obvious."

"Yeah? You think so?"

"Oh, come on, Karyn!" he said angrily. "You've seen the way she looks at him."

"Oh, yeah, sure," she replied. "She's stuck on *him*, that's obvious. But I don't think he's stuck on her."

"Hey, don't you think he's screwing her?" They crossed the street and approached the fast-food restaurant.

"Sure he is. I mean, I assume that he is. But haven't you ever screwed a girl you didn't give a shit about?"

"Well, sure, of course," he lied. Jeremy had never had sex with anyone, but he certainly would never admit it, especially not to Karyn or Lucas.

"Well, there you are," she said. "Simon's no fool. If this girl is gonna be bad news for him, he'll dump her so fast she won't know what hit her." Karyn laughed grimly. "If! Jesus, I'll bet he's dumped her already. He doesn't need me or anybody else to talk him into it, unless he's really stupid, which he ain't!" They entered the Burger King.

At that moment Lucas jumped to his feet in the motel room as he heard his father's voice out in the corridor. As Simon entered the room, Lucas ran over to him. "Dad," he cried. "What happened? What happened?" Rowena ran past him and threw her arms around her father's neck and began to weep.

Simon hugged his daughter tightly. "Take it easy, honey, everything's okay." Gwendolyn Jenkins walked up behind him, smiling coldly, and Adrienne Lupescu came behind her,

183

trembling, pale, steadying herself by leaning her hand against the wall of the corridor.

"What happened?" Lucas repeated.

Simon sighed, half with weariness, half with relief. "Heart attack, pure and simple. They kept us at the station until the autopsy results came back."

"So you're not in trouble?" Rowena asked.

"No, not at all," her father replied. "No charges against any of us."

"Oh, Daddy, that's great, just great," Rowena gushed and embraced him once again. She looked past him at Gwendolyn. "What about you? I mean, you caused him to have a heart attack, right? Why aren't you in jail?" It was obvious that Rowena wished that she were.

"He did not die from a weak heart," Gwendolyn said with confidence. "'Twas the hand of Satan which struck him down."

"Oh, Lord," Rowena muttered.

"Listen, honey," her father said, "the guy was fifty-four years old, fifty pounds overweight, and he smoked two packs of cigarettes a day. There's no way any district attorney could blame the heart attack on Gwen."

"I am wearied, Simon," Gwendolyn said. "I must sleep a little time." She turned and walked toward the room where she and Simon had been staying for the past few days.

Rowena watched Gwendolyn leave the motel room, and then she said to Simon, "Daddy, that woman is nuts. You've gotta get rid of her, you've just *got* to!"

Simon patted her gently on the back. "Come on, now, Row, she didn't do anything. This is all just a very weird coincidence, that's all. She was just putting on an act—"

"Daddy, she wasn't putting on an act!" Rowena said firmly. "Oh, I know she didn't kill that man with any spell or anything, but she thinks she did, she honestly thinks she did. She's crazy, Daddy. She's dangerous!"

Simon smiled down at his daughter. "It's nice to know that somebody cares."

Lucas stood nearby, watching quietly. Then he said, "Hey, Dad, I care too."

Simon smiled at his son, more warmly than he had ever done before. "Thanks, Lucas. It helps to hear that."

"Daddy—" Rowena began again.

"Row, I have to go and talk to Gwen about all this. Do me a favor, will you? Keep an eye on Adrienne. She's still pretty shaken up." Simon left his daughter's room and walked toward his own.

Adrienne had been largely ignored throughout the day, but for the hysteria into which she lapsed when she learned of the impending interrogation, and it was only after Simon's comment that Rowena took the time to study the other girl closely. She looked terrible, almost as if she teetered on the edge of a breakdown. Rowena went over to her and took her hand gently. "Adrienne? Are you okay?"

Adrienne looked at her with frightened, panicky eyes. "I did nothing wrong, I swear I did nothing wrong!"

Rowena felt like weeping afresh, she felt so sorry for the poor girl. "Of course you didn't," she said kindly. "Everybody knows that. And everything's okay now, so you don't have to worry about anything."

Adrienne took hold of Rowena's hand and gripped it tightly. "I was so frightened, so frightened! I feared they would imprison me, I truly feared it!"

Rowena smiled at her. "Adrienne, you have to calm down! Everything's okay. Nothing's wrong now. You're not in any trouble. So try to relax a little, okay?"

The girl clutched her desperately, as if seeking to derive strength and repose from her. "Yes—yes—" she echoed. "Everything is fine now—everything is fine—"

"Look, me and Lukie are waiting for Jeremy and Karyn to come back with some food. Why don't you wait here in our room with us? I'll bet you're kinda hungry, aren't you?"

Rowena's kindness and infectious cheer broke through Adrienne's anxiety, and she smiled weakly. "In truth, I have neither dined nor supped this entire day. I am famished!"

"Okay, so eat with us. I think Lukie has some brandy, or bourbon, or something. I think you could use a drink."

"I think we could *all* use a drink," Lucas said from the doorway. "Come on, let's break into the bottle."

Rowena helped Adrienne into a chair, supporting her with one arm around her waist as if she were an invalid. "Whatcha got, Lucas?"

"I don't know," he said, examining the flask which he had earlier placed on the dresser. "It's brown."

Two rooms away, Simon was saying, "Goddamn it, Gwen! What the hell's the matter with you, pulling something like you did today?!"

Gwendolyn Jenkins was reposing seductively on the bed, her long black hair spread out on the pillow, her arms raised above her head and resting upon her hair. "What do you mean, my love?"

"You were supposed to—"

"I said I would cast a spell on him and destroy him, and so I did. What then is disturbing you?"

"For Christ's sake, Gwen, don't you realize what almost happened today?! What if that guy hadn't had a heart attack? We'd all have ended up looking like a bunch of assholes!" He paused. "Will you listen to me? I'm relieved that a man had a heart attack and died! My God, what's happening to me?" He ran his hands through his hair nervously.

Gwendolyn rose slowly from the bed and walked over to him. She took his troubled face in her hands and looked lovingly into his eyes. "You have yet to release the bonds of moral foolishness which still hold you in their grip. That man offended you, and so he earned my wrath." She smiled at him and frowned as one might at a foolish but deeply beloved child. "Simon, Simon, dear sweet man! That fat pig died not from a weakness in his heart, but from a weakness in mine." She kissed him passionately.

Simon pushed her gently away. "Look, Gwen, I'm really bushed. This has been a hell of a day, you know? I think I need a good night's sleep."

She smiled at him through half-closed eyes. "Aye, I am weary as well." She leaned forward and kissed him again, with less intensity. "How many days must pass until we begin to travel about the land?"

"The tour?" he asked. "We're scheduled to open at the Garden on December second. Why?"

She shrugged. "We will need much rest, then." She yawned. "And 'tis a good time to begin getting it."

"Yeah," he said, sitting down on the edge of the bed and pulling off his boots. "Let's turn in, okay?"

"As you wish, my love," she murmured, undoing her belt and chain and allowing them both to drop to the floor. Simon watched her as she slipped the dress down around her knees, and he felt an unexpected surge of desire as he watched her, naked but for her fishnet stockings and garter belt, bend over to pick up the various articles of clothing. She stood up and grinned at him with brazen impishness.

He smiled wickedly at her. "Come here," he said softly.

As Simon and Gwendolyn began their repeated explorations of each other's bodies, Rowena and Lucas were finishing filling Karyn and Jeremy in on what had transpired. "So everything's okay, I guess," Rowena was saying.

"Damned lucky," Karyn said as she began removing the fast-food supplies from the brightly colored bags. "Jesus, what a day!"

"Yeah," Lucas said, his voice slurring a bit. Whatever the brown liquor was in the flask, he had downed most of it, and it was having its expected effect. Adrienne had taken but one draft, and Rowena none at all. "Dad lucked out again."

"Strange kind of luck," Jeremy observed, taking a hamburger and a small bag of fries from the largess which was being spread out on the dresser. "I mean, a guy died today, you know?"

"But Daddy didn't have anything to do with it," Rowena said quickly.

"Right," he nodded, taking a healthy bite of the lukewarm sandwich. "That's what I mean. Strange kind of luck."

Adrienne was sitting quietly in a chair beside the dresser, fidgeting nervously, her hands turning one over the other in her lap. Rowena smiled at her kindly and asked, "Adrienne? You want a hamburger?"

She snapped her eyes toward Rowena, and the terror which had been residing in them dissipated slightly as she gazed at the friendly face of the younger girl. "Wh—what?" she asked.

"You want a hamburger and some fries?" she repeated. Adrienne stared at her blankly, so Rowena reached over and took one of the cardboard bundles and opened it. She handed the sandwich to Adrienne and said, "I think fast food is junk, but Burger King is probably the best. I mean, at least they don't fry everything, you know?"

Adrienne regarded the hamburger quizzically and then took it from Rowena's hand. She nibbled at it tentatively at first and then, apparently satisfied that it was edible, she took a bite. "'Tis a tasty bit," she said appreciatively.

"Good," Rowena smiled. "You want a Coke?" She stuck a straw through the lid of one of the small wax cups and handed it to her.

Adrienne took the cup but was unable to manipulate both it and the sandwich, and pieces of lettuce and onion began to drop from beneath the folding, soggy bun and fall upon her lap. "Mercy," she muttered.

"Hold on, I'll get you a napkin," Rowena said.

"So what's your father gonna do now?" Karyn asked. Her mouth was stuffed with food as she spoke.

"I don't know," Rowena said. "I hope he's gonna—" She broke off the expression of hope that Simon would disengage himself from Gwendolyn, not knowing how such a statement would affect Adrienne. "Well, I just hope he's gonna be more careful."

187

Adrienne placed the half-eaten hamburger on the dresser and said, "By your leave, I think I need to sleep." She rose to her feet.

"Sure," Rowena said. "You must be exhausted. Heck of a day!"

"A terrible day," she said sadly, shaking her head. "A terrible day." She left the room slowly, her weakness evident from her unsteady gait.

They watched her leave and after the door closed behind her, Lucas said, "Something's wrong with that chick."

"Don't be mean, Lukie," Karyn said. "After what she's been through today, anybody would—"

"I don't just mean today," he interrupted. "I mean, there's just something wrong with her."

"She's the nervous type," Rowena said. "That's all."

"She's afraid of her own fuckin' shadow," he countered. "I mean, you say 'Hello' to her and she looks at you like you just pulled a gun."

Rowena nodded at Lucas as she took a bite from a sandwich. "Listen to this," she said sarcastically. "Mr. Mental Health over here!"

"Well, shit! I don't jump out of my shoes every time somebody says 'Boo!'"

"Hey, Lukie," Karyn broke in, not wishing to hear any more bickering, "you bring any dope with you?"

"Yeah," he muttered. "I got a few joints."

"Well, let's do some weed, hang out a little while, and then fall out. I'm really tired."

Rowena regarded her irritably. "You know, Karyn, I don't mean to be pushy or anything, but you really shouldn't smoke that stuff while you're pregnant. I mean, it's bad for—"

"Look, kid, when you're pregnant, you can live on wheat germ, you know?" she snapped. "Don't bug me, okay?"

Rowena pursed her lips and said coldly, "Sure. Sorry." She stood up and took one of the bags of food. "I'm gonna go see if Dad wants something to eat." She walked quickly from the room.

"Oh, shit," Karyn muttered and followed her out into the corridor. "Hey, Row, wait a minute, wait a minute." Rowena stopped walking and turned to face her. The look on Rowena's face bespoke anger and hurt, and Karyn said, "Look, I'm sorry I snapped at you, really I am. I'm just tense, you know? I mean, after today and everything. And I'm tired, you know? I didn't mean it."

188

Rowena gazed at her impassively for a moment and then relented. "I know. It's been a bad day for everybody."

"Yeah, right." Karyn grinned. "Say hi to your dad for me."

"Okay, I will," Rowena replied and continued on down the hallway.

As she walked back into the room where Lucas was busily engaged in finishing his food, Karyn thought to herself, After all the shit I gotta put up with from this fuckin' family, I'd better get a wedding ring outta this!

Rowena reached the door of her father's room and raised her fist to knock on it. But she paused as the sounds of creaking bedsprings and impassioned moans drifted out from behind the door. And after everything that's happened today! she thought dismally. Daddy, what are you doing, what are you doing. . . .

She turned away from the door and began to walk slowly back toward the room where Jeremy and the others were finishing their meals. As she passed Adrienne's door, she heard a strange and disturbing sound filter through from the interior to the hallway. She stopped and listened carefully. It was low, like the mournful groan of a wounded cat. She knocked softly on the door. "Adrienne? It's me, Rowena. Are you okay?" There was no response. She knocked again. "Adrienne? Adrienne? It's Row. Are you okay?"

Still no answer. She tried the doorknob and, finding that the door was not locked, she turned the knob and pushed the door open. The room was pitch black, and she reached to the light switch on the wall beside the door as she entered. She looked around the room. "Oh, Adrienne," she said sadly.

Adrienne Lupescu was huddled in a corner, weeping and whimpering, her knees pulled up tightly against her chest and her lips moving in gasps of unintelligible words. "I didn't . . . ," she muttered. "It wasn't . . . I didn't . . . I didn't . . ."

Rowena knelt down beside her and took her in her arms, holding her tight, stroking her hair, and murmuring soft reassurances to the poor girl. "Shhhh," she said softly. "I'm here, Rowena's here. Everything is all right. You're safe. Shhhh. Shhhh."

"I didn't mean it . . . ," Adrienne wept quietly. "It wasn't me . . . it was her, it was her—"

"Shhhh—Shhhh—"

"She made me. . . . She made me. . . . I didn't want to . . . I didn't want to—"

189

"Shhhhh—"

"I didn't want to lie. . . . I didn't want to lie. . . . She made me, she threatened me. . . . She made me do it. . . . It's all her fault, it's all her fault—"

"Shhhhhh," Rowena said gently, continuing to hold Adrienne and stroke her hair. She had no idea what the girl was talking about, and it did not matter to her. She felt so much pity and so much concern that all she was thinking about was the poor, frightened, disturbed girl in her arms. She held her and stroked her hair and whispered to her until she seemed to be falling asleep. Then she helped her over to the bed. As she switched off the light and closed the door softly, she thought, You poor thing. You poor, poor thing.

She returned to Lucas and Karyn's room, and after another hour of meaningless conversation, she retired to her own room. She slept soundly until morning. She did not hear the intermittent gasps of fear and terror which filtered through the wall between Adrienne's room and her own throughout the night.

⟦ CHAPTER THIRTEEN ⟧
November 24

ADRIENNE LUPESCU'S BODY was covered with a thin film of cold sweat as she tossed about in restless, exhausting sleep. The few faint moans and whimpers which broke free from her thin, trembling lips would have been meaningless to any listener not privy to the nightmarish memories drifting through the troubled girl's dreams. The fear and the terror and the pain had been so long ago, so very long ago, and such greater fear and terror and pain had been visited upon her since that the memory of her ordeal at the hands of the authorities had remained submerged and unremembered.

But the events of the previous day, the experience of being taken into custody and brought to what she assumed to be a jailhouse, had brought the events of three centuries past back with a horrifying clarity. The memories now tortured her in her sleep.

Her dreams reminded her of Elizabeth Proctor's arrest, of John Proctor's impotent rage, of Abigail's self-satisfied smugness at her impending triumph. She remembered being summoned once more to testify before the witchcraft tribunal in March of 1692, on the day when the game which she and Abigail and the others had been playing ceased to be a game.

In her dream she sat nervously upon the bench in Jonathan Corwin's house, her fidgeting fingers folded in her lap, her eyes moving from one face to another, from Corwin to Judge Hathorne to John Proctor to Deputy Governor Danforth to Marshal Cheever to Elizabeth Proctor. She was trembling with terror, visions of the hangman's noose dancing in her mind, only half able to hear the words being addressed to her by Judge Corwin. She snapped her head attentively toward him when she heard her name spoken. "I—I beg your pardon, sir?" she asked tremulously.

"I said answer the question, girl!" Corwin demanded.

"The—the question? I— I—"

"Is it or is it not true that Goodman Proctor brought you out of a fit by a simple slap upon the cheek?"

"It—it was happenstance, your lordship." She felt tears beginning to come and willed them to stop. She failed, and a few salty beads rolled down from her eyes.

"Happenstance!" Corwin said angrily, his cold gray eyes glaring at her from beneath pencil-thin brows. "And how was it happenstance that for weeks you have had fits in this very room, you and the other girls, denouncing people as witches; but that when Goodman Proctor strikes you, your fit ceases! How is that happenstance?"

"The—the fit went away all by itself," she whimpered. "Mr. Proctor struck me, 'tis true, but it was happenstance that he struck me just as the fit went away." Stupid thing to say, she told herself. No one will believe that.

Corwin leaned forward. "Mary Warren, listen to me very, very carefully, and heed well what I am about to say. This court has already condemned people to death, and relegated others to prison. Martha Corey, Sarah Good, Rebecca Nurse, George Burroughs, John Willard, and George Jacobs are all awaiting the gallows. Giles Corey, Martha Carrier, and Elizabeth Proctor are all under indictment. And the most significant evidence presented in these trials has been the testimony of you girls. If you are making sport with this court, you shall pay for it dearly, I warn you, here in this life and in the life beyond."

She swallowed hard, refusing to contemplate the true nature of the fraud she and Abigail and the other girls had been perpetrating. "I am afflicted, sir," she said. "The Devil and his servants have afflicted me."

"Ha!" John Proctor spat. "If you are afflicted, 'twould be a great blessing for you to be afflicted to death!"

"Mr. Proctor! If you please!" Judge Hathorne said.

"She goes to bring out innocent people and lead them to the gibbet!" Proctor said emphatically. "Good sirs, no possession by the Devil is ended by a slap on the face! 'Tis a pretense only, a sport, a silly game of silly girls!"

Danforth leaned over and whispered in Corwin's ear. He nodded and then himself leaned in the other direction and whispered to Hathorne, who nodded in turn. Corwin sat back. "Marshal Cheever," he said.

The village constable, in truth a simple farmer elected to a part-time job by the church council, stepped forward stiffly. He seemed all too aware of his own importance in the midst of this scandal. "Sir?" Cheever asked.

"Are the tongs heated without?"

"Aye, sir."

"Fetch them."

"Aye, sir." Cheever spun about on his heel and walked quickly from the room.

Corwin looked at Mary Warren. "I had hoped that we might avoid this, girl, but your words do not ring true to me, and too many lives hang on your testimony for us to risk any error."

"I—I do not understand, sir," she stammered.

"You'll understand soon enough, you little liar!" Proctor said angrily. "No innocents shall be slaughtered for your silliness."

"Oh, no, sir," Mary wept. "That could not happen!"

"Goodman Proctor, please be silent," Judge Hathorne said. "The court will conduct this interrogation without your assistance, by your leave."

Proctor sat down beside his shackled wife, fuming silently. Cheever walked back in a moment later, holding a pair of tongs in his heavy, thickly gloved hands. The pincers at the end of the tongs were red-hot, glowing in the dimly lit room. Mary stared at the tongs and gasped, realizing what they were for.

"Mary Warren, for the last time, will you tell us the truth?" Corwin demanded. "Are these fits of your own making? Or are they possession? Has someone sent his or her spirit out against you, or are you doing this to yourself?"

What can I answer? she thought desperately. If I say that the

Devil is responsible, they will tear me with the pincers. But if I say that I have done it myself, they will cast me into prison, possibly hang me! But perhaps they will only hurt me if I admit to a pretense! Perhaps if I maintain my position even in the face of these threats, they will believe me! What to do . . . what to do—

"Mary Warren, answer me! Now!"

"It—it—" She shook violently from her fear. "It—it was the Devil and the servants of the Devil. I swear—I swear—"

"She's lying," Proctor said, jumping to his feet. "Can't you see that she's lying?!"

"John Proctor, be seated and be silent!" Corwin growled. "I shall not ask you again!" Proctor sat down, intimidated by the magistrate, and Corwin turned his attention back to Mary. "I cannot tell, I cannot tell. You may be lying and you may be speaking truth. We will have to put it to the test." He nodded at Cheever.

"NO!" Mary screamed as two of Cheever's associates grabbed her by the arms and shoulders to keep her seated and relatively immobile. "NO! JESUS, PLEASE, HELP ME!" Cheever opened the pincers and walked toward her, the glowing metal jaws seeming ready to clamp down upon her at any point on her body. "NO! NO! I'LL SAY WHATEVER YOU WANT ME TO SAY! I'LL SAY WHAT—" She shrieked as Cheever clamped the fiery tongs down upon her right cheek, pinching her soft flesh between the burning teeth of the pincers. The odor of roasting meat permeated the room, and Mary Warren fell into a dead faint.

She came slowly back to consciousness in extreme pain. She opened her eyes to see a woman—was it Goody Cheever?—carefully, gently touching her wounded cheek with dollops of butter. Mary Warren cried bitterly, and the consequent movement of her facial muscles increased the pain in her cheek and thus her weeping as well. She bent over, weeping, crushed.

"Now then, girl," Hathorne said. "The truth."

She sighed through her tears. " 'Twas as Mr. Proctor says. 'Twas sport, pretense."

"Repeat, girl!" Corwin demanded. "Repeat your words, louder!"

" 'Twas pretense only," she wept.

"And no one ever sent his spirit out against you?"

"No sir."

"And you never saw anyone with the Devil, not Goody Nurse or Goody Corey, no one at all?"

"No sir, no one, not ever."

"And all the girls have been lying?"

"Aye sir. . . . Well, at times 'tis easy to believe, when the fits come on you—"

"What are you saying, girl?" Corwin shouted. "Do you pretend to have these fits or do you not?!"

"Pretense, sir, 'tis pretense, but sometimes the sport cannot be controlled."

Corwin sat back in his chair and studied her wounded face intently. "Perhaps they cannot control them, but you can."

She looked up at him through her tears. "Wh—what, sir?"

"Yes," he said darkly, "perhaps we have been looking in the wrong places for the Devil's servant. Perhaps it is *you*, Mary Warren, *you* who have bewitched these other girls!"

She felt herself slipping into a swoon, and she fought to remain awake. "No sir, I swear to God, I swear to God!"

"Then who has bewitched them?"

"No one, sir, no one, no one! 'Tis sport and pretense, sport and pretense!"

"And whose idea is it, this sport and pretense, if not yours, Mary Warren? Is not that a form of bewitchment, to seduce others into sin?"

"No sir, I swear, I swear—!"

Corwin turned back to Cheever and nodded. "Again, Mr. Cheever, if you please."

"NO!" she screamed. "IT WASN'T ME, IT WAS ABBY, IT WAS ABBY!"

Hathorne sat forward quickly. "Abigail Williams? Are you saying that Abigail Williams is responsible for this?"

"Yes!" she screamed, weeping bitterly.

Corwin waved Cheever back. "Mr. Cheever, go and bring in Abigail Williams." As an afterthought he added, "And bring in the other girls as well." He turned back to Mary. "Your friends are all waiting without. We shall see how they respond to this revelation of yours." The tone of his voice clearly indicated that he doubted her.

Cheever returned a moment later with Abigail, Mercy, Suzannah, and Betty. They filed in quietly, each of them blanching when they saw the swollen, blistering burn on Mary's face. "Girls, listen to me very carefully," Corwin said. "Mary Warren has told us that the bewitchments from which you suffer are of your own device, that you are making sport with this town and this court, that you are knowingly sending innocent people to the gallows, and that you, Abigail Williams, are the leader of this disgusting conspiracy."

Abigail drew herself up haughtily. "And do you believe these lies, sir?"

"My mind is open, Abigail," he replied evenly, "but I am curious to hear your response."

"Hear this, then," she said, her voice calm and confident. "I have always doubted Mary's sincerity, always wondered whom she truly served, the Lord or the Devil."

"Abby!" Mary gasped. She wouldn't denounce me! She wouldn't!

Mercy Lewis threw herself suddenly backward and fell onto the floor with a resounding thud, screaming, "Mary, Mary, stop! No, no, please don't!"

A second later Betty Parris doubled over as if in pain and began to scream, "She's stabbing me, she's stabbing me! Mary, why, why? Mary, I've done you no wrong!"

"Mary Warren!" Corwin shouted. "What are you doing to these poor creatures? Stop it at once, do you hear?"

Mary stared at the two girls with openmouthed astonishment and confusion. Suzannah and Abigail began to throw themselves against the walls of the room, screaming out Mary's name and begging for mercy, for pity. For an instant Mary's eyes locked with Abigail's, and there was a clear message in the cold green orbs which seemed to bore into Mary's mind: Betray us and we will denounce you. Tell the truth and we will see you hang as a witch. Put us in jeopardy and I shall kill you.

"No," Mary muttered. "No—it isn't true—it isn't true—"

"What are you saying, Mary Warren?" Corwin demanded. "Speak up, girl!"

"I lied," she wept, "I lied. 'Twas the Devil, the Devil, he bewitched me, he bewitched all of us." The girls ceased their gyrations and Mary threw herself forward at Abigail, grasping her about the knees and weeping, "I'm sorry, Abby. I'm sorry, I'm sorry!"

"Mary Warren," Corwin demanded, "did you see Sarah Good with the Devil?"

"Yes," Mary wept.

"And Martha Corey, and Rebecca Nurse, and George Jacobs, and the others? Did you see them with the Devil?"

"Yes," she wept.

"And is there anyone else, as yet unnamed?" Corwin asked imperiously. "Did you see anyone else with the Devil?"

Mary was kneeling in front of Abigail, clutching her knees as if for support and comfort, but Abigail had not responded to her gesture of reconciliation, her silent plea for help. Mary looked up into Abigail's cold emerald eyes and withered under

195

their steady, merciless stare. *You know what you must say*, the eyes were telling her. *You know whose body I wish to see dangling from a rope. You know who it is who must hang, you know whose husband I want for my own. Tell them, Mary, tell them.*

"Mary Warren!" Corwin repeated. "Answer me! Is there anyone else as yet unnamed whom you saw with the Devil?"

Mary buried her head in Abigail's skirts and cried out, "Yes! Yes! There, there is the Devil's servant, there is his chief witch!" Her eyes were pouring their tears into the hem of Abigail's skirt, and she pointed, without looking, in the direction of Elizabeth Proctor. "Many times have I seen them together, many times!"

Her head snapped up at the sound of a struggle, at the sound of curses, oaths, and heavy chains. She heard Abigail laugh and whisper, "Good! Good! He must denounce her now, to save himself!"

Mary had not pointed at Elizabeth Proctor. She had pointed at John, at whom Abigail now gazed with a look of vindictive triumph.

"Mr. Proctor . . . ," she muttered in her sleep, "I'm sorry . . ."

For three and a half months, Mary Warren had been bound in fetters in the basement of Judge Corwin's house, seeing the light of day only when she was dragged forth to testify in court, to be examined in court, to be interrogated, to be tortured. She had denounced John Proctor as a witch, and had almost immediately recanted her denunciation. Corwin and the others could not decide if she was a poor innocent under Proctor's diabolical control, or a witch herself trying to snare and destroy other truly innocent people. At times they would be tending to believe that she, along with the other girls (whose honesty and innocence they never doubted), was struggling to tell the truth when she denounced Proctor, and she in her fear and her pain would follow their lead and restate her accusation. At other times they would grow suspicious of her, consider the possibility that she herself was Satan's servant, and behave as if her denunciation of Proctor was itself an act of the Devil; and when their moods swung in this direction, she would again succumb to fear and pain and would again recant, saying that she had never seen John Proctor with the Devil. The swings back and forth from one position to the other served merely to increase the suspicions of the judges, leading to further torture, further threats, further fear, and thus repeated denouncements and recantations.

Of all the people suspected of witchcraft in Salem, only Mary Warren was tortured. Of all the people who denounced others as witches, only Mary Warren's testimony was considered so unreliable as to warrant validation under torture. She wept and screamed, she begged and pleaded, she said whatever they wanted her to say, swore to whatever truth or falsehood they presented to her, she denounced everyone, she absolved everyone, she denounced Abigail and Mercy and Betty and Suzannah, she absolved Abigail and Mercy and Betty and Suzannah, she denounced John and Elizabeth Proctor, she absolved John and Elizabeth Proctor, she cried and shrieked and bled.

There was a strange logic to the opinion which the judges ultimately fixed upon as true. All of the girls had accused Elizabeth Proctor of witchcraft, and all steadfastly maintained that they had seen her with the Devil on numerous occasions. Is it reasonable, the judges asked themselves, to believe that a wife could have traffic with Satan without her husband's knowledge? And could he have had this knowledge and not acted upon it without consenting to it? And if Elizabeth Proctor was a witch, as was generally assumed to be true, would she have so controlled Mary Warren so as to put her own husband in jeopardy? Is it not more reasonable to assume that Mary's denunciations were true, and that her recantations were false? If so, then the girl was innocent and must be released. The alternative, of course, would be to hang her and release John Proctor. But could they release John Proctor and not release Elizabeth Proctor? Could they release Elizabeth and not release Tituba and Rebecca Nurse and Sarah Good and George Jacobs and all the others?

It was a simple equation. One either believed the girls, all of them, Mary included, or one did not. True, only Mary had denounced John Proctor; Abigail and the others maintained that none of them had ever seen him with the Devil. But this only testified to the subtlety and dangerous intelligence of John Proctor, who had apparently masked his devotion to Satan so well.

So John Proctor was a witch, they decided, as was his wife and over two dozen other people in Salem Village. And, as the Bible inexorably commands, thou shalt not suffer a witch to live.

Corwin leaned forward and stared into the dull, numb eyes

of the broken girl who sat before him on the stool. "Mary Warren, are you prepared to sign the deposition?"

"Yes," she said weakly, her voice little better than a hoarse whisper.

"You know that to sign your name to an untruth is perjury? You are certain that what you have told us is the truth?"

'Yes," she repeated. Anything, she thought, I'll sign anything, only let me go, don't hang me, don't hurt me anymore.

Corwin held a piece of paper in front of her face and asked, "Are these your words, written down exactly as you spoke them?"

She tried to focus on the page, but the black letters danced about before her eyes. "I—I cannot—I cannot read them."

Corwin handed the paper to Cheever and said, "Read aloud the words of the witness. Listen carefully, Mary. Make certain it is accurate."

Marshal Cheever cleared his throat and began to read the deposition:

"Mary Warren versus John Proctor: The deposition of Mary Warren aged twenty years here testifieth. I have seen the apparition of John Proctor Senior among the witches and he hath often tortured me by pinching me and biting me and choking me, and pressing on my stomach till the blood came out of my mouth and I also saw him torture Mis Pope and Mercy lewis and John Indian upon the day of his examination and he hath also tempted me to write in his book and to eat bread which he brought me, which I refusing to do, John Proctor did most grievously torture me with a variety of tortures, almost ready to kill me."

Corwin turned back to Mary. "Are those your words, Mary Warren?"

"Yes," she whispered.

"And you swear to their veracity, upon your immortal soul?"
"Yes."

"And you are prepared to sign your name to this document in the presence of witnesses?"

She sighed. "Yes."

Corwin and Hathorne exchanged satisfied glances, and then Corwin said, "Marshal Cheever, give her the quill."

Mary watched with impassive dullness as Cheever dipped the tip of the feather in the inkwell and then handed it to her. She took it with a weak and trembling hand. A few droplets of ink dripped from the quill as she moved it toward the bottom of the page, but no one moved to blot it. Mary wrote her name on the bottom of the deposition, the irregular, uneven signature bearing mute testimony to her condition.

Judge Corwin released a contented sigh and said, "My friends, let us bow our heads in prayer." All heads in the room inclined and all hands folded piously, all save Mary's. She sat motionless, staring at the paper which she had just signed. "Oh Lord," Corwin intoned, "we thank Thee that in Thy mercy and Thy wisdom Thou hast enabled us to strike a blow against Thine enemy. We humbly beseech Thee that Thou mayest turn the curse of Thy wrath from this village, and grant unto Thy faithful servants the buttress of Thine arm in this grave struggle."

The prayer went on and on, but Mary paid no attention to it. She remained motionless and mute, as if her feelings had been cut from her.

And she dreamed on, remembering that black day in June of 1692.

Mary Warren walked slowly toward the solitary figure which stood motionless before the gibbet, the solitary figure which gazed silently upward at the body which dangled above it from the end of the rope. "Abigail?" she whispered.

"Aye," came the quiet reply.

"Abby, 'tis all over now. Come, let us go." She reached out and took Abigail Williams gently by the arm. She did not look up at the mortal remains of John Proctor.

"Let us go?" Abigail laughed bitterly. "Let us go where, Mary? Shall we return to the Proctor cabin? We cannot, for it is deserted. Perhaps we should go to the Corey home. Oh, mercy, I have forgot. Martha is hanged and Giles is pressed beneath stones." She turned and gazed at Mary with cold, emotionless eyes. "Perhaps we should go to the Parris house, to my uncle—oh, no, wait, he is gone, is he not, dismissed by the congregation? Dear, dear me. Where shall we go, Mary?"

"Abby, I'm sorry that—"

Abigail Williams swung her arm around and struck Mary in the face with a closed fist. "Damn you, Mary Warren! Damn you!"

Mary remained on the muddy ground where she had fallen under the impact of Abigail's blow. "Abby, please. I'm sorry for what has happened, truly I am."

"And does your sorrow give me back my John?" she wept.

"Will your sorrow give me back my love?" She looked up at the body of John Proctor as it swung slowly from the rope in the summer breeze. "Look what you've done, Mary Warren, look what you've done!"

Mary pulled herself to her feet. "Abby, if there is anything I can do, anything—"

Abigail Williams grabbed her by the arm and began pulling her away from the gallows. "Aye, there is something you can do, Mary."

"Where—where are we going?" she asked.

"You shall see," Abigail muttered. She did not release her grip on Mary's arm. She dragged her down the muddy main street of Salem Village, out past the town boundaries, along the deserted road far from the farms and the houses. She left the road and, still dragging Mary behind her, went deep into the woods, walking with a steady determination until they came to a small clearing in the midst of the woods.

Abigail then released her grip and said, "Kneel down." Mary knelt obediently. Abigail stared at her hatefully. "You owe me, Mary Warren. You owe me more than you can ever pay me. Do you understand that?"

"Yes," she wept. "I'm sorry, Abby."

"I'm not interested in your sorrow. Just be quiet and do what I tell you to do." She reached into her bodice and pulled out a small wooden cross, obviously one hastily and crudely fashioned. She stuck it cross-end down into the soft earth. "Repeat what I say, Mary," she ordered.

"Yes—yes, Abby, I will. But what are you—?"

"I am going to make a pact with the Devil, Mary Warren, and so are you. We shall offer him our souls in exchange for my love. He will give me back my John and we shall be the Devil's servants, in truth, not in pretense."

Mary stared at Abigail with shock and disbelief. She's taken leave of her senses, Mary thought. She is mad!

"You are in my debt, Mary!" Abigail said through trembling lips. "You will do this thing, do you hear?"

"Yes, yes, of course," Mary said nervously. Humor her, humor her. She is just upset today. John Proctor was hanged today. Give her time and she'll be right again.

"Very well," Abigail muttered. "Repeat the words which I say." She bowed her head reverently. "Hail, Satan, lord of the world."

"Hail, Satan, lord of the world," Mary repeated dutifully.

"We come before you as supplicants, begging your aid and your friendship."

"We come before you as supplicants, begging your aid and

your friendship." Mary glanced over at Abigail. The other girl was shaking with the intensity of her prayer.

"Come to us, Satan, make us your own."

"Come to us, Satan, make us your own."

"Come to us, Satan."

"Come to us, Satan."

"Come to us!"

"Come to us!"

Mary Warren looked with pity at her poor friend, and then turned her head at the sound of approaching footsteps. She leapt to her feet and screamed, backing away from the unexpected visitor. The tall man was smiling, laughing, as he drew closer to them, and there was a madness, a cruelty in his face which terrified her.

But it was not the demonic visage which had caused Mary to scream. The man who was walking toward them did not have feet. He had hooves.

She screamed aloud in her sleep. Rowena, slumbering in the motel room next door, did not hear her. The torturous dream went on.

Nine and a half years, Mary Warren thought sadly. Nine and a half years living on the streets of Boston, selling her body to strangers, opening herself to disease and danger. Twice already had she been afflicted by the pox, and four times given birth to bastards, which she left on the steps of the foundling home in the wee hours of the morning. Abigail Williams had fared no better in the degrading trade into which she had forced Mary to join with her. Six times had she had the pox, and five times spawned bastards for the foundling home.

Mary was still chronologically a young woman, but she seemed old, tired, worn out. She was having an increasingly difficult time finding customers to partake of her fading charms down by the docks and warehouses. She was gaunt and emaciated, redolent of sweat and grease, radiating illness, disease. Her face might have been pretty still, might have held some attraction, but for the deep, ugly scar on her cheek and the unhealthy thinness of her lined and jaded countenance.

Now, in 1702, she was hard pressed to find a man who would throw her tuppence for some bizarre perversion. It had been easy—horrible but easy—back in 1693 when the two girls had first come to Boston, to find a man willing to give a few shillings for the privilege of spearing her beneath her skirts and fumbling awkwardly with her small breasts; but as the time passed she was drawn deeper and deeper into the morass of perversity, forced by the imperative of survival to do things which she as a child in the country had never even imagined people doing, things with her mouth, with her anus, even at times with Abigail, for the amusement of wealthy, cruel onlookers.

The years had passed without joy, without peace, without expectations. She and her friend—no, she and her creditor, she and her mistress, she and her owner—had spent the years living in broken-down, abandoned buildings, selling themselves to filthy strangers, hiding from the constables and the clergy. They spent each night seeking out ploughs for their furrows, and ended each night by praying to the Devil, often stealing an infant or a child and butchering it as a sacrifice to the Dark Lord.

"You shall serve me in this world and the next," Satan had told them that day in the forest. "You shall sin and sin greatly, for great sin pleases me. You shall burn with the souls of the damned for countless centuries, and then, at my pleasure, in the fullness of time, I shall return you to the earth and give you each yet another life to live. You, sweet Abigail, shall have your Proctor to love or destroy, and you, little Mary, shall be her servant. And when I have returned you to the world of living men, you shall have power, and pleasure, and wealth. . . ."

That was nine and a half years ago, Mary thought sadly as she foraged through the garbage of the inn on the high street, looking for something edible. She found an apple core, brown and covered with bugs. She shooed away the bugs and brushed off the snow and bit into the rotting fruit.

"Mary," she heard Abigail say from behind her. "I have been thinking."

She turned to see Abigail Williams approaching her. Abigail's once beautiful black hair now hung down in matted clumps. Her once voluptuous figure had resolved itself into starchy obesity. Her once lovely face was now marked with pox scars and blackheads. "Thinking about what?" Mary asked.

"Come with me." Abigail led her away from the garbage and walked briskly toward the stable directly across the street. Once inside she lighted a lantern and pointed up at the rafters. "See? What do you think?"

Mary gazed upward. Abigail had slung a rope over the sturdy central beam. The rope had been plaited on each end into nooses. "Abigail!" Mary said. "What means this hangman's rope?"

" 'Tis a simple thing," Abigail said. "The sooner we die, the sooner will come the day when we are given back new, fresh lives, the sooner I will have my John and the sooner we will both have wealth and power and pleasure." She looked Mary steadily in the eye. "We must hang ourselves, Mary Warren."

Mary backed away from her. "Hang ourselves! Abby, don't speak nonsense!"

" 'Tis not nonsense," she replied earnestly. "Sin pleases the Master. Suicide will please him greatly!"

"But Abby, I don't want to die!" she began to weep. "I'm too young!"

"Oh, Mary," she laughed, an insane glow in her eyes, "are you indeed? How many years left before we both starve to death, or end up dying of the pox, or get caught sacrificing a child and end up on the end of a rope anyway? Does your life please you so much that you cherish it and fear to leave it? Are you looking forward to tonight's strangers spilling their seed in you? Did you enjoy your garbage supper so much?"

"But to take your own life, Abby!" she said, weeping still. "God damns suicides!"

"We're damned anyway, you silly ass!" A sudden look of comprehension flooded over Abigail's face. "Oh, I understand now, I see! You have some foolish hope of salvation, of confession on your deathbed, don't you!" She reached out and grabbed Mary by the hair. "Well, do not delude yourself, Mary Warren. You are damned, and that's the end of it. You have sold yourself to the Devil and you have signed his book, and that's the end of it! God has turned His back on you. The only hope either of us has is for the second life Satan will give us on earth, sometime in future years, at his pleasure. So stop all this wailing about damnation. Suicide or no suicide, be it that you die by starvation or disease or execution, you are damned, just as I am damned." She tried to straighten her ragged skirt. "You know that what I am saying is true."

Mary sobbed. It was true. It was undeniably true.

Abigail climbed up onto one of the two footstools which she had placed beneath the nooses. She had apparently measured the rope quite carefully, for when she slipped her end of it over her head the other end dangled just over five feet above the other stool. Mary approached the other stool slowly, weeping quietly. "You don't know for sure," she sobbed.

"What are you talking about?" Abigail demanded.

"He didn't love you, Abby. Maybe the next time will be the same."

"He will love me," she said emphatically. "And if he does not, then he will have more to fear than a hangman's rope!" She sniffed. "Now hurry up, Mary Warren! Let's be done with this!"

Mary stepped up onto the stool and placed the noose around her neck, her fingers trembling and her eyes pouring forth tears of sorrow and of fear. Both women were standing on tiptoe upon their self-designated gallows. "Good-bye, Abby," she sobbed.

"Oh, be quiet, Mary Warren," Abigail snapped. "We're both going to hell, aren't we? There is no need for good-byes!"

She pushed Mary backward and then an instant later jumped off the stool. Mary dangled at the end of the rope, watching as Abigail kicked and gasped and thrashed on the other end. She felt the rope cutting into her throat, tried to cry out through empty lungs and a broken windpipe, clutched impotently at the noose as it choked her to death.

Darkness swept over Mary Warren. Then, for an instant, there was nothing.

And then there was pain, unending pain, and the echoes of Satan's mad laughter wracking her tortured soul.

She shrieked in her sleep and did not awaken. As the deep, dark hours of night slowly moved onward toward daybreak, she lived her life over and over again in her tormenting dreams. There was no escape in wakefulness and no escape in sleep, for she knew what she was, she knew what she had been, she knew what she would be again. And the terrible memories paled into insignificance when she dreamed of the inevitable future, when she would once again return to the eternal darkness, when she would once again be the blind, shapeless thing floating in unending agony upon the burning lake of hell.

⟨ CHAPTER FOURTEEN ⟩

November 25

THE NEXT MORNING all the news wire services carried the story of the televised death of Ludwig Eisenmann. The videotape of the incident was shown on the local news broadcasts and was almost immediately released to the networks. CBS and NBC had reservations about showing it on the nightly news, but after ABC decided to air the footage, the other two networks followed suit.

The next day, the issue of witchcraft in popular culture was raised on three of the nationally televised morning talk shows, and the tape of Eisenmann's death was shown on two of them. The Christian Broadcasting Network devoted two full hours of programming to the problem of satanism in America, and before evening a cry of outrage had been raised by clergymen, educators, and parents' organizations nationwide. That night the American Civil Liberties Union, fearful that this outburst of parochial fury might pose a threat to other small and eccentric religious groups, contacted Simon Proctor to inform him that their services were available to him should he need them.

The day after that, owners of record stores began to notice evidence of an unusual demand for the records of Simon Proctor and Witch's Sabbath. They promptly arranged to have more of the records shipped to them by the distributors.

By the end of the next day, advance sales for the upcoming concert tour of Witch's Sabbath had been sold out, and Harry Schroeder was busily engaged in arranging additional bookings in other cities throughout the nation. The original tour had been limited to bookings in cities east of the Mississippi, but Schroeder now expanded the itinerary to include the West as well.

The film which Simon Proctor had bankrolled, *Satanists of Salem*, was released the day after that. Lines of people were queuing up to see it in such great numbers that the film company rushed through the production of additional prints, and the film was sent off to additional theaters.

Two days after that, Simon Proctor was interviewed by *Rolling Stone* magazine.

One day later, Gwendolyn Jenkins agreed to pose for a photo spread in *Penthouse* magazine. She agreed verbally in the presence of witnesses, but refused to sign a contract or a model's release.

"Many years ago I signed the Devil's book," she explained. "I have signed nothing since, nor shall I ever."

The next day, the concert tour began. Witch's Sabbath played to a standing-room-only crowd at Madison Square Garden.

And the money began rolling in.

III

WINTER SOLSTICE

The dog turns back to his own vomit, and
the sow is washed only to wallow in the
mire.

—II PETER 2:22

[CHAPTER FIFTEEN]
December 2

"ONE ROAD leads to your lover's room,
Your lover's room, your lover's room.
The other road leads to a cold hollow tomb,
Where Death's gonna dance on your grave. . . ."

The instrumental conclusion to Simon's old hit "Pathfinder"
echoed through the vastness of Madison Square Garden, and
the packed audience began cheering and whistling even before
the last notes faded into silence. He stood motionless, drinking
in the adulation, repressing his urge to jump up and down with
glee as he surveyed the multitude before him. Not one empty
seat, he thought. Standing Room Only. Filled to capacity. And
Harry says it's going to be the same in Philly, in Chicago, in St.
Louis, everywhere, everywhere.

Almost everyone in the audience was going wild with
applause. Rowena Proctor, who was sitting off in the wings
with Jeremy, Lucas, and Karyn, was not. She sat uneasily upon
the metal folding chair and watched with undisguised unhappiness as her father executed a formal bow to the cheering
throng. Jeremy leaned over to her and said, "Come on, Row.
Try to make the best of it."

"I do *not* want to take a whole month off from school," she
replied. "Daddy is so selfish. Doesn't he realize how long it's
gonna take me to make up all the work I'll miss?"

"You can do it easily," he said. "You're smart!"

"That's not the point, Jeremy!"

"Besides, it's only two weeks, not a month. Half of it is over
your Christmas vacation anyway." She sniffed, refusing to be
reasoned with. "Look," he continued, "Adrienne is an important part of this new act of your dad's, right? And she just can't
seem to function unless you're around."

"So that's supposed to be my problem? Jeeze! If she can't
handle things unless there's somebody around who treats her
like a human being, then she should have dropped out of the
act and stayed with me in Bradford."

"They need her harmonies," Jeremy said patiently for the

hundredth time. "You know that. Besides, I thought you liked her!"

"I do like her," she snapped. "I like her and I feel sorry for her, and if you ask me the best thing for Adrienne would be to get away from this concert tour, away from this witchcraft crap, and away from Gwendolyn!"

Lucas was sitting next to Jeremy, and he leaned across him to say, "You still bitchin' about having to go along?"

"Oh, shut up, Lucas," she muttered.

"Poor kid," he said with mock sympathy. "Gotta take a couple of weeks off from school to go along on a national tour with a rock band. How will you ever be able to face your friends!"

Karyn nudged him in the ribs. "Lukie, leave her alone."

"Ahhh," he snarled as the stage lighting changed from a red to a bluish tinge. "Shut up. Here comes the new stuff."

Simon Proctor raised his hand commandingly and the deafening cheering diminished. "Hear me!" he said, his bass voice resonating throughout the hall. There was relative silence. "Not long ago I met two women, two witches—" a few scattered cheers, "—who have chosen to serve the Dark One by singing for you songs of mystery and evil. Allow me to present them to you now." More cheers and a steadily building applause. "My children, welcome Adrienne, a witch from the wilds of Transylvania, and Gwendolyn, the daughter of a druid, a witch from the mountains of Wales."

Madness descended upon the audience, and deafening applause drowned out the last few of Simon's words. The tape of Gwendolyn casting a spell on Eisenmann had been seen by most of the people present, and she had become a pop heroine in advance of this, her second public appearance. The two women walked onto the stage. To be more precise, Adrienne walked nervously to her position before a standing microphone to the side of the band, and Gwendolyn combined a slink with a strut as she moved to center stage. Both were attired as they had been on the Campbell show, and numerous rather crudely phrased expressions of appreciation drifted from the boys in the audience up to Gwendolyn's ears. She smiled and waited for the cheering to diminish.

When at last it did, she spoke into the microphone in as sensual a tone as she could manage and said, "I am Gwendolyn."

The cheering resumed, and she raised both hands to quiet it. "I have been introduced to you as a witch and the daughter of a druid, which I am. But I am also a sssss*suc*cubus." She hissed the last word, emphasizing the "suc" syllable. The boys in the crowd went wild. "Do you know what a sssss*suc*cubus is? 'Tis a demon in the shape of a woman, sent to earth by Satan to seduce and delight."

Numerous volunteers waved to her from the audience.

"Adrienne, Simon, and I shall sing you an old song from the distant past, a song about a succubus. The song is hight 'The Unquiet Grave.'"

Mark Siegal's drums set the beat for the song, and Herricks, Strube, Mahoney, and Adrienne, who was playing the lute, came in on cue. The delicate plinking sound of the old instrument, amplified electronically, combined in a bizarre but pleasant manner with the thudding bass and the buzzing lead guitar.

Simon strummed the rhythm guitar while Gwendolyn, the sole figure on stage without an instrument, stood arms akimbo before the microphone. She and Adrienne began to sing.

"Cold blows the wind to his true love,
   And gently drops the rain.
He never had but one sweetheart
   And in the greenwood she lies slain,
   And in the greenwood she lies slain.

He did as much for his sweetheart
   As any young man may.
He sat and mourned upon her grave
   For a twelvemonth and a day,
   For a twelvemonth and a day."

As she watched the performance from the wings, Rowena leaned to Jeremy and asked, loudly so as to be heard over the music, "Do you really think the kids out there are gonna like this stuff?"

He shrugged. "I don't think anybody really listens to the words, not many people, anyway. It's the general sound, the atmosphere in the hall, the visual images, stuff like that. I mean, it's a pretty melody, isn't it?"

"I'll grant Gwendolyn that," Rowena said. "The songs she comes up with are pretty. It just seems so odd to hear them rocked up like this. You know?"

"Yeah," he nodded. "But it's an interesting sound. I think they like it. Hell, I like it!"

"When the twelvemonth and one day was past,
　　Her ghost began to speak.
'Why sittest here all on my grave
　　And will not let me sleep?
　　And will not let me sleep?'

'There's but one thing I want, my love,
　　But one thing that I crave.
And that's a kiss from your cold white lips,
　　And I'll go from your grave,
　　And I'll go from your grave.'"

Strube began a lead guitar interlude which was a variation
on the melody, and as he played Gwendolyn began to dance
about the stage, swirling about and projecting an image of
licentious abandon. Her gyrations elicited cheers and catcalls.

"'My breasts they are as cold as clay,
　　My breath smells earthy strong,
And if you kiss my cold clay lips,
　　You shall not live for long,
　　You shall not live for long.'

The man lay down upon the ghost
　　And gave to her his seed.
And when his body they did find,
　　The man was dead indeed,
　　The man was dead indeed."

The loud, searing music blasted at the audience, and there
was a raw and unrestrained energy in the frenzied cheering
which erupted as soon as the final cymbal clashes signaled the
end of the song. Simon leaned over to Gwendolyn and cupped
his hand over the microphone as he said, "They love you,
babe!"

"And I thee," she said softly. He did not hear her. He was
gazing out at the thousands of cheering people, dollar signs
rushing around in his brain. "Sweet man," she murmured, not
caring that he did not hear her.

Adrienne looked off to her right and searched the faces in
the wings. Rowena, seeing her look nervously about, waved
and smiled at her. Adrienne saw the wave and, upon seeing
the smiling face, flushed slightly and returned the wave,
reassured, a bit calmed. Rowena shook her head. She isn't

going to be able to take a whole tour, she thought. Her nerves won't take it.

Gwendolyn's voice broke into her musings. "And here now a song of the highlands of Scotland, from the days when the ghoulies still prowled about the moors. . . ."

December 4

THE CROWD IN Philadelphia was even more enthusiastic than the ones they had encountered at their two performances at the Garden in New York. The numbers were smaller because the concert hall was smaller, but there was not an empty seat in the house.

"See you not that bonny bonny road
    Which winds about the fernie brae?
That is the road to Elfinland
    Where you and I this night maun gae.
Come and go,
    Come along with me,
Thomas the Rhymer. . . ."

It was Adrienne's first attempt at carrying the melody, and she managed to get through it without incident. Her tremulous soprano was again nicely balanced by Gwendolyn's alto and Simon's bass, and the overall effect was magical. Though it was doubtful if the largely teenage audience could decipher the thick Scots dialect in which the song was sung, they responded enthusiastically to the heavy sound and announced theme of the song. "Here now a song of Thomas the Rhymer," Gwendolyn had said, "a man kidnapped by the queen of the elves and given the gift of prophecy. . . ."

"'But Thomas, you must hold your tongue,
    Whatever you may hear or see,
For if a word you chance to speak,
    Never go you back to your country.'
Thomas got a cloak of the elfin cloth,
    And a pair of shoes of velvet green.
And until seven years were gone,
    Thomas on earth was never seen.
Come and go,

212

Come along with me,
Thomas the Rhymer. . . ."

The crowd went wild.

December 6

CHICAGO WAS COLD, colder even than Bradford, but the snow
and the ice and the bitter, biting wind did not have an adverse
effect upon attendance at the concert. Simon Proctor and
Witch's Sabbath did five encores, and it was clear to all that
Gwendolyn Jenkins was the center of attention and the star of
the show. In the past, in his youth, Simon might have been
jealous, might have been resentful of the easy way she
upstaged him, but at this point in his life he had no concern
other than the amount of the box office receipts.

After the final encore, as the curtain closed and the
houselights rose, Simon turned to his associates and began to
dance a merry little jig, to their general amusement. "Back up
on top, boys," he sang merrily, "back up on the tippy-top!"

"Yeah, so when do I get a raise?" Herricks asked glumly.

"You made the choice," Strube said as he unslung his guitar
and handed it to a member of the road crew. "We all had the
same choice, straight salary or percentage. You chose salary."

"Don't remind me," he grumbled. "Fucked again."

"I am *up*, I am *up!*" Simon said, hopping about the stage. "I
should be exhausted, I should be dead on my feet, but I am
up!"

"Yeah, me too," Mark Siegal said. "Let's go out and do
something."

"Are you kidding?" Herricks said. "It's colder than a—" He
stopped himself. "I mean, it's, like, real cold out there."

"He's right," Mahoney said. "Let's just send somebody out to
get some booze and we can party down in the hotel."

"The hotel has booze, you asshole," Herricks muttered. "All
you gotta do is call room service."

"Sure," Simon replied, "and pay five times what it would
cost to buy a bottle yourself!"

"Hey, listen to the rich man over here!" Herricks said,
nodding in Simon's direction. "You're a hit again, or haven't
you noticed?"

"Let's head back to the hotel," Mahoney broke in. "I got

some grass, we can send out—or call up, for some booze. I really feel like unwinding, you know?"

"Yeah, me too," Strube said. "I hate to admit it, but I was just a little nervous before the opening in New York. Sort of like this was our last shot, you know? But now—"

"Now are your fears quieted," Gwendolyn said as she wrapped her black cloak about herself. "And I agree, 'tis a time to make merry."

They left the concert hall en masse, and piled into the waiting limousines which were parked out in the rear. The crowds of yelling, screaming fans were held back by a cordon of Chicago policemen, whose irritated faces indicated that they were not pleased at being out in the cold in order to insure the safety of this band of misfits. Simon, Gwendolyn, and the band leapt into one automobile, as Rowena, Adrienne, Lucas, Karyn, and Jeremy entered another. They proceeded to speed through the white, windy streets back to their hotel.

"Up to Simon's suite!" Mahoney intoned jovially as they entered the hotel lobby. He turned to the desk clerk. "Please send an assortment of liquors up to Mr. Proctor's rooms. Only the best!"

"And you?" Adrienne asked Rowena. "They intend to make merry. Will you join them?" Her pleading eyes and apprehensive voice made it clear that she dreaded the prospect.

"Are you kidding?" Rowena said. "All I want to do is watch some TV and go to sleep."

She sighed in relief. "I do not wish to attend either. Can I stay with you a while?"

"Sure," she smiled. "What about you, Jeremy?"

He shrugged. "I don't know. I thought I'd kind of like to go to the party—I mean, if you don't mind. I'd like to have a few drinks, maybe—"

"Hey, what are you doin', askin' fuckin' permission, for Christ's sake?" Lucas said with disgust. "Come on, Sloan, just come with us and party down."

Rowena cast her brother an annoyed look, and then turned her eyes coldly to Jeremy. "Do what you want. I'll see you tomorrow." She turned and walked toward the elevator with Adrienne scampering behind her.

"You know what I think?" Lucas asked as he watched the elevator doors close.

"What?" Jeremy asked.

"I think Adrienne has the hots for Row."

"Oh, Lukie," Karyn said from beside him, "that's ridiculous! She isn't gay!"

"Yeah?" he asked skeptically. "How the hell do you know? Did you try to find out or something?"

"Funny, real funny," she said. "She just likes Row, that's all. Row makes her feel safe. Hell, nobody else even pays any attention to her, 'cept when Gwendolyn bosses her around."

"Yeah, maybe," he conceded. "But I still think that chick is nuts, the way she always looks like she's about to flip out, the way she follows Rowena around like a little puppy dog."

"Yeah, yeah, right," Karyn said impatiently, not at all interested. "Let's go up to your dad's room and have some fun."

Jeremy looked at her increasingly swollen belly. "Hey, Karyn, don't you think maybe you should take it easy? I mean, it's—"

"Goddamn it, Jeremy, don't you start with me!" she snapped.

As the elevator doors opened, Rowena fished around in her purse for the key to her room and said, "You sang real pretty tonight."

"Thank you," Adrienne said, apparently quite pleased at the compliment.

"I've read about that guy Thomas the Rhymer in English class. He was a character in one of Walter Scott's novels. Have you ever read it? It's called—oh, I can't remember the title."

"But I am sure that it is unknown to me," Adrienne said. "I have read very few novels. My parents did not approve of frivolous pastimes."

Rowena laughed as she unlocked the hotel door and pushed it open. "Well, Sir Walter Scott is hardly Sidney Sheldon!" she said. "There are lots of real good books, good novels. Surely your parents didn't disapprove of all of them."

"Nay, but they did," she said sadly. "Oh, I wanted to read, to learn things, to find pleasure in stories, but they were withheld from me."

"Boy, that's weird," she said. She tossed her purse and coat on the bed and switched on the television. "Was it a religious thing? I mean, you're probably Orthodox, right? Isn't that the religion in Romania? Orthodox?"

"I am a witch," she reminded her. Rowena looked at her deeply for a moment, and then wordlessly began to search through the channels on the television.

"Hey, here's an old *Columbo* episode. You like *Columbo?*"

"Anything you wish is fine," Adrienne said, unwrapping her cloak and placing it upon the back of the chair upon which she proceeded to sit. Anything is better than being with the others, she thought, especially with *her*.

They watched the show in silence, Rowena stretched out upon the bed and Adrienne staring at the picture screen without seeming to watch it. Nearly an hour went by, and then a loud knocking was heard on the door. Rowena went over and said, "Who is it?"

"Hey, like, open up!" It was Lucas, and his slurred words indicated that he was very, very drunk.

"What do you want?" she asked, being in no mood to admit him.

He pounded again upon the door, more forcefully. "Hey, Row, open the fuckin' door!" he shouted.

She opened the lock and swung the door open quickly. "Lucas, will you keep your voice down? Jeeze! It's late! People are trying to sleep!"

He waved away her rebuke. "Ah, fuck 'em." He looked past her to Adrienne. "Hey, Gwendolyn wants you to come to the party. She sent me down here to get you."

Adrienne sighed and trembled slightly. "Very well," she muttered.

"Hey, wait a minute," Rowena said. "Why do you take orders from her? If you don't want to go, don't go! She isn't your owner!"

Adrienne shook her head. "I must do as she requests." She stood up and smoothed out the skirt of the flowing white gown she still wore from the night's performance.

"Well, dammit!" Rowena said. "I'm going to go and give that bitch a piece of my mind!"

Lucas laughed as if he were guarding some dark secret. "Uh, Row, I don't think you should go to this party."

"Why not?" she asked bitterly. "You don't think I know that you're all a bunch of perverted junkies?" She stepped into her shoes and said, "Let's go. Somebody has to put that woman in her place!" She stormed out of the room, with Lucas and Adrienne following behind her.

They rode the elevator up two more floors in silence. As the doors opened, Rowena turned to Adrienne and said, "They passed the Thirteenth Amendment a long time ago, you know!"

"I—I beg your—?"

"Abolition of slavery," she muttered, furious at Adrienne for her weakness, furious at herself for not telling Gwendolyn off long before this, furious at her father for a multitude of reasons.

216

She threw open the door to her father's suite of rooms, and the words she planned to say died upon her lips as she surveyed the scene before her. The room was murky with smoke, tobacco and marijuana mingling in the atmosphere. In one corner, Siegal, Herricks, and Strube were sitting on the floor with four naked girls, snorting a white powder through a rolled-up dollar bill. The girls were members of the vast throng of willing, nubile, brainless young women who follow rock bands around the country, camp followers of a drug-soaked army. Another girl was kneeling on the couch, her face pressed down into the cushions, her rear thrust obscenely upward, as Tom Mahoney bounced merrily up and down upon her. Jeremy Sloan sat alone at a table, holding a can of beer and watching the surrounding activities with undisguised discomfort. And in the middle of the room, Simon Proctor was lounging back in a soft easy chair, his hands behind his head, as a naked Gwendolyn Jenkins knelt in front of him, her face buried in his crotch.

"Daddy!" she cried, her voice filled with shock and pain.

Her father looked over at her absently, his red eyes able to open only halfway. He tried to focus on her, but could not. "Huh?" he muttered.

Gwendolyn looked up and grinned maliciously. "Ah, the virgins have arrived!" she cackled. She stood to her feet and released her grip on Simon's erect organ. Rowena turned her eyes away. "My dear little friend," she said to Adrienne, "you are not in truth a virgin, as we both well know."

"Gwendolyn—please—" Adrienne whimpered.

"Our friend Larry has made a most impolite observation," she said, ignoring her and strolling over to Herricks. He took the rolled-up bill from his nose and got unsteadily to his feet. "He made the comment that this night was—how did you say it, my dear Larry?"

He blushed slightly. "I didn't mean nothin'. It's just an expression."

"Colder than a witch's tit, I believe those were the words." She laughed and, grabbing both his hands, placed them upon her breasts and squeezed them hard. "I have already demonstrated to him that my bosom is warm, but I think he wonders still about yours." She released Herricks's hands with a laugh and turned back to Adrienne. "It is up to you to defend our kind, my dear friend." The smile remained on her face, but it became suddenly cold and hateful. "You will give yourself to this man, here and now."

"Please," she moaned. "I don't—"

"Remember who you are, and who I am," Gwendolyn said sternly. She pointed to an empty spot on the carpet. "There. Right now. Obey me!"

Rowena exploded at her. "Who the hell do you think you are, Goddamn it!"

She laughed. "Oh, He will, no doubt, no doubt!"

Adrienne reached beneath her dress and pulled her underpants down to her ankles and then stepped out of them. She began to walk slowly, mournfully over to the place which Gwendolyn had indicated.

"Adrienne, stop it!" Rowena shouted. "You don't have to do this!"

She felt a hand on her shoulder and spun around to see Karyn, staggeringly drunk, her blouse open, her breasts and belly both protruding outward, standing there and smiling insipidly. "You know, kid, no offense, but you belong in, like, a convent or something, you know?"

Rowena grabbed her hand and thrust it violently from her. "Karyn, you're disgusting!"

As Lucas reached around Karyn from behind and began roughly kneading her breasts, she giggled, "Nobody's perfect."

Adrienne lay down upon her back, wordlessly, her eyes closed, her pale face frozen into a blank, impassive, distant expression. "Adrienne, no!" Rowena shouted.

"Becalm yourself, child," Gwendolyn said. "Our dear friend Adrienne has not known a man for many years. She fights it, but she feels the need burning deep within her. And so must you."

"You—you—*bitch*!" Rowena spat.

"Aye, that and much else." She nodded in mock agreement. She gestured over toward Jeremy. "There is a man whom you desire, who desires you. Both your loins burn with desire for each other, do they not? Does not your womb need to be filled by him? Give yourself to him now, and stop this childish play!"

"You—I—I—you—" Rowena stammered, growing red with fury and embarrassment.

Herricks stumbled over toward them, his eyes glaring at Adrienne with a bestial need. She pulled her dress up past her waist, and bent her legs at the knee, spreading them wide apart. Her face was a frozen mask, waxlike, blank.

"Adrienne, stop it!" Rowena cried. "I'll leave, I'll go home, so help me God I will!"

"Then go and begone!" Gwendolyn said, laughing. "Hell has no need of nuns!" She turned to Herricks. "She is yours."

As Herricks leapt upon Adrienne and impaled her roughly, Rowena cast one last desperate look at her father's besotted face and then ran from the room, slamming the door loudly behind her. She ran down the two flights of stairs, too upset to stand patiently and wait for the elevator, and then rushed into her room, weeping bitterly.

"Daddy, I'll never speak to you again," she wept to herself. "You're a horrible man, horrible! I hate you!"

She grabbed the telephone from the night table beside the bed and dialed the desk. Pull yourself together, she thought. Calm down.

She waited a few moments and then said, "Yes, this is Rowena Proctor in room 432. Please connect me with USAir." She waited. "Yes, I'd like to arrange for a ticket from Chicago to Burlington, Vermont. As soon as possible." She waited again. "That will be fine. . . . No, not round trip. One way. One ticket."

"Two," Jeremy said from the doorway. "Make it two tickets, Row."

She looked at him and began to weep afresh. "Two tickets, please. Two one-way tickets to Burlington." He walked over to her and they hugged tightly. She was barely able to concentrate on the voice which spoke to her on the phone. "I love you, Jeremy," she said.

"And I love you, Row. I love you very much. And I'm very sorry about this whole damned thing. I've had it with this bullshit, honest I have." He kissed away her tears. "I'm gonna go back home and get a job and start acting like a normal human being, okay?"

"Okay," she sniffed. She snapped her attention to the phone. "I'm sorry, what did you say? . . . Fine. That will be fine. Thank you." She placed the phone down. "We have to pack. The plane leaves in two hours. We can call Gramps from the airport in Burlington. I'm sure he'll come and get us."

"It'll be awful early in the morning."

"He won't mind, not when it means we're coming home." They embraced again, and she continued to weep, and he continued to soothe her. "I hate them," she muttered. "I hate all of them!"

December 8

IT WAS WHAT Southerners refer to as sweater weather in St. Louis, Missouri, and it was a welcome change from Chicago's blustering, biting cold. The troupe had arrived in the self-proclaimed Gateway to the West late in the evening of the previous day, generally hung over, washed out, and miserable, and most of them were taking the opportunity to sleep and rest. The concert scheduled for the coming night would be the first ever Simon Proctor and Witch's Sabbath had played this far west, and all were hoping that it would be as great a success as the others thus far on the tour. It seemed that almost overnight they had gone from being a regionally known band on the brink of catastrophe to a national news item; but they were professional enough and experienced enough to know how quickly such luck could dissipate. So they slept and rested, anticipating the evening with anxiety and eagerness.

Most of them slept, that is. As the morning sun rose over the city and its rays began to dance upon the brownish waters of the Mississippi River, Adrienne Lupescu strolled quietly and morosely along its banks, ignoring the rude catcalls of the dock workers and the wolf whistles which followed her along the shore. She walked with her head down, her hands thrust into the pockets of her long cloak, the cool morning wind whipping through her brown hair. She heard the sound of light footfalls behind her, and she stopped and turned. Gwendolyn Jenkins was following her some twenty yards away, and she stopped also. The two women stared at each other for a few moments, and then Adrienne walked on. She could hear the footsteps recommence from behind her, and she strove to ignore them.

She came to a railing which bordered an observation deck overlooking the river, and she stopped and leaned against it. Gwendolyn stopped walking for a moment, and then slowly came closer. She stopped about six feet away and imitated Adrienne in leaning against the railing and gazing out at the muddy water. Neither spoke for what seemed a long while. At last Gwendolyn said, "The water seems impure, sullied."

"This age is impure and sullied," Adrienne muttered.

Gwendolyn shrugged. "It is as any age."

220

They fell silent again. Then Adrienne spoke, without turning her eyes toward the other woman. "Why did you do that to me?"

"You know why," she replied.

"'Twas unkind and unfair," Adrienne said.

"Aye," came the reply, "and what you did was unkind and unfair. All would have been well, but for your weakness and fear."

"Then you should have chosen another," she spat. "I'll not apologize for being what I am!"

"Chosen another!" She laughed incredulously. "And when did I choose you?! You chose to be part of the plot, you joined the scheme from its first day! I never chose you, my dear. You chose *me*, me and Betty and Mercy and the others! You chose *us*!" She sniffed. "All would have been well, had you not been one with us."

Adrienne did not reply. They leaned over the railing and stared down at the river bank as the sluggish waves lapped upon it. They stood silently as the sounds of the awakening city reached their ears. Adrienne sighed. "You needed not to shame me before the girl."

"What matter? The girl is of no importance."

"She is my friend," Adrienne said weakly, tears beginning to well up in her eyes.

"You have no friends," Gwendolyn said bitterly. "Once you had friends, as you may recall, but you abandoned us when we needed you. Or at least, you attempted to abandon us."

"I miss her. She went home to New England." Adrienne wept.

"Then make it a good miss, for she has no place in this, neither she nor that eunuch she loves." A grim chuckle. "He will be best man, I think, when I marry Simon Proctor. We'll be needing a virgin's blood."

"I want to go home," Adrienne cried. "I want to go home!"

"Home! Whither be home?! Mean you to New England, or to your more recent abode?"

Adrienne grew visibly more pallid. She did not reply.

"No more of this nonsense. Come, return with me. We perform again tonight."

"I don't want to sing tonight."

Gwendolyn Jenkins turned and faced her, folding her arms angrily across her chest. "Oh, indeed! And when was your opinion asked?" She walked slowly, threateningly toward her, and Adrienne recoiled from her approach. "I asked not for your opinion!"

"And—and yet, I may have one," she muttered timidly.

"No, you may not!" Gwendolyn hissed. "No more than you asked my opinion before denouncing me in court as a liar! No more than you asked my opinion when you strove to put my neck in a noose! Nor did you ask Mercy Lewis or Betty Parris for their opinions before you put their lives in jeopardy!"

Adrienne was walking backward, away from her, trembling. "I was afeard—I was afeard—"

Gwendolyn stopped walking, and laughed. "Then, now, always. A rabbit you are, silly girl, a frightened little rabbit." She shook her head. "Come," she said evenly. "Let us return." She turned and began to walk purposefully back along the route they had just come. Adrienne watched her for a few moments and then followed at a slower pace, wiping the tears from her cheeks.

December 10

PEOPLE TEND TO think of New Orleans as a relatively normal city, except, of course, for the brief annual outburst of madness of the Mardi Gras. But this attitude falls far short of the truth, as anyone who has ever spent time in New Orleans can attest. It is a city of perpetual carnival, of perpetual merrymaking, and Mardi Gras is but a highly publicized example, albeit in an extreme form, of a perennial view of life.

Thus it was that Simon Proctor and Witch's Sabbath approached their New Orleans concert with some trepidation. This would be a difficult crowd to entrance, shock, amuse, or surprise. This would be a crowd which had seen it all and done it all. Winning them over would not be easy, especially inasmuch as the band was still a relatively unknown commodity in this part of the country.

They need not have worried. The Orleansoisie were predisposed to drink in the bizarre and the arcane, and the stage show presented to them that night was like liquor to an alcoholic. They sucked upon the musical pipe and Simon filled it with audio and visual opium. From the moment Gwendolyn sauntered onto the stage, the cheers and shouts were almost continuous, all but obliterating the lyrics and the blasting music. The old, chilling sea chantey which Simon sang dripped with violence, hatred, and death, but it was the frenzied, lascivious dance which Gwendolyn executed hither and yon upon the stage which aroused the crowd. She banged a tambourine above her head and upon her thrusting hip as she spun about in time to the old song of murder and pillage.

"Sailed I have on the open sea,
   Waging war on the ships of kings.
Skilled I am at piracy.
   'Tis a skill that battle brings.
Long have I sailed this outlaw hull
   'Neath the flag of the bone and skull,
Sailing o'er the blood red waves
   Of a sea of dead men."

The words were largely unknown to the audience, and would doubtless remain so, as they remained largely unheard over the din of the frenzied crowd; but the atmosphere and attitude of the song communicated themselves, and tumult arose from the multitude when key words reached their ears through the maelstrom of cheers.

"Give me a cutlass sharp and bright,
   Give me a swab to cool my gun.
Give me a hot and a lusty fight,
   Give me grog and give me rum.
Like a plague I roam the world,
   Killing the men and raping the girls,
Stealing silver, gold, and gems
   From the hands of dead men."

The Caribbean rhythm which Mahoney and Siegal imparted to the song on bass and drums merged in an odd but somehow compelling manner with the language of the seventeenth-century ruffians who had once sung the song to the rhythm of raising sail or hoisting anchor. Gwendolyn seemed to snap her hips abruptly from side to side with each heavily accented beat of the song.

"When I die and go to hell,
   I will sit on Satan's knee.
What a tale of terror I'll tell
   Of my life of piracy.
Many are the thieveries I've made,

223

Rape and murder my stock in trade.
I have turned my path into
A road of dead men."

During the musical frenzy which Strube tore into before the last verse, Gwendolyn picked up a prop skull from behind the amplifiers and began to prance about the stage, holding it aloft, pretending to taunt the grinning sardonicus with her lips and her bosom. Then she spun about madly until she came to rest beside Simon and joined him in the chorus.

"Fifteen men on a dead man's chest,
  Yo ho ho and a bottle of rum!
Drink! and the Devil be done for the rest!
  Yo ho ho and a bottle of rum!
Raise the Jolly Roger high!
  Fly the skull in the crimson sky!
Fifteen thieves drinking rum in a toast
  To the souls of dead men!"

The song ended with an abrupt, ear-splitting blast from all the instruments, and the audience, startled, allowed almost two seconds of silence to intervene between the final note and the mad applause which then ensued. Simon stood imperiously upon the stage, a king, as it were, surveying his kingdom, and he called out into the microphone, "For you, Lafitte! For you, Jean Lafitte, cutthroat, pirate, buccaneer! For you, demon of the high seas!"

The ovation was deafening, cries of ecstatic, intoxicated enthusiasm for Simon and the band mingling with shouts of praise for the infamous Louisiana pirate of whom, were the truth to be known, very few of the people in the audience had ever heard. But that was of no matter. The cheers went on and on.

December 12

SIMON DRUMMED his fingers impatiently upon the wall beside the hanging telephone and then glanced up at the wall clock which hung above the stage door entrance. He listened to the unanswered ringing on the other end of the line and muttered, "Shit!"

Then he heard the receiver being picked up and Rowena's voice, distant and a bit fuzzy, say, "Hello?"

"Hi, Row? It's your dad. Listen, honey, I wanted to—"

She hung up.

Simon breathed heavily, anger mixing with embarrassment and guilt, and he dialed the number once more. Goddamn dial phones! he thought irritably. Takes five seconds to call a number on a push-button phone, and here I gotta wait for the fuckin' dial to spin back. . . .

He waited, listening to the clicking as the connection was made. Once again he heard the phone ring, and once again heard the receiver being picked up. "Hello?" Rowena said.

"Rowena, don't hang up! Listen to—"

She hung up.

"Goddamn it, Row!" he shouted into the dead phone. He dialed again, ripping the dial around angrily. He waited again, listened again, continued to drum his fingers on the wall.

The receiver was picked up. "Ay-yah?" said old Floyd.

"Dad? That you?"

"Ay-yah."

"Dad, listen to me. Can you put Row on the line and keep her from hanging up? I gotta talk to her."

"Sorry, boy, I can't do that."

"What do you mean? Put Row on the line!"

"Nope."

Simon took the receiver from his ear and stared at it in astonishment. Then he said, "Damn it, Dad, I want to talk to my daughter! Will you put her on and keep her from hanging up?"

Floyd hung up.

"Dad? Dad? Goddamn it!" he shouted. He slammed the receiver back into its holder and closed his eyes, trying to calm himself. He was tired, very tired. The flight from New Orleans to Dallas had followed a very late night at the concert hall, and Gwendolyn had kept him awake until after dawn that morning. He had another show that night, and the strain of the constant schedule of flights and performances was beginning to tell on him. Not twenty-five anymore, he reminded himself. Can't party until dawn, drink so much, snort so much coke, screw so much. Gotta slow down.

Gotta straighten things out with Rowena.

He dialed the phone number of the old Proctor Inn in Bradford once more, slowly, almost painfully. He waited and listened. He heard the receiver once again being picked up.

"Ay-yah?" Floyd said.

"Dad, listen to me—DON'T HANG UP!—I'm calling from two thousand miles away on a stage courtesy phone, but all the calls are being charged to the rental fee of the hall, so this is costing me a small fortune here! Okay? So listen, okay?"

A pause. "What do you want, boy?" Floyd asked coldly.

Simon sighed. "Dad, I know that Row's angry, but I have to talk to her and try to—"

"She ain't angry, boy," his father said heatedly. "She's disgusted and she's ashamed!"

"Oh, for Christ's sake, Dad—"

"Listen, boy, what the hell'dya expect was gonna happen? Row's a good girl, a normal human being! How'dya expect her to feel after what she was subjected to?"

Oh, great, Row, he thought. Run home and describe everything. "Look, Dad, I'd had a little too much to drink, and I—"

"Simon, you're a disgrace. You've been a source of shame to me all your worthless life, and now you're shamin' your daughter. She doesn't want to talk to you, she doesn't want to hear any apologies, she doesn't want to have anything to do with you."

"Oh, really!" he said, offended and annoyed. "That's gonna be damned hard, with us living under the same roof!"

"Simon, listen to me. You shouldn't come back here. You should—"

"What the hell do you mean I shouldn't come back there! It's my goddamn house, for Christ's sake!!!"

"Boy, if you come back here after the concerts are over, she's likely to do something foolish, like run off and marry the Sloan boy. And she's too young for that."

"What are you talking about?" he shouted. "I told Jeremy that I didn't want—"

"They're keepin' company real close, boy. Ever since they come back they been with each other every day. He stays over sometimes."

Simon saw red. "WHAT DO YOU MEAN HE STAYS OVER? JESUS, DAD—"

"Oh, he sleeps on the couch downstairs," Floyd said easily. "He ain't like you, boy. He's a good boy. Worth twice of the likes of you."

Simon took a deep breath and counted to ten. Then, forcing calmness, he said, "Dad, listen to me very carefully. You tell Row that I'll be home in about two weeks. Tell her that I have to talk to her and explain things. Tell her that I expect her to be

226

home when I get there. And you tell Jeremy Sloan that if he lays a hand on my daughter, I'll break his fuckin' neck! You got that?" No answer. "Dad? You got that?"

Floyd sighed. "Thank God your momma isn't alive to see—"

This time it was Simon's turn to hang up on somebody. Goddamn stupid old fool, he thought bitterly. You think I like truckin' around the whole goddamn country like this? I'm keeping a roof over your head, you stupid old man!

He felt a hand on his shoulder, and he turned around to see Mark Siegal standing there, looking concerned and just a bit frightened. "Hey, Simon, I think we got a problem."

"What's the matter? It isn't Adrienne, is it?"

"Oh, no, no. She's okay."

"I mean, ever since that night, she's been weirder than usual."

"How can you tell?" Siegal laughed slightly.

Simon laughed also, but humorlessly. "No kidding, Markie. Every night when we go onstage, I expect her to—well—"

"Flip out?" Siegal finished for him. "Forget it, man. People don't have nervous breakdowns that easily."

"I guess not," he agreed. "But sometimes I wonder about her, and about Gwen too. I mean, neither of them are exactly normal people. They're both space cadets." He and Siegal laughed again, and then Simon asked, "So what's the problem?"

"We got a massive demonstration outside. The stage manager—what's his name—?"

"Sokolowsky," Simon reminded him.

"Whatever. He put in a call for the cops, but the city's kind of annoyed at so many of their guys being assigned to us as it is."

"What kind of demonstration is it?" Simon asked. "We talkin' fans, or what?"

"Hardly! We got a crowd of pulpit-thumpers out there."

"Shit!" Simon spat. "Are they blocking the ticket booth?"

"Of course they are. That's why they're out there. They got signs and loudspeakers and all that stuff."

Gwendolyn walked up behind them. "Is aught amiss?" she asked.

"What?" Simon spun around. "Oh, hiya, Gwen. You and Larry work out the chords for the golem song?"

"The what?" Siegal asked.

"Tell you later." To Gwendolyn, "Worked out okay?"

"'Tis fine," she said. "But your face is troubled."

"Oh, it's nothing. There are some demonstrators outside, screwing up ticket sales. It doesn't matter, really. The concert's practically sold out already anyway."

"Then why are you troubled?" she asked.

He shrugged. "Just bothers me, that's all. I don't need a bunch of Holy Rollers giving me bad PR right now. We've never done a gig this far west, and—"

"What are Holy Rollers?"

"You know, Bible Belt bigots."

She considered this for a moment, trying to sift through his rather imprecise description and arrive at a meaning. "Mean you ministers?"

"Yeah, sure, there's gotta be ministers out there. Right, Markie?"

"Oh, yeah, absolutely. There's some guy out there on a platform, waving a Bible around and screaming bloody murder."

Gwendolyn's eyes narrowed and her lips pursed. "Damn all ministers," she muttered darkly. "I hate them, my love, I hate them with every fiber of m'body. Be damned to all of them."

Simon laughed uneasily, surprised at her vehemence. "Yeah, well, it's not all that important. Besides, they're just trying to protect their—I don't know, their 'flocks' from our influence. Just ignore them. They don't matter. They're fighting a losing battle in this society, anyway."

Gwendolyn was not listening. Her balled fists were beating very lightly at her sides, and her eyes flashed a steely light. "Take me out unto them!" she commanded.

"Hey, Gwen," Siegal said. "Forget it. It isn't that important. Really, just forget it." Even though it was his concern which had brought the situation to Simon's attention, he did not like the look in the woman's eyes.

"I will go out to them," she insisted. "If you will not accompany me, then I shall confront them alone!"

"Gwen," Simon laughed nervously, "there isn't any need to confront anyone at all. Just forget it!" The phone beside him rang, startling him. He reached for it impulsively. "Hello? Rowena?"

"Simon? That you?" said the distant, tinny voice.

He was disappointed. "Oh, hiya, Harry. What's up?"

"They told me I could find you at this number, so I—"

"Yeah, yeah, right. What's up?"

Harry Schroeder's words were unintelligible as Gwendolyn said loudly, "Simon Proctor, I will go out to them. Are you coming or not?"

"Wait a minute, Gwen, wait a minute." To Schroeder he said, "Harry, are you at your office?"

"Yeah. Why?"

"Let me call you back. We got a situation here."

"Yeah, sure, okay. Don't forget, okay? It's important."

"Okay, okay. Talk to you later." He hung up and turned to Gwendolyn. "Listen, Gwen—"

"Bah!" she spat in disgust. "Do you fear ministers?!"

Simon stiffened. "Hey, look, I lived in Brooklyn for ten years. I ain't afraid of anything!"

"Fine!" she said. "Then accompany me!" She spun about on her heel and began to walk toward the corridor beside the stage which would take her to the front of the concert hall. Simon cast Mark Siegal a pained look and reluctantly followed after her.

Siegal watched them leave. "Their first fight," he muttered to himself with amusement.

Gwendolyn walked to the entrance doors of the hall without looking back to see if Simon was following her. She knew he was. She pulled open the large metal doors and walked out into the angry, shouting crowd. If she felt any fear, she was successful in masking it, for her face bespoke nothing but arrogance, anger, confidence, and pride.

"That's one of them," a voice in the crowd rang out.

"That's the one who says she's a witch!" another shouted.

"There's Simon Proctor! There's Simon Proctor!"

"Get out of Texas!"

"Go back east!"

"Sinners! Sinners!"

"Leave our children alone!"

Simon came up behind Gwendolyn and said, "Look, this is nuts! Let's go back inside. This is dangerous!"

She turned to him, a look of annoyance and disappointment flashing at him. "I trust my Master, Simon Proctor. If you cannot trust him, then at least trust me."

A middle-aged man approached them through the crowd, pushing his way to the front, parting the sign-carrying, shouting throng. His clear brown eyes blazed with righteous indignation and wrath, and he held an old, tattered Bible before him as if it were a shield. He came to a halt in front of Gwendolyn and stared at her with disgust. Simon stood behind her, attempting to remain calm, fighting the urge to cower or flee.

"I am Ted Earl, pastor of Calvary Church," he said in a loud, booming voice. The crowd quieted down instantly, listening to their leader with rapt attentiveness. "Mr. Proctor, we've come here today to demand that—"

"It is I who have come out to meet with you, not he!" Gwendolyn interrupted. "Do not ignore me, minister, for the power of Satan moves through me, not through him!"

"Yes, I know who you are," Earl said angrily. "I've seen the news shows. I saw you frighten a man to death. You belong in prison, or in a mental institution, not on a stage corrupting our children." His remarks were followed by a frenzied outburst of cheers and imprecations from the crowd.

"So you know me," she shouted over the din as the crowd began to close in upon them threateningly and Simon's face began to lose its color. "Then you must also know that I am powerful and to be feared!"

"You are to be pitied and to be shunned!" the minister cried out. "You are come among us as a leper, a moral leper! You are a woman possessed, a poor, loathsome tool of Satan!" More shouts and cries of agreement.

Gwendolyn smiled and her eyes went wide as she nodded. "Well! At last I meet someone who has some inkling of the truth!"

"You are—" Earl began.

"I am Gwendolyn Jenkins!" she outshouted him. "I am a servant of Satan and a witch, and I defy you to test your powers against mine!" There was a stunned silence. "You claim to serve the Almighty God, do you not?"

"I have been washed in the blood of the Lamb," Earl said. "I have come here to stop this blasphemy from polluting our city. I have not come here to engage you in a contest of tricks!"

"Ha! Tricks, is it! Do you remember the story of Elijah and the prophets of Baal, minister? Is your trust in your feeble God so much less than his?"

This statement brought cries of outrage from the crowd, and Simon felt a few hands shove him roughly forward into Gwendolyn. He began to tremble, terrified at the mindless presence of what was rapidly becoming a mob.

"Elijah was a prophet of God!" Earl shouted. "I am but His lowly servant!"

"And as big a fool," she laughed harshly. "The power in this world belongs to the lord of this world, not to your silly, petulant deity!"

The hands which began to grab at her were thrust imperiously away, but there were too many for her to resist them all. "You are a blasphemous animal!" Earl shouted. "You will *not* be permitted to spread your perversions here among our children!"

Simon felt a fist thud into the small of his back, and then another struck him in the face. He fell backward, jolts of pain radiating from his mouth and spine. The sound of the police siren and the commanding voice from the bullhorn, ordering the crowd to move aside, seemed to him to be like the bugle of the cavalry in the midst of an Indian attack. He managed to pull himself to his feet, and grabbing Gwendolyn roughly by the arm, he stumbled back to the doors of the concert hall and ran inside.

A policeman followed them in, a young man with a square jaw and an overly officious manner. "Are you two injured?" he asked.

"No, no, I'm okay," he stammered.

"I am unharmed," Gwendolyn said evenly. The officer nodded curtly and then returned to the fledgling riot without. She turned to Simon and said, "Damn all ministers!"

He took her shoulders in his hands and shook her. "What the hell is wrong with you?!" he shouted. "Were you trying to get us killed or something?!"

"Tosh," she said easily. "No harm is done."

"Yeah, sure, because the cops showed up! If they hadn't, we might both be on our way to the fucking hospital right now, if we weren't beaten to death!" He released her and turned away, shaking his head in amazement. "My God, Gwen! You don't say the things you said to a mob like that!"

She shrugged. "You are too timid a man, Simon. You must be stronger, more forthright, like your—" She stopped speaking abruptly.

"Like my what?" he asked.

She studied him for a moment and then smiled. " 'Tis of no matter. I love you as you are. Naught needs changing."

Siegal and Mahoney came running up to them, Adrienne following behind them nervously. "What the hell happened?" Siegal asked. "I heard a lot of shouting and then the siren—"

"Miss Congeniality over here nearly got us killed just now!" Simon spat, jerking his thumb at Gwendolyn. She smiled patiently.

"No shit!" Siegal exclaimed. "You okay?"

"Some Holy Rollers belted me a couple of times, but I'll survive." He turned back to Gwendolyn. "Listen to me good!

231

You pull anything like that again, and we're through, you got me? We're yesterday's news, we're finished!"

She reached up and stroked his cheek, grinning with amusement. "And do you think I would be so easy to dismiss?"

"I'm not kidding, Gwen!"

She nodded, still smiling condescendingly. "Yes, yes. Very well. I am sorry."

He stood for a few moments, staring at her. He had not expected an apology, and he did not quite know how to react to it. Then he sniffed and said, "I gotta go call Harry." He walked away from them, back down the corridor toward the back of the stage.

Gwendolyn watched him go, still smiling. Mahoney asked, "Hey, Gwen, what the hell happened out there?"

She shrugged. "A trifle. 'Twas nothing."

"Yeah? Simon didn't look like it was nothing!"

"He was frightened and upset." She began to follow Simon.

"Hold on," Mahoney said, starting after her. "What happened?" Siegal and Adrienne followed a pace behind him.

"A crowd of enemies threatened us and denounced us, and I stood up to them," she said over her shoulder, continuing down the corridor.

"Enemies—what—?" Mahoney began.

"Like Moral Majority types," Siegal explained. "They were demonstrating out there, carrying signs and stuff like that."

Mahoney laughed with disbelief. "And you started an argument with them?! Are you nuts?!"

Gwendolyn stopped short and turned viciously on the slender bass player. "I'll not be rebuked by you, nor by any man! Guard your tongue!" She spun around and continued to walk away.

Mahoney's Gaelic temper rose to the surface. "Hey! Who the hell—?"

"Shhh, no," Adrienne said, taking him gently by the arm. "No, Tom. Leave her be. Ignore her. She is strong willed and dangerous."

"Yeah, but, shit! All I did was—"

"I know, I know," she soothed. "I have known her for many years, and you must heed me when I say that it is useless to spar with her."

Mahoney's anger began to subside. "Well—"

"Please," she said, a hint of fear and desperation creeping into her voice. "It will but worsen matters."

He shrugged as if reluctantly allowing himself to be pacified. "Oh, well—okay, okay."

They walked on toward the back of the stage in silence, and they found Simon babbling excitedly into the telephone with Gwendolyn standing beside him, gazing at him quizzically. Whatever it was which had made him so excited, it was obviously information to which she was not as yet privy.

"Okay. . . . Okay, yeah, sure," he was saying with enthusiasm. "Yeah, the itinerary's the same. . . . No, no problem. . . . Let them edit it themselves. . . . Yeah, day after tomorrow in Phoenix'll be great. . . . Right. . . . Twelve noon. . . . That'll give 'em plenty of time to set up." He paused as Harry Schroeder spoke to him at length. "Holy shit! That's a great idea, a great idea! Are you sure we can get permission from—?" Another pause. "And they agreed?! . . . Fantastic! Fantastic! This'll make a fortune, Harry, a fortune!" Another pause. "I'm not getting carried away at all! I just know how these things work, how much dough they make. Harry"—and he laughed into the phone—"you are a genius, a genius! Yeah. . . . Yeah. . . . Okay. . . . Okay. . . . Right, day after tomorrow, noon, at the hall. Okay. Bye." He hung up.

Mark Siegal grinned questioningly. "What happened, Simon? You win the lottery or something?"

He turned to them eagerly. "Where are Larry and Carl?"

"Working out an arrangement," Siegal said. "Why?"

"Go get 'em."

"Why? What's—"

"Markie, just go get 'em!" Siegal shrugged and then ran off to find the other two members of the band.

"Hey, Simon, what's the big news here?" Mahoney asked.

"Hold on, hold on," he said happily. "I want everybody to hear this." He took out a cigarette, lighted it, and smoked it in silence. A few minutes passed, and at last Siegal returned with Herricks and Strube in tow.

"Okay, so here they are," Siegal said. "So what's going on?"

"Okay, listen," Simon said seriously. "Harry Schroeder has set up a deal with Shalcom—"

"Shalcom?" Herricks asked. "Aren't they the people who produce all those concert videos?"

"A concert video?" Mahoney said. "We're gonna make a concert video?"

"That's terrific!" Strube exclaimed. "There's a lot of money in videos." Gwendolyn and Adrienne listened attentively but said nothing.

233

"Lots and lots and *lots* of money," Simon grinned.

"Is this part of the arrangement we have now?" Herricks asked.

"What do you mean?"

"I mean, is this part of the tour, with all rights to the video company, or is a new contract going to be signed?"

"Oh—" Simon was momentarily nonplussed, "I'm sure a new contract with them is necessary. Shit, I should have asked Harry—"

"Then I want a *percentage*, not a fuckin' salary," Herricks said bitterly. "I ain't gettin' stiffed again!"

"Yeah, yeah, whatever," Simon said petulantly, annoyed at being interrupted. "They're gonna meet us in Phoenix day after tomorrow and start filming concert footage. They'll come with us for the rest of the tour—"

"And use the best performances for the video!" Strube finished for him. "Great!"

"Simon," Gwendolyn said, "I do not understand. What will be happening?"

"We'll be making even more and more money, that's what'll be happening," he said happily. Then, to everyone, he said, "And there's more. You know the way the tour's been set up— we go to Los Angeles from Phoenix, sweep up to Seattle, then across the country to Milwaukee and Toledo and Buffalo, right?"

"Right," Siegal and Mahoney answered in unison.

"Well, the last concert date is in Boston on the twenty-second. The next day, the twenty-third—"

"The solstice," Gwendolyn observed.

"The what?"

"The winter solstice, December twenty-third," she said. "The last day of the world's death, the first day of the world's birth. 'Tis a date of great sanctity to the followers of the old religion."

Simon stared at her dumbly and then his eyes went wide and he began to jump up and down gleefully. "No shit? No shit? A holy day for witches? That's great, that's great! We can use it! We can use it! That's *great!*"

"Use it for what, man?" Herricks asked.

"Okay, listen," he said, reining in his enthusiasm. "We're gonna conclude the video with a performance we stage—like, set up, you know?—not from a concert."

"Why?" Siegal asked. "What's the purpose of that? Won't it kind of break into the whole idea of a concert video?"

234

"Not at all, not at all," Simon smiled, feeling cocky and triumphant, even though the coup had been Harry's and Harry's alone. "Harry has managed to get us permission—he's paid the fees, gotten the license, all that shit—to set up and film a song in—get this, now!—a museum in Salem, Massachusetts—"

Gwendolyn shivered and Adrienne went white.

"—in a museum they call the Witch House, a place where a guy named Jonathan Corwin used to live—"

Gwendolyn's jaw clenched and Adrienne's hands went to her mouth.

"—and he was one of the judges at the Salem witch trials! Some of the people accused of witchcraft were even interrogated in that very house! Isn't it a great idea? Isn't it a perfect setting for a video?"

Gwendolyn Jenkins reached out and steadied herself against the wall, her face blank and impassive, frozen into inscrutability as if by an act of will.

Adrienne Lupescu fainted, falling face-first onto the hard wood floor.

⟦ CHAPTER SIXTEEN ⟧
December 23: Winter Solstice

THE VILLAGE OF Salem, Massachusetts, prefers to be remembered as a center of the old whaling trade. It prefers that the nation think of it as the location of numerous interesting historical sites and a village where artists congregate and local theater companies perform.

All of this is true, of course; but it is for none of these things that Salem is known, for when the name of the town is mentioned the immediate association made is with the events of 1692, when fear of witchcraft descended like a shroud upon the community.

The Jonathan Corwin Museum had been dubbed the Witch House in popular parlance so many years ago that the name became official, and a visit to the old seventeenth-century home had long since become the central purpose of most visits to Salem. The old wooden structure stood between Essex and North streets, a caped, square building constructed of wood which had been warped slightly by the centuries of rain and snow and wind, so that now it presented an appearance of incongruity so slight as to be undetectable, but sufficiently prominent to have an effect of subliminal disconcertment. It was a twisted house, a house of horrors, a house whose dry wooden walls had absorbed the shrieks of tortured prisoners, innocent and guilty alike, a house where Judge Jonathan Corwin and Judge John Hathorne and Deputy Governor Thomas Danforth and others had interrogated, terrified, tortured those residents of Salem who had been accused of witchcraft by a small group of hysterical girls. It was today a museum, nothing more; but the wood had soaked up the cries and the terror and the pain. They were all still there somewhere, buried deep in the grain.

It was beside the entrance door that Simon Proctor stood staring at the telephone receiver in his hand. He was not thinking about the witch trials of three centuries past, nor was he reflecting on the innocents condemned to death in this room. He was thinking about the prospect of spanking his daughter and punching her boyfriend in the mouth.

Rowena had just slammed down her phone, and Simon stood for a few stunned moments before doing the same thing. "Damn it all, anyway!" he muttered. His anger at the way his daughter had spoken to him mingled with feelings of guilt. His actions were responsible for her attitude, and he knew it. "Damn it all," he repeated bitterly.

"Hey, Simon, you 'bout ready?" he heard Mark Siegal ask.

He turned and looked at his drummer. Siegal, like Simon, Mahoney, and Herricks, was dressed in the black and white, austere clothing of the seventeenth-century Puritan, from the narrow, flat-domed hat to the silver-buckled shoes, from the high white stockings which disappeared beneath the pant leg just below the knee to the fluffy white neck cloth which rested upon the long black coat. "Yeah, yeah, Markie, I'll be right in. Everything set up?"

Siegal walked forward. "Yeah, but look, Simon, I'm not sure about Adrienne. I don't think she's gonna be able to do this."

Simon frowned. "What the hell is wrong with that chick, anyway? Jesus, she's been acting like a—" he was about to say "like a mental case," but thought better of it.

"It ain't just her," Siegal said. "Gwen's been real skittish too, like this is some ordeal for her or something. I don't get it."

"They won't explain anything to me either," Simon said as he and Siegal left the anteroom and entered the large central room of the museum. "The only thing I can think of is that they take all of this satanism stuff seriously—"

"Well, they do. We all know that."

"—and so this place is like, I don't know, Dachau would be to a Jew or something."

Siegal tried to imagine his own reaction to a visit to a Nazi concentration camp museum. He shook his head. "I don't know. It would upset me, but not like Adrienne."

Simon shrugged. "Who knows. They're a couple of loony tunes anyway. Let's just hope we can make it through a rehearsal and the filming without either of them screwing up."

"Yeah, let's hope," Siegal agreed quietly. Both women were in the room with the other members of the band, and he did not want them to hear their conversation. He took his seat behind the drums and waited for Simon to speak.

"Okay, listen up. The dramatic bit here should be pretty easy, if everybody remembers their lines. The song, of course, we've done a dozen times over the past few days. We're gonna run through it once, let the technicians get sound and light levels straight, and then we'll do it for real. Okay? Everybody ready?" They all nodded except for Herricks. "Larry, what's the problem?"

"I can't fuckin' breathe, that's what's the problem," he grumbled. "I don't know why we gotta wear these dumb fuckin' suits!"

"Accuracy, my boy, accuracy," Siegal said. "When we decided to try a little drama, we all agreed to dress this way."

"Well, I didn't know it was gonna be so fuckin' uncomfortable."

"Don't gripe, Larry," Strube said. "You're getting a percentage of this video, remember."

"Ahhh," he muttered, continuing to tug at the collar of the Puritan outfit.

Simon turned to the technicians and asked, "Are you guys ready?"

"Whenever you are," came the reply. "Just ignore us. We'll be measuring levels, setting up camera angles, stuff like that."

"Okay." He looked at Gwendolyn and Adrienne, who were standing off to one side, whispering to each other feverishly. "Ladies? Ready for a run through?"

"Yes, Simon," Gwendolyn said. She looked meaningfully at Adrienne. "We're *both* ready."

The Corwin House was typical of dwellings in seventeenth-century New England. The small anteroom led into one large single room, off to the side of which were a privy and a kitchen. The upstairs, at one time little more than a loft, had been expanded years before into a full second story, but the main museum exhibits were displayed in the large central room downstairs. The museum's custodians had removed most of the exhibits, but had left the large oak desk and a few chairs in place. The drawings and judicial paraphernalia which hung from the walls had been allowed to remain, but a guard remained as well to keep an eye on them.

The room was large, but seemed now rather cramped. Instruments and amplifiers, light tripods and cameras, wires crisscrossing the floor—all combined with the seven musicians and the four technicians and the guard to make the room seem depressingly small. Still, there was room enough for the instruments to stand off in one half of the room, across from the old oak desk and the chairs.

"Okay," Simon said. "Let's run through it. We fade in on Gwendolyn sitting in one of the chairs. Tom, behind the desk. Larry, you lead me and Adrienne in. We start with the drum roll and the bass riff in the background. Mark, Carl, whenever you're ready."

A military roll on the snare drum and an ominous series of low bass notes began the little play Simon and the others had put together. Gwendolyn looked into the camera lens and began to speak as Simon and Adrienne, each holding their hands behind their backs as if they were bound, were led slowly across the room behind her.

"I am sitting in the home of Jonathan Corwin," she began, "a man who condemned many people to the gallows in Salem, Massachusetts, during the spring and summer of 1692. This is the Witch House. And I am Gwendolyn Jenkins. I am a witch."

She looked over her shoulder. "See them led to the seat of justice, that farmer, John Proctor, his servant, Mary Warren, witches, both of them."

"John Proctor, you have been accused of witchcraft by Abigail Williams. How do you respond?" Mahoney said imperiously and on cue.

"I am what I am, nothing more, nothing less," he replied.

"This is really stupid," Herricks muttered.

Simon spun around and yelled, "Goddamn it, Larry, we've got to get this whole thing down perfect before we film it! Will you stop screwing around?"

"I ain't screwing around, man!" he replied testily. "I just feel like a goddamn asshole dressed up like this and acting like this!"

"Typecasting," Siegal muttered, but he was unheard on the other side of the room.

"Larry, listen to me good!" Simon said angrily, his face flushing. "We're gonna do this and we're gonna do this right, you hear me? Now try to get into it and *stop screwing around!*"

"All right, all right," Herricks said with a snort. "Jesus!"

"Where were we?" Simon asked. "Oh, yeah, right. I am what I am, nothing more, nothing less." He dropped easily back into the role.

"Marshal Cheever," Mahoney said to Herricks, "have either of the prisoners said anything to each other on the way here from the jail?"

Herricks sighed and responded. "They talked about the spells they was gonna cast on the accusers." His voice was a bored and unconvincing singsong.

Simon slammed his fist down upon the desk. "Goddamn it, Larry!"

"What's the matter now? What'd I do?"

"You can try at least, can't you? I mean, I've seen Sunday school Christmas pageants with better acting than that!"

"Okay, so go hire some little kids!" he spat. "I'm not kiddin', man, I feel like a goddamn asshole doin' this!"

"Well, for Christ's sake, Tom's doin' it, I'm doin' it, Gwen's doin' it! What makes you so special?"

"Hey, what about Mark and Carl? All they're doin' is sitting over there playin' their instruments, which is what we should *all* be doin'!"

"We want a bass and drum background, not a piano," Simon shouted. "Besides, there weren't any black or Jewish Puritans!"

"So what? There weren't any Irish Puritans either, but Mahoney's playing the judge!"

"Goddamn it, Larry! You can't tell if somebody's Irish just by looking at him!"

"And you can't tell if somebody's Jewish just by looking at him!"

Simon Proctor pounded his fists upon the desk to accentuate his shouted words. "*We need drums, not piano!*"

"So let me play the drums and give Siegal this stupid role!"

"You can't play the drums!"

"Anybody can play the drums! It's a retard's instrument!"

"Hey," Siegal shouted. "Don't be so ignorant, Larry!"

"It's true, man!" Herricks shouted back. "Look at Ringo Starr! Luckiest man in the whole fuckin' world, a third-rate talent hooked into the world's biggest group!"

"Yeah, yeah," Siegal bristled, "you're an expert on third-rate talents!"

"Ah, fuck you!"

"Hold and be silent!" Gwendolyn Jenkins stood to her feet and placed her balled fists upon her hips. She and Adrienne were both dressed in the typical garb of the Puritan woman, and she tore the white cap from her head and threw it emphatically upon the floor. "This is foolishness," she said evenly. "We will not proceed as we had planned."

"Hey," Simon said. "I'm in charge of—"

"Be quiet!" she snapped. Her manner was commanding and imperious, and Simon fell silent. "Adrienne, go and fetch the harp and the lute." As Adrienne hastened to comply, Gwendolyn returned her attention to Simon and said, "What was being done was foolishness. Hear now what we shall do, which is not foolishness. This day is the solstice, the day of the rebirth of the sun, and we should be celebrating rebirth, not witch trials and executions. I shall speak of rebirth and resurrection and then Adrienne and I shall sing a song of old Salem. You may make a record of it as you wish." She glanced over at the amused technicians. "I have no knowledge of these machines. But if a record you must have, then a record you shall have, to sell to the curious and those who seek diversion."

"Gwen," Simon began, "now listen to me. The little dialogue we—"

"Silence!" she commanded. "Then after the song of old Salem, I shall speak again of the solstice, and then shall we all sing the song we had planned to sing." Adrienne scampered back in at that moment, carrying with her the two black cases containing the harp and the lute. "Open them," Gwendolyn commanded. To the other musicians she said, "Assume your positions with your instruments. I will signal when to begin the final song."

"Damn it, Gwen!" Simon said heatedly. "We've spent a long time planning this thing!"

"And 'twas silliness you planned, Simon Proctor," she replied evenly. "Now go and stand with the others." Simon stood defiantly for a moment, and then slowly walked over to the instruments. Tom Mahoney and Larry Herricks followed him as Adrienne handed Gwendolyn the harp and then took out her lute. They spent a few moments getting the instruments in tune, and then Gwendolyn turned to the technicians and said, "Commence."

They looked at Simon and he shrugged. "What the hell," he muttered. "Roll 'em."

A camera was moved into position, the lights switched on and the sound level checked. Then one of the men said, "Whenever you're ready, miss."

Gwendolyn looked into the camera, as she had seen Simon do during the filming of the concert performances. "I am known to you as Gwendolyn Jenkins, daughter of a druid, a witch and servant of the Dark Master. I sit now in the home of Jonathan Corwin, a judge in Salem Village, a man who condemned dozens of people to death for witchcraft."

She strummed absently upon her harp. "Some were innocent, some were truly witches, but that is of no matter. This day is December twenty-third, the day of the winter solstice, the day of rebirth, the day of winter's death and spring's nativity. This day shall we sing you two songs, the first a dirge of bitter memory, the second a hymn of joyous hope, the first a song of Salem, the second a song of the solstice, the first a song of loss and defeat, the second a song of victory."

She began to pick out a slow, lilting melody on her harp, and Adrienne joined in with her customary contrapuntal plucking of the lute. When they began to sing, the sadness and beauty of the mournful melody and harmony held even the jaded onlookers in thrall.

"Fair was Lizzie Proctor, dark was Abigail.
    Both they loved the same man, and both they loved
        him well.
Late it was in winter of sixteen ninety-two
    When Abigail decided what mischief she would do.
She and Mary Warren, Mercy Lewis and the rest
    Swore to send Elizabeth unto eternal rest.
For Abby loved John Proctor, loved Lizzie's wedded man,
    And she did swear to have him any way a woman can.
So she and Mary Warren did wickedly conspire
    To send the quiet Lizzie unto the judge's ire.
They said she served the Devil, they swore it on their
        lives,
    And so condemned to hanging that most faithful of
        wives."

They paused in their singing and played a musical interlude, the deep and resonant harp winding about the gentle plinking of the lute. Mark Siegal leaned over to Simon and asked, "Hey, have you ever heard this song before?"

He shook his head and whispered, "No, never. It's new to me."

"Is it true? I mean, is the stuff they're singing about really what happened back in Salem? That *is* your ancestor she's referring to, isn't it?"

"Well, I'm descended from John Proctor, and the other names are right—Abigail, Mary Warren, Elizabeth Proctor. But I've never heard this song before."

Siegal nodded. "Creepy."

"But the court became a madhouse and John instead did
    die.
  They placed a noose around his neck and then they
      hanged him high.
So Abby in her sorrow did call on Satan's power
  And offered her soul to him in that benighted hour.
She swore to be his servant in this world and beyond,
  If only she could once again embrace her darling John.
She did the Devil's wishes in Boston's chilly clime,
  And in the deepest hellfire does Abby bide her time.
For fair was Lizzie Proctor and dark was Abigail.
  Both they loved the same man, and both they loved
      him well.
Both they loved him well,
  In heaven and in hell."

Gwendolyn and Adrienne ended the song by repeating the final line three times and then allowing the final minor harmony notes to fade slowly into silence.

Gwendolyn's eyes had been gazing vacantly off into space as she sang, and she was trembling slightly as she returned her attention to the camera. Adrienne had been standing behind her, and as soon as the song ended she moved quickly off to the left, breathing heavily and erratically as if on the verge of an asthmatic seizure. Gwendolyn's cold green eyes fixed on the camera as she said, "Abigail Williams sold herself to the Devil in exchange for a promise that someday she would again hold her lover in her arms, a promise of rebirth, of regeneration, of another life to live in the world of the living."

She stood up, placing the harp upon the chair. "And all

prayers are answered when they are addressed to the Dark Master. Each year the sun seems to die, sinking lower, ever lower against the horizon, bathing the earth in its warmth for an ever shorter period of time each day, and from time out of mind druids and witches and shamans and priests have prayed for the sun to return. Each year, on this day, the sun is reborn, as we are all reborn. The solstice day, all hail! The world is new!"

Her last words were the refrain of the song the band had been rehearsing, and they recognized it as a cue. Herricks played an ascending piano riff which culminated in a deafening blast from all the other instruments. The cameras swung away from Gwendolyn toward the band and she pranced over and whirled around Simon as he began the first verse of the song.

"See now the sun is rising high,
    Mounting the ladder of the sky.
Now let every boy mount every girl.
    Now let life abound throughout the world.
The solstice day, all hail! The world is new!"

Adrienne stood stiffly near the drummer, her hands clapping to the rhythm of the song, but she neither sang nor danced. Her eyes darted around the room nervously, as if each wall and each plank of wood threatened her with accusation and danger.

"Sprite and fairy float in misty air.
    Troll and gnome awake in earthy lair.
Elf and goblin through the forest creep,
    And old Jack the Froster goes to sleep.
The solstice day, all hail! The world is new!"

Gwendolyn danced as was her custom, but there was a difference to her movements and her gait. She seemed never to take her eyes from Simon's face, seemed in fact to structure her movements so that she would be able to look at him, stare at him, study him, no matter what the direction in which he or she moved.

"No more need we fear sun's early set.
    Hail fellows, we embrace you all, well met.
Sing and dance with joy in this fair hour.
    With your bodies worship nature's power.
The solstice day, all hail! The world is new!"

The song ended with a descent into boisterous, joyous bedlam, and the sheer pleasure of the playing and singing elicited howls of delight from the musicians. They laughed and hopped up and down, slapping each other on the back and cheering. Part of this was no doubt related to their awareness that it was all being filmed, but at least some elements of their actions were honest. Simon grabbed Gwendolyn by the waist and lifted her up, spinning her joyously about. She smiled impassively down at him.

He turned to the film crew. "Did you get all of that, start to finish?"

"Every bit, Mr. Proctor," was the reply. "It'll look great!"

"That's terrific," Simon said happily. "Still, I can't help but think that the little play—"

"Simon, it was great the way we did it," Siegal said. "I hate to have to agree with Larry, but I don't think the dramatic bit would have been very good."

"We'd have looked like jerks," Mahoney agreed.

"Well, I suppose," Simon said. "Anyway, that song you two did was great." He put his arms once again about Gwendolyn's waist. "Where did you learn that, anyway? I never heard it before. Is it real? I mean, really an old folk song about my family?"

She smiled and said softly, "Aye. 'Tis true and an old song."

"So where did you learn it?"

Gwendolyn snaked her arms up around his neck and kissed him passionately. "Perhaps later I will tell you. Perhaps it is time."

"Time for what?" he asked.

"Time for everything. Time for the truth, for revelations."

He grinned. "Secrets, huh? Hiding things from me?"

She giggled. "A few little things, perhaps."

"Hey, are we done here?" Herricks grumbled. "It's, like, nearly seven o'clock. I'm starving." After the brief euphoria of a few moments before he had reverted to his customary mood.

"Yeah, me too," Mahoney chimed in. "Let's call it a day."

"A day!" Simon said. "Let's call it a tour! We're done, boys, finished and done."

"And when do we get paid?" Strube asked. He shot an amused and vindictive glance at Herricks and added, "Those of us not on salary, I mean."

"Let's go back to the hotel, get washed up, and go out for some food. After dinner I'll call Harry and see what's happening on the financial end of the whole thing. One thing's for sure," Simon laughed, "we've made a fortune this time out, a fortune. Twice as many gigs as we'd hoped for, not an empty seat in any of them, record sales up, people lining up to see that ridiculous movie . . ." He grabbed Gwendolyn and began dancing around the room with her, singing, "We're in the money, we're in the money. . . ."

Four hours later the group had wined and dined and, after nearly a month on the road, were all in their respective hotel rooms, each sinking into what was to be the first of many long, deep sleeps. The tour had been a rousing success, as Simon had said; but as he had noted to himself many times in the past, he was not twenty-five anymore, and neither were his friends. He, and they, were worn out by the travel, the tension, the constant movement, the schedules, the exhausting process of public performance. By the time the last bottle of wine had been emptied at the Salem Guest House that evening, drooping eyelids and wide yawns were being traded infectiously around the table.

Even Gwendolyn seemed tired, though she and Adrienne were by decades the youngest members of the troupe. Adrienne's mood seemed to brighten measurably the farther they went from the Corwin Museum, and she seemed even to enjoy herself at dinner, laughing at Mahoney's foolish jokes. But Gwendolyn seemed as worn as the others, as if the effort she had expended had been so much more intense than theirs that it had a deeply draining effect upon her. As soon as they returned to Simon's suite—how nice that sounded, Simon had thought, after so many years of rattrap rooms; a suite!—as soon as they returned, Gwendolyn had indicated her intention of going immediately to sleep, and she dragged herself unceremoniously into the bedroom. Simon went in after her, believing himself to be too excited, too exhilarated to sleep; but as he lay down beside her, still fully clothed, as was she, he felt his eyelids growing suddenly, irresistibly heavy. Sleep washed over him in an instant, and he and Gwendolyn lay motionless and calm upon the bed.

Simon heard a voice, an angry voice, speaking to him, and he attempted to open his eyes, attempted to rouse himself to consciousness, but found that he could not. Didn't I lock the door? he asked himself. Who could have gotten into the room?

He was not aware of himself awakening and sitting up, but he found himself suddenly sitting upon the edge of the bed, looking at the angry face of a plain but wholesomely attractive woman in her late thirties. She was dressed oddly, somehow antiquely, and her blond hair was tucked carefully beneath the rim of the plain white bonnet which matched the white apron which girdled her waist. Her balled fists rested angrily upon her hips, and the folds of her rather austere black dress rippled as she stamped her feet.

"I'll *not* have that whore resting beneath my roof one more night," the woman said furiously.

Simon rose to his feet and began to ask her who she was and what she was doing in his hotel room, but the words died in his mouth as he realized that he was no longer in that room. He looked around in confusion at the log walls, the unvarnished wooden floor, the crude but sturdy table and chairs, the blazing fire which burned in the fireplace. "Wh-what—?" he stammered.

"And I'll thank you to give me your attention when I'm speaking, John Proctor!" the woman demanded.

Simon looked down at the bed, and found both that it was not the bed in which he had fallen asleep and that Gwendolyn was nowhere to be seen. He looked back over at the woman. "What—?" he repeated, "What are you talking about—?"

"'Tis a bit late for games, husband," the woman said firmly, her nostrils flaring. "You have confessed your sin to me, and I am warmed by that. But it cannot be as 'twas before. I want that harlot out from beneath my roof this day, else I shall depart myself!"

Simon opened his mouth to speak, but the words which he heard pouring forth from his lips were not the words he was attempting to say. "As you wish, Liz," he heard himself saying. "I'll do naught to hurt you more."

The woman sniffed back a tear. "Nor should you," she said, seeming to retreat from anger into slightly mollified sorrow. "Send her out today. I'll get Mary to take her place." She laughed bitterly. "She is plain enough to be safe in your company."

"Liz . . . ," Simon heard himself saying, and then a sudden blast of cold wind assaulted his face. He spun around, panicking, confused, and frightened at finding himself standing in an open, barren, snow-covered field.

"But you said that you loved me!" a voice said from behind him.

He turned around and faced a distraught, weeping Gwendolyn, her face somehow younger and more innocent than the face he had kissed so often of late. "Gw—" he began, and then once again lost control of his voice. "It does me no happiness, Abby," he heard himself say. "In my sin and my weakness have I used you ill and betrayed my wife. No words you can say to me will be any worse than the words which I've said to myself."

"But you said that you loved me!" she wept.

"Abby—" he heard himself saying, "don't, please—"

"I gave my maidenhead unto you!" she cried. "I gave you all my hopes and all my trust and all my joy! I cannot live without you, John, I cannot!"

"You cannot love another woman's husband," he said firmly. "It is contrary to the laws of God and man. It is my sin, Abigail, it is my sorrow."

"Your sorrow!" she cried, her voice mingling pain and confusion with anger and astonishment. "And what of my sorrow? What of me? I gave you my love, I gave you my innocence, and you cast me off like a strumpet?! What of me?!"

"I am sorry, Abigail," Simon heard himself saying, "but I am wedded to another."

"Aye, you are," she spat, "but that can change, that can change!"

"Confess, Goodman Proctor!" he heard a voice shouting. "There is yet time! Confess now, and save your life! Confess, and save your soul!"

Simon tried to turn around and find the voice which was shouting at him, but he found that he was being held stationary by two brawny men, one on either side of him. He turned his head to the left and felt a peculiar and unfamiliar scratching on his throat. He began to tremble when he realized that he was standing upon the platform of a gallows, and that a noose was around his neck.

"Confess, Goodman Proctor!" the voice cried.

"Aye, John," he heard Gwendolyn say, "confess to me that you love me, and I shall save you! Confess to me that you have no love for your wife, and we shall see her swing from the rope, not you! Confess to me that it has always been me you've loved, swear to love me forever, pledge yourself to me, and I shall save you from the hangman! I can do it, John, none other but me!"

"Confess, John Proctor!" the other voice cried. "I'll not hold up the execution longer! Confess!"

"Love me or die, John!" Gwendolyn said. "There is no third choice! Love me or die!"

Simon felt the wooden platform upon which he stood drop suddenly out from under him and he fell feet-first into nothingness. He felt the rope snap tight about his neck, and then he bolted from his bed and slammed himself into the night table of the hotel room.

He fell backward from the sharp edge of the small piece of furniture and landed upon the floor with a resounding thud. He was drenched with sweat and his arms and legs were shaking violently. He placed his hand upon his chest, attempting instinctively to still his racing heart and calm his rapid breathing.

"Jesus Christ!" he whimpered. "God Almighty!"

"Nay, 'tis another whom you should invoke," Gwendolyn said quietly, a hint of amusement in her voice. He looked up at her as she raised herself up on her elbows near the edge of the bed upon which she was lying, and she smiled down at him. "Do you understand, my dear love?"

"Wh—what? Understand what?"

"Do you understand your dreams?"

"My—my dreams? What the hell are you talking about?" He got up from the floor and rose unsteadily to his feet.

She held out a hand to him and said, "Come, sit beside me. I have a tale to tell you."

Simon sat down upon the edge of the bed and gazed into her deep green eyes with confusion. "Look, Gwen," he said shakily, "I'm sorry, but I just had one hell of a nightmare, and I don't really feel like—"

"'Twas no nightmare," she said softly. "'Twas a memory, of sorts. My memory, not yours. I sent my spirit out to you, and you did dream."

His distress was being replaced by irritation. "Gwendolyn, let's just go to sleep, okay?"

She shook her head slowly. "No, Simon, not yet, not now. 'Tis time for the truth. I have not been honest with you, my dear. I have told you half-truths and untruths, but I did so for love of you, not from a desire to deceive you." She moved from a prone to a sitting position beside him, and she placed her hands upon his arm. "Simon," she said, her voice steady and calm, "I am not who you think me to be. I am not Gwendolyn Jenkins. Gwendolyn Jenkins is dead. So is Adrienne Lupescu. They died last All Hallows' morn. We killed them, took their places, for we knew you were expecting them to show up at your door."

"Killed—! Gwen, what the *hell* are you talking about!" He

frowned, confused, annoyed, and strangely frightened of the woman who sat beside him.

"Listen to me well, Simon Proctor," she said. "My name is Abigail Williams. Our friend, whom you have called Adrienne, is Mary Warren."

Simon began to laugh despite himself. "Gwen, are you smoking something you haven't been sharing with me?"

"Be quiet and listen," she hissed, and the ferocity of her tone silenced him immediately. "Three centuries ago I lived in Salem Village in New England. I was the niece of the town's minister, Samuel Parris, and I earned my keep as a house-keeper and a serving maid." She took his hand and squeezed it gently. "I loved your ancestor, John Proctor. I loved him more than my own life, more than my own soul. I lied and cheated and did perjury that I might have him."

"Gwen," he said gently, "cut it out, will you? I know the whole story. I know that Abigail denounced John's wife Elizabeth as a witch, I know that their maid Mary Warren accused John of witchcraft, and I know that he was hanged and that his wife survived. That's all family history to me." He shook his head. "I really don't understand why you're trying to—"

"You do *not* know the whole story, Simon," she said evenly, a bitterness underlying her tone. "You do not know that my anger was so great and my despair so deep that I struck a bargain with Satan. You do not know that I, who had sent so many others to the gallows by my perjured testimony, sold my soul, sold myself. I swore that I would serve the Devil in this world and the next, if only he would grant me the answer to my prayers."

Simon gazed into the emerald eyes and noted with growing discomfort a mad glow, a staring wildness, an unblinking, insane intensity. My God! he thought. Harry was right! This chick is nuts! "Uh, Gwen—" he began.

"Abigail," she corrected him. "My name is Abigail."

"Yeah, sure, right," he said quickly. "I think that maybe we'd better talk about this tomorrow, after we've had some sleep, after we've let some of that wine wear off—"

"Simon," she said, unsmiling but not unkind, "I know that this is all very hard for you to accept or understand, but you must try, you must listen and believe. I am *not* Gwendolyn Jenkins. I have never been Gwendolyn Jenkins. 'Twas but a role I played, a name I took, to enable me to become close to you, to enable me to see if my prayer would be answered in the way I hoped or in the way I feared."

"And what prayer was that, may I ask?" he inquired gently, as if he were speaking to a patient on the brink of a breakdown.

"Know and understand," she said bitterly, "that I loved your ancestor and I hated him. I hated the Proctor name and I longed to make it my own name. I would have done anything for him, anything. I would have killed for him, I would have died for him, but he used me, he lied to me, he robbed me of my innocence, he polluted my purity! . . ."

She was beginning to tremble violently and tears were welling up in her eyes, and Simon put his arms around her. "Hey, come on, take it easy! Calm down!" I don't believe this! he thought to himself. I finally hook onto something which seems about to make me a rich man, and it ends up depending on a crazy woman. Great. That's just great. My luck strikes again.

She continued as if she were almost unaware of his presence. "So I prayed to Satan to grant me a boon. I sold him my soul, and Mary sold hers with it, in exchange for his promise."

"His promise to do what?" Simon asked, stroking her hair sadly and feeling very sorry for himself, visualizing piles of money shrinking into nothing.

"His promise either to give me back my beloved whom they hanged in Salem, or to give me leave to destroy his breed, to wipe the Proctors from the face of the earth!"

Simon looked at her warily, realizing for the first time that Gwendolyn's delusion might be a source of danger to him. "I, uh—I hope that you don't feel that—I mean, uh, it seems to me—"

She smiled at him warmly. "It was love which I had hoped for, and the opportunity for vengeance which I had feared. Had you not loved me, then my wrath would have been horrible, and I would have swept you and your family away like chaff beneath the broom. But the Master granted me what I hoped for, not what I feared. You love me, Simon Proctor, and my joy grows daily in your embrace."

I never said I loved you, you poor thing, he thought to himself, looking sadly into her intense eyes. "But I'm not John Proctor, Gwen," he said gently. "I'm not that man. I'm just his descendant."

She slid from the edge of the bed onto the floor and knelt before him, placing her hands upon his knees and gazing up at him with adoration. "But you are he," she whispered. "His blood runs in your veins. His face is your face, his voice is your

250

voice. I do not believe in reincarnation, Simon, for I know it to be false; and yet I feel that only if your body actually housed the soul of John Proctor, only then could you be any more like unto him, only then could you be any more the man I loved three hundred years ago."

He shook his head sadly. "Jesus, Gwen," he said in a soft, sorrowful voice. "You need help, honey, you need care—"

"I need *you*," she said earnestly. Her lips tightened as she whispered, "I have spent the past three centuries in hell, suffering the torments of the damned, burning in a lake of fire, blind, deaf, speechless, in horrible agony, in horrible pain. I made my pact with the Devil and I suffered for it, but 'twas worth it, 'twas worth every moment of it, for I knew that someday, somehow, my Master would fulfill his end of the bargain."

"Gwen—"

She seemed not to hear him. "And fulfill it he did, last Eve of All Hallows. 'Twas a Proctor's lust which ruined me in Salem, a Proctor's wife who drove me from my home to the streets of Boston; and then, in the fullness of time, 'twas a Proctor's child who summoned me forth from the pit, me and Mary Warren with me—"

"A Proctor's child! What are you talking about?"

"Lucas," she said simply. "'Twas he who read the words and said the prayer. He called us forth into the physical world, not knowing that he was doing Satan's bidding." She smiled warmly at him. "And now has Satan blessed me with a Proctor's love—nay, not just a Proctor; a mirror image of my John, my John reborn, my dear, sweet John alive again!" She began to weep freely, and she leaned her head against his knee. "Oh, Simon, how I love you, how I love you!"

Simon pushed her away, a bit more roughly than he had intended. "Jesus, Gwen, are you listening to yourself?!" he asked. "Don't you realize how crazy this is? You are not Abigail Williams! Abigail Williams was a girl who lived and died centuries ago. You are Gwendolyn Jenkins! And Adrienne is Adrienne, not Mary Warren!"

She smiled up at him, sadly, patiently, lovingly. "'Tis hard to understand, I know. But someday you will understand. I have faith in that, my dear, sweet love. Trust and understanding will grow from year to year, once we are wed."

Wed! he thought. Wed! My God!!! Very, *very* gently, he said, "Gwen, please listen to me. I have a great deal of affection for you, I really do, and I want to do what's best for you. But you have to understand that you need help, professional help!"

She laughed softly. "Now hear me, Simon Proctor. You and I are destined to be man and wife. 'Tis fate, 'tis what must be. We shall be wed according to the old ritual, the satanic ritual, and Satan shall bless our union. We shall be wed privately, secretly, without any of the fanfare and flourish which you relish so greatly. No disbelieving eyes shall gaze upon our nuptials, no money shall be made from them. This will not be entertainment, not be a performance before the public. It is too imporant to me to allow it to be used in such a manner." She ran her hands gently up and down his legs from knee to hip. "You must promise me this, Simon. If you love me, you will wed me in the manner I wish."

Entertainment? he thought. A performance?

A tear dropped from her eye to his knee as she whispered, "I have suffered the agonies of hell for you. I have given myself to Satan for you. All that I have done has had but one object, my dear Goodman Proctor. I would be your wife. I must be your wife." She fell silent and gazed up at him expectantly, seeming to hold her breath as she awaited his response.

As Simon looked down into her wide green eyes, as her words echoed in his ears, an idea began to germinate in his mind and an ever increasing flow of dollar signs began to drift through his interior vision. No, hold on a minute, he told himself. That would be a terrible thing to do, a cruel, heartless thing to do.

Marry her according to a satanic ritual.

Film it!

Tack it onto the end of the concert video!

No, no, that's a horrible thing to think of doing! I can't take advantage of this poor, sick girl! It would be inhuman, inhuman!

Of course, a person with this kind of a delusion needs psychiatric help, and that costs money, lots of money. I certainly couldn't be faulted for trying to help her make some of it, could I? Why, it wouldn't even be a legal marriage.

It'd be a great scene. We didn't do the little skit we worked out for the Corwin Museum, so why not do this instead? Sort of like a climax to the whole video. The kids'll eat it up. They'll love it! A marriage made in hell. That's it, that's it, that's the hook! A marriage made in hell! Fantastic!

Wait a minute, wait a minute! What are you thinking of?! This girl has been sitting here telling you that she's a resurrected witch from three centuries ago! This girl is crazy, she needs help! She needs therapy, she needs care! You can't exploit her illness like this! It would be monstrous! What kind of a cold-hearted bastard would you be if you took advantage of her?!

Have to film it secretly, of course. Can't let Gwen know about that. She takes it all much too seriously. She can't find out that the whole thing would be essentially a publicity stunt. Have to hide cameras and microphones around the place where we do it, film it secretly. Someday, when she's cured, she'll thank me for doing it, getting her the money for a good psychiatrist, a good rest home. Yeah, and one for Adrienne too. She's probably as daffy as Gwen is.

Film it secretly! Are you nuts? Use her like that, abuse her like that, lie to her, take advantage of her illness, exploit her emotions, just to make a few more bucks?

Nothing wrong with a few more bucks. . . .

She's gonna need expensive therapy. . . .

Not my fault that she's nuts. . . .

You can never have too much money. . . .

Got to strike while the iron is hot. . . .

Nothing ventured, nothing gained. . . .

She'd be even more upset if I didn't agree to marry her. . . .

So we film it. So what? She'll get over it. . . .

Won't be a real marriage anyway. . . .

Simon Proctor smiled down at Gwendolyn Jenkins and took her hands gently in his. "My dear," he grinned, "you may set the date."

Gwendolyn sprang up from her knees and threw herself into his lap. She covered his face with kisses.

But what about the dreams? a voice buried deep in Simon's mind asked him. What about the dreams? . . .

Simon ignored the voice and dismissed the dreams as irrelevant as he began to unbutton Gwendolyn's blouse.

⟦ CHAPTER SEVENTEEN ⟧
December 24

ROWENA STOOD precariously upon an old stepladder, carefully draping tinsel from the boughs of the large evergreen tree which occupied the far corner of the large sitting room. Without turning around she asked, "Jeremy? Have you found it?"

Jeremy Sloan was searching through a large cardboard box, whose discolored hue and tattered flaps bespoke years of use. "Not yet," he replied. "You sure it's in here?"

"Gotta be. We've used the same star on top of the Christmas tree for as long as I can remember, and we always keep all the ornaments in that box."

"Well, I don't—" He paused and smiled. "I got it, I got it. It's in a little box with lights and other stuff." He took out the small, delicate glass star and handed it to Rowena. She reached up toward the very top of the evergreen, but she could not quite reach it. "Hold it, Row," he said. "Let me do it. My arm's longer."

"Okay with me," she said. "I get nervous on ladders." She descended carefully.

"Right," he laughed. "I mean, you might fall two or three feet from a stepladder!"

"Oh, shut up," she said good-naturedly, punching him lightly in the stomach. "Just put the star up there."

Jeremy hopped up onto the top step of the ladder and deftly affixed the star to the top of the tree. He jumped off and said, "You want me to plug in the lights?"

"Hold on, let me get Grampa and your uncle." She walked out of the room and went down to the kitchen where the two old men were having lunch. Jeremy made a few last-minute improvements upon the decorations, moving an ornament or two and lifting a string of lights so as to fill in a gap, and then stood back and appraised it. Not bad, he thought. He smiled. I've decorated a lot of trees in my day, but it's never been as much fun as this. Must be the company!

Rowena returned shortly, followed by Floyd Proctor and Reverend Wilkes. "Okay, let 'er rip!" she said merrily. Jeremy went over to the wall and knelt down to plug the cord into the outlet. The tall evergreen burst immediately into bright, blinking color.

"Looks great, Row," Floyd said.

"Real pretty, real pretty," Wilkes smiled, not entirely honestly. His Puritan forebears had regarded Christmas as a pagan holiday, and they had not celebrated it. The passing of the centuries had softened this attitude, but Wilkes, as a Congregationalist minister of decidedly antiquated predilections, still felt just a bit uneasy during this season of the year. Christmas should be celebrated, he believed, as a commemoration of God's gift of His Son; but the orgy of consumerism which the season engendered, coupled with the decorated trees, rosy-cheeked Santas, talking snowmen, and heroic reindeer, rubbed his old Calvinist fur the wrong way. Still, he thought, no need to make an issue of it. Save the sermons for Sunday. Let the boy and girl enjoy themselves.

"It looks pretty as a picture," Jeremy said, gazing at the tree which stood off to the left of the large picture window which overlooked Bradford's street. "Like a painting or something. The tree all decorated, and all the snow out there in the background and everything. You know what I mean?"

"Yes," Rowena sniffed, "but the painting just got messed up."

"Huh?"

"Look," she said, nodding toward the window. Jeremy looked outside to see Simon's car approaching the old Proctor Inn along Bradford's street, followed very closely by a battered old van which Rowena recognized as belonging to Mark Siegal. "The children are back," she muttered.

Reverend Wilkes glanced out the window and then, turning to Floyd, said, "I mean no offense, but I'm not in the mood to make social pleasantries with your son and his friends at the moment. I think Jeremy and I had best be going."

Floyd nodded. "I know just what you mean, Fred. If this weren't my house, I'd be leaving with you."

Wilkes walked toward the door. "Come along, Jeremy."

Jeremy cast Rowena a pained look and shrugged. "It's getting near suppertime anyway," he said. "I'll come back over later on tonight, okay?"

"Sure," she smiled. She gave him a warm kiss and said, "I'll see you later."

Jeremy followed his uncle out of the house and Rowena watched them cross the street to the parsonage just as Simon

255

and Mark pulled their respective vehicles to a stop in front of the old inn. Expressions of annoyance formed on the faces of Rowena and her grandfather as they watched the doors of the car and the van swing open and their passengers began to step out into the cold New Hampshire air. Simon had driven Gwendolyn, Karyn, and Lucas in his car. Adrienne had ridden with the four other musicians. Rowena noticed that it was Simon, not Lucas, who assisted Karyn in her departure from the vehicle. *How much longer until the baby comes?* Rowena thought. *Another six weeks maybe. It figures that Lucas doesn't even know enough to help her. What a jerk.*

The front door was unlocked and the sounds of footsteps, laughter, and cheerful conversation reached the sitting room from the foyer. Gwendolyn preceded Simon into the sitting room, and she smiled broadly at the decorated tree. "Ah! An evergreen! And so nicely adorned!"

"Thanks," Rowena grumbled. "And Merry Christmas, for all that means to you."

"Nay, but it is a joyous solstice, child," Gwendolyn laughed. "The sun is reborn and soon the powers of the world will burst forth in new life upon the branches of the trees and in the fields and meadows."

"Please," Rowena muttered. "Spare me. And don't call me child."

"And how then should I call you?" Gwendolyn grinned unkindly. "I have never had a stepdaughter before, nor," and she looked at Floyd, "a father-in-law."

They stood in silence, at first not comprehending the implication of her words. Then Rowena said, "What?!" It was an expression of disbelief, not a question.

Floyd looked angrily at Simon, who had removed his coat and was just now entering the room. "Boy, what the hell's goin' on here?"

Simon shrugged nervously, defensively. "Well, uh, Gwen and me—that is, well—"

"Simon!" Floyd bellowed. "What the hell did she mean by that!"

"We shall be wed within the week, Father," Gwendolyn said, smiling. She grabbed Simon's arm and squeezed it to her body happily, her face radiating joy and ecstasy.

For a very brief moment Rowena thought she looked almost normal; but the moment passed quickly, and she shouted, "Daddy, you can't be serious! You just *can't* be serious!"

"Row, take it easy. I'll explain everything to you later."

Simon winked at her, trying to communicate the idea that all was not as it seemed. She either did not notice the wink or did not understand its import.

"Damn it, Daddy!" she shouted, beginning to cry. "What in the world is wrong with you!"

"Simon, Simon," Floyd shook his head in disgust. "You can't mean this! You just can't mean this!"

"Hold on, here, everybody," Simon said with annoyance. "If I want to marry Gwen, that's my business, no one else's." He looked from Rowena to Floyd. "I'll explain everything to you later, in private."

"What the hell is there to explain?" Floyd shouted. "If you're serious about marrying this—" he groped for a sufficiently derogatory word, and could not find one, "this *woman*, then I have nothing to say to you, now or ever again."

"Hey, come on, Dad. You told me yourself that I should get married again, settle down with—"

"I mean you should marry a normal woman, not someone like this!"

Gwendolyn disliked being discussed as if she were not present, but she repressed her anger. "Mr. Proctor," she said with as much kindness as she could muster, "I shall be your daughter-in-law. I shall strive to be a good wife to your son. Will you not strive to accept me into your family, as a daughter? I have done you no harm, sir, none whatsoever. I—"

"You say you're a witch," Floyd snapped, "not a make-believe witch like Simon, right? A real, dyed-in-the-wool witch, right?"

"I am a witch, 'tis true." She nodded. "But I fail to—"

"Well, if you think you're a witch, then you belong in a padded cell somewhere, not sitting at my dinner table, not sleeping under my roof, with my son!"

She laughed, arching her eyebrows in amusement. "Mr. Proctor, becoming your son's wife has nothing to do with sharing his bed. I have done that already."

Floyd stood immobile, glowering at her. Then he muttered a few words in disgust and, pushing his way past Simon, stormed out of the room. Rowena followed him out, shaking her head and weeping. Simon turned to Gwendolyn and said, "They'll settle down. Don't let it bother you."

She laughed again. "It bothers me not at all, my love."

He glanced at the door of the sitting room. "Look, I think I'd better go and have a few words with them, try to get them to see things our way."

"Yes, do so. I must speak with Adrienne—" she stopped and chuckled, "I mean, with Mary. There is much we must do in preparation. When shall we be wed?"

Simon thought quickly. Got to get video and audio equipment up here, get it hidden in—in what room? Maybe the old barn out back. Yeah, yeah, the old barn'd be great! We could fix it up real spooky! Take a day or two to fix it up, a day for the installation—— "How about in five days, on the twenty-ninth? Can you wait that long?" He grinned at her.

She slid her arms around him and hugged him tightly. "I have waited for nearly three hundred years. I can wait five days."

He pecked her lightly on the lips. "Okay. Go find Adrienne. I'll—"

"Mary," she reminded him. "Mary Warren."

"Yeah, right. I'll go talk to Dad and Row." He kissed her again quickly and then left the room. She watched him leave, her eyes following him with unabashed adoration.

Simon found his father and his daughter sitting in the kitchen. Rowena was still weeping, and Floyd was pounding his closed fist softly upon the table, his face slightly purple with rage. "Now listen to me, both of you," Simon said sternly.

"Boy, I got nothing to say to you," Floyd spat.

"I don't want you to say anything. I want you to listen!"

"I don't want to listen to you either," the old man said. "If you're gonna go'n marry that little slut, then I don't—"

"Pop, will you shut up!" Simon shouted. He glanced over his shoulder to make certain that Gwendolyn was not hovering near the door of the kitchen. "Of course I'm not going to marry Gwen!"

Rowena and Floyd stared at him dumbly. Then Rowena said, "But you just told us you were!"

"Row, just be quiet and listen. There's a lot more to this than you know." He pulled a chair from beside the table and seated himself in it. "I've been thinking about these past few months a lot lately. Doesn't it seem at all strange that those two were so eager to join up with my band? Doesn't it seem odd to you that Gwen went after me so fast, so intently?"

"Yeah, I guess so," Rowena said. "So what?"

"So there's a reason for it. Listen. . . ."

Simon took about ten minutes to explain everything to his father and daughter. They listened in silence, the expressions on their faces reflecting at first confusion, then disbelief, then astonishment. When Simon finished his discourse, he sat back and awaited their response.

Rowena spoke first. "Daddy, you can't be serious! I can't believe what I'm hearing!"

"Yeah, I know," Simon nodded. "I know exactly what you mean. I knew that Gwen and Adrienne were weird, but I never knew how weird until she spun out her fantasy for me."

"I don't mean that at all!" she said. "Daddy, you can't take advantage of her like this! It's terrible!"

This remark stung, and his tone of voice reflected his hurt. "Are you kidding? I'm hearing this from somebody who hates Gwen?"

"You can't hate a cripple for not being able to walk," Rowena replied. "I had no idea she was crazy—I mean, really crazy, not just screwy! And Adrienne! Poor Adrienne! Are you sure she believes this stuff too?"

"Yeah," Simon said defensively. "I talked to her about it. She's convinced that she's really Mary Warren."

"Boy," Floyd said, shaking his head, "you can't do this. These girls need help."

Simon stood up and gazed at them in disbelief. "What the hell is going on here? I thought you two would be relieved when you heard the truth! Look, don't you understand? I'm not really going to marry her! It's all just an act, a show. When we've made some more money, we can get them both some therapy, some help. What's the big deal?"

Rowena stood up and walked toward the door of the kitchen. "Daddy, if you can seriously ask that question, there's nothing I can say to answer it that you can understand."

"Hey!" he called after her. "Who do you think you're talking to, young lady?" She continued out of the room, leaving her father staring stupidly after her. "Goddamn kid!" he muttered.

"Simon," Floyd said, "listen to me. Think, boy, think! What you're plannin' to do is wrong, it's just plain wrong! You can't use people like this. It's just plain *wrong!*"

"Oh, cut the shit, Dad," he said angrily. "I'm trying to keep a roof over our heads, and I'm doing it the best way I know how."

"I kept a roof over your head for quite a while, remember. But I never done nothin' like what you're planning to do."

"You never had to!" he spat. He strode furiously out of the room after his daughter, calling her name as he went. Simon looked in the sitting room and found it empty, but he glanced out the window to see Rowena walking across the street toward the parsonage. He rushed out to the foyer, grabbed a coat from the closet, and went to the front door.

"Simon," he heard Gwendolyn ask as he turned the doorknob, "where are you going?"

"Oh, uh, nowhere, nowhere. I'll be back in a few minutes." He left the old inn and bounded down the steps. He could see the front door of the parsonage swinging closed behind Rowena. Simon quickened his pace as he leapt over a small roadside snowbank into the street, and found to his chagrin that the ice patch upon which he had landed afforded him no traction. He fell on his back and slid a few feet forward.

He pulled himself cautiously to his feet and then stood motionless for a few moments. Calm down, he told himself. Relax. Take it easy. No reason to be upset, no reason to be angry at Row or Dad. They don't understand, that's all. Give them time. They'll realize eventually that this whole plan is okay, that nobody's going to be hurt. Just take it easy.

He placed his right hand on the ache just above his tail-bone. "Damn," he muttered. "That's gonna be sore for a while."

He felt a hand upon his shoulder and turned to see Gwendolyn standing behind him. "Are you injured?" she asked anxiously.

"No, no, I'm okay. You go back inside."

"But where are you going?"

Simon placed his hands gently upon her waist, feeling the taut flesh even through the heavy cloak. "Row's upset about you and me, Gwen, that's all. It's natural for a daughter. You know what I mean, don't you?"

"I suppose so," she shrugged.

"I have to talk to her some more. She just stormed out of the house and went across the street. It's no big deal, nothing to worry about. I'm just going over to talk to her."

Gwendolyn smiled at him and leaned forward, kissing him deeply. "Hurry back," she breathed.

"Yeah, yeah, I will, I will." He resumed his movement across the street, more slowly and carefully this time. Gwendolyn watched him go and waited until he had entered the parsonage. Then she followed after him.

Simon mounted the steps to the upstairs apartment and pushed the door open. He was prepared for a confrontation with Rowena and had determined to remain calm, to understand her feelings, to listen to her and attempt to reason with her as an adult. But when he opened the door he found his daughter tight in the embrace of Jeremy Sloan. She had her face buried in his chest and was weeping freely. He was stroking her long blond hair gently, whispering soothingly into her ear.

Simon became suddenly, irrationally angry. "Well, I see you've found a sympathetic ear!" he spat.

Rowena looked over at him. "Daddy, will you just go away? I can't stand the sight of you!"

Simon walked over to them and grabbed Rowena's arm. He pulled her away from Jeremy roughly, saying, "I thought I told you once before to keep your hands off my daughter!"

Jeremy looked back at him apprehensively, but with a clearly discernible element of anger. "Cool it, Simon," he said evenly. "I was just—"

"Yeah, I know what you were doing, and I know that you've been staying over nights at my place, and I don't like it one bit, you hear me?" He moved threateningly closer to Jeremy.

The young man did not retreat. "I love Rowena, I love her very much. I would never do anything to—"

"Don't try to bullshit me, boy!" Simon hissed. "I know what you've got on your mind. I was your age once, I know what—"

"You don't know anything," he said. "I finally got your number, Simon, back in Chicago, in your hotel room." He leaned forward slightly. "All you ever think about is your bank account and your dick, Simon. You don't really give a damn about anybody but yourself."

Simon stared at him blankly for a moment, and then his face contorted in fury. He swung his fist at Jeremy, but the younger, stronger, more agile man deflected the punch easily. Simon found himself falling forward while Jeremy merely stepped easily to one side. Simon righted himself and then turned to Rowena and said, "Row, get back to the house. Now!"

"No!" she said emphatically. "Why on earth should I? So I can keep your crazy girlfriend company until the men in the white coats come to take her away?"

"Goddamn it, Rowena! Do as I say!" he shouted.

"Simon," Jeremy said, "Row just told me what you're planning to do. It's disgusting."

"Hey, when I want your moral evaluation of my actions, I'll ask for it, okay?"

"Well, you're gonna get it whether you ask for it or not," he replied. "Simon, I used to look up to you, used to think you were so great, so cool, you know? I never realized what a heartless, selfish, greedy son of a bitch you are."

"Who the hell do you think—?" Simon began.

"Don't act like you're offended, man," Jeremy said. "Row just told me what you're gonna do, pretend to marry Gwen

261

just so you can make some more money. Jesus, Simon! Don't you have any sense of right and wrong? You should send Gwen to a mental hospital. She needs professional help. Adrienne needs professional help." He shook his head. "When I think about what you let Gwen do to her back in Chicago—" He shook his head again. "Jesus, Simon!"

"Now wait just one goddamn minute here!" Simon shouted. "I don't have to justify my actions to you or anybody else, you little bastard! And don't change the subject! I didn't mind it when you came along on the tour with Lucas, but I do *not* want you putting your hands on my daughter!"

"Daddy, your mind's been in the gutter for so long it can't climb out!" Rowena shouted. "And he isn't changing the subject! The subject is the terrible thing you're gonna do to Gwendolyn!"

They all turned toward the door as they heard Gwendolyn's throaty laugh. "And is it so terrible to be wed?" she asked with amusement. She unbuttoned and removed her cloak, swirling it about with a flourish and sending it flying onto a nearby chair. "I am touched, child, that you are so concerned for my well-being."

Rowena regarded her cautiously. "Yours, and Adrienne's," she said. "Daddy has told me—"

"Told you that I am a madwoman? Told you that I believe myself to be some reincarnated ghost?" She laughed disparagingly. "Rest easy, child. I love your father, and he loves me, and we shall be wed, and all shall be well."

"Really!" Rowena said. "And did Daddy tell you that he plans to film the wedding and stick it onto the end of the video of the concert?"

Gwendolyn shook her head. "'Tis not true. Our marriage will be a public joy, but the wedding will be private." She turned to Simon. "Our nuptials will not be a spectacle for the idle eyes of gaping onlookers, will it, my love?"

"Of course not," Simon said nervously. Rowena, he thought, shut the hell up, will you?!

"He's lying, Gwen," Rowena said. "He's—"

"Hold your tongue, girl!" Gwendolyn said. "I know my man, and I know the worth of his word to me."

"Listen to me, Gwendolyn!" Rowena shouted. "He just told me—"

"I said, hold your tongue!" Gwendolyn shouted in return. "I'll not listen to such calumny! Be silent, if you value your life!" Her face was growing red.

262

"What's going on up here?" Reverend Wilkes stumbled out of his bedroom, his eyes half open and bleary with interrupted sleep. "Jeremy? What's all the shouting about?"

Jeremy spoke without taking his eyes from Simon. He was watching the older man suspiciously, tensely. "It's nothing, Uncle Fred. Sorry we woke you up."

"Nothing! When I hear people shouting at each other in my home, it isn't—" He noticed Gwendolyn. "Do I know you, miss?"

"This is Gwen Jenkins," Simon said, turning his eyes toward Rowena and Jeremy. "She and I are getting married in a few days." He continued to stare at them defiantly.

Wilkes's face wrinkled up into a broad smile. "Well, Simon, that's fine, that's fine! I'm very pleased—" He narrowed his eyes at the young woman and his smile faded. "Wait a minute. Aren't you—? Didn't I see you here a few weeks ago? Aren't you the one who—?"

"I am a witch," she said coldly. "And you are Jeremy's uncle?"

"Yes," he said gruffly, all signs of friendliness gone.

"You are the minister," she stated.

"I am proud to wear that title, yes."

She nodded. "I hate ministers. I hate all ministers."

"Hey, Gwen," Simon said quickly, "there's no need to . . ."

"'Tis not a personal thing," Gwen said matter-of-factly. "I do not know you, sir. But if you are a minister then you are my enemy, as you are the enemy of my Master."

Rowena stepped forward between Gwendolyn and old Reverend Wilkes. "Gwen, why don't you just go away, get out of here! And you go with her, Daddy!"

"Calm yourself, child," Gwendolyn said, grinning slightly. "I am a warrior in an old war, and this man and men like him have been our enemies since time out of mind. Three hundred years ago, 'twas ministers who hanged my John." She turned to Jeremy. "I too had a minister for an uncle. Samuel Parris he was, minister of Salem Village, and a more mean-spirited, cruel man never walked the—"

"Gwen, cut it out," Simon commanded. "Let's just go home. There's no need to explain anything to these people." He looked at his daughter. "Rowena! Come home, now!"

Rowena glared at him coldly. "Daddy, you can go straight to hell!"

"Rowena!" Reverend Wilkes said sternly. "I understand your anger. But remember God's commandment to honor your father! You must not speak to him in such a manner."

Gwendolyn laughed. "Ah, so little has changed since I was a child! The ministers still vomit platitudes and sit in judgment seats, and I have no doubt but that they still salivate over the pain and agony of those poor souls whom they profess to pity!"

"I beg your pardon, young lady!" Wilkes said.

"And well you might, minister," she chuckled. "I have spent three centuries in hell. You might be surprised how many of your esteemed company I have seen there!"

Wilkes frowned at her, confused. "What on earth are you talking about?"

Simon took Gwendolyn's arm and tried to pull her toward the door. "Gwen, come on, cut it out, will you? Let's go home."

She pulled her arm free of his grip and continued to face the elderly clergyman. "'Tis a simple story, minister. I am a three-hundred-year-old witch, returned to earth this last Eve of All Hallows." She grinned at Jeremy. "Your nephew has not told you of me? I am surprised, for 'tis an enchanting tale."

Wilkes shot Jeremy a quick glance but then returned his attention to Gwendolyn. "Young woman," he said gravely, "I'm not certain what you're trying to say. But I can tell this much: you are deeply disturbed, and you are far from the Lord."

She laughed loudly. "Far from the Lord! Aye, that I am! Far from the Lord!" And she laughed again, deeply, loudly.

Wilkes moved closer to her and placed his hand gently upon her arm. She withdrew it immediately and stepped back, as if his touch were distasteful to her. He ignored her gesture and said, "Don't you know, girl, that God loves you?"

She laughed again, but there was a defensiveness, a nervousness to her laughter. "I think not, minister. He must hate me as much as I hate him."

"He does not hate you, child. He gave His only Son to die for you, that you be not condemned to perdition for your sins."

She snorted, her expression one mingling disbelief with disgust. "Spare me your sermons, minister. I have heard them all before. There is no love in this world, none at all. All who exist are either masters or slaves. There is no third station. You have chosen to serve a weak, simpering god, a foolish and silly god, a god for infants and weaklings. I have chosen to serve a god of physical pleasure, a god of power and pain. Satan is the Master of this world, not your jackass Jehovah!"

Wilkes's face grew slightly flushed. "Girl, you must not speak blasphemy! You are a creation of the Lord God, you are His child, you are His daughter!"

Gwendolyn seemed to regain the small element of her

composure which she had lost. She sidled up to Wilkes, her hands clasped behind her back. "His daughter, am I?! Allow me to tell you of my family, minister! My father was a slave trader out of the English town of Shelbourne, and my mother was a Dutch whore. My father spent his life in prayer and bitter agonizing over his sins as he bought and sold human flesh and took his pleasure with the pox-ridden bodies of outcast women."

Wilkes gazed at her impassively, and his voice tried to hold a sympathy he did not feel. "You poor girl. You must not think—"

"And my uncle, Samuel Parris. Ah, there was a servant of God indeed! Shall I tell you what sorts of punishments he inflicted upon me when I was a child, when I had misbehaved? All throughout my childhood I thought 'twas proper that my uncle pinch and grab me beneath my skirts." She laughed bitterly. "Ministers!"

"Child," Wilkes's voice boomed, "God's grace and forgiveness are freely offered gifts! Accept them before you are lost!"

Gwendolyn swung her hand upward from her side and grabbed Wilkes by the crotch, squeezing hard and mercilessly. "Aye, and my cunny is a freely offered gift. Take it, if you would."

Wilkes staggered backward as Jeremy pushed Gwendolyn roughly away from his uncle, saying, "Gwen, you're disgusting! Get the hell out of here. You too, Simon! Move it!"

Simon took Gwendolyn once again by the arm and pulled her toward the door. "Rowena, come home!"

"No!" she spat and turned away from him.

Simon stood motionless for a moment, glaring at his daughter, contemplating taking her with him by force. He saw Jeremy's dark eyes staring at him, challenging him to try, his balled fists trembling slightly in anticipation of conflict. Simon turned, threw open the door and dragged Gwendolyn behind him down the stairs. As they descended, Gwendolyn called out, "I shall see you again, minister! Damn you, minister, I shall see you again!"

Rowena, Jeremy, and Reverend Wilkes stood in silence for a long while, all staring at the vacant doorway. Then Jeremy said, "I'm sorry, Uncle Fred."

Wilkes shook his head. "You've done nothing wrong, boy. But that woman!" He shook his head again. "Poor Floyd! To have that creature for a daughter-in-law!"

"Try on the idea of having her for a stepmother," Rowena grumbled.

Wilkes turned to her and hugged her paternally. "I'm sorry, child, sorry for your hurt. You should stay here with us for a while. That house isn't fit for a decent girl to be in."

"Yeah, Row, stay here," Jeremy said eagerly. "You can sleep in my room. I'll stay on the sofa."

She smiled at him, sadly, affectionately. "Jeremy, I'm not gonna evict you from your own bed. I'll take the sofa."

"Don't be silly," he replied. "I know how to be a good host."

"Well, we'll discuss it later." She sighed. "God, this is so screwed up!"

"Yeah," Jeremy said, nodding. "And I think things are gonna get worse if Simon goes through with this."

Wilkes turned to Jeremy and frowned. "Boy, what was that poor woman talking about?"

"Huh?"

"She said she was three hundred years old. What was she talking about?"

Jeremy looked at Rowena and took a deep breath. "Uncle Fred, it's a long story."

Wilkes sat down at the table. "I got time," he said.

⟨ CHAPTER EIGHTEEN ⟩

December 24, continued

THE NIGHT WAS dark and still, moonlit by the indistinct silver orb which floated half hidden behind the thick black clouds. Gwendolyn came to the parsonage and opened the front door very gently, hissing slightly at the creak of the hinges. She tiptoed up the stairs, went to the door of the parsonage apartment, and pressed her ear against it. She froze in place, listening, but even her sensitive hearing could detect nothing more pronounced than a few gentle snores. She remained frozen in place, smiling maliciously, and then carefully, oh so carefully, turned the doorknob and pushed the door open. She crept into the dark and silent room.

Jeremy had fallen asleep upon the sofa, worn out by his day of labor and the excitement at home which had followed it. She could hear a soft humming issuing forth from the rear bedroom where Rowena was straightening up her boyfriend's messy abode in preparation for her own habitation. A light crept out from beneath the closed door of the bedroom, and a soft voice was coming from the room next to it. Reverend Wilkes was sitting at his desk, reading softly aloud from his Greek New Testament as was his after-dinner custom.

"En archain ain ha logos," he said quietly, *"kai ha logos ain pros ton theon, kai theos ain ha logos . . ."*

Rowena was busy, Wilkes was preoccupied, and Jeremy was asleep. There would be no better time than now for what she was planning. A virgin's blood. One must have a virgin's blood.

She moved silently from the doorway to the sofa, her gentle footfalls making nary a sound upon the old, worn carpet. She knelt down beside the sleeping boy, smiling at him cruelly. "Jeremy," she whispered. She leaned her face close to his and whispered again, "Jeremy." He opened his groggy eyes, but before full wakefulness could arise in him his semiconscious mind was drawn deep into the eyes which stared into his, the two orbs burning with green fire which seemed to bore into his soul. "Jeremy," she repeated.

"Y—yes—?" he muttered.

"You are sleeping, Jeremy," she whispered. "You are dreaming. You are dreaming of peacefulness and calm, of warm sunshine and quiet, cool breezes."

"Yes," he whispered, "yes. . . ."

He seemed to be lying upon a blanket of cool grass in midsummer. The warm sun was beating down upon his bare skin and a gentle, soothing wind was sweeping over his body.

"You are happy, Jeremy," she said. "You are happier than you have ever been in your whole life. You are happier than you have ever imagined you could ever be."

"Yes. . . ." He smiled. Such joy! Such contentment! He could see his own face somehow, and his expression was one of uninterrupted happiness, of imperturbable peace.

"When you hear my voice speak to you of peacefulness and calm, then shall you go to the place of warmth and rest. Then shall you go because I send you there. You must heed my words and obey them, that you might go there."

"Yes . . . yes . . . ," he whispered.

"Soon, my dear Jeremy, very, very soon, I shall come to you, or Adrienne shall come to you, and you shall listen and you shall obey. Do you understand?"

"I . . . understand. . . ."

"Then shall you be taken to a place of warmth and light and ease and joy, a place of endless happiness and warmth and pleasure."

"Yes," he whispered. "Happiness . . . pleasure . . ."

He rolled over on the cool grass and the summer sun beat gently down upon his bare back as he reached out to embrace Rowena. She was lying beside him, smiling and murmuring wordless expressions of love and desire and need. He ran his hand over her warm belly and soft breasts as she entwined her fingers in his hair and pulled him closer to her.

"Row," he muttered. "Row . . . I love you, Row. . . ."

"Jeremy," she breathed in Gwendolyn's voice, "pleasure, calm, happiness, if you heed my commands."

"Yes," he whispered. He placed his lips upon hers and she responded eagerly, parting her lips and drawing his tongue deep into her mouth. He squeezed her breasts gently at first, and then tightened his grip as he felt the need grow within him, as his loins began to burn with desire.

And then her face changed. It was no longer Rowena whom he held. A rotting human skull gazed up at him from a decaying and cadaverous body, and the creature's grip on him was viselike and unrelenting. One bony finger reached over and plunged into his throat, releasing a flow of blood which seemed to inundate the field. But he welcomed the assault, he welcomed the hideous laughter, he welcomed death.

"Jeremy!" Rowena said, shaking him roughly. "Jeremy! Wake up!"

He sat up on the sofa and looked at her stupidly for a moment. Then he blushed slightly and smiled. "Row! I just had the weirdest dream!"

She sat down beside him and kissed him lightly on the lips. "So I gathered. You were groaning in your sleep."

"Yeah, I'm not surprised," he laughed. He noticed that she had donned her coat. "You going out?"

"Just across the street. I figure I'd better go over and get some things if I'm gonna be staying here for a few days. It looks pretty quiet over there, and I'm kind of hoping that everybody's gone. I really don't want to meet any of them, especially Daddy or Gwen."

"Makes sense." He looked around the room. Rowena had switched on a table lamp. "Where's Uncle Fred?"

"In his room, reading," she replied. She rose to her feet. "Look, I'm gonna go over there now. I'll be back in a few minutes."

"Okay. I'll wait up for you," he said. Jeremy watched her close the door behind her and then fell almost immediately back to sleep. In a few moments he was snoring soundly.

Rowena walked out into the cold night air and pulled her collar tight around her throat. She crunched her way through the snow and glanced quickly through the front window of the old inn before pushing open the door. She entered the house quietly, not wishing to meet or speak with anyone, wondering where her grandfather was, wondering if she would have the opportunity to speak with Adrienne, wondering if she really wanted to. She mounted the stairs to her bedroom and once inside closed the door softly behind her.

Rowena sighed, partly from relief and partly from unhappiness, and then took a small suitcase from her closet. As she was filling it with clothing and books, she heard the door open behind her. Damn it! she thought. She turned around apprehensively.

Karyn Johannson waddled into the room. She was pale and weary, but she managed a smile. "Hiya, kid. Hot times over at the parsonage today!"

Rowena returned her attention to her suitcase. "No kidding."

Karyn chuckled. "Your father was fit to be tied when he came back this afternoon. I understand that Gwen didn't get along too well with that old man over there."

Rowena turned and faced the other girl, noting with distaste that Karyn's long, stringy red hair was matted and unwashed, that she exuded a slight but detectable odor of sweat. "You know, Karyn, I don't understand you at all."

Karyn sat down heavily on the edge of the bed. "What do you mean?"

"I mean, good Lord! You're pregnant by a guy who hasn't said one thing about marrying you, you drink like a sailor on shore leave and do all kinds of drugs all the time. I *know* that you think all of this witchcraft stuff is nonsense, but you seem to get a kick out of all this!"

Karyn laughed easily. "Look, Row, I love Lukie, okay? I know he's an asshole sometimes, but so is everybody else. I'll do whatever he wants to do, and hang around with whoever he wants to hang around with. I mean, it don't make no difference to me, you know?"

"But your baby!" she said with exasperation. "God, Karyn, all those drugs, all that liquor—!"

Karyn got awkwardly to her feet. "Jesus, Rowena! I just came in to say hi and make nice, and you start a goddamn lecture!" She waddled out the door, saying, "You're as much fun as a fart in a space suit."

Rowena closed the door which Karyn had left open and then finished packing. As she took her toiletries from the top of the bureau, she remembered a small bottle of perfume which she had purchased for Adrienne as a Christmas present. Despite all that had transpired, she still felt sorry for the girl, still felt an urge to protect her from herself and others. She could not forget that night in the motel room when she had held and soothed and comforted the frantic girl. I might as well give it to her, Rowena thought. I'm sure she's around somewhere. I don't want to run into Daddy or that bitch of his, but maybe she's in the room she stayed in before, by herself.

Rowena took her suitcase in hand and stuffed the bottle into the pocket of her parka. She opened her door carefully and leaned out into the hallway. She neither saw nor heard anyone. Probably all went out to eat or something. Karyn probably didn't have the energy to go with them.

She tiptoed down the hallway and peeked into her grandfather's room first. Old Floyd was sitting in a chair by the window, staring morosely out at the fields which stretched out behind the old inn. "Gramps?" she whispered.

Floyd turned his head and smiled at her. "Hello, honey," he said softly. "I thought you—?"

"I'm staying at the parsonage for a while," she said. "I just can't stay here with all these horrible people here. I hate Gwendolyn, I hate Daddy, I hate his band, and I just can't stay here."

He held his old hand out to her and she stepped forward and took it. She leaned over and kissed him on the cheek. "I'm sorry, Grampa. I don't want to leave you here all alone like this."

He patted her hand gently. "It's the best thing to do, Rowena. I don't want you to be here right now anyway. Not with all these goings-on."

"Why don't you come over too? I'm sure Reverend Wilkes can put you up. In fact, he'd be happy—"

"No," Floyd shook his head. "I've lived in this house all my life. I ain't gonna let my son and his sick friends drive me out of it. But you go back over to Fred's. You stay there till they all leave."

"Okay," she said and kissed him again. "Where is everybody, anyway?"

"Went over to Piermont, most of 'em. Karyn stayed here. So did that other poor girl."

"Adrienne? Where is she?"

He shrugged. "I don't know. Don't care much, either. You go on and git, Rowena." He turned away from her and stared once more out the window, lost in thought, lost in regret and sorrow, in anger at himself and in fury at his son.

She left his room quietly and then went to the room where she hoped she would find Adrienne Lupescu. She pushed that door open and looked inside. Adrienne was sitting on the bed, sewing. "Hi, Adrienne," she said as she entered.

Adrienne looked up, startled, and then smiled warmly. "Oh, Rowena, it's so good to see you! I've missed you so!"

Rowena felt her heart go out to the poor, lonely girl. "Are you all right? I mean—"

"Aye, all is well with me," she sighed. "They did not touch me after that night."

She knew what it was to which Adrienne was referring, but she chose not to discuss it. She remembered having become angry at Adrienne that night and now regretted it, realizing that the girl was not responsible for her actions. It was her mental illness which had forced her to obey Gwendolyn's orders and submit to Herricks's assault. "What are you doing?" she asked. "You making something?"

"Aye," she replied, holding up a black lace cloth. " 'Twill be part of Gwendolyn's trousseau."

"It's lovely," Rowena said politely. Black for a bride, she thought. It figures.

"The wedding will be in a few days, and there is much to do." She resumed her sewing.

Rowena put her suitcase down and reached into her pocket. She took out the perfume bottle and handed it to Adrienne. "Merry Christmas," she said.

Adrienne stared at her for a moment and then took the bottle from her. "For me? A gift?"

"Yes," she laughed. "It's a Christmas present. Merry Christmas!"

Adrienne stared at the bottle with disbelief and then began to weep softly. "I—I have no words—"

"You can say thank you," Rowena said.

"Th—thank you," she wept.

Rowena sat down beside her on the bed. "Hey, jeeze! Don't

cry! I just wanted to get you a little something. It isn't much!"

Adrienne hugged her impulsively. "You are so kind, Rowena. You are so good."

Rowena blushed, growing uncomfortable. "Come on, cut it out. It's just a bottle of perfume, for Pete's sake!"

"'Tis the kindest thing anyone has ever done for me, truly the kindest thing!" She hugged Rowena tightly and continued to weep.

Rowena felt tears rising to her eyes as well. What a life this poor thing must have had, she thought sadly, to get so worked up over a cheap bottle of perfume. "Come on, Adrienne, take it easy. Take it easy!"

"I am sorry," she said. "It is just that you are so—" She shook her head and brushed away a tear. "I am sorry."

Rowena gazed at her for a moment and then said, very, very tentatively, "Look, Adrienne, I'm staying across the street with Jeremy and his uncle. Why don't you come with me? You shouldn't stay here. Gwendolyn isn't good for you, she's bad for your nerves."

Adrienne laughed sadly. She took a small handkerchief from her sleeve and blew her nose loudly. "I cannot, Rowena. I am bound to her in all things. It is my debt, my punishment, for what I did in Salem three hundred years ago."

Rowena took her hand. "Adrienne, I know all about this delusion you and Gwen have, but you must understand that none of it is true! You are Adrienne Lupescu. You have never been anyone else."

She shook her head. "I am Mary Warren. I was born in Salem in 1672. Abby and I hanged ourselves in a stable in Boston in 1702. I was returned to earth last Eve of All Hallows."

Rowena sighed. "Adrienne, dammit, that isn't true! Daddy is just taking advantage of your illness. You have a problem, and you need help. All that you're doing by staying here is making yourself worse, making your sickness worse!" She squeezed her hand. "Come with me, over to the parsonage. Please."

Adrienne shook her head again. "I cannot. But you should go back there. This house is not fit for you. You are too good for it." She returned her attention to the lace.

Rowena stood up and took her suitcase in hand. "If you change your mind, just come on over, okay?"

"Yes. Thank you. And thank you for the gift." Adrienne seemed to be avoiding her eyes.

Rowena left the room and walked quietly down the hallway. She took no precautions, having been informed by her grandfather that Simon and company had gone into Piermont. Drinking, most likely, she thought. That's where Lucas always goes.

She left the inn and walked across the icy street toward the parsonage, holding her parka closed against the cold wind. The door of the parsonage opened before she reached it, and Reverend Wilkes walked out into the night air, all cloaked and scarfed and earmuffed. "Rowena," he called out. "Did you get everything you need?"

"For a few days, at least," she said. "Where are you going, Reverend?" They met in the middle of the street.

"To the church," he answered. "I leave it open all day in case anyone wishes to come in and pray. Got to lock it up for the night."

"You shouldn't be going out in this weather," she said solicitously. "Why doesn't Jeremy go and lock it up?"

"Oh, he does," Wilkes said. "But now that he's got himself a job, and a hard one at that, I don't want to keep asking him to do little chores for me."

"Well, gee, I'll go and—"

"No, no, child, you go upstairs." He smiled. "The walk will do me good. It's a nice night, anyway. I'll be home soon."

"Well, okay," she said without conviction. "If you're sure—"

"Go upstairs, Rowena." He smiled. "I'll be fine." He began to walk unsteadily up the street on his arthritic legs. She watched him for a moment and then went into the parsonage.

Wilkes grimaced as the pain in his knees intensified, and he stopped for a moment, hoping it would subside. Pride, he thought to himself, foolish pride. You should have let the girl lock up the church. You shouldn't have left it unlocked in the first place, for that matter. No one left around here to attend it, no congregation anymore. Last Sunday service I prayed with two women as old as I am. Didn't even preach.

He started walking again, slowly, feeling the cold seep into his old bones, and reached the church in a few minutes. Thank the Lord this is a small town, he thought as he opened the door and reached in to switch off the few dim ceiling lights which he had left on during the day. Then he closed and locked the door.

He turned away and began to walk painfully back toward the parsonage when he heard a distant voice call out, "Minister! Reverend Wilkes!" He turned in the direction of the voice and saw a motion across the street. The full moon's light filtered through the clouds sufficiently to reflect from a metallic object moving somewhere in the middle of the old town cemetery. Wilkes squinted his eyes and peered into the darkness. "Minister!" the voice called again as he once more saw the glint of moonlight upon metal. No one was supposed to be in the cemetery at night, he thought angrily. Some young vandals, he thought, kids up to mischief. His fists clenched as he began to cross the street and walk over toward the old graveyard.

The Bradford cemetery did not belong to the Bradford Congregationalist Church in any legal sense, for both belonged to the town; but as the town's minister, Wilkes had cared for the old graveyard for many decades as if it were part of his duties. No one had been buried there for years, no one in Wilkes's own lifetime, for that matter; but this was of no importance. The cemetery was the place of repose for those who had gone before, and it needed to be respected and tended to, and Wilkes had done both. There had been very little vandalism in the old graveyard over the years, but he had read about such things elsewhere, stones defaced and overturned, old markers uprooted and carried off as souvenirs and conversation pieces. He quickened his pace as best he could and tried to ignore the shooting pains in his knees.

Wilkes found the gate open. It was never locked but it was always closed. Now it was open wide. He squinted his eyes again and saw once more the glint of moonlight on a moving object. He walked toward the motion and soon was able to see a black-robed figure wielding a shovel, digging into the cold, stony ground. He moved toward the figure and said loudly, "You there! What do you think you're doing?" He was ignored and he drew closer. When he was not five feet from the figure he repeated, "What do you think you're doing? Stop that immediately. I said stop that im—" The blade of the shovel swung suddenly upward and struck him in the head, sending him sprawling onto the ground, dazed and stunned but not mortally injured. He lay motionless, struggling not to lose consciousness.

Gwendolyn Jenkins reached into the pocket of her cloak and drew forth some rope and a long strip of cloth. She tossed the shovel aside and dropped to her knees, acting with feverish haste. She wrapped the rope around the old man's ankles and then tied his hands together behind his back. She wrapped the long cloth around his mouth several times and knotted it behind his head. Then, smiling, she returned to her digging.

Wilkes managed to drag himself back up to full awareness very quickly, and felt a surge of panic when he realized that he was bound and gagged. His eyes darted frantically around and he struggled impotently against the ropes. Gwendolyn threw shovel after shovel of dirt onto the ever expanding pile beside the ever deepening hole, hopping at last into the hole and continuing to dig. Wilkes tried to scream, tried to cry out for help, but the gag muffled his cries. His wrists became bloody from his struggle with the bonds, but the knots were too tight for him to escape them. He writhed about on the cold ground like a trussed and terrified animal.

Gwendolyn threw one last shovel of dirt from the hole and then climbed out. Wordlessly, ignoring his frenzied, spasmodic motions, she rolled him over a few times and then pushed him into the pit. She stared down at him unemotionally, watching as he shook his head in an attempt to free his eyes of the dirt, watching as he struggled, listening to the muffled cries, gazing impassively into the angry, frightened eyes. Then she smiled coldly, inhumanly, and laughed. "Ministers!" she said. "How I *do* hate ministers!"

She picked up the shovel and began to throw dirt into the pit. Wilkes felt his heart rising to his throat as the cold stones and flakes of earth struck him in the face and fell heavily onto his chest and legs. He tried to scream, and found that terror had rendered him dumb.

"Shall we pray together, minister?" Gwendolyn asked. "'Tis your last chance this side of the grave." She continued to toss the dirt back into the hole. "Come, let us pray. Our Father, who art in heaven—come now, minister! I can't hear you!— Our Father, who art in heaven, hallowed be Thy name . . ."

Wilkes jerked his body in frenzied, desperate movements, as if he hoped he could snap the thick ropes with his old, tired muscles. His heart began to beat faster and faster. Pains shot through his chest.

". . . Thy Kingdom come, Thy will be done on earth as it is in heaven . . ." Gwendolyn continued to toss the dirt onto the old man's face and chest and legs. ". . . Give us this day our daily bread and forgive us our trespasses, as we forgive those who trespass against us . . ."

The cold earth was smothering him, weighing down upon him, impeding his futile, senseless struggle. The woman's voice was becoming muffled and indistinct as she filled in the grave, as the heavy dirt filled his ears and eyes and nose. He struggled to breathe, and inhaled only the smell and substance of mold.

". . . Lead us not into temptation, but deliver us from evil, for Thine is the Kingdom . . ."

He tried to draw air into his lungs. There was no air.

". . . and the power . . ."

Wilkes tried to move, but each motion caused the loosely packed dirt to fall in on him more tightly. He was at last immobile.

". . . and the glory . . ."

His chest exploded in pain as his old heart succumbed to the terror.

". . . forever and ever. Amen."

Gwendolyn Jenkins piled the dirt high over the impromptu grave, and then stood back to admire her handiwork. "I thank you, minister," she said softly. "I hated my uncle so, and never had the chance to kill him. He was a minister, like you. So you stand in his stead." She laughed bitterly. "So many ministers in my life—like unto that fool who insulted us a few days ago—and so few opportunities for vengeance. I thank you, Reverend Wilkes. Meeting you today was a great pleasure for me."

She looked up at the sky and smiled at the dark clouds which drifted over the face of the moon. "I do believe 'twill snow tonight, minister," she whispered. "Your silly God shall give you a white blanket for your final bed."

She gazed intently at the pile of earth, watching for any movement. The dirt seemed to settle slightly, being compacted by its own weight. She laughed softly and vindictively and then spat on the grave. "Ministers!" she muttered.

She picked up the shovel and left the cemetery quickly, tossing the tool casually into the bushes which bounded the cemetery entrance. She moved quietly down the cold, deserted road, seeming at last to disappear into the darkness. And then the old town was silent once more, but for the low moan of the wind.

〔CHAPTER NINETEEN〕
December 29

MARK SIEGAL BREATHED deeply as he stood back and surveyed the end result of all his labors. When Simon had decided to use the old ramshackle barn which had been decaying for years behind the old Proctor Inn, it had fallen to Siegal to oversee the renovation. Of course, renovation was the last thing Simon Proctor intended for the barn. In its present state, it was a perfect setting for the wedding ceremony as he had envisioned it. The silent, lofty timbers, the cracked and weathered planks of the walls, the rust and the dust and the gloom, were ideal surroundings for a satanic ritual. Such renovation as Siegal had done related merely to the shoring up of several potentially dangerous beams and wall sections. For the rest, his job had been twofold: to decorate the barn in an appropriately macabre manner, and to assist the cameramen in the process of hiding film equipment at various places around the interior of the old structure.

As he swept his gaze from right to left, he had reason to be satisfied with the job he had done. The interior of the barn was, of course, a large, open rectangular room, and he had placed a long narrow table at one end to serve as an altar. He had draped the table with purple cloth and placed a candelabrum at each end to balance on each side the large, free-standing gold-painted pentagram which stood in the middle of the table. He had found a carpenter over in Piermont who had been able to produce the symbol quickly and well, and who had wondered who would want a five-pointed star enclosed in a large circle carved from wood and painted gold. Siegal offered no explanation, and the carpenter had not pressed the matter. He was paid in cash for his labor, and that was sufficient.

The rear wall of the barn, directly behind the table and pentagram, had been decorated with a large inverted cross which was painted a bright, brilliant red. Siegal had objected, saying that the absurd combination of colors—purple, bright red, gold, black, and so forth—was jarring rather than atmospheric, bizarre rather than macabre, but Simon had been insistent. Simon had absolutely no sense of the visually aesthetic. It seemed as if all his artistic sense had been channeled into music, leaving nothing for the other muses to work with.

Siegal complied without serious argument. It was, after all, Simon's pseudomarriage, not his, and the video would sell and rent by the hundreds of thousands regardless of the colors of the decorations. Simon had arranged with the television people to obtain the clip of Eisenmann's death on the Campbell show, and small payments to the late professor's few distant relatives had made it possible to include it in the final version of the video. It would begin with the Campbell show, go through the tour and the songs in the Corwin Museum, and end with the wedding.

Well, he may not have much of an eye for color, Siegal thought, but he certainly has a mind for business. We're all gonna make a fortune out of this.

He continued to examine the interior of the barn. The wedding was to begin very shortly, and any last-minute changes needed to be made now. He saw nothing which needed his attention. The artificial cobwebs which he had brought with him from the theatrical props store in Manhattan were strung between the rafters and the walls; the hideously ugly gargoyles which he had managed to find in antique shops stood at judiciously chosen spots around the room; the entire barn would be lighted by candles for the ceremony, and the two hundred black candles he had managed to purchase were awaiting the lick of the flame.

Looks good, he thought. Good? It looks horrible! But that's what we want.

Siegal then turned his attention to the important, the crucial elements of the preparations: the recording equipment. He and Simon had decided to limit the film crew to two people, one of whom would be secreted in the shadowy recesses of the loft until the beginning of the ceremony, the other of whom would be in a hastily constructed shed connected to the west wall of the barn, where he could film through a hole which had been drilled in the wall. They had briefly contemplated using two more cameramen, but had decided not to risk it. Gwendolyn had been very clear about the seriousness of this ceremony, and she would be furious if she knew it was to be filmed and used for commercial purposes.

So two cameramen, no more. They had hidden microphones in a dozen places around the barn so as to be able to record every sound, every word, no matter where spoken. The camera in the loft would be able to take panoramic shots, and the exterior camera could handle profile close-ups. Full face would have been better, but more cameras and more people would have endangered the secrecy.

Siegal was satisfied. He left the barn after calling out a muted good-bye to the two cameramen and walked out into the cold evening air. Sunset in fifteen minutes, he thought. The wedding in a half hour. Then we can all go home and forget all this nonsense. He indulged himself in a few minutes of self-pity. I'll bet Charlie Watts doesn't have to do this kind of shit for Jagger!

He jogged across the white ground, listening to the hushed crackle of the snow as it was crushed beneath his boots. How the hell can Simon like it up here? he wondered. Gets more snow in one day than New York City gets in a month!

He pushed open the side door of the old Proctor Inn and then shut it behind him quickly, grateful for the warmth of the interior. Siegal stamped his feet a few times to dislodge the snow from his boots and then walked over to the doorway of the sitting room. "Anybody seen Simon?" he asked.

The other band members were sitting around impatiently, smoking cigarettes and joints, drinking bourbon and wine, wishing they were all home, wishing that this day were over. The tour had been long and hard and harried, and this unexpected extension of their working commitment had pleased none of them. They were all already attired in their Witch's Sabbath costumes (except for Herricks, who had none), and Siegal could tell by the expressions on their faces that they were not in the best of moods. Herricks exhaled a blue cloud of intoxicating smoke and answered, "He's upstairs gettin' dressed."

"Thanks," Siegal said and began to walk toward the stairs.

"Hey, Markie," Strube called out, "you wanna blow some weed?"

"Not now, Carl. Maybe later." He turned and moved toward the stairs.

"Hey, Siegal!" he heard Herricks call out. "Tell Simon to get his ass in gear, will you? I want to get the hell out of here, get back to civilization."

"Yeah, yeah," Siegal said testily as he bounded up the stairs. He went to Simon's room and opened the door. He entered to find his friend seated on the wooden chair which had been moved to a position in front of the dresser. Simon was staring absently into the mirror, gazing into his own eyes. Siegal smiled. "Admiring your own beauty?"

Simon jumped slightly at the unexpected voice. "Oh, Mark. You startled me. I didn't hear you come in. Is everything ready?"

"Yup," he replied, pulling up a chair and sitting down. "All we gotta do is light up the candles and roll the cameras."

"Shhh!" Simon said quickly. "Gwen and Adrienne are in the next room!"

"Sorry," he shrugged. "They almost ready?"

"Beats me," Simon replied, returning his gaze to the mirror. "They won't let me in to check on them. Can't see the bride before the wedding, and all that stuff." He reached beneath the cowl of his black monk's robe and scratched the back of his neck. "They should be ready pretty soon, though."

"Good. The guys are all waiting downstairs, bored to death. And they're smoking a lot of dope down there. I mean, your old man's got to smell it!"

Simon shook his head. "Dad's over at the parsonage with Row and the Sloan kid."

Siegal laughed. "Getting away from his guests?"

"Yeah," Simon grinned, "partly. He really just wants to keep an eye on Jeremy. He likes that little bastard."

"So does Rowena."

He snorted. "Don't remind me."

"His uncle ever turn up?"

"Hmmm?" Simon was staring at his own reflection.

"The old minister, his uncle. He ever turn up?"

"Nope. Nobody can figure out what happened to him. Just seemed to vanish." Simon's goatee felt a bit loose, and he pressed it hard against his chin. "That's really why Dad's over there. The boy is real upset."

"Can't say I blame him. No clues, no note, nothing?"

"Nothing." Simon slumped down in the chair and sighed slightly. "Maybe he got assumpted or something."

"Got what?"

"Whatever the word is. Taken up into heaven by God or something. Who knows? Who cares?"

Siegal took out a cigarette and lighted it. "I take it he wasn't on your ten favorite people list."

"Far from it. I wasn't on his, either." He paused. "Funny that we both used the past tense."

Siegal shrugged. The conversation was growing tedious. "You want to go over to the barn, check it out?"

"No," Simon replied, shaking his head. "I trust you, Markie. I'm sure you did it up good." He squinted his eyes at his own reflection. "Enough makeup, you think?"

"Yeah, sure. You look great." Siegal studied him closely for a moment. "Simon, is something bothering you?"

He shrugged. "No. I don't know."

"Hey, come on, man," Siegal said, reaching over and punching him familiarly on the shoulder. "You look depressed! And on your so-called wedding day!"

They both laughed. "Yeah, right," Simon said. "My wedding day!"

"Oh, damn!" Siegal slapped his forehead. "I totally forgot!"

"Forgot what?"

"We didn't throw you a bachelor party!" He laughed again. Simon just smiled, and then he sighed. "Come on, Simon," Siegal said seriously. "What the hell's the matter?"

He stood up and began to pace the room, the oversized monk's robe trailing behind him. "You know, Markie, when I first thought this up it all seemed so easy, such a good idea. But everybody keeps telling me that I'm doing something terrible to Gwen, and it's starting to get to me."

He shrugged. "I haven't told you that."

"No, but Dad has, and Row. Even Jeremy and his uncle. Of course, you got to expect it from a minister, I suppose, but—"

"You talked to the minister about it?"

"Not personally. He sent me a hellfire and damnation warning through my father." He found Siegal's tone odd. "Why do you ask?"

"Just curious. I mean, the old guy has disappeared, after all."

"Yeah, yeah, the cops asked me all about it. Last time I saw him, me and Gwen were arguing with him."

"The cops suspect you of doing him in?" He grinned at the joke.

"No, of course not. I was with everybody else, drinking over in Piermont, remember? You, me, Gwen, Lucas, everybody."

"Yeah, yeah. Sorry I asked. Just curious."

"But anyway, I'm starting to feel, I don't know, guilty or something. I mean, this girl really thinks she loves me. And I don't love her, not really."

"You screw her often enough," Siegal pointed out.

"What's that got to do with it?"

Siegal shrugged. "Nothing, I guess. But look, Simon, the chick is really crazy, right? She thinks she's some old-time

281

witch, right? So marry her for the video, and maybe someday she'll decide that she's somebody else, and take off and that'll be the end of it. Why worry?"

"Yeah, yeah, I know." He sighed again. "Still makes me feel funny."

"So call it off," he suggested.

Simon laughed. "Hey, it doesn't make me feel *that* funny!"

"I didn't think so," Siegal said, joining in the laughter. "I think we stand to make a bundle off this whole video thing."

"Yeah, probably." He paused. "I think maybe it's time to take the money and run, you know?"

"What do you mean?"

"I think we should call it quits after this video. I mean, we've made money on the tour, more money than we've ever made. This video should make us a lot more, and that dumb movie is doing really well. Maybe we should just quit while we're ahead."

"What do you mean 'we'? Except for Tommy and his rock club, the rest of us are still just working stiffs! Maybe you can afford to retire, but we can't!"

"Listen, Markie, you're gonna see at least a hundred grand from the tour and the video, maybe more. That's enough for anybody to lay back and cruise on."

"Okay, sure, but two hundred grand is better than a hundred grand, and three hun—"

Simon laughed softly, refusing to take his friend's concern seriously. "Easy, Mark. You don't want to make too much money too quickly."

"Hey, it beats making too little too slowly," he muttered. "Look, man, I'm serious here! If we don't—"

He stopped speaking as the door swung open and Adrienne Lupescu leaned her head into the room. "Excuse me," she said quietly.

"Hiya, Adrienne," Simon said. "Come on in."

"No, by your leave," she said. "Gwendolyn asked—I mean Abigail asked me to tell you that she is prepared. You should await us in the place which has been made ready."

Has to try to remember to say Abigail instead of Gwendolyn, Simon thought. I wonder how much of this resurrection crap they really believe? "Okay, fine," he said. "You'll be right over?"

"We shall," Adrienne replied. "We lack but one element for the ceremony. When I have fetched it, I shall come. Gw—Abigail says that she will follow soon after you when you go." She withdrew and pulled the door closed.

Simon turned to Mark Siegal. "Well, let's do it." He rose to his feet.

"Wasn't that what Gilmore said?"

"Huh?" Simon walked out of the room and Siegal followed him.

"Gary Gilmore, the guy who was executed in Utah a few years ago. Weren't those his last words, 'Let's do it'?"

"Funny, Markie, very funny," he said as he descended the stairs. "If this were a real wedding, you might even be making me nervous."

Herricks, Strube, and Mahoney had heard them coming and were waiting at the bottom of the stairs. "Let's get this show on the road," Herricks said.

"Yeah, right," Simon responded. "Okay, let me run through it for you again."

"For Christ's sake, Simon, we know what to do!" Mahoney said. "It isn't all that hard, you know?"

"I know, but I just want to make sure everybody knows what to do and when to do it, so listen up. . . ."

Simon's band only half listened to him as he reviewed for them the procedure for the ceremony. Their boots made muted crunching sounds on the snow as they walked from the old inn to the barn, each of them nodding in turn as Simon made mention of some individual directions. When they entered the barn, Simon smiled. "Markie! Great job!"

"Thanks," Siegal replied. "Should we light the candles?"

"Maybe we should wait for the girls."

"Yeah, but the cameramen have to get light readings. Remember, we can't treat this like a dress rehearsal. It's a one-shot deal, you know?"

Simon nodded. "Of course. Are they all set, except for the light?"

"Yeah," Siegal replied. "They got the sound level a while ago. They'll start rolling as soon as we give the word."

"Great." He addressed the others. "Guys, everybody start lighting candles. Everybody got matches?" They all searched through their pockets and each found at least one book. A group of such inveterate devotees of tobacco and marijuana was never short on such things.

They walked around the large, high-roofed barn without coordination, lighting candles randomly. After a few minutes the interior was illuminated by two hundred flickering flames which danced atop two hundred tall black candles. The wavering, trembling light reflected from the golden pentagram

283

and the inverted cross, and seemed to shimmer upon the cobwebs. Simon looked around and grinned. "Fantastic!" he muttered. "Fantastic!"

"Looks goddamn stupid to me," Herricks muttered.

"Shut up, will you, Larry?" Siegal said. "It's atmospheric."

"Yeah, I suppose," he said and lighted a cigarette on one of the candles. "I just wish we could spend our time making music and not doin' this shit."

"You're making money," Strube said, "so stop bitching."

"Come on, everybody, just shut up," Simon said. "Tom, why don't you go to the door and keep an eye out for the girls. We'll start rolling as soon as you see them coming from the inn."

Mahoney walked to the door and peered out. "Well, then, start rolling. Here they come." He squinted against the glare of the sun upon the snow. "They got somebody with 'em."

Simon ignored the last remark. "Okay, start filming. Everybody to the door. We'll walk in one at a—"

"We know, Simon, we know, we know!" Herricks spat. "Jesus!"

They moved to the door. They stood in silence.

The cameras began to roll.

Tom Mahoney walked slowly forward and took his place to the right of the table which was serving as the altar. Carl Strube waited until Mahoney was at his appointed spot and then he too walked from the rear of the barn, coming to a halt to the left of the altar. Siegal and Herricks followed suit, the latter on the left, the former on the right.

Simon Proctor then came forward, walking with exaggerated solemnity, his hands clasped upon his breast, his head bowed. He moved to a position directly in front of the altar and stood motionless. Then he turned toward what he knew was the clandestine side camera and spoke, striving to lower his already low bass voice, rolling his vowels and looking up from beneath his dark brows. "We gather here to celebrate and to worship. I shall this day wed Gwendolyn Jenkins according to ancient ritual. Satan shall bless our union and make fruitful her womb."

He turned from the camera and stood in motionless silence, his eyes fixed upon the door at the other end of the barn. Come on, he thought, hurry up, hurry up. I know we can always edit the film so the time gaps are gotten rid of, but I want to get this over with. Hurry up, Gwen, will you?

The barn door creaked open.

Lucas Proctor and Karyn Johannson walked in. "Hiya, Dad," Lucas said easily. "Everything just about ready?"

"Cut!" Simon shouted. "Lucas, what the hell do you think you're doing?"

Lucas's face registered hurt confusion. "Comin' to the wedding, of course. What did you think I—"

"Where's Gwendolyn? Where's Adrienne? And what the hell are you two doing here? I told you this was supposed to be just the seven of us."

Lucas leaned forward and smiled. "Does that include the cameramen, Dad?" he whispered.

"Shut up, Lucas! Goddamn it all! Where—"

"Gwen's waiting outside. Adrienne had to get something. When she gets here, we can start."

"What do you mean, 'we'?" Simon said. "I thought I told you that I wanted to make a big thing out of the number seven, all that numerology stuff! You two can't be here for this! It messes up the whole idea!"

Karyn coughed. "'Scuse me," she said. "Look, I didn't really want to come to this thing, y'know? but Adrienne said that Gwen wanted us both here. I mean, she's the one who planned the whole ceremony, right?"

"No, she did not!" Simon exclaimed. "I worked out the whole ceremony myself."

"Yeah?" Karyn grinned. "Well, you shoulda let Gwen in on it, 'cause she's got her own plans."

"What the hell are you talking about?" Simon said. "I told her that I would arrange a ceremony, and all she had to do was repeat the words as I say them."

"Yeah, right, I know, she told me," Karyn replied. "And what did she tell you?"

"Well, she said that—" Simon paused. "Well, okay, she said that she had some things she wanted to do, and I said it would be okay, as long as—"

"As long as she used your vows, right? Well, that's the way it's gonna be. Your vows, her ceremony."

"Shit!" Simon muttered. "This screws up everything!" Shoulda had a rehearsal, he thought. But how could I have explained that to Gwen without telling her that I'm having it all filmed? "Shit!" he repeated.

He heard Gwendolyn's voice from outside the door, faintly, as if she were still standing some distance from the barn. "Mary Warren approaches," she said. "Make ready within."

Make ready within, Simon thought as he returned to his

place in front of the altar. Well, if Gwendolyn ever does decide that she's somebody else, at least I won't have to listen to the ridiculous way she talks anymore!

Why are you so annoyed at her? he asked himself. She hasn't done anything. She takes this ceremony seriously. She thinks she's marrying you. Let her do it her own way. What difference does it make?

"None," he muttered softly and then said in a stage whisper, "Roll the cameras, fellows. Don't stop, no matter what happens." A soft whisper of assent reached him from the loft. It'll be okay, it'll be fine, he thought. So we don't do it my way. So what?

The door swung open again and Gwendolyn Jenkins entered. She was wrapped in her black cloak and had pulled the hood tightly around her head. She took Karyn by the hand and whispered something into her ear. Karyn nodded and walked to the altar, discarding her coat before she reached it. She was, of course, not in costume. Simon struggled not to be annoyed.

Adrienne Lupescu walked in through the still-open door, trailing a rope behind her. A moment later, Jeremy Sloan entered, the rope's end tied around his wrists. His face was blank and expressionless, and he walked somnambulistically behind Adrienne. She came to a stop and removed her cloak. She was dressed in the same flowing white gown which she had worn on stage during the past month, and her braided brown hair had been piled fetchingly upon her head. As she walked forward and stood off to the left of the altar, Jeremy followed, impelled by the rope and stood dumbly beside her, his empty eyes staring off into the distance.

Lucas Proctor took his place beside Karyn. His father leaned toward him and whispered, "What the hell is he doing here? And what's wrong with him?"

"Gwen hypnotized him," Lucas whispered in reply. "Adrienne says she wanted him to be here, and that was the only way to get him to come."

"Okay, but why is he here?"

Lucas shrugged. "Beats me. Adrienne says he has a role to play in the wedding ceremony."

"Where's Rowena? Does she know about this?"

"Are you kidding," Karyn laughed. "She'd pitch a fit if she knew he was here."

"So where is she?"

Karyn shrugged. "Last I saw of her she was talking to that mailman. You know, that guy you—"

"Yeah, yeah, I know what a mailman is!" Simon snapped. "Damn! This gets more and more screwed up by the min—"

He stopped speaking as Gwendolyn strode slowly forward. She unbuttoned her cloak, drew the hood back from her head, and dropped the garment to the floor. Simon's eyes were riveted upon her. Her wedding gown consisted entirely of black lace which hugged her voluptuous form from breasts to thighs and then parted, a long slit running up her left leg. The lace was in like manner tight about her upper arms to the elbow, then flowed down in long, loose sleeves which hung down nearly to her knees. Beneath the lace she was naked.

Simon heard Strube whisper "Nice dress" and heard Mahoney giggle, but he ignored them. He could not take his eyes off her as she walked up to him. A silver chain girdled her waist, sloping seductively down about her right hip. The slope of the chain lent an exaggerated undulation to her gait as she walked. A smaller chain hung down from the larger one, and from the smaller chain was suspended what Simon thought at first glance was a cross. As Gwendolyn drew closer, he saw that it was a dagger.

Gwendolyn's eyes were fixed upon Simon's, and the half smile, half smirk upon her lips indicated that she had made the impression upon him which she had intended to make. She walked up to him and glided her arms up and around his neck, reaching upward and kissing him deeply. "My love," she whispered, "my love, my dear one."

"You look beautiful," he whispered in reply, "absolutely beautiful!"

She smiled her thanks for the compliment and then turned to the others present, keeping her hands still clasped behind Simon's neck. "The joining of man and woman is an expression of nature's most ancient and profound power. By bearing witness to our union, you partake in our joining and the power which it generates. Do you understand?" No one made reply, so she continued. "Lust is the essence of love. Lust is the essence of power. And lust is the primordial force which drives all life. You all shall partake of our union by each partaking of the flesh of the others."

"Uh, Gwen," Mahoney said, forgetting the rolling cameras for a moment, "are we talking cannibalism here? Because if we are, you can count me out—"

She laughed. "Cannibalism! Tosh, such nonsense! I talk of lust, physical lust. Simon and I shall fold our hands upon Karyn's belly, and shall say our vows, and then each of you in

287

turn, beginning with my husband—" she looked at Simon and smiled, "my husband! 'Tis a lovely word! Each of you, beginning with my husband, shall take your pleasure with me. The field well furrowed needs must be generously sown." She allowed her arms to slide down from around Simon's neck. "And then each man must take unto himself another woman, that we may worship the lord of the flesh with a sacrament of the flesh."

"Gwen, there's five guys and only three girls," Strube pointed out.

"Unfortunate, but unimportant. Mary Warren can accommodate you all, even as I shall." Adrienne Lupescu's face betrayed no emotion at Gwendolyn's words, but she blanched and trembled slightly. Her face remained as impassive as Jeremy's. "Karyn's womb is bursting with new life, new flesh, and is thus a sealed chamber. But Mary's field will accept your ploughs."

Might have to edit this out, Simon was thinking. The X-rating for the movie was one thing, but we want the concert video to get as much play as possible. No matter, no matter. What's left will be great.

"Karyn," Gwendolyn said. "Stand before the altar, and bare your belly to us."

Karyn glanced at Lucas, who was staring at Gwendolyn with a look combining apprehension and anticipation, and she sniffed. "Okay, but I ain't doin' no perverted stuff, you get me?"

Gwendolyn smiled. "All you need do is stand still as we make our vows upon your womb."

Karyn shrugged her unenthusiastic assent, and pulled her oversized tee shirt up to just below her breasts. Gwendolyn gently reached out and began to pull down the elastic waistband of the sweat pants which Karyn was wearing. "Hey!" she said, thrusting Gwendolyn's hand aside. "Cut that out!"

Gwendolyn smiled at her, but her eyes were hard and showed neither patience nor kindness. "Permit me," she said, but it was a command, not a request. "Your belly must be exposed."

"It *is* exposed!" Karyn insisted.

"*Fully* exposed," Gwendolyn said evenly, and reached again for the waistband. Karyn flushed slightly, but did not resist as Gwendolyn pulled the sweatpants slightly downward. Karyn's round and protuberant stomach seemed to hang outward from her body, framed by the bottom of the shirt and the top of the pants. Gwendolyn knelt down in front of her and held her hand out to Simon. "Kneel beside me, my love."

Simon did as he was asked, and he whispered, "Gwen, the vows I worked up for us are—"

"Dismiss them from your mind, Simon," she interrupted. "Repeat the words as I say them, even if you do not understand them. Remember that I am a servant of Satan, and know better than you how to call his blessing down upon our union."

"Yeah, but—"

"Shhh!" she commanded. "Place your hand upon her belly." He did so and she placed her hand atop his. She closed her eyes and her lips moved slightly as she prayed silently. Then she said, "*In nomine Satani, introibo ad altare diaboli.*"

"*In nom*—" Simon began. "What was that? Say it again, will you? I didn't—"

"Shhh!" she said angrily. "Just be quiet, then." She closed her eyes again and began to chant, "*Judica me, Satanas, et discerne causam mean de gente sancta. Ab homine sancto erue me. Emitte tenebram tuam et dolum tuam, ipsa me deduxerunt et adduxerunt in montem insanctum tuum, et in tabernacula tua.*"

"Gwen," Simon whispered, "say it in English, say it in English. Everybody here has to understand what you're saying for this kind of ceremony to be valid." Everybody watching the film has to understand what you're saying, or else they'll get bored, he thought.

"Very well," she said irritably. "But be quiet, Simon. Do not interrupt me further."

"Okay, okay."

She closed her eyes again and repeated her opening prayer in English. "In the name of Satan, I will go unto the altar of the Devil. Give judgment for me, Satan, and decide my cause against a holy people. Deliver me from holy men. Send forth thy darkness and thy deceit, for they have led me and brought me to thine unholy hill and thy dwelling place."

Tom Mahoney leaned over to Mark Siegal and whispered, "Hey, that's the Roman Catholic Mass!"

"You're kidding!" Siegal whispered back. "That can't be, Tommy. I'm not a Catholic, but I know you guys don't pray to the Devil!"

"No, no," he whispered, "the name of God has been replaced with Satan, holy changed to unholy and like that. But everything else—"

"A Black Mass," Siegal said softly. "A real Black Mass! This is great! What a sequence! I don't think it's ever been done in a m—"

"Shhh!" Adrienne Lupescu said.

"Introibo ad altare Satani, ad diabolum qui laetificat corpus meum," Gwendolyn chanted. "I shall go to the altar of Satan, to the Devil, the joy of my flesh. *Adjutorium nostrum in nomine Satani, qui regnat infernum et terram.* Our help is in the name of Satan, who rules hell and earth. *Ave Satanas, ave Satanas, ave Satanas.* Hail Satan, hail Satan, hail Satan." Gwendolyn began to sway slowly back and forth, as if mesmerized by her own chant.

Larry Herricks turned to Carl Strube and said in a voice just slightly too loud, "That is one fucked-up chick, man!"

"Shhh," Strube said. "Don't screw up the fil—" He stopped himself before finishing the sentence.

Gwendolyn continued to sway back and forth, but she opened her eyes and said, "Accept our devotion, father of lies, accept our worship, lord of the flies, accept our bodies, lord of the grave, thou who destroyest, thou who canst save. Bless thou our union, Master of hell, who makest wombs of all women to swell, whose rod is the fruit tree, whose seed is the rain, bless thou our union, master of pain." She glanced at Simon. "Repeat what I say, line by line." He nodded his assent, and she continued. "All that I am, I offer to thee, *ave Satanas, ave Satanas.*"

"All that I am, I offer to thee," Simon repeated, his hand flat against Karyn's round belly, *"ave Satanas, ave Satanas."*

"All that I have, I offer to thee, *ave Satanas, ave Satanas.*"

"All that I have, I offer to thee, *ave Satanas, ave Satanas.*"

"Grant thou my prayer, thou Master of hell, *ave Satanas, ave Satanas.*"

"Grant thou my prayer, thou Master of hell, *ave Satanas, ave Satanas.*"

"Inflame thou my lusts, thou lord of the flies, *ave Satanas, ave Satanas.*"

"Inflame thou my lusts, thou lord of the flies, *ave Satanas, ave Satanas.*"

"Praise to thee, Lucifer, praise to thee, Lucifer."

"Praise to thee, Lucifer, praise to thee, Lucifer."

"Ave Satanas!"

"Ave Satanas!"

Gwendolyn looked down at the floor of the barn, as if addressing her prayer down at the bowels of the earth. "Joined we are, this man and I, here and forever, above and below."

She waited for Simon to respond, and glanced at him urgently when he did not.

"Oh—uh—joined we are, this woman and I, here and forever, above and below," he said.

"On earth wilt thou aid us, in hell shall we serve."

"On earth wilt thou aid us, in hell shall we serve."

"An unholy covenant, he, you, and I."

"An unholy covenant, she, you, and I."

"*Ave Satanas.*"

"*Ave Satanas.*"

Gwendolyn rose to her feet and Simon did likewise. Karyn pulled her shirt down and her pants up and walked away from the altar without being bidden, obviously pleased that her role in this charade was at an end. She walked over to Lucas and whispered, "Baby, if she's for real like she says she is, she needs a —"

"Shut up, will you?" Lucas said. "Have some respect."

"Have some respect!" she repeated quietly. "Are you kidding?"

"Shhh!"

Gwendolyn turned to Adrienne and said, "Bring him forward."

Adrienne tugged gently on the rope and began herself to move to the front of the altar. Jeremy Sloan followed numbly behind her, his vacant eyes registering nothing, his blank face remaining expressionless. Adrienne's face was white and drawn, and her lips trembled as she said, "Abby, 'tis not necessary, 'tis a—"

"Hush!" Gwendolyn said. "Hand me the rope."

Adrienne extended the end of the rope hesitantly toward Gwendolyn and then retreated a few steps, looking from Gwendolyn to Jeremy and back again, the trembling of her lips seeming to spread to the rest of her body. Gwendolyn pulled the rope gently and Jeremy moved in response, shuffling numbly forward until he stood in the same spot which Karyn had occupied a moment before. Simon leaned over to Gwendolyn and whispered, "Gwen, what are you doing?"

"Be silent!" she snapped.

"But—"

"Simon, we are in the midst of a ceremony of great significance. Be quiet and strive to be worthy of it." She walked up to Jeremy and put her face close to his. "Jeremy Sloan," she said in a quiet but firm voice, "can you hear my voice?"

"I hear you," the boy murmured.

"Open your shirt," she commanded.

Jeremy's hands moved slowly and mechanically upward to the row of buttons, and he began to release them one by one. When he had unbuttoned the last of them, his hands fell heavily down to his sides and he stood motionless. Gwendolyn reached out and pulled the shirt open, baring his smooth, muscular chest. She lowered her eyes reverently and said, "*Suscipe, Pater insancte, potens aeterne diabole, hanc immaculatam victimam, quam ego indigna ancilla tua offero tibi.* Accept, unholy father, powerful and eternal Devil, this pure victim, which I, thine unworthy servant, offer to thee—"

"Hey!" Simon said very loudly. "What are you talking about?! What do you mean about a victim? Gwendolyn—!"

"Jeremy!" a high voice screamed, and Simon turned his head to see his daughter Rowena rushing toward them from the entrance of the impromptu place of worship. "Jeremy! What do you think you're doing?! Gwendolyn, get away from him!" The expression of hurt anger on her face shifted in an instant to one of terror as she drew close and saw what was about to transpire.

Simon turned back to Gwendolyn and began to speak, but whatever words he had been intending to say stuck in his throat as she ripped the dagger from the silver chain and raised it high above her head, her large green eyes flashing madly as her throaty voice continued to intone its arcane supplication. He made a jerky, spasmodic motion toward her, as if seeking instinctively to obstruct her even as his brain attempted to comprehend her actions.

He moved too slowly.

The glinting dagger swept downward in a murderous arc and the cold blade tore with an audible rip through Jeremy's chest. A spring of purple blood was loosed, and it began to spurt out and drench both Simon and Gwendolyn in its sanguine flood. A sudden glimmer of awareness filled Jeremy's eyes, and then the light of consciousness died in them as the boy slumped to the floor and lay motionless in the crimson puddle which was spreading out upon the floor beneath him.

Gwendolyn fell to her knees and scooped some blood up with her cupped hands. She lowered her head to her palms and licked up some of the liquid. Then, laughing, she spread the rest over her breasts and thighs as she screamed, "*Ave Satanas!*"

Not five seconds had passed, but to Simon it had seemed an eternity. He shook his head and blinked his eyes, as if he were attempting to rouse himself from a dream, and he had the distinct, conscious physical sensation of having just passed from the then into the now, from a vaguely fuguelike state into one of horridly clear awareness.

He looked down at the floor.

It was real. It was true. She had just killed the boy.

A split second of stunned and total silence was followed by pandemonium as Rowena's screams were joined by screams and cries and shouts of disbelief from all sides. Mark Siegal fell to his knees and grabbed Jeremy's wrist with one hand while pressing down upon the bloody slit in his chest with the other. He was seeking both to find a pulse and to keep the wound from spilling any more blood. Both attempts were futile and desperate, for there was no pulse to be found, and the eruption of blood had ceased the moment that death had descended upon Jeremy. The blade had struck deep, between the ribs, into the heart.

"My God!" Simon muttered. "My God!"

So deep was his shock, so profound the disbelief which had fixed his eyes on the pale body which lay at his feet, that he was oblivious to the loud crash of the camera as it dropped from the hands of the stunned cameraman up in the loft and fell to the floor of the barn. But Gwendolyn was not thus distracted, and she turned her eyes toward the loft, her quizzical expression rapidly becoming one of anger. She turned to the side when she heard a scream of shock come from behind the west wall, noticing for the first time a hole through which she could discern movement. She spun Simon around to face her, her hands displaying a physical strength which surprised him. "You have betrayed my trust!" she screamed.

Simon gazed at her numbly as Rowena threw herself upon Jeremy's lifeless body, as Strube ran from the barn to call the police, as the cameraman in the loft sidled down the ladder and then rushed out the door, as Siegal upon his knees and Mahoney and Herricks and Lucas and Karyn upon their feet remained in impotent, stunned silence.

"You have betrayed my trust!" she repeated.

Adrienne Lupescu knelt down beside the body and placed her arm comfortingly upon Rowena's shoulder. So great was the girl's grief and confusion that she did not think to refuse the solace which was being offered her by one who had played a role in the murder.

Gwendolyn's hand swung around and landed a resounding slap upon Simon's face. It was sufficiently forceful to knock him off balance, and he stumbled to the side. "You have betrayed my trust!" she said for a third time. "I told you, Simon Proctor, that this was not to be for public eyes! Do you think I am so silly and easily tricked that you could ignore my wishes?" She was trembling with anger and her face was flushing red. She closed her eyes and clenched her jaw as if attempting to calm herself, and when her eyes opened again a moment later and she spoke, her tone was gentler and less excited, though it was apparent that her anger remained. "If we are to be wedded, dear Simon, we must not attempt to deceive one another. I have been honest with you in all things, and I expect—"

The stinging pain upon his cheek seemed to rouse Simon from his shock, and his face contorted in fury as he grabbed Gwendolyn by the shoulders and began to shake her mercilessly. "Do you realize what you've done?!" he screamed.

She pushed his hands from her easily. "Aye, right well! I fear that I have given my trust to a man who cannot be trusted!"

"You maniac!" Simon shrieked. "You just killed a man!"

"Do not take that tone with me!" she said firmly, her barely repressed rage bubbling to the surface. "I offered a sacrifice to the Master, a sacrifice to call his blessings upon our marriage." She folded her arms imperiously upon her breast. "And if you cannot bring yourself to commit yourself to the service of the true ruler of this world, then I fear that our wedded road will be a thorny one! There is no room for doubt or halfhearted devotion, Simon. Our devotion to the Master must be as firm and full as our devotion to each other. We must—"

"Devotion!" he spat. "Devotion! I'm not devoted to you, you goddamn mental case! I would never marry a lunatic like you!"

She gazed at him with blank incomprehension. "What— what are you—?"

"This isn't a marriage ceremony, you stupid fool! This is another video, another film, another performance!"

The meaning of his words slowly became clear to her, much as she seemed to struggle against them. "No," she stammered, "no—you love me—you must love me, as I love you—you must—"

"I don't love you!" he shouted, placing his hands upon her shoulders and pushing her roughly away from him. "Are you kidding? Me, love a nut, an insane asylum outpatient? You mean money to me, Gwen, money, nothing more than that!"

She stared at him coldly. "Such a fool I am, such a fool! Money! All you care about is money! How dare you, Simon Proctor!"

"Goddamn it, Gwendolyn!" he shouted back at her. "You just killed Jeremy! Don't you understand what you've done?!"

She replied as if she had not heard him. "You could have had wealth, and power, and me, *me*, and yet you chose to betray me and use me—*use me*!—like a foolish serving wench!"

"Gwendolyn, for Christ's sake, will you shut up?" he screamed. "This isn't a fucking game here! You just killed a human being!"

"One of many, Simon Proctor!" she spat. "Murder is not new to me. From the day my actions led your ancestor and eighteen others to the gallows, I have served as the angel of death to many of the—"

Simon struck her across the face viciously. She recoiled but did not fall as he shouted, "You fucking maniac! You goddamn fucking nut!"

"Guard your tongue!" she said. Tears seemed to be welling up in her eyes, but none poured forth, as if her white-hot anger was evaporating them unshed. "I have suffered too much for too many years to be treated thus by you or any man, especially by a Proctor! For three hundred years I have—"

He grabbed her by the shoulders. "Listen to me, goddamn it! You are Gwendolyn Jenkins. You are *not* Abigail Williams. You are mentally ill, you are crazy, you have some insane delusion about yourself, about me, about the Devil, about all of this! You are Gwendolyn Jenkins, Gwendolyn Jenkins! You are not Abigail Williams. You are not a witch! There is no such thing as witchcraft! There is no Devil, no Satan! It's a game, it's all a game, nothing but a game, nothing but a way for us all to make money! My God, don't you understand?!"

She pushed him away from her and stepped back. Her voice was cold and hard as she spoke. "So. I see. All is for sport, all is pretense. You think me a madwoman, and you used me to line your purse and warm your bed, and you have no feelings for me."

"Hey, if you're trying to make me feel guilty, if you're looking for sympathy or something, forget it!" he spat. "You just committed a murder, Gwen! Can't you understand what that means? Don't you realize what's going to happen to you now, what's going to happen to me? Jesus, Gwen, wake up! This is reality!"

She laughed bitterly. "Ah, no, Simon Proctor, 'tis but a game, 'tis but a hard and bloody game." She turned and walked away, grabbing her cloak from the floor. As she wrapped it around herself she said, "I play games with great skill, Simon, and I never lose them. I play by rules, and I play honestly. But if I am cheated, then the rules be damned!" She

295

strode to the door and flung it open with an angry snap of her arm. "I told you, but you would not listen. I explained, but you did not understand. Satan answered one of my two prayers, and I had believed it to be the prayer I wished answered, not the prayer I feared answered. Remember my other prayer, Simon Proctor, remember it well, for it is your death warrant!"

"Don't you threaten me!" he shouted, his body trembling with rage.

"Your ancestor John used me to gratify his lusts and then cast me aside like so much soiled linen unworthy of the washing! Elizabeth Proctor, your ancestress, caused me to be driven out of Salem, led me to be cast upon the streets of Boston where I had to sell my body to strangers in order to stay alive! So great was the misery those Proctors caused me that my life ended at the end of a noose which I had plaited myself! And you, most recent of Proctor bastards, you have used me and abused me, lied to me and laughed at me!" Her green eyes blazed. "But no more, do you hear me? No more! This breed of Proctors has plagued me long enough! I shall wipe you from the face of the earth, all of you! I shall visit upon you all the pain which your family has caused me to suffer, all the torments I have endured! Count your days, Simon Proctor! They are few!" She spun around and walked out into the cold winter air. Adrienne Lupescu scurried after her, grabbing her cloak and exiting without putting it on.

Simon ran to the door of the barn, shouting, "Come back here, goddamn it! Where the hell do you—?" He stopped the moment he stepped out into the snow. Neither Gwendolyn nor Adrienne was anywhere to be seen. It was as if they had simply vanished.

Simon walked slowly back to the altar. Rowena was lying upon Jeremy's chest, her tears mingling with the already drying blood, her face pressed against his cold skin. Simon knelt down beside her and placed his hand upon her arm. "Row—" he said gently.

"This is your fault!" she screamed at him with a sudden ferocity. "This is all your fault!"

"Rowena, try to calm down," he said softly. "This is a terrible thing, a terrible, tragic thing, but we have to—"

"You go to hell, Daddy!" she screamed, and then collapsed in tears upon the body of her boyfriend. Simon remained beside her on his knees, not knowing what to do. He looked at his hands and he shuddered. They were covered with Jeremy's blood.

⟦ CHAPTER TWENTY ⟧
December 29, continued

THE TWO VALIUMS the doctor had given her were not working. Rowena lay in her bed restlessly, always feeling herself on the brink of blissful slumber, always being wrenched back to full wakefulness by the memory of the afternoon. The image of Jeremy's face filled her thoughts, the sound of his voice filled her ears, and tears continued to stream forth from her sore, red eyes. She had never known it to be possible for one person to produce so many tears, and still the tears came.

Never to hear his voice again. Never to feel his arms around her again, his lips upon hers. Never to make love with him. Never.

Her father was still down at the police station, and she hoped that she could fall asleep before he returned. Great as her anger was, she knew that he was in serious trouble, and she was worried about him. Half of her mind fought to sleep, half fought to remain awake. She hated her father and she feared for him, blamed him and pitied him, wished he would die and feared for his life.

Gwen said she was going to kill him, she thought. She said she was going to kill all of us. Something must be done, something must be done. She's crazy, she's dangerous. The police have to get her, they have to punish her, they just have to! She can't just get away with this! They have to get her before she hurts anyone else, before she hurts Daddy, or Lucas, or me. They have to get her!

She rolled over onto her side and tried to sleep, prayed that the drug would take effect and give her some respite from her sorrow and her fear. She knew that her grandfather was asleep already, even though he had become so upset that she worried about his heart. He had wept and wrung his hands when Simon told him what had happened, he had prayed and cursed, and she had comforted him as he had comforted her, both of them ignoring Simon, both of them blaming him, both of them damning him with their eyes and their words.

But when she had gone to Floyd's room a few hours ago, the old man had already taken his nightly libation and was snoring contentedly. Nothing short of a war could keep old Floyd awake after ten, and perhaps not even that.

The scent of hashish told her that Karyn and Lucas, who had gone to the station with Simon and the others, had returned and were seeking slumber in their customary manner. There were no sounds coming from their bedroom, and Rowena assumed that they had already fallen asleep.

Time dragged on endlessly, and the dark house was silent but for the muted snores from her grandfather's bedroom. Rowena felt herself at last drifting off, felt the thoughts in her mind growing indistinct and foreign. She hovered between sleep and wakefulness, when she heard a voice.

"She means to destroy you all," Adrienne Lupescu said.

Rowena looked around her. She was sitting in a rowboat upon a misty, placid lake. No birds winged through the gray sky, no insects buzzed about in the still air, no fish moved through the silent waters. She floated in a boat upon a dead lake in a dead world.

"She means to destroy you all," Adrienne repeated.

Rowena sat in the bow of the boat and Adrienne in the stern. The older girl wore a long black dress with a white collar and a small white hat. She sat with her hands folded in her lap and her knees pressed tightly together above the severe black shoes with the silver buckles. She looked as if she had just stepped off the *Mayflower*.

"Why?" Rowena asked.

"Vengeance," Adrienne replied, her voice a monotone, devoid of expression, her face blank but for the hint of sorrow about her eyes. "Vengeance upon John, upon Elizabeth, upon Simon, upon all of you."

"I have done her no harm," Rowena said.

"You are a Proctor," Adrienne pointed out. "In her anger and her hurt she has sworn to wipe your family from this world. She means to destroy you all."

Rowena paused, knowing somehow that there were questions she had to ask. "How?"

"She will gut you as a butcher, tear you from bosom to belly."

Another interim of silence as the mist which hovered upon the face of the lake began to grow thick and dense, enveloping the small boat. "When?" Rowena asked.

"In thirty-four days."

The mist was now a fog, and Rowena struggled to see Adrienne through the thick clouds. Adrienne seemed to be drifting away from her without moving. "Why then? Why thirty-four days from now?"

"There are four nights of the year when the powers of the underworld are at their height," said the soft, fading voice. "The Eve of All Hallows in October, Walpurgis Night in April, Midsummer Eve in June. The fourth is Candlemas Eve, thirty-four days from today. She means upon that evening to destroy you all."

Rowena could see nothing but fog. Even the boat in which she sat had become invisible. "Adrienne? Adrienne? Wait!"

"I am here," said the distant voice.

"Why are you telling me this?"

"Pity. Sorrow. Regret."

"Adrienne? What can we do?"

Rowena's eyes snapped open, and she sat up in her bed, shaking and perspiring. She looked wildly around the room and, suddenly terrified by the darkness, she switched on her table lamp. The sight of the familiar surroundings calmed her slightly, and she closed her eyes and heaved a heavy sigh.

And then she heard Adrienne Lupescu's voice, quite clear and distinct, say, "Flee!"

She jumped from the bed and backed over to the door of the room. She was alone. "Dreaming," she whispered to herself. "I was dreaming. I must have been dreaming."

"Flee, Rowena," the voice said again, and the girl bolted from the room, slamming the door loudly behind her and then leaning against it out in the corridor, her heart racing and her knees shaking violently.

She heard the front door open and close and then heard soft, muted voices drifting up from the foyer. She recognized her father's voice, and Mark Siegal's, and assumed that the other voices belonged to the members of his band. She pulled her nightgown tight around her neck against the strange chill she felt in the warm house, and went downstairs.

She found her father sitting pensively in a chair in the sitting room just off the foyer. He had removed his coat and was staring off into space. Herricks, Mahoney, Strube, and Siegal stood around him, making pointless small talk, glancing at their watches and looking uncomfortable and eager to leave. She entered the room and leaned against the wall beside the door, ignoring their delicate greetings, not responding when they said good-bye, not turning to see if they closed the front door behind them when they left.

She and her father were silent in the now empty room. A

long time seemed to pass before he said, without looking at her, "I'm sorry, Rowena. I'm so sorry." She did not answer him. "I never, never meant to hurt anybody. I was just trying to make money, trying to be successful, trying to keep a roof over our heads." He looked over at her, and as their eyes met she noticed how old he seemed to have become, how deeply lined his face was, how his lips trembled as he spoke. "You're supposed to want to be successful, aren't you? Everybody wants to be successful." She still did not answer him, and he looked away. "I had no idea that Gwen was so crazy. No idea."

"What did the police say?" she asked at last.

He sighed. "Took our statements, got descriptions of Gwen and Adrienne. They believed us when we told them the whole story, but there may still be charges against me. Reckless endangerment, something like that. Maybe they just said that to scare me, to make sure I was telling the truth. I don't know."

The silence descended once again. Rowena walked over and sat down upon the sofa. She sighed. "Oh, Daddy!"

Simon began to weep. "I'm sorry, honey, really I am. I'm so sorry!"

She shook her head. "That doesn't help, Daddy. That doesn't help one bit."

He buried his face in his hands. "I don't know what else to say."

They were silent for a few more moments and then Rowena said, "Adrienne came to me in a dream."

"Huh?" Simon sniffed. "You dreamed about Adrienne?"

"That's not what I said. I said she came to me in a dream."

Simon stared at his daughter and thought, Jesus, Row, don't lose your grip. "What do you mean?"

"She warned me to get out of here. She said that Gwendolyn will kill us all in thirty-four days, on Candlemas Eve. She told me to flee."

Simon rose from his seat and walked over to her. He sat down beside her and took her hand. It was cold, limp, unresponsive to his touch. "Row, honey, it was just a dream."

"She kept telling me to run away, even after I woke up."

"Honey—"

"Daddy, I was standing up, wide awake, in the room with the light on, and I still heard her." She looked into her father's eyes and her face assumed an aspect of fear and desperation. "I wasn't dreaming that I heard her voice. I don't know who or what she and Gwendolyn are, but they aren't just crazy
300

people. Daddy, we have to get away from here before Candlemas Eve!"

"Okay, okay, Row," he said comfortingly, patting her hand, "we'll talk about it in the morning, okay? Why don't you go and try to get some sleep."

She nodded, suddenly very tired. "Yeah, okay." She rose without another word and walked slowly back upstairs.

Simon watched her go and then walked over to the liquor cabinet near the window. He took out a bottle of bourbon and, without bothering to get a glass, uncorked it and poured some of the fiery liquid down his throat. He felt warmed and comforted by the bourbon, and he gazed out the window and sighed.

Poor Rowena, he thought. I hope this is just a temporary thing. Her emotions are all twisted up right now . . . well, of course they would be, wouldn't they, seeing her boyfriend murdered like that? Of course, of course. She'll probably be okay tomorrow. Adrienne came to her in a dream! He laughed humorlessly. The poor kid.

The sitting-room window resounded with a sudden, jarring thud, and Simon leapt back, startled. He felt his heart rise into his throat, and then settled in relief as he saw the cause of the sound. Calm down, he told himself. No murdering psychopaths. No witches out there. No ghoulies, no ghosties, no long-legged beasties. Just a bird.

A bird had lighted on the outer sill of the window and had knocked into the glass, doubtless tossed there by a sudden gust of wind. Simon heaved a sigh of relief. Just an animal, just a bird. Gotta take it easy, he thought. Gonna start jumping at every sound. He walked back over to the window and looked at the bird. He smiled.

His smile faded as the bird gazed back up at him with its blank expression. The bird raised one leg, balancing itself precariously upon the other, and placed its talons upon the outer face of the window. The bird scraped its claws slowly and threateningly down the surface of the glass. Simon and the bird stared intently at each other for a few moments, and then the creature flapped its wings and flew off into the night.

Simon Proctor reached out to steady himself against the wall, feeling his knees grow weak and his body begin to tremble. He stumbled backward away from the window and sat down heavily in the chair.

"My God!" he whispered, his voice shaking, his hands shaking, his entire body shaking. "My God! My God!"

Simon had been born and raised a country boy, and had spent many boyhood hours in the woods and fields and mountains of New Hampshire. His familiarity with the wildlife of the region was thus extensive, and he knew many things about the creatures which inhabited the White Mountains of New England.

He knew some things about ravens.

They did not have green eyes.

IV

CANDLEMAS EVE

My days are consumed like smoke,
and my bones are burned like an hearth.
By reason of the voice of my groaning
my bones cleave to my skin.
I am like a vulture of the wilderness:
I am like an owl of the desert.
Mine enemies reproach me all the day,
and they that are mad against me are sworn against
     me.
For I have eaten ashes like bread,
and mingled my drink with weeping.

—PSALM 102

⟦ CHAPTER TWENTY-ONE ⟧
January 29

"WELL, I THINK he's nuts," Larry Herricks said as he poured another stream of warm beer down his throat. "Out of his fuckin' mind, you know? A goddamn space cadet, if you ask me."

Herricks looked for agreement in the faces of the other members of the band as they sat pensively at the now-deserted bar of "Tom's basement." Mark Siegal was buttoning his jacket as he tossed the last few drops of bourbon into his mouth and set his glass loudly down upon the bar top. Carl Strube and Tom Mahoney were each nursing their beers. None of them nodded in response to Herricks's statements. Siegal sighed. "Look, Larry, I don't think it's true either, and I don't know if Simon really believes it. He may just be on edge, like, real nervous about this whole thing, you know?"

"Nervous!" Herricks laughed. "I'll say he's nervous! On his way to a fuckin' nervous breakdown!"

"Maybe so," Strube said. "But there are certain facts here. We all saw Gwen murder that kid. That's a fact. And we all heard her say she was gonna wipe out Simon's whole family. That's a fact too. We know that she is capable of murder, and we know that she threatened them with murder." He sipped his beer. "Reason enough to get the hell out of there, if you ask me."

"Yeah, right, sure," Herricks said sarcastically. "A month later, right? The day before holy fuckin' witch's day or whatever it is, right? Warned in a dream, right?" He spat with disgust. "Gimme a break, man! This is nuts!"

Siegal finished buttoning his jacket. "I don't know why you're so annoyed about it, Larry. I'm the one going up there to help them move, not you. So what's the big deal?"

"The big deal," he replied heatedly, "is that just when we start making money, real money, for the first time in the past few years, Simon throws the whole thing overboard because he's scared of witches! No video, no more records, no more concerts! I mean, Jesus!"

"He thinks it may be a matter of life and death," Mahoney pointed out. "He's scared, man. Wouldn't you be scared?"

"Nah, of course not!" Herricks replied. "You think I'd let a couple of schized-out chicks freak me out like that?"

"Okay, John Wayne," Strube said tiredly. "What do you think he should do?"

"Get 'em arrested, lock 'em up! Get some other chicks for the act! Shit, there's gotta be thousands of chicks can wiggle their tits like Gwen. I mean, what's the big deal, you know?"

"The big deal," Mahoney repeated, "is that it may be a matter of life and death."

"It's bullshit," Herricks said glumly and finished his beer. He grimaced. "Hey, Tommy, ain'tcha got nothin' cold around here? Why do we always gotta drink warm beer in this place?"

"Cold stuff's for people who pay for it," Mahoney replied pointedly.

"Tom," Strube said, "let's go downstairs and bring up some cold brew. Maybe it'll shut him up."

"Fuck you," Herricks muttered.

"Look, I gotta go," Siegal said. "I'll probably see you guys day after tomorrow, after I drop them off at the airport."

"Try to get here before the last show's over," Mahoney said. "I got a new group from Long Island booked, starting tomorrow. You gotta hear them. They're damn good."

"Yeah, sure, I'll try," Siegal said as he walked toward the door. "See you."

"Take it easy," Strube said.

"Bye," Mahoney waved. Herricks said nothing. "Come on, Carl. Let's go get Weeping Beauty here a cold beer." Mahoney and Strube laughed as they went to the rear door of the room and proceeded downstairs to the cellar. One of the drawbacks to the club was the absence of taps for beer kegs, so that only bottled beer was available for the customers. Refrigeration facilities upstairs in the bar were limited, so that Mahoney or his employees had to make frequent trips downstairs throughout a business night to replenish the stock of cold beer.

Herricks watched them go. "Assholes," he muttered. "Dumb, stupid, fuckin' assholes." He got unsteadily to his feet and meandered from the bar over to the DJ's platform in the corner of the large room. Listen to some music, he thought to himself. Cheer myself up. He grabbed an album at random without looking at it and pulled the disk roughly from the dust cover. Witches, he thought as he dropped the album onto the turntable and switched on the system. Christ Almighty! Witches! What an asshole Simon is!

He walked back to the bar and sat down heavily upon the stool as the loud music began to reverberate through the room. He ran his fingers absently up and down the empty beer bottle as the unfamiliar rock group boomed from the speakers.

"Have you ever wondered what it means when people say,
  'To the Devil give his due,' or 'There'll be hell to pay'?
Have you ever wondered why the mighty human brain
  Which could create such peace and joy makes misery and pain?
There's a power working.
  Beneath the surface there's a power working.
You can turn your heart to heaven,
  You can give your soul to hell.
Either way there's a power working."

"Shit," he muttered as he rose to his feet. "Doesn't anybody sing about sex and drugs anymore?" He ambled over to the DJ's platform and pulled the arm of the turntable roughly from the record, sending a screech tearing through the room. He chose another album, more carefully this time. "*Year of the Cat*," he muttered. "Al Stewart. That's good. Mellow me out a bit." He put the album on the turntable and returned to the bar. Where the hell are those guys? he asked himself. Wish they'd hurry up.

He drummed his fingers on the bar top as the music filled the room. He was not listening to it. He was thinking. Three-hundred-year-old witches! Incredible! How can Simon actually believe shit like that? Sure, the chicks are nuts, anybody can see that. But to run away from them, and to Idaho, of all places! He frowned and shook his head as Al Stewart's voice drifted around him.

"It seems to me as though I've been upon this stage before,
  And juggled away the nights with the same old crowd.
These harlequins you see with me, they too have held the floor,
  As here once again they strut and they fret their hour.
I see those half-familiar faces in the second row,
  Ghost-like, with the footlights in their eyes.
But where or when we met like this last time I just don't know.

It's like a chord that rings and never dies,
For infinity."

It's impossible, he thought to himself. More than impossible. It's ridiculous! When you die, you're dead, and that's the end of it. Nobody comes back from the dead, nobody lives again or anything like that. No heaven or hell, no rebirth, no reincarnation, no afterlife. It's bullshit, it's all bullshit.

"And now these figures in the wings with all their restless
tunes
Are waiting around for someone to call their names.
They walk the backstage corridors and prowl the dressing
rooms,
And vanish to specks of light in the picture frames.
But did they move upon the stage a thousand years ago,
In some play in Paris or Madrid?
And was I there among them then, in some traveling
show,
And is it all still locked inside my head
For infinity?"

But what if? he thought. What if there is something, some, I don't know, some part of us which lives on after death? What if hate lives on, or love lives on, or something like that? What if there really was somebody from back in Salem, centuries ago, who made a deal with the Devil? . . . What if there really is a Devil? . . . Nah . . . nah, that's stupid, stupid. Nuts, that's all. They're just a couple of nuts.

"And some of you are harmonies to all the notes I play.
Although we may not meet, still you know me well,
While others speak in secret keys and transpose all I say,
And nothing I do or try can get through the spell.
So one more time we'll dim the lights and ring the curtain
up
And play again like all the times before.
But far behind the music you can almost hear the sound
Of laughter, like the waves upon the shore
Of infinity. . . ."

"Bullshit," Herricks muttered. "Nothin' but bullshit." He shook his head vigorously and glanced over toward the rear door of the room. Where the hell are those guys? he wondered. If they're doin' a joint and trying to cut me out, I'll flatten 'em!

He slid off the stool and weaved his way back toward the door. He pushed it open loudly and called out, "Hey! Carl, Tommy! What the fuck you guys doin', brewin' it fresh down there?" There was no answer. "Hey! What the fuck you guys doin'?"

He waited a moment for a reply, but none was forthcoming. "Shit," he muttered again and began to descend the stairs to the cellar. "Hey, Tommy! What the hell are you guys doin'?" He attempted to sound friendly. "Look, if you're blowin' some weed, save some for me, okay?"

He reached the bottom of the stairs and knocked on the cellar door. "Hey! You guys in there? Hey, Tommy? Carl?" He knocked again and then detected a strange, slightly repellent odor. He stepped back a few feet from the door and heard his boots make a soft squishing sound as he moved them. Herricks looked down and saw that he was standing in a thick pool of—of—

"Jesus Christ!" he shouted and jumped up onto the bottom step. "Tommy! Carl! *Mahoney!*" There was no reply. Herricks stepped back into the red pool and carefully pushed the door open. He leaned his head inside and looked around the dimly lighted cellar. "Hey you guys!" he called out. "Are you okay? Are you in here?" He stepped cautiously into the storeroom and squinted to see in the dim light. "Hey, guys, this isn't funny! What'd you do, kill a chicken down here or something? Tommy? Carl?"

He walked a few feet farther into the room and then stopped, frozen, horrified by the sight which presented itself to him, stunned and nauseated by what he saw upon the floor of the cellar.

Larry Herricks screamed at the top of his lungs and turned to run, his feet slipping on the blood beneath them. He did not make it to the top of the stairs.

⟦ CHAPTER TWENTY-TWO ⟧
January 31

IT HAD TAKEN them more than a month to persuade old Floyd
to abandon the family homestead. Rowena and Simon were
ready to leave weeks before, and Lucas and Karyn, both more
shaken up by the events of the so-called wedding day than
either of them liked to admit, were eager to join them. But
Floyd was adamant in his refusal to run away from what he
regarded as a couple of madwomen, and weeks had gone by
before Simon and Rowena had worn down his resistance. Thus
it was that they were making ready to leave just one day before
the day about which Rowena had been warned in her dream.

She was still buttoning her coat as she descended the stairs
of the high school and walked out into the cold, clear air. She
had taken care of all her last-minute academic concerns that
afternoon, returned her books, arranged for the guidance
department to send a transcript to her at a post office box
number. As she walked away from the school, she did not
bother to look back.

She searched for Mark Siegal's van and saw it parked along
the narrow road which bordered on the school building. It was
nice of Mark to drive her to school that morning, nice of him to
pick her up now. Heck, it was nice of him to drive up here to
help them move. Of all weeks for Simon's old car to break
down! They would all fit in Mark's van with no trouble. They
could get to Kennedy Airport in New York by sunset and could
be in Idaho before midnight, before February first. Before
Candlemas Eve.

Idaho, she thought. The Rocky Mountains. Am I ever going
to live anywhere where it doesn't snow like crazy? Of course,
Idaho was a good choice for relocating, she knew that well.
She, Lucas, and Simon had discussed possible places at great
length. They had settled on Idaho because old Floyd would
feel comfortable in the mountains, because it was far distant
from New England, and because it was a very unlikely place
for Gwendolyn, or Abigail, or whoever the hell she was, to
look for them. It would have been better had they been able to
get a direct flight from the airport in Burlington, Vermont, to

Boise, but they could not. No matter, though. Mark Siegal would get them to Kennedy in plenty of time.

"Hi, Mark," she said, attempting to sound chipper as she climbed into the passenger seat of the van.

"Hiya." He smiled. "All set? You take care of everything?"

"Yup," she replied. "Handed in my books, got a copy of my transcript, cleaned out my locker."

Mark felt sorry for the girl, having to abandon the only school she had ever attended, the only town she had ever lived in, the only home she had ever had. "Burned all your bridges, I guess," he said gently.

She sighed. "Every last one." She sat in silence as he started the engine and began to drive back toward the river, beyond which she could see the town of Bradford, New Hampshire, one last time. Mark tried to make conversation, but Rowena's monosyllabic responses soon caused him to abandon the attempt.

They pulled into the driveway beside the old Proctor Inn a few minutes later. Rowena avoided looking at the For Sale sign which the realtor had planted on the front lawn. Great old house, she thought to herself. Don't see why we have to sell it. I know that Daddy doesn't want anything left here which can connect us with another address, and he doesn't want any letters or anything sent here which would be forwarded or anything, but I still don't see why we have to sell the old house just to avoid that. I think he wants a clean break with the past, that's all.

She and Mark left the van and climbed the few steps to the front door. As they entered the house she heard her brother's voice saying, "Listen, baby, everything's gonna be okay, honest to God! We got nothin' to worry about!"

She walked back toward the kitchen where Lucas and Karyn were obviously arguing about something, and she said, "Hi. Everything okay?"

"No, everything isn't okay!" Karyn snapped. Rowena could see from the rings around her eyes that she had either been sleeping poorly or crying recently or both. "Everything sucks, if you want to know the truth."

Rowena sat down at the table beside Karyn. "What's the matter?"

Karyn whipped out a cigarette and lighted it with trembling hands as Lucas answered, "She's scared, just like the rest of us."

310

"Not just like the rest of you," Karyn insisted. "I'm the pregnant one around here, not you. What if I go into labor on the airplane, or in the van? What if I go into labor up in fuckin' God's country in Idaho? Idaho! Where the hell *is* Idaho, anyway?" Her eyes were darting madly around the room. "What the fuck am I doin' movin' to Idaho?! I don't even know where the fuckin' place is, for Christ's sake! What am I doin' in this fucked-up situation? Some nut is gonna try to kill me because I got a fuckin' Proctor bun in the oven? This is nuts, this is nuts!"

"Karyn," Rowena said, taking her hand, "calm down. Getting upset like this isn't going to help anybody."

Karyn pulled her hand away. "How can you be so goddamn calm? Don't you realize that there's a crazy person out there someplace who wants to kill all of us?"

"Sure I realize it," Rowena said evenly. "We all realize it. That's why we're getting out of here today." She took Karyn's hand again and this time the older girl did not pull it back. "Listen, Karyn, you know that I had that dream, the one with Adrienne in it, telling me that we had until February first. Well, I'm convinced, and Daddy's convinced, that it wasn't a regular dream at all. I don't know who Gwen and Adrienne really are—I mean, we know they aren't normal people, that's certainly obvious—and I can't bring myself to believe what Daddy believes, that they're a couple of witches come up from hell, but I do believe that they have some powers of some kind, and I believe that Adrienne was trying to warn me. We're safe here until tomorrow, and by tomorrow we'll be three thousand miles away, living somewhere where nobody knows us." She squeezed Karyn's hand reassuringly. "Lukie's right. Everything's gonna be okay, it really is. You have to believe that."

Karyn looked intently at Rowena and seemed to smile slightly. "Yeah, I guess so. I'm just—I don't know, a little funny. I'm just about due, you know?"

"Sure, of course. I understand. Look, you really seem worn out. Why don't you go and lie down for a little while. It's only two-thirty and we're not gonna leave until four or so, so you can catch some sleep."

"No, I shouldn't," Karyn said. "There's so much to do, packing and closing up the house and stuff. I mean, I know it isn't my home, but I've lived here for a couple of years, and I kinda feel that I ought to—"

"Don't be silly," Rowena said. "We can do whatever needs to be done. You go and rest a while, okay?"

Karyn smiled. "Yeah, okay. I'm really tired. But listen, you guys wake me up if you need my help with anything."

"You bet," Rowena said. She watched as Karyn rose awkwardly to her feet and left the kitchen. She turned to Lucas. "When is she due?"

"Due to do what?" he asked.

Rowena gritted her teeth in annoyance. "Due to give birth!"

"Oh. I'm not sure. Sometime this week." He paused. "Hey, how come you can calm her down so easy? I been tryin' to do that for over an hour. Why does she listen to you and not to me?"

"Because she knows that you're a jerk and I'm not," she replied.

"Hey, fuck you, Row, y'know?" he muttered.

"Cut it out," Simon said darkly as he entered the kitchen. "We're all in this together. We can't afford any arguments just now." He was carrying a shotgun in his arms and as he drew near to his son and daughter he slid the gun onto the table.

"What's that for, Dad?" Lucas asked.

"That's for you," he said as he reached into his pocket and drew forth a handful of shotgun shells. "Row, I have a pistol that I want you to carry. It's only a .22, but it's a weapon anyway."

Rowena and Lucas looked at each other, and then Lucas said, "Dad, I don't know a goddamn thing about guns, you know that. If I ever tried to use one I'd probably blow my own head off."

"Daddy," Rowena added, "I'm terrified of guns."

"Yeah, and we can't take these things on the plane with us! They'll think we're trying to hijack the plane or something."

Rowena giggled. "We could pull a gun on the pilot and say, 'Fly this plane to Idaho!'" Her brother joined her laughter.

"Be quiet!" Simon commanded. There was not one iota of humor in him at the moment. "Pay attention. We can ship the guns by plane. We just can't carry them on board, so that's no problem. We'll still have them when we get to where we're going, and even if we don't, we'll have them until we get to New York. Lucas, you used to shoot when you were a little kid, so don't tell me you don't know how."

"Hey, Dad, I haven't held a gun since I was, like, seven years old, and even then it was only a .22 rifle, a squirrel gun!"

"A gun is a gun," his father replied. "You point it at whatever you want to shoot and you squeeze the trigger. The only difference is the force of the recoil. Rowena, you should never be afraid of anything which exists to help you. In our situation, guns are means of defense. You will carry the pistol."

"Daddy, I'm afraid of guns, honest to God I am! I don't think I could even fire one in self-defense! Honest!"

Simon stared at her for a moment. "Row, if you had been holding a gun when you came running into the barn last month, what would you have done?" She did not answer and he did not press her to. The point was made. She looked away.

Floyd Proctor entered the kitchen a moment later, saying, "Boy, I can't find that old Winchester anywheres."

"It doesn't matter, Dad," Simon said. "We have three shotguns, a rifle and a pistol. That'll be enough."

"Coulda sworn it was up in the attic. Thought I saw it there just a few years ago."

"Dad, forget it. It doesn't matter."

"My pa give me that gun when I's a boy," Floyd said. "Hate to go off and leave it. Hate to go off at all, for that matter!"

"Dad," Simon repeated patiently, "just forget about the Winchester. It really doesn't matter. We have enough weapons already."

Floyd's pensive frown suddenly smoothed out. "Hold on, now. I remember. Back in—when was it?—two, three years ago. Yeah, yeah, I lent it to Fred Wilkes. He was holding that turkey shoot the week before Thanksgiving, to raise money for his church, you remember?"

"I remember that," Rowena said. "Jimmy Groverson's mom had a turkey already bought, and when his dad shot a turkey at the turkey shoot he ended up taking turkey sandwiches to school for lunch for a month."

"I'll betcha that old gun's over t'the parsonage somewheres. I'm gonna go over'n look around."

"Dad," Simon said, "we really don't need—" He stopped speaking as Floyd disappeared down the hallway.

"Daddy, let me ask you something," Rowena said.

"Go ahead," he replied, sitting down in a chair by the table.

"What's the purpose of carrying guns? I mean, either Gwen and Adrienne are just a couple of crazy people, or they're three-hundred-year-old witches. If they're just nuts, we don't need guns. We just need to get out of here." She paused. "For that matter, if they're just nuts, we just have to wait until the police locate them. And if they do have special powers of some sort, what good are guns going to do against them?"

Simon paused before replying. "Look, Row," he said at last, "I don't know what'll be effective against those two. If I thought garlic would drive them away, I'd give you both garlic. Do you understand?"

"No," she said.

"Well, I know that guns can injure living things. If they're alive, then guns'll hurt them. And if they're not alive, not like you and me are alive, then—" He stopped speaking. "Then I don't know what to do. Just carry the gun, use it if you have to. Why take any chances."

"Makes sense," Lucas nodded. "Makes sense."

"Fine," Rowena said testily.

Her father smiled at her with understanding. "Row, we don't have any choice. Hey, listen, we probably won't have to use the guns. We probably won't even see Gwen and Adrienne. We're gonna be leaving in an hour and a half or so, and we'll be thousands of miles away by tomorrow."

She nodded, resigned to his logic. "I guess so. I just hate guns!"

Mark Siegal walked into the kitchen and said, "Simon, if you're just about done packing, we could start loading up the van. I got a luggage rack for the roof yesterday, just in case we need it."

"All we got left to pack up are the instruments down in the basement. Lucas, give me a hand with them, will you? Row, why don't you and Mark start carrying the suitcases outside?"

"Okay," she replied. "Oh, Daddy?"

"Yeah, honey?"

"It went real well today."

He frowned. "What went real well?"

"My last day at school. You know, saying good-bye and stuff."

He smiled at her, amused. Her high-school career was the last thing on his mind at the moment. "That's nice, honey, real nice." He walked out and went down the hallway toward the basement stairs, with Lucas following close behind him.

The next hour and a half was spent loading up the van, trying to fit the accumulated possessions of an entire family into the limited available space while leaving room for the people themselves. Suitcases stuffed to bursting with clothes, heavy cardboard boxes filled with mementos and sundry private treasures of no intrinsic value, records, books, musical instruments, photograph albums—all were fitted, moved, forced into place in the van. By four o'clock Mark Siegal's vehicle was filled from back door to luggage rack, overfilled, perhaps; but everything had been allocated a place, and room

314

still remained sufficient for Mark, Simon, Floyd, Rowena, Karyn, and Lucas.

Simon and Mark stood back and surveyed the van. "Looks to me like we're ready," Mark said.

"Yeah, looks that way. What time is it?"

Siegal looked at his watch. "Ten to four."

"Good, good." Simon placed a hand on Siegal's shoulder. "Markie, I can't thank you enough for this, for all your help."

Siegal grinned and made a gesture of dismissal. "Skip it. Next time I'm being chased by witches, I'll expect your help."

Simon laughed. "Yeah, sure. Go tell everybody that we're ready to leave, okay? I want to—well, I'll wait here."

"Okay, Simon." Siegal ambled back toward the house.

Simon Proctor sighed as he looked up at the old white building which had been his home, and that of his father, and his grandfather, and his great-grandfather, and so on all the way back to that day in the late seventeenth century when Elizabeth Proctor had migrated from Salem Village to this backcountry river valley. A damned shame, he thought to himself. Never realized how much I love this old house, this boring little town, these mountains. I hate to leave, I truly hate to leave. Must be even worse for Dad. Floyd's never lived anywhere else, never known any other kind of life.

He repressed the feeling of guilt which was assailing him. It's full circle, that's all, he thought. Full circle. Elizabeth's life seemed to have been ruined back in Salem, ruined by witchcraft, but it wasn't. She came here, found herself a new husband, a new life. That's my story too. Witchcraft. Making me leave Bradford, making me get out, go to Idaho. A new life for me, for Row, for Lucas. Dad'll adjust soon enough, I'm sure. Hell, he's gonna have a great-grandchild pretty soon. That oughta put a sparkle in his eye.

Still, he thought, I hate to leave. I love this old house.

"Daddy?" he heard Rowena say from the window, "where's Grampa?"

"Isn't he—? Oh, yeah, he's probably still over at the parsonage, looking for that old gun of his. I'll go get him. Everybody else ready to go?"

"Everybody except Karyn. She's sound asleep, and Lukie doesn't want to wake her until we're just about to leave."

"Good idea. Wait until I find Dad. Then you can help her get herself together. Okay?"

"Okeydokey," Rowena said, and disappeared from the window.

315

Simon walked across the street to the parsonage. As he mounted the narrow staircase which led to the upstairs apartment, he felt a pang of sorrow, of grief. Poor Jeremy, he thought. Poor kid. Wish I'da been nicer to him. Wish I hadn't gotten him into this. First his uncle disappears, then he's killed . . . horrible, horrible. My fault. All my fault. I guess we'll never know what happened to old Reverend Wilkes. Probably dead. My fault. My fault.

He shook his head as if to dispel the unwanted thoughts. "Dad?" he called out as he opened the door to the apartment. "Dad? You in here?" There was no answer, and he began searching the rooms. Floyd was not in the apartment. Maybe up in the attic, Simon thought. He pulled down the attic ladder which was embedded in the ceiling above the top of the stairs and climbed up into the small, sloping room just below the roof of the house. "Dad? Dad?" No reply.

Simon left the parsonage and walked back over to the old inn. He's probably wandering around, getting a last look at things, visiting an old friend or two, something like that, he thought. He went into the house and found Lucas, Rowena, and Mark having coffee in the kitchen. "Can't find him anywhere. Did anybody see him leave?"

"Just when he went over to look for the gun," Lucas said. "I ain't seen him since."

"Probably making a few good-byes in town," Simon suggested.

"I wonder if he's upstairs with Karyn?" Rowena said. "I heard some voices up there a while ago. I figured it was probably Lukie up there talking to her, but I guess it couldn't have been if he was in the basement with you, getting the guitars and stuff together."

"Why would he be talking to Karyn?" Lucas asked. "He can't stand Karyn!"

Simon smiled. "It's amazing how a baby can change people's opinions of each other. Maybe he's trying to make friends with her or something. I'll go up and see."

He walked from the kitchen to the stairs and proceeded up to the bedrooms. He saw that the door to Lucas and Karyn's room was closed, and he knocked on it softly. "Karyn?" he said. "You awake?" He turned the knob and pushed the door gently open. His father was not in the room, but the loud snores which emanated from beneath the blanket on the bed told him that Karyn was sleeping soundly. He turned to go, but then thought, She has to get up soon anyway, and maybe she's seen Dad. Couldn't hurt to wake her up and ask.

He walked over and sat down on the edge of the bed. "Karyn? Wake up. Time to go." The blanket moved above the reclining form and a soft yawn arose from beneath it. "Wake up, Karyn," he said. "We're gonna be leaving soon." He pulled the blanket gently from her.

His heart jumped into his mouth as Gwendolyn Jenkins reached up and grabbed him by the throat, laughing horribly. He tried to tear her hand away from him, but her grip was like a vise, her fingers were as hard as rock, her steely skin was as cold as ice, sepulchral, inhuman. He swung his fist wildly at her, tried to strike her in the face. His fist moved through her body as if through steam, leaving wispy traces trailing behind it, but touching nothing, only a thin film of cold moisture upon his skin serving as proof that something, *something* was there. Only her iron grip seemed real.

"I have a new song for you, my love," she whispered as her grip tightened upon his windpipe. "You can use it for your next *concert*"—and she squeezed—"you can make *money* with it." She squeezed harder. "Listen carefully. I shall only sing it for you once. Are you listening? Good." She began to sing softly. "Tick-tock, tick-tock, hear the ticking of the clock, tick-tock, tick-tock, hear the crowing of the cock, tick-tock, tick-tock, Peter doth betray his Master, tick-tock, tick-tock, the day of doom approacheth faster, tick-tock, tick-tock, carve the woman on the bed, tick-tock, tick-tock, see the old man lose his head, tick-tock, tick-tock, burn the boy and slice the girl, tick-tock, tick-tock, wipe the Proctors from this world." She smiled sweetly at him. "Do you like my song, Simon dear?"

Simon felt himself fall down hard upon the floor as the choking grip suddenly disappeared. He was alone in the room. She had vanished completely, instantly. He was tempted to persuade himself that it had been a hallucination, but he knew that it had been real. He could still feel the cold, rigid fingers upon his throat, and he was gasping for air.

He heard footsteps running up the stairs. A moment later Lucas, Mark, and Rowena rushed into the room and ran over to him. "Daddy," Rowena said, "what happened?"

Mark and Lucas helped him to his feet, and Mark said, "We heard a thud, like something fell."

"Are you okay, Dad?" Lucas asked. "Did you fall down or—" He looked around the room. "Karyn? Where's Karyn?"

"She must have her," Simon said hoarsely, his body shaking violently. "She must have her. She must have Dad too."

"What are you talking about?" Siegal demanded.

"Gwendolyn!" he tried to shout through his injured throat. "She was here, just now, in this room!" Mark, Rowena, and Lucas stared dumbly at him, the color draining from their faces. Rowena's hands went to her mouth. "We've got to find them, we've got to find them!" Simon shouted. "She's going to kill them!"

"Jesus!" Rowena prayed. "Jesus!"

"Everybody get a gun," Siegal said. "Simon, you and Lucas search one end of town, Rowena and I will search the other."

"What good are the guns?!" Simon screamed hysterically. "I tried to hit her, to punch her, but she wasn't even *there!*"

"Damn it, let's not waste time arguing about it!" Siegal snapped. "Let's just do it! Come on, Rowena. Get your pistol." Siegal ran from the room and Rowena followed quickly after him.

Lucas grabbed Simon's arm. "Come on, Dad. We can't just stand here! We have to go look for them!" Lucas pulled his father after him as he ran from the room and bounded down the stairs. They went to the van where Siegal and Rowena were busily rummaging about in search of the weapons. Siegal tossed Simon a shotgun and then found one for Lucas. Rowena already held the .22 pistol. Once he had taken a rifle for himself, Siegal began to run toward the nearest house. Rowena ran after him.

"Hold it, Mark," she said. "Let me knock. Nobody around here knows you. You can't run up with a rifle in your hands and start asking questions!"

"Okay, okay, right. Go ahead."

As Rowena went to the door and began to knock on it, Simon and Lucas ran in the other direction. They began to search house by house. None of the local residents thought it prudent to refuse entry to such obviously distraught, armed people.

Five o'clock.

They broke into the Grange hall and searched through the offices, the closets, the basement, the storage rooms. As the sun began to set, they went back to the inn to find flashlights and lanterns. The Grange hall was searched again, just in case they had missed anything in the dim twilight without lights to assist them. Nothing. They were gathered together by the state police, who had been summoned by the townspeople to quell the disturbance, and the officers were eager to assist them in their search when Rowena explained that two people were missing, kidnapped by a maniac. But when Simon began to jabber away about witches and a family curse, the police drove away with irritated disgust, after ordering them to refrain from any further disturbance of the peace.

Six o'clock.

The old Congregationalist church had been locked and boarded up ever since the disappearance of Reverend Wilkes, and it took the combined muscles of Simon and Lucas and the aid of a crowbar wielded by Siegal to break down the barriers. They burst into the church, calling out for Floyd and Karyn, searching the pews, the office, the cellar, the bell tower. They were not there.

Seven o'clock.

They sped to the state police station, begging for help. Simon shouted that the woman who had killed Jeremy Sloan was going to kill them all, and to placate him the police reissued the already standing all-points bulletin on Gwendolyn Jenkins and Adrienne Lupescu. It was clear to Simon and the others that the police thought he was mad.

Eight o'clock.

They wandered over the fields and farms of Bradford and the surrounding towns, crying out for Floyd and Karyn, sweeping the beams from their flashlights and lanterns ahead of them as they moved, jumping nervously at every sound, crying out in fear at each shadow which they themselves were creating with their lights. Each distant scarecrow elicited a mingling of hope and terror, hope for what it might be, terror of what it might be. There was nothing. The weathered, frozen scarecrows were nothing more than strands of rags keeping silent vigil over snow-covered fields, dead guardians of dead land in a dead season.

Nine o'clock.

They stumbled through the woods amid the evergreens and the naked elms, falling over protruding roots, frightened of the hooting owls and the distant growls of wildcats, listening for the sound of human voices other than their own, hearing none. Their cried of "Dad," "Floyd," "Karyn," echoed through the naked forest, and were unanswered.

Ten o'clock.

They searched again through the old inn, through the barn, through the cellar and the attic and the bedrooms.

Ten-thirty.

They pounded on doors throughout the town, forced entry into a few houses, saw doors pulled shut and window shades drawn and lights extinguished by the few residents of Bradford.

Eleven o'clock.

They tore through the Grange hall yet again, assaulted the church yet again, broke into people's barns yet again, calling out the names with an ever increasing urgency, a growing panic.

Eleven-thirty.

Eleven forty-five.

Simon Proctor stood before his house, breathless, sweating in the cold night air, his face and hands bleeding from his falls in the woods, his coat and hair covered with snow, his eyes wide and wild, his lips trembling, his hands opening and closing spasmodically upon the stock and barrel of his shotgun. "Lucas, Rowena, get into the van. Markie, get them the hell out of here, get them away from here."

"You're coming too, Simon," Siegal said.

He shook his head. "No. I'm staying here. I'm facing her."

"Dad," Lucas said firmly, "I'm not leaving here without Karyn."

"And I'm not leaving without you and Grampa," Rowena added.

Simon screamed. "Goddamn it! Do what you're told! Get away from this town, now!"

"Daddy, I'm not going to leave you here to—"

"Rowena," he shouted, dropping his gun and grabbing her by the shoulders, "do what I tell you to do! I want you and your brother safe, I want you away from here!"

Lucas bent down and picked up his father's gun. He handed it to him and said, "You said earlier that we're all in this together. Well, nothing's changed, except now my girl's missing and my grandfather's missing. I'm sorry, Dad. I ain't no hero. Far from it. But I can't just run away and leave her here, and leave you here."

"Lucas, will you please pay attention to me!" Simon screamed, throwing the gun away. "Get in the goddamn van and get the hell out of here! This is my fault, my respons—"

Three sounds assailed his ears simultaneously, stopping his mouth and sending shivers up his spine. The four people looked around them, seeking to find the source of the sounds.

They heard the church bell, which had not been in usable condition in living memory, toll twelve.

They heard an earsplitting, rending shriek of incredible agony, a shriek of terror and pain.

And then, wafting slowly toward them, borne upon the frigid wind, was deep, throaty, vindictive laughter.

They stood for a moment as if frozen in place, and then began to run toward the church. The church bell had tolled; there had to be someone pulling the rope.

Lucas led them, his eyes wide and wild with fear and anger in equal measure. Rowena followed behind her father and Mark, not wanting to go to the church, not wanting to be left alone.

The church door was open wide, as they had left it not long before. They rushed into the dark building and stood in the aisle between the pews, listening carefully for sounds. The laughter began again and Simon said, "The bell tower! She's in the bell tower!" He led them back toward the narrow, winding staircase which led from behind the narthex to the top of the tower. They stumbled over their own feet as they leapt up the stairs, gun stocks thudding against the old wooden encasement, heavy breathing mingling with furtive whispered prayers. The laughter grew louder as they wound their way up toward the bell tower.

Simon pushed open the trap door and scrambled onto the platform which formed a floor just below the peak of the spire. Mark, Rowena, and Lucas followed immediately after him. They stood together, guns leveled, staring at Gwendolyn Jenkins.

The woman was leaning back against the wooden wall, looking from face to face, laughing softly, confidently. "All come to services at once?" she laughed. "I'm sorry, but the church is closed for repairs."

"Gwen, where are they?" Simon demanded. "What have you done with them? Answer me!"

"Gwen?" she asked with mock confusion. "Who be this Gwen? I know no such person. I am Abby, my dear, sweet Simon, don't you remember?"

"Damn it, where are they?!" he shouted.

"Oh, I do believe they've gone to pay their respects to the minister, that boy's uncle," she smiled. "Such good neighbors they are, the two of them, going to the grave this late at night."

"What grave?" Simon said. "What the hell are you talking about?"

"Why, the minister's grave, of course! He's buried not a stone's throw from here, in the cemetery across the way."

"In the cemetery! Gwen, there—"

"Abigail, if you please!"

"—hasn't been anybody buried there in years."

"Nay, but I buried him myself, not seven weeks ago!" She smiled wickedly. "'Twas a lovely service, my dear. A great pity you could not attend."

Simon stared at her furiously, and then opened fire. The sound of the gunshot seemed to act as a catalyst for Lucas and Mark, and they too began firing at her. She laughed merrily as the bits of hot, burning metal passed through her insubstantial form and tore through the wood behind her. "Death comes but once to us all," she laughed. "I died three hundred years ago. Think you to kill me again?" Her laughter began to fade as her form began to fade, slowly, silently disappearing into the cold air and darkness. "Go to your father, Simon Proctor!" said the faint and fading voice. "Go to your woman and child, Lucas! 'Tis a bad night to be alone in a graveyard!" The laughter and the image faded into nothingness and were gone.

The four people stood in silence, gazing at the now empty spot where Gwendolyn Jenkins had stood a moment before.

Where Abigail Williams had stood a moment before. . . .

"Daddy," Rowena said, tugging on the sleeve of Simon's coat, "come on, come on!"

"Huh?" he asked. He felt numb, drained.

"We have to go to the cemetery, now! She said that's where Grampa and Karyn are! Maybe it isn't too late, maybe they're still okay. Daddy! Come on!"

Simon shook his head vigorously as if to clear it. "Yeah, yeah. Let's go." They descended the winding staircase and ran from the church urgently, reloading their guns as they ran, knowing that the weapons were useless but feeling the urge to have them at the ready nonetheless. They entered the small cemetery quietly, cautiously, looking around them with trembling faces and terrified eyes. Soft laughter seemed to dance upon the naked limbs of the trees which stood just outside the fence. Simon pointed toward the rear of the old graveyard and said, "Look over there. I think I see a light."

Mark squinted through the darkness. "Dim glow. Lantern, maybe, with a low wick?"

"Maybe." Simon moved slowly and carefully toward the light. Mark was right behind him, and Lucas and Rowena, arms around each other, followed. As they drew close to the light, Simon smiled. "Dad! Thank God!"

Floyd Proctor was standing behind an old, weathered, granite tombstone, the plain type which local notables had chosen for themselves in past centuries, a simple upright slab with rounded top and deeply chiseled name and dates. Floyd was leaning against the stone, his left hand folded over his right, his eyes staring ahead of him at his son as he approached. "Dad, where's Karyn?" Simon asked, drawing near to his father. "Dad? Are you okay? Dad?"

Floyd neither replied nor moved. As Simon came close to him, his eyes did not follow his son's motion, but rather stared off at the same spot as before, motionless, expressionless. Simon felt a feeling grow upon him of utter *wrongness*, of something—something—terribly, terribly wrong. He reached out and placed his hand gently upon his father's hand. It was cold and hard to the touch. "Dad?" he said, and then noticed that Floyd's throat, seen indistinctly in the glow of the dim lantern which sat upon the ground at Floyd's feet, seemed bruised and battered, bloody. "Dad? Are you all right?" Simon shook his father gently by the shoulder.

Floyd's severed head, which had been carefully balanced upon the stump of his slit neck, fell forward and bounced once, rolled a few feet, and then came to rest face down in the snow. His body, which had been propped up upon the tombstone, slipped slowly to the ground.

Simon gasped and jumped back as Rowena's scream cut through the silence of the graveyard. He stared down at the back of his father's head, his eyes blinking as if to dispel the horrid vision, and he reached out to Mark Siegal, seeking to steady himself upon his friend's arm. Siegal was no longer behind him. Simon turned to see that neither Mark nor Lucas nor Rowena were facing him, that none of them had as yet seen old Floyd's head drop from his body, that Rowena's scream was unrelated to the butchery before them. They were looking off to the left, to the sturdy, thick branch of a snow-covered oak tree.

Karyn Johannson's legs, bent at the knees, were folded over the branch and were tied by ropes which bound her ankles to her thighs. Her legs were twisted and disfigured, broken in numerous places, pulled wide apart from each other. She was naked but for the scarf which seemed to be dangling from her head, swaying and swinging slowly back and forth between her arms which extended downward toward the ground from her inverted body. A massive, horrible slit had been cut into her flesh from just below her breasts to the crevice of her womb, and the blood which covered her from belly to head testified to the fact that she had been hanging upside down when the knife had torn through her. The blood was no longer flowing, but it had bathed her chest, her arms, her head, even her scarf before death and drainage ceased its flood.

But it was not a scarf which Simon saw dangling from her. It was her long red hair, made redder and thicker with gouts of blood. Her hair hung down straight and tight, as if weighted down. Simon's eyes drifted down from her mutilated form to the end of the ruddy tresses. They had been plaited into a noose, and from them dangled the lifeless, strangled body of her unborn, never to be born, child.

Lucas fell onto the cold ground in a faint as Rowena screamed and screamed and screamed. Mark and Simon fell back into each other, repelled by the vision of massacre which confronted them, and Mark inadvertently kicked his foot against Floyd's head. The head rolled a few feet through the snow and then came to rest upon the stump of its neck. It gazed up at Simon with motionless, lifeless, accusatory eyes.

No time now, Simon thought. Can't mourn, can't cry. No time, no time. "Come on," he said hoarsly. "We have to get out of here."

Rowena was still screaming, her fingers thrust into her mouth, her body trembling so violently that her legs seemed about to give way. Simon grabbed her roughly by the shoulders and shook her. "Rowena! Snap out of it! We have to get out of here!" He turned to Siegal, who was staring dumbly at Karyn's body as it swayed gently to and fro in the wind. "Mark! Get Lucas! Try to bring him around! Mark!!"

Siegal blinked as if awakening and then, suddenly aware and efficient, grabbed Lucas and slung him over his shoulder in a fireman's carry. He began to run awkwardly from the grave-yard, bent by his burden. Simon dragged the hysterical girl along with him as he too ran madly toward the street.

They reached the van in a few minutes and Mark tossed Lucas into the back unceremoniously. He hopped into the driver's seat and began to race the engine as Simon pushed Rowena into the passenger seat and then leapt into the back of the van, securing the door behind him. "Move, Mark, move!" he shouted.

Siegal threw the engine into gear and hit the accelerator hard, causing the tires to whip against the snow-covered ground for a few moments before they found traction and impelled the van out of the driveway and onto the street. He turned the wheel hard to the left and the van seemed on the verge of tipping over as Siegal struggled to right it. They screeched and slid up the street, shattering the silent winter night with the sound of the frantic engine.

They sped toward the highway along the empty road,

traveling at a speed far in excess of the limit, almost spinning out once and always in danger of tipping over when they hit a curve. Something from the luggage rack on the roof broke free and fell onto the road behind them, but Siegal neither stopped nor looked back as Simon kept saying, "Faster, Mark, faster! Get to the highway! Hurry!"

The van swerved suddenly, sending Simon thudding against the pile of suitcases which lined the rear compartment. "Rowena," Mark said rapidly, "put on your seat belt."

She looked over at him, a dazed, numb expression on her face. "Huh? Wh—what—?"

"Put on your seat belt! Hurry up!" He swerved again and the van skidded wildly on the snow-covered road surface.

"What the hell are you doing?" Simon asked. They were speeding along a straightaway, and Simon had felt the telltale smoothness of a skid as the van had swerved.

"Simon, look out front!" Mark Siegal said urgently. "Look out on the road ahead of us!"

Simon pulled himself forward and grabbed the headrest of Rowena's seat. He peered out through the windshield into the darkness and saw a figure standing at a distance in the middle of the road. It was Gwendolyn Jenkins, or Abigail Williams, or whatever the creature was now after so many centuries with its body in the earth and its soul floating upon the lake of fire. It was she, and it was not she. It was a human form, but it was somehow insubstantial, translucent, the beautiful countenance which Simon had kissed so many times now appearing to be a mask of sculptured glass covering a rotting and decaying skull. She raised her arms as if in greeting as the van sped toward her, and as Siegal swerved again and passed by her, Simon could clearly see the bones of her arms and hands moving beneath the cloudy, transparent skin.

"She keeps ahead of me somehow," Siegal said. "This was the third time. I don't know how the hell she's doing it."

"She isn't doing it," Simon muttered. "Satan is doing it. There isn't any other explanation."

"Save it for the stage act, man," Siegal spat. "I'm scared enough. I don't need no Devil shit right now."

"I'm not kidding, Mark."

"I don't give a shit, Simon! I just want to get—" He swerved again and Gwendolyn-Abigail's laughter drifted in and then out of the interior of the van. "Jesus Christ!"

Simon thought quickly. "Don't try to avoid her."

"What?!"

"Don't try to avoid her. Run her down."

Mark nodded dubiously. "Might not help."

"Can't hurt."

"Those bullets went right through her back in the bell tower. Didn't even muss her hair."

"Okay, so maybe we'll go right through her too. Listen, man, she may—shit!" he cried as Siegal swerved again to avoid the grotesque figure which had appeared once again in the middle of the road. "Damn it, Mark, run her down! She may be trying to make us drive off the road and wrap ourselves around a tree or something. If she passes through us as we run at her, then no harm is done. And maybe we won't. Maybe we'll leave her spread out on the road. Jesus, Markie, try it, will you?!"

Siegal nodded. "Okay, okay." He paused. "There she is again."

The phantasm stood motionless upon the solid yellow line in front of them, a hundred yards away. Her arms were raised and her laughter reached them even from the distance, even over the roar of the engine. Siegal gritted his teeth, accelerated, and aimed for her. The motionless figure seemed to rush at them as they approached, and as they struck her and felt no impact, heard no sound, Simon allowed himself a sudden hope that he had been right, that her insubstantial form presented no physical obstacle to them.

And then he saw that as the van had passed through her she had entered it, that she was there with them, that she was sitting on Mark Siegal's lap, her legs straddling him. She laughed through the glass mask of human features, through the rotting teeth and decaying skull, and a funereal voice said, "Thank you for giving me a ride, kind gentlemen." It was not Gwendolyn's voice. It was not a woman's voice. It was not a human voice. The bony fingers reached up and grabbed Mark Siegal's temples. He screamed when the cold appendages grasped him, releasing the steering wheel and struggling impotently against the unrelenting grip. The van began to rock back and forth uncontrollably as his knees struck the steering wheel repeatedly in his struggle with the specter. She gazed down at him with amusement, and then gave his head a mighty twist, cracking the neck, turning the head around once, twice, three times, leaving it staring backward at Simon, an expression of shock, pain, and unutterable fear emblazoned upon the staring face.

Simon's screams mingled with the insane laughter of the

creature as the van careened off the road and struck a large tree head-on. He threw his arms over his face as he felt himself thrown forward against the rear of the front seats, felt himself skim painfully over them and crash through the windshield. He hit the ground hard, missing the tree itself by inches, and he skidded across the snow and the rocks and the naked branches, coming to rest at last against a bank of snow.

He lay there, dazed and injured, numb and cold. He heard a low moan from behind him and he tried to turn over to look, but the excruciating pain in his side told him that he had broken a few ribs. He was able to move, however. At least his spine was intact. Slowly and painfully, he moved upon his stomach, swiveling around so that his face would point in the direction of the van. When at last the battered vehicle was in view, he was able to see in the dim moonlight that Rowena was moving in the front seat. "Row . . . ," he said softly, feeling his entire frame rack with pain from the simple act of speaking, from the simple effort of breathing. "Rowena," he said again, and saw her turn her face toward him from behind the shattered windshield. She slumped forward, unconscious, still held in place by the seat belt she had so fortuitously affixed. "Lucas," he called out. "Lucas. . . ." There was no answer from the interior of the van. Simon turned his head to the side and saw Mark Siegal, his head still facing backward, impaled through the chest upon a branch of the tree.

He heard footsteps, numerous footsteps, moving slowly closer, crunching upon the hard snow. His heart began to beat wildly and his fingers scrabbled upon the ground, seeking to impel his injured body away from the approaching footsteps. He saw three figures moving stiffly through the dark woods, the moonlight dancing in their eyes as they drew near. Panic mounted in his brain and then was replaced by a sudden flood of relief.

"Tommy," he tried to call out. "Larry, Carl. Over here. We're over here."

Mahoney, Herricks, and Strube lumbered over the uneven ground and sidled between the bare trees.

"I don't know what you guys are doing here, but you couldn't have come at a better time," he said joyfully. "You won't believe what's happened tonight. Jesus, I don't half believe it myself!" Larry Herricks bent down and grabbed Simon beneath the arms, pulling him to his feet. "Ouch! Hey, take it easy, Larry! I think I cracked a couple of ribs!" He looked into Larry Herricks's eyes. They were cold, empty, expressionless. "Larry? . . ." Simon felt his panic return. He struggled to free himself from the cold grip, pushing himself away from Larry Herricks. He was not able to break free, but he was able to push himself far enough away to see the gaping hole in Herricks's chest where once his heart had beat.

Herricks was dead, Strube was dead, Mahoney was dead, their hearts torn from their bodies, their corpses animated by some infernal power, their deaths certainly orchestrated by Simon's mortal yet immortal enemy. Herricks threw Simon across his shoulder and began walking slowly, steadily back up toward the road. Simon could see Mahoney tear the seat belt from its mooring and drag the unconscious Rowena from the seat as Strube ripped open the back of the shattered van and pulled Lucas out into the cold night. Mahoney cradled Rowena almost lovingly in his dead arms as he followed Herricks back up toward the road, and Strube, draping Lucas across his shoulder in the same manner as Herricks had done with Simon, followed behind.

The strange procession moved in line along the deserted country road, only the dim moonlight illuminating their movement, only Simon's terrified weeping breaking the stillness and the silence. An occasional hoot from a hungry owl and the distant howl of a dog enraptured by the moon were the only other sounds.

The three dead men and their burdens entered the sleeping town of Bradford and moved silently up the single narrow street. Simon's cries for help were not heeded by the villagers. For one thing, he was so weak, so injured, and so frightened that he could barely raise his voice above a whisper, and in addition, he and Mark and Lucas and Rowena had spent so many hours that night running around the town and making noise that even if people had heard him, they would have ignored him. Simon tried to talk to Herricks, tried to talk to Strube, to Mahoney, tried in desperation to awaken some human response in them. It was of no avail. They were not under the witch's control as Jeremy had been the day of his death; they were not living men whose wills had been taken from them, whose lives were still theirs and might yet be reclaimed. Dead men, walking corpses, animated dust. That was all.

They proceeded up the dark street, past the old gas station, past the Grange hall, past the Proctor Inn and the general store above which once Jeremy and Reverend Wilkes had lived, past the old residences. They came to the spot in the

328

road between the church and the graveyard, the graveyard where Karyn's body still hung from the tree branch and swayed in the cold wind, the graveyard where Floyd Proctor's head still gazed blankly up at the starless sky, the graveyard where, somewhere, the remains of Reverend Frederick Wilkes were mingling with the soil.

But they did not turn to the graveyard. The three dead men slowly turned toward the church and began to walk steadily toward it. As they drew near, Simon thought he heard music; as they entered the old colonial building, he was certain that he heard music, the music of a harp and a lute, blending in gentle, delicate harmony. Simon tried to shift his position on Herricks's shoulder, tried to look in the direction in which he was being carried, tried to discover what was awaiting him in the front of the old church. And then his heart thumped loudly in his chest as the lute and the harp were joined by two female voices.

"A sad time for lovers, so they say.
　'Tis a sad time for lovers, so they say.
For the leaves have all fell down
　And the body's in the ground,
And we're meeting one last time on this dark day.

The death snow has fallen on the grass,
　And the death snow has fallen on the grass.
The life is almost done
　And the course is almost run,
And the bell tolls the eve of Candlemas."

Simon Proctor began to weep.

⟦ CHAPTER TWENTY-THREE ⟧
February 1: Candlemas Eve

THE THREE DEAD men shuffled down the aisle between the pews. Piles of rope were resting on the floor directly in front of the altar, and each grabbed a coil. As Herricks began with stiff fingers to bind Simon hand and foot, Simon looked to the

329

right, to the space before the pulpit. Gwendolyn and Adrienne—Abigail and Mary—were sitting on two folding chairs, singing.

Strube tied the ends of two strands of rope to Lucas's wrists and then tossed the other ends up into the air. They looped over the rafter of the old wooden building and then fell back toward the floor. Strube pulled easily, mindlessly upon them both, hoisting Lucas upward, and then tied the ends to the base of the lectern at the left of the altar. The unconscious boy, still deep in shock from the sight of the mutilated body of his girlfriend, dangled two feet from the ground.

"A tear for the damned, and mourn them well.
    Shed a tear for the damned, and mourn them well.
And sing a sorrow song
    For the time will not be long
'Ere they greet the lord of darkness deep in hell."

Abigail and Mary, eyes closed, ignoring the proceedings, sang on. Mahoney tore Rowena's clothing roughly from her body, and she seemed to rise slowly to consciousness as the cold hands touched her warm skin, but she was too confused, too injured to resist. When she was naked, Mahoney threw her onto the communion table and began to tie her hands to one set of legs and her ankles to the other. She tried to rise to a sitting position, but he thrust her roughly down upon her back and then completed his task. She lay helpless upon the altar, arms stretched out behind her, legs stretched out in front. When she came fully awake and understood her situation, she began to weep. "Daddy," she cried, and Simon's heart seemed to break.

"On All Hallows' Eve the wind is high,
    And on All Hallows' Eve the wind is high,
The Midsummer moon is bright
    And 'tis dark on Walpurgis Night,
And on Candlemas Eve the children die."

The two women continued to play their instruments, humming the melancholy melody, and Simon watched as they began to grow indistinct, as they began to fade into the gloomy, candle-lit darkness of the interior of the old church. Their images and their music seemed to disappear simultaneously. They were gone.

Simon was lying, bound, in the front pew. He struggled to rise and found that the ropes which had been affixed to his hands and feet had been attached by another rope to the pew itself. He could sit up, but he could not move from his position. In front of him, Rowena lay motionless upon the communion table, motionless but for the trembling of her breast as she wept. To the side, Lucas hung from the rafters, and the low moan which escaped from his lips told Simon that his son was alive, injured, and awakening. Mahoney, Strube, and Herricks stood against the wall beside the lectern, completely immobile, no movement in their dead eyes, their chests unmoved by breathing.

"Daddy?"

Simon sighed and sniffed back his tears. "I'm here, baby."

Rowena leaned her head in his direction. There was a bruise upon her forehead at the point where she had struck the dashboard of the van, and a small trickle of blood stained the right side of her lip. "Daddy, what are we gonna do?" she asked, her voice broken and frightened.

He shook his head. "I don't know, baby, I don't know. I don't know if there's anything we *can* do!"

They were silent, but for Lucas's repeated moans. The cold wind whistled through the old rafters, caused the candle flames to dance upon the wicks, sent flickering ghostly shadows drifting upon the walls and floor. The candle flames danced in the open, staring, dead eyes of the three bodies which stood against the wall, stood as if waiting, stood as if ready to obey their next commands.

Simon took a deep breath. "Gwendolyn!" he shouted. There was no response. "Gwendolyn!!" he shouted again, and only silence replied. "Gw—" he paused. Then he sighed and said softly, "Abigail?"

"Welcome, Simon dear," Abigail Williams said from behind him. "So happy you could come tonight." Simon Proctor turned his head to see the two women he had known as Gwendolyn Jenkins and Adrienne Lupescu walking down between the pews toward the front of the church. Abigail and Mary drew close to him. Both were attired in simple black dresses with white collars and small white caps, and as they came to a stop in front of Simon, Abigail flared her skirt outward at the sides with her hands and spun about prettily. "Do you like it?" she asked. "I wore it just for you."

"Gwen—"

"Tosh! And just when I thought you'd finally learned to call me by my true name!" She clicked her tongue and shook her head. "So disappointed I am in you, Simon Proctor! Truly I am!"

"Okay, then, Abigail! I beg you, I *beg* you, to have pity, to have mercy, if not on me then at least on my children." Tears began to roll down his cheeks. "They've never done anything to you, they've never hurt you or lied to you. I'm the one who you should be mad at, not them!"

She sat down beside him on the pew and stroked his brow affectionately. "Poor fellow, you still don't understand, do you? I am long-suffering, but when I take revenge, my revenge is inexorable. Do you see your friends over there?" She nodded at the three corpses against the wall. "I killed them two days ago. And do you know why?" She paused. "I killed them because it would hurt you to see them dead! I killed them just to hurt you!" She smiled again. "Don't you understand? Killing Lucas and Rowena will pierce you to the heart, Simon dear."

"Abigail—please—"

"Shall I tell you how I killed them?" Her green eyes twinkled merrily. "I sent out my spirit against them, as I had done before against that damned minister."

"Wh—what are you—?"

"Oh, you did not know of that? Aye, when you and I and the others were drinking and making merry in the tavern across the river, I sent my spirit out against the minister." She laughed. "I buried him alive. 'Twas delightful!"

"No—you couldn't have—you—"

"But I digress. Where was I? Ah, yes, I sent my spirit out against your friends and ripped their hearts from their bodies. They were most upset. And, by the way, your friend Mr. Herricks has quite a foul mouth!"

Simon stared at her with disbelief, more terrified of the cold, conversational tone of her speech than the content of her words. "How—how can you do things like this?" he stammered. "What kind of creature are you that you can do these things?"

"I told you, months ago," she replied easily. "I am a witch."

"But—"

"And more than a witch, 'tis true," she nodded, looking down pensively and then looking back into his eyes, a sudden fury suffusing her face. "I am a woman who is sick to death of Proctors! I am a woman who destroyed herself three hundred years ago for love of a Proctor, who was driven from her home by the vindictive hatred of a Proctor, who spent three hundred years suffering the agonies of hell for hope of a Proctor's love, who was dragged up from the pit by the stupid incantations of a Proctor child this last All Hallows' Eve, who gave herself once again to a Proctor, and who was once again betrayed by a Proctor! *That* is what I am, Simon, my darling," she hissed, "my dear, sweet love!"

"But you can't—" he wept, "you can't—"

"Ah, but I can, and I shall. I shall free myself of you and your damnable family, and live out the rest of this life as I wish. I am returned to the world a young woman, and I shall dwell again upon the surface of the earth and live out another life, doing what I will, going where I will, taking what I will! Someday I shall die, someday return to hell, but what of it? Three centuries ago I signed my name in the Devil's book, and it cannot be erased, so I shall not waste this life fearing the approach of death. Indeed, I shall revel in death! I shall be a harbinger of death, a black angel, visiting vengeance and destruction upon all who anger me!"

Simon tried to jump to his feet, pulling against the tight, abrasive ropes, shouting, "Let me go, goddamn it, let me and my kids go! I'll marry you, if that's what you want, I'll marry you for real, but just let us go!"

"Marry you!" she said, surprise and offense in her voice. "Marry you! After all which has gone between us! You flatter yourself, Simon Proctor, truly you do!" She glanced over her shoulder. "Mary Warren, come here." Mary approached obediently. "Sit beside our friend Simon and comfort him. He is about to become very, very upset." She laughed and turned away. Abigail knelt in the midst of the church, facing away from the front, away from the cross, and she bowed her head and began to mutter supplications to her dark lord.

Mary sat beside Simon and looked down at the floor, avoiding his eyes. Simon whispered desperately, "Untie me, Adrienne, please untie me!"

"Mary," she corrected him sadly.

"All right, all right, Mary! Untie me, quickly, please!"

She heaved a mighty sigh. "I cannot. I am sorry."

"Yes you can, damn it, yes you can! You don't hate me, do you? You don't hate Lucas. You like Rowena, I know that for a fact! Help us, please!"

She shook her head sadly. "You do not understand, Mr. Proctor, and I cannot truly explain it to you. I am bound to obedience to Abigail. I was bound to her when first we both lived in Salem, and I am bound to her still. I owe her a debt, and—"

"A debt! Are you crazy?! What kind of debt could you possibly owe her to make you obey her like this?! Untie me, for Christ's sake!"

She shook her head again. "'Twas I who ruined her plan to kill Elizabeth Proctor. 'Twas I whose foolishness led John Proctor to the gallows. She has never forgiven me. I am under Satan's curse and God's wrath." She began to weep. "I am alone, all alone in the world, with no one, with nothing. Satan plagues me for my weakness, God damns me for my sin, Abby torments me for my error." She looked up at him. "Don't you understand? I have no choice, no choice! I am bound to her, bound to her, her bidding is my will! Can't you understand?"

"Excuses, Mary Warren?" Abigail said, rising from her knees and walking menacingly forward. "Explanations? And to him?" She grabbed Mary by the hair and pulled her to her feet, gazing furiously into the weeping, sorrowful eyes. "Truly am I happy not to have been your school teacher! You never learn your lesson!" She pushed Mary back into the pew and then turned to Simon. "'Tis a night for learning lessons. I shall now teach one to you, foolish man. You sold your soul to the Devil without even knowing it, without extracting from him any boon or benefit in exchange. Well, then, let me show you what awaits you. Let me give you—what is it the Christians say about their bread and wine?—let me give you a foretaste of the feast to come."

Abigail sauntered over to Lucas and smiled almost lovingly at him. The boy's head was rolling from side to side and his eyes were blinking painfully as he tried to rouse himself to full consciousness. Abigail slapped him gently on the cheek. "Lukie? Lukie! Wake up! It's time to get up!" She giggled as Lucas Proctor's blurry eyes tried to focus on her face. "That's better." She turned to Simon and smiled. "Now watch carefully, my dear love." She looked up at Lucas and the smile faded from her face. She stepped back a few feet, never taking her eyes off him, and she extended both her arms toward him, fingers straight and taut. Abigail stood motionless for a moment and then screamed, *"In nomine diaboli, incende!"*

Lucas looked at her uncomprehendingly, and then his eyes went wide with pain and shock. His body began to shake violently and beads of perspiration began to roll down his face. He looked wildly over at Simon, and tried to speak, tried to cry out, but instead of words, billows of smoke issued from his mouth.

The smoke poured from his mouth, his nose, his ears. His

arms and legs, wrapped still in clothing, began to sizzle audibly beneath the wool and cotton, and a few delicate licks of flame burst through his sleeves. A horrible shriek managed to escape his lips, and it was followed by a rolling ball of fire which leapt outward and then enveloped his head and shoulders. His body jerked and shuddered as the inferno consumed him from within, as the flames crept down his legs and up his arms and spread over his chest. The ropes which bound him to the ceiling caught fire and then snapped, allowing the heap of charred bone and melting flesh which had been Lucas Proctor to drop to the floor.

Simon screamed and Rowena screamed, but Abigail's laughter drowned them out. "*Satanas laudamus!*" she laughed.

"Lucas!" Simon wept. "Lucas, Lucas!" Rowena wept also, but could not bring herself to speak. She was almost paralyzed with fear.

Abigail smiled triumphantly at Simon. " 'Twas a bit chilly in here. We had need of a fire." She laughed again, madly, and then reached beneath her skirts. She slowly drew forth the knife which she sheathed against her thigh and then walked toward Rowena. "Ah, and what have we here?" she asked with amusement. "Why, 'tis yet another Proctor womb! Now, we cannot have this lying about, breeding more Proctor vermin, can we, my dear?"

"Daddy! Help me!" Rowena managed to cry out.

"Get away from her!" he screamed, choking on his own tears. "Please, Abigail, I'll do anything, anything you want, anything!"

"Good!" she grinned. "I want you to watch!" She placed the tip of the blade between Rowena's breasts and, without exerting any pressure other than the weight of the blade, drew it down her body to the petals of her nether lips. A thin line of red became visible in the blade's wake, and a few drops of blood beaded up at several points along the knife's path.

"Daddy—!" her voice broke.

Abigail pulled the blade away and stepped back, still smiling down at the terrified girl. She turned to Mary Warren and tossed the knife to her. Mary was not prepared to catch it, and it clattered loudly on the floor. "Pick it up!" she commanded. Mary bent down and retrieved the knife. "You must learn your place, Mary Warren. You must learn that you are mine, and Satan's, and must do our bidding without making excuses or offering explanations." She stepped back and pointed at Rowena. "Gut her!" she ordered.

Mary Warren began to weep and her back bent with sorrow, but she nonetheless began to walk toward Rowena. She stood over her and placed the tip of the blade at the upper end of the thin red line, tightening her grip upon the hilt. She avoided Rowena's desperate, pleading eyes. "I am sorry," she whispered sadly.

"Adrienne—Mary—please—please—" the girl stammered.

"I must," she sighed. "I must do as I am told."

"No you don't," Rowena wept. "You do *not* have to do whatever she tells you to do, you do *not*!" The girl was trembling violently from her terror, and her wide, frightened eyes were fixed upon the blade whose tip rested upon her breast just below her throat. "We were friends—we were friends—you couldn't do this to me—you couldn't—"

"I am sorry," Mary repeated.

"When you were all upset and scared—in the motel—I held you and you cried on my shoulder—"

"I remember," Mary whispered, weeping.

"And at Christmas—" Rowena said, talking just to talk, her mind wildly trying to maintain a grip on sanity and reason in the midst of the madness which was beginning to engulf it, "at Christmas—I gave you a present, remember?"

"I remember."

"And I—I tried to help you when Larry—when Gwendolyn made you—I tried to help you—"

"I remember."

There was the slightest hint of pressure beginning to be brought to bear upon the knife, and Rowena screamed, "Oh God, please! Please!"

"I have no choice," Mary said sadly, wiping away a tear with her free hand. "I have no choice."

"Everyone has choice," Rowena screamed, "everyone has choice."

"No, not everyone. Not I." The pressure increased slightly.

"You *do* have a choice," Rowena wept. "You can still choose between doing what is right and doing what is wrong." Rowena tried to ignore Abigail's piercing laughter at her last statement. "You can still choose!" she repeated, as firmly as was possible with her broken, trembling voice.

"I made that choice centuries ago," Mary whispered. "I cannot undo the choice I made then. There is no going back for me now."

"Mary, listen to me," Rowena said urgently. "I know what happened back in Salem, I know what happened to *you* back in

Salem, I've read all about it—oh, God, PLEASE!—listen to me, Mary, LISTEN to me!" She felt the cold tip of the knife pierce through the outer surface of her skin, just slightly, just barely, and felt her panic increasing rapidly. "You chose to do wrong, but you were pressured into it, intimidated, terrified into it. It was Abigail's fault, not yours, it was her fault, her fault! When you had to choose between telling the truth and supporting her lies, she forced you to make the wrong choice, she threatened you, she made you lie along with her and all the others."

"One cannot make another sin," Mary said quietly. "The choice was mine."

"No, it wasn't yours, you *had* no choice, you were a frightened, terrified, lonely girl and you were bullied into it, forced into it! Mary," she screamed, "don't you understand? It's happening to you again, right now, right now, just like it happened to you before! You have to choose between good and evil, and she's trying to force you to choose evil, just like she did in Salem three hundred years ago!"

"Enough!" Abigail spat. "Silence her, Mary Warren! Silence her immediately, do you hear?!"

"She destroyed you, Mary, don't you see?" Rowena cried. "She destroyed you just as surely as she destroyed John Proctor and all the other innocent people killed in Salem, just as surely as she destroyed Jeremy and Lucas. Everything that happened to you, everything, *everything*, is her fault! Don't let her do it again, Mary, don't let her do it to you again! Choose good, Mary, choose good, choose God!"

Mary froze in place. The blade did not withdraw from Rowena's breast, but neither did it descend.

"Mary Warren!" Abigail commanded. "Strike, damn you!"

Mary did not reply. She was gazing off into the distance, her brow furrowed.

"Try to remember, try to think back to—to when you were— oh, Mary, try to remember what it was like before you met Abigail, what *you* were like before you met Abigail!" Rowena saw Mary's indecision and dared to focus her hopes upon it. She rushed on urgently, desperately, her voice filled with a terrified mixture of panic and prayer. "Try to remember, Mary, oh, please try to remember! Before she corrupted you, before she made you part of her own corruption! Please try, Mary, please! Please!"

"Strike!" Abigail repeated.

Mary Warren did not answer her. She was not listening to her. She was thinking back. She was remembering.

She was remembering her childhood. She remembered sitting upon her mother's lap, snug and secure as her mother sang her a lullaby. She remembered holding her father's hand as they walked from their simple cabin through the autumn forests of old New England, on their way to the meeting house for Sunday services. That was before the Indian attack, she thought, before Mother and Father were killed. Mother pushed me into the root cellar, beneath the trapdoor in the floor of the cabin. She stood on top of the trapdoor when the Indians broke in. She died there on that spot, protecting me, hiding me.

Mary remembered. She remembered how innocently she had fallen in love with young Matthew Hopkins, the blacksmith's son. She remembered how innocently he had returned her love. She remembered their awkward, trembling hands the first time they touched, children holding hands at an August picnic. And that first, gentle, fleeting kiss, their only kiss, their only intimacy, more intimate in its pristine innocence than any other kiss she had ever received.

She remembered what it was like to love and to hope and to dream.

She turned her head slowly in Abigail's direction and gazed at her coldly through narrowed eyes.

She remembered how much she had admired Abigail Williams, the minister's niece. She had so many of the qualities which Mary had lacked: self-confidence, poise, an easy manner, and a glib way with words. She had so wanted to be Abigail's friend. She wanted her friendship so much that she would have done anything—did do anything . . .

She remembered that day in the forest with Tituba, that day when the small group of girls had assembled to cast a spell upon Elizabeth Proctor. It had been Abigail's idea to cast the spell.

She remembered that she and Abigail were the first to disrobe, the first to stand naked in the freezing forest. It had been Abigail's idea that they be first, they two.

She remembered the demonic possession which they pretended to be experiencing, the convulsions which eventually they were unable to control. Abigail had led her into that absurd pretense, absurd in every way except that it was taken seriously by their elders.

She remembered her fear and her pain at the hands of the judges at the trial of Goodwife Proctor, and she remembered trying, at long last attempting, to tell the truth, that there were no witches, that there were no devils possessing them, that it was all sport, all pretense, all a foolish and wicked game.

And she remembered Abigail leading the other girls in an accusation against her! She remembered casting herself at Abigail's feet, she remembered being sucked back into the lies and the evil and the murderous perjury.

It was Abigail, it was all Abigail, it was always Abigail!

She remembered that day in the forest, that day when John Proctor was hanged on the basis of her own perjured testimony, that day when Abigail, when *Abigail* forced her to give herself to Satan, when *Abigail* forced her to swear the oaths which would condemn her to eternal damnation, when *Abigail*, when *Abigail* turned her from a weak and foolish girl into a murdering witch.

It was *Abigail*, it was *ABIGAIL*!

She remembered the whoring in Boston, and it was Abigail's idea that they be whores. She remembered kidnapping and butchering the infants as sacrifices to the Dark Lord, and it was Abigail's idea that they offer up the bloody gifts. She remembered that moment in the abandoned stable, that last moment of her previous life, as they stood upon their tiptoes with nooses around their necks. She remembered Abigail pushing her backward, killing her as she killed herself. She remembered that it was *Abigail* who wanted to end their lives quickly, so as to have their second lives all the sooner, so as to have a second chance for a Proctor's love or a second chance at vengeance upon a Proctor, and it had been *Abigail's* love and *Abigail's* vengeance, not hers, not Mary Warren's.

She looked down at the terrified, trembling girl who lay bound before her. And this is what we were in such a hurry to do, she thought. To kill this kind, innocent child who never showed me anything but sympathy and generosity and love.

I have been two people, Mary thought, two people. I have been a quiet, shy, timid, pious little girl, and I have been a murdering Satanist whore. And what was the link, what was the bridge?

"Abigail," she muttered softly.

Not hearing her softly spoken word, Abigail Williams repeated for the third time, "Strike, damn you!"

Mary Warren was gazing down at the desperate, pleading face of Rowena Proctor as she slowly pulled the tip of the knife away from the girl's breast. She turned to Abigail and said, in a quiet but strangely firm voice, "No."

Abigail glared at her. "Mary Warren, I warn you—!"

"No," she repeated. "I'll not have more innocent blood on my hands." She threw the knife away, and it clattered loudly against the floor of the church, echoing starkly against the old wooden walls. "What the girl has said is true, Abigail," she said evenly and without fear. "I never made a choice without you, I never chose but with your threats and demands pressing upon me. But now I shall choose, despite you. I shall not kill her." She reached down and began to untie the ropes which bound Rowena to the communion table. "And neither shall you."

Abigail Williams stared at her furiously. "Shall I not!" she said and walked over to the spot where the discarded dagger lay.

"Abby, stop!" Mary commanded. "This is not sport! I am not pretending!"

"Ah, but this is sport indeed!" Abigail said. "Our dear Simon has said so repeatedly, haven't you, my love?" She looked over at Simon Proctor, who was sitting bound, weeping, shaking, terrified, horrified, in the front pew. "All a game, is it not?" she asked. Abigail bent down and picked up the knife. "All a delightful game!" She stepped over the ashes of Lucas Proctor and lifted the knife high above her head as she approached Rowena. "Get out of my way, Mary!" she commanded.

Mary was still laboring on the tightly tied knots. "No, Abby," she said. "You shall not kill her."

"Oh, but I shall!" Abigail laughed darkly. "And then I shall make you pay for this, Mary Warren, I swear I shall!"

"I have paid for all I have done," Mary screamed, spinning around and facing her, a sudden fury taking possession of her. "I have paid for everything you have done to me, for everything you forced me to do!"

"Your guilt is your own, you silly ass!" Abigail spat.

"My guilt, my sin, was in listening to *you*, Abigail," she cried. "I listened to you and sent innocent people to the gallows. I listened to you and I sold myself to the Devil. I listened to you and I killed babies in Boston, I whored on the streets, I took my own life!" From her anger she drew strength, and in the bitterness of her misery she began to move slowly, menacingly toward Abigail. "But not again, Abby, no more. You shall *not* kill this girl! I say you shall not!"

Abigail grabbed Mary by the hair and pulled her forward and then flung her out toward the pews. "Indeed! Well, watch me, then, Mary! Watch me!" She walked to the side of the communion table upon which the bound girl lay and raised the dagger once again high above her head, preparing to strike deeply, with all her strength.

A motion to her side distracted her and she paused as she glanced toward it. Mary Warren crouched slightly and then threw her arms upward as she leapt from the floor. Simon and Rowena watched in mute astonishment, their terror momentarily forgotten, as Mary seemed to shrink and shrivel in midjump, as her arms drew in close to her rapidly compacting body, as her head and legs shrank and grew thin and inhuman. In an instant Mary Warren was gone, and in her place a cawing crow flapped its wings in the air above them, a crow which rose slightly higher into the air and then dove at Abigail, its extended talons embedding themselves in her face.

Abigail screamed and fell back, away from the communion table, blood streaming from her cheek and forehead. She flailed her arms wildly at the bird as it withdrew and attacked, withdrew and attacked, again and again and again. The bird tore clumps of flesh from her face and arms, and its yellow claws were red with blood. Abigail managed to grab hold of the crow and throw it from her, and in that moment—before the crow was able to right itself, fly upward, and attack again—she crouched and jumped up at the rafters of the church. In an instant there was a raven circling the room, flapping its wings madly as it rose above the rafters and then attacked the crow. The crow flew to a higher position in the air and, still flapping its wings, raised its talons to meet the raven's attack.

The heavy thud which resonated from the rafters mingled with the cawing of the crow and the croaking of the raven as the birds slammed into each other, as their talons raked each other's wings, as their sharp, cruel beaks sought to tear at each other's shiny black breasts. They tumbled through the air, locked in combat, separating only to fly again into the heights and then resume the battle. Bloodstained feathers drifted gently down toward the floor as the birds stabbed and bit each other.

And then the crow managed to grab the raven's head in its talons and tore at it, sending the raven spiraling downward to the floor. It landed on its side, and its right wing broke with an audible snap. It tried to drag itself away from the incessant attack by scrabbling upon the wooden floor with its claws and one good wing, but it could not escape the determined crow. The raven crawled beneath a pew and then reassumed a human form. Abigail crawled out, her face torn and bloody, her right arm hanging useless from her side, a large section of hair torn from her head. The crow dived at her again and again and again, and Abigail tried to protect her face with her one good arm. At length she retreated on her knees into the corner and stayed there, battered, bloody, her wounded face contorted in fury.

The crow hovered near her and then seemed to expand downward without actually moving. It was as if the crow were dripping Mary's body down from its belly. In an instant the crow was gone and Mary, bloodied and breathing hard, stood there in its stead. "It is over, Abby," she panted. "It is ended."

"No!" Abigail screamed. "I shall have my vengeance!"

Mary shook her head. "No, not now, not ever."

Abigail turned her frenzied eyes to the three dead men whose bodies were leaning against the wall. "Seize her!" she shrieked. "Kill her!"

The limbs of the dead men began to move spasmodically, but Mary raised her hand and commanded, "Be at rest. Remain at rest." The bodies of Strube, Mahoney, and Herricks seemed for a moment to be shuddering, as if torn between two contending forces, and then each in turn fell forward and lay motionless upon the floor.

"Arise!" Abigail screamed. "Arise! Obey me! Obey me!" They did not move.

"Stop it, Abby," Mary said. "It is ended. Accept it."

"Never!" she shouted as she raised her left hand above her head. It looked to Simon and Rowena as if she were grasping at something behind her, but there was nothing there to grasp. And then Abigail thrust her hand forward as if to throw something at Mary. A fireball appeared out of nowhere and hurtled toward the other woman, who stood calmly in place, awaiting it.

Mary Warren raised her hands before her and held them palms outward. When the flaming missile struck her hands, it dissipated, it disappeared, leaving nothing but a smoky wake and a faint scent of fire. Mary shook her head. "It is useless, Abby. We are the same, you and I. You cannot destroy me."

"Nor you me," Abigail replied. "I can wait, Mary Warren. I have waited for centuries. I can wait longer. I shall have my revenge!"

"Never, Abigail," Mary said quietly. "It is ended. No more evil must be allowed to issue forth from us. We must surrender these new lives. We must return to—we must return to—" She could not bring herself to say the word. She simply sighed and said, "We must return."

"Not I, Mary Warren!" Abigail said. "I have another life to live, and I intend to live it—"

"And to do more harm to innocent people?" Mary asked. "To commit more murders? To continue to do Satan's bidding?" She shook her head. "No, I cannot permit it."

"You cannot permit it! *You* cannot permit it!" Abigail laughed incredulously. "You think that you have such power, Mary Warren? Why, you stupid little fool!"

Mary ignored her. She closed her eyes and spread her arms outward. Her body tensed as if she were bracing herself, and then she cried out, "Send us back whence we came! Our time is ended! Send us back whence we came!"

"Stop it, Mary!" Abigail shouted. "Stop it this instant!"

"Let it end here, let it end now! Send us back to the pit!"

"Mary Warren! Stop it!" Abigail struggled to her feet, wincing from the pain of her broken arm. "Stop it, damn you!"

"I surrender my life, I surrender her life. Our time is ended. Send us back whence we came!"

Simon Proctor had been sitting in silence as the strange conflict had progressed, his attention riveted upon the two witches. But a sound coming from the open door of the old church caused him to look away from them. He saw what was making the sound, and he screamed.

Two figures were slowly, stiffly approaching them from the door of the dark church, moving forward awkwardly but with determination. Simon blinked, fearing that the candles were playing a trick on his eyes. They were not. The approaching figures were precisely who he thought they were.

Karyn Johannson moved with an ungainly swaying motion up the aisle upon her broken legs. The baby was still hanging from her hair and the gouge in her flesh from belly to breast had been pulled even more horribly open by the movement of her shattered body. Her face was still frozen into the last shriek of agony which she had emitted before she died. Her dead eyes stared wildly, lifelessly, ahead of her.

Behind her, a black cleft in the forehead of his decayed and putrescent face, trailing ripped strands of rope from his wrists and ankles, his mouth still open and still covered with cold earth, was the Reverend Frederick Wilkes.

The dead approached slowly. They ignored Simon as they passed him, they ignored Rowena as they drew close to the corner near the pulpit where Abigail was cowering. Wilkes moved with a steady, stiffened gait. Karyn seemed to be stumbling from side to side but never faltered.

The two corpses came to a stop in front of Abigail, and then the body of Karyn reached out its cold hand and grasped her

343

by the wrist of her broken arm. Abigail screamed in pain as Karyn pulled her out of the corner, into the open space in front of the communion table.

"This is your doing, Mary Warren!" she screamed through her tears. "I'll not forget this, I'll not forgive this!"

Mary sighed. "Oh, Abby, don't you understand? I cannot allow you to do further harm, so our pact is void. We must return. We'll not be doing Satan's work upon earth, and so our second lives are forfeit. These poor things," and she waved her hand at the two walking dead, "are but escorts."

"It isn't too late, Mary!" Abigail screamed. "You and I can still—"

She shook her head. "It was too late for me centuries ago, Abigail. It was too late for me when I first became your friend."

Abigail tried to break free from Karyn's grip, but the mangled corpse seemed to be made of stone. It stood immovable, a statue holding Abigail tightly in its granitelike grip. Abigail soon ceased her struggle and stood, trembling, frightened, confused, staring at the frozen mask of agony which held her and returned her gaze with lifeless eyes. There was a profound silence in the old church.

And then, very softly and indistinctly, a voice could be heard drifting through the large, silent room. Abigail looked around her, attempting to locate the source of the voice, but saw no one speaking. Abigail looked to her right and blanched as she realized that the voice was drifting upward from deep within the body of Reverend Wilkes. But it was not his voice which spoke so softly and distantly, no words were being formed by his dead lips, no breath was being passed from the decaying lungs to the rotting vocal cords. The voice came from elsewhere, even though it drifted out from the open, speechless, dirt-encrusted mouth.

"A . . . bi . . . gail," the voice said.

Abigail Williams gasped, and a mighty shudder smote her frame. She looked around madly, seeking some other, *any* other source for the voice which addressed her, but she found none. The voice was most definitely coming from the body of the dead minister.

"A . . . bi . . . gail," the voice repeated, a bit stronger now.

"No," she said, "no, it can't be—it can't—"

"Abigail," the voice said, quite clearly and distinctly, though echoing slightly as if it were reverberating in the empty vessel of dead flesh.

"J—John?" she whimpered. "Is that you, John?"

"It is I, Abby," said the voice of John Proctor. "I am here."

She struggled to smile as she felt her heart rise up into her throat. "John, my dear, my love!"

"Nay," the voice said, "never that, Abby. A sinner and a fool, a weakling and a blind, silly man, but never your love."

"But you are here, you are come to me in some manner," she said hopefully. "The Master has released you to me!"

The corpse moved its head slowly, awkwardly, from side to side, in pathetic imitation of a living man shaking his head. The putrid skin ripped and cracked upon its neck as it moved. "We serve different masters, Abby. I speak to you from this body because my Master forbids the eyes of the damned to behold the forms of the blessed."

"Wh—what are you—? I don't understand," she stammered.

"Mary has been heard, Abigail," said the voice of John Proctor. "You must return whence you came. Mary has surrendered your life."

Abigail renewed her struggles against the relentless grip of the dead girl. "No! No! 'Tis not true! I have another life, another chance! The Master promised! Mary cannot break the Master's word!"

The cold, dead, lifeless eyes stared blankly at her as the voice replied, "There is a balance between the two worlds, Abigail, between the world of eternity and the world of time. You and Mary left eternity together. If she returns to eternity, you cannot remain in time."

"But the Master gave his word!" she screamed. "It isn't fair! It isn't fair!"

"Mary has been heard," the voice of John Proctor repeated. "She has surrendered her life. Yours is now forfeit."

A strange smell began to permeate the room, and Simon, who had been watching the strange scene wordlessly, his eyes wide with fear and wonder, crinkled his nose. It smells like something. . . . I can't quite place it. . . .

Then he recognized the odor.

It was sulfur.

A reddish glow was becoming visible, a ruddy circle beneath the spot upon which Abigail stood in Karyn's relentless grasp. The wood of the old church floor seemed to fade into nothing, not to burn up but merely to fade, as the glowing circle became a platform of flame which rose up around the knees of the two women, the one living and the other dead. "No!"

345

Abigail cried as the flames licked up at her. "NO, wait! It isn't fair!" She and Karyn seemed to be sinking into the sulfurous circle, descending slowly into the flames. "NO! NO! I HAVE A LIFE TO LIVE! I HAVE A LIFE TO LIVE!!!" She and the corpse sank downward inch by inch and Abigail felt the sulfurous atmosphere of the depths crawl up and tear into her flesh, burning and blistering her. "HE PROMISED ME!" she shrieked. "HE PROMISED ME ANOTHER LIFE!"

"Even as you surrendered Mary Warren's life to Satan three hundred years ago, so today has she surrendered your life to him." The voice of John Proctor paused. "And so the circle is closed."

"BUT HE PROMISED ME ANOTHER LIFE!!!" The flames burned into her terrified face. "HE PROMISED ME ANOTHER LIFE!!! HE PROMISED ME!!! HE PROMISED ME!!!"

"The Devil," the voice reminded her, "is the father of lies."

Abigail Williams emitted an ear-rending scream of incredible agony as she sank out of sight into the billowing flames, and then the flames seemed to fall in upon her, away from the surface. The glowing circle began to fade and the wood floor began to reappear. In a moment, the glow was gone, the odor had dissipated, and the old church was filled with silence.

Mary Warren felt her knees weaken, for she knew that what she had just seen happen to Abigail was going to happen to her. She sank to the floor and began to weep as the body of Reverend Wilkes walked over to Rowena and snapped the thick ropes which were still binding her to the communion table. He tore the ropes free with one quick motion of his dead hand and then repeated the movement to free her ankles. The corpse turned and approached Simon, staring above his seated form with dead, empty eyes, and then the cold hands reached out and snapped his bonds. Simon knew that he should rush to his daughter and care for her, but he was too terrified to move.

The dead man turned to Mary and inclined his head toward her huddled form. There was an audible cracking sound as the bones of the dead man's neck bent forward. "Mary Warren," he said.

She looked up at the corpse's face through her tears. "I know, Mr. Proctor. I must return also. But I have stopped Abigail and I have saved Rowena. It is fair, it is just. I am ready to go."

And then the corpse of Reverend Wilkes began to glow

brightly. Mary gasped and threw her arms over her eyes, expecting a reappearance of the flaming gateway to the inferno, but the glow was not sulfurous. As the glow intensified, she looked up with dread at the face of the dead man. Rowena slipped off from the communion table onto the floor and watched in stunned fascination as the glow grew brighter. Simon, finding enough strength to move his legs, stumbled forth from the pew and crawled to his daughter. He enveloped her in his arms, and they watched wordlessly as the glow became almost blindingly intense.

The corpse fell backward onto the wooden floor. In its place stood a glowing phantasm, a rippling, translucent human form. Simon gasped. It was an image of himself.

His ancestor, John Proctor, smiled down at the frightened, weeping girl. The ghost asked softly, "Do you remember, Mary, when you were a child and read the Bible, what the Lord said about the greatest love?"

Mary Warren's memory searched back over the years, over the centuries, to her childhood in Salem. "I cannot," she said sadly. "I cannot. . . . I cannot remember. . . ."

"It was something Jesus said to His disciples shortly before He was crucified," the ghost reminded her. "'Greater love hath no man than this, that a man lay down his life for his friends.'" He paused, allowing the words to penetrate her fear and sorrow. "And do you remember the parable of the man who hired workers for his fields and paid those who worked but a little time the same wage as those who had worked the entire day?"

Mary Warren began to weep even more bitterly. "Do not play with me, Mr. Proctor," she cried. "I do not understand you."

The ghost knelt down and took her hand in his. His touch was cool and soothing. "You chose to do what was right, Mary Warren, with no hope for forgiveness, no hope for reward. Though you were convinced that you were eternally lost and abandoned by God, you made a moral choice." John Proctor smiled at the frightened, confused girl. "You made the right choice." He was silent for a moment. And then he spoke again.

"You are absolved."

He stood up and opened his arms to her. Mary gazed up at him with disbelief and then, a cry of joy bursting through her tears, she jumped to her feet and threw herself into the spirit's embrace. He hugged her tightly to his bosom and looked over at Simon and Rowena. "Are you too old to learn lessons, my descendant?" he asked.

Simon tried to say something, but no words came from his lips. Rowena answered for him. "He isn't too old to learn."

"Then learn," the ghost warned him. "He who has ears to hear, let him hear." He hugged Mary more tightly and then they both faded away into nothing, dissolved into the silent emptiness of the old church.

Simon and Rowena did not move for a long while. They remained huddled in an embrace upon the floor in front of the communion table as the first rays of the morning sun drifted in through the cloudy windows of the church. They wept and did not speak. Simon wrapped Rowena in his coat, and together they stumbled out onto the still-empty street of the still-sleeping town, making their way wearily and painfully back toward the old inn.

Once inside they went into the sitting room, too exhausted and too numbed to attempt the stairs, and fell into a deep sleep, Simon on the floor and Rowena on the sofa. They slept through the morning, through the afternoon, into the night, through the night. Rowena was the first to awaken the following morning, the morning of February 2, as the sunlight streamed through the large window and bathed her face in warmth. Simon awoke also, moments later. They looked at each other wordlessly and then embraced again, and wept again.

It was February 2, which the church calendar names the Feast of Candlemas.

It is the festival of purification.

⟦ EPILOGUE ⟧

HARRY SCHROEDER COUGHED nervously as he sat on the waiting room sofa beside Rowena. He had been attempting to make light conversation with her all day and had found her chillingly unresponsive. He knew that she bore him no ill will, knew full well that anyone who had gone through what she had gone through would not be in the mood to discuss television shows, records, movies, or any of the other neutral topics which he had attempted to raise with her. He also knew that she was not cold toward him as a matter of conscious decision. She was distracted, understandably, and her distraction expressed itself in perfunctory smiles and curt, brusque responses to his meaningless prattle.

Schroeder looked up at the clock on the hospital wall. Three o'clock already, he thought morosely. I sure wish somebody else was around to ferry the kid back and forth.

He knew that there was not, of course. The details of the events which had transpired in Bradford were not clear to him, were not clear to anyone, really, but he understood enough to know that her boyfriend was dead, her brother and his girlfriend were missing and presumed dead, her grandfather was dead, the old minister was dead, the members of the band were dead. No one was left other than the girl and her father, and with her father being held here in the hospital, under court-ordered psychiatric observation, that left no one other than him to see to the poor girl's needs.

Her demands upon him were few enough, to be sure. As Simon's manager, he had limited access to Simon's bank accounts, so that he was able to provide Rowena with whatever money she needed from week to week. Inasmuch as she was seventeen years old, the fact that the court had appointed him as her guardian was a mere formality. She was to remain in Bradford, and he had neither the inclination nor the obligation to move to New Hampshire from New York. It was only on days such as this that his responsibility for the girl seemed inconvenient, when he was asked by her to drive her from Bradford to Boston, which entailed, of course, the six-hour drive from New York to Bradford, two hours from there to Boston, two hours back, and another six hours back home.

349

But there's nobody else to do it, Schroeder thought. After what the poor kid's been through, I can't very well tell her to hop on a bus.

"Miss Proctor?" the nurse said from behind the reception desk. Rowena rose quickly to her feet. "Your father is waiting for you in visiting lounge four. Please leave your purse with me, and I'm afraid that I must ask you to empty your pockets."

"Yes, I understand," she said, having gone through this each time she came to visit her father, both in Concord, where the court had originally assigned him, and here in Boston, where he had been remanded for extensive observation. Security measures, she thought. Makes sense from their standpoint. To them, Daddy is obviously a deeply disturbed man. Can't let him get hold of anything he could hurt himself with.

As she emptied her pockets into the small wooden box which the nurse had provided, Schroeder said, "Tell your dad that everything's going okay with the legal end of this. He should be out of here and home within a month, if everything works out right."

"That's great, Mr. Schroeder," Rowena said without enthusiasm. "I'm sure he'll be happy to hear that."

"Of course, nobody's gonna believe his story about witches and all that stuff. Sounds too much like a publicity stunt, and—well, you know your father's reputation and everything."

"I know," she said quietly as she handed her purse over for safekeeping.

"But with all the other evidence, the stuff that happened on the Campbell show, your own statements about those two crazy people—well, the lawyers think that the court's gonna just declare the whole thing homicide by person or persons unknown. I'm sure the cops'll keep looking for Gwen and Adrienne, but I doubt they'll ever find them."

Rowena laughed softly. "I'll go along with that, all right."

She began to walk toward the doors at the end of the corridor, and Schroeder walked beside her until they reached the sign which said Authorized Persons Only beyond This Point. "I know it was hard for you not to back your dad up at the hearing, but everybody understood your situation. I mean, when you started agreeing with him about all that supernatural stuff, the judge was very patient and tolerant."

"Yes, he was," she agreed, eager to go through the doors and see her father but not wishing to be rude to Harry Schroeder. She waited impatiently for him to finish his needless monologue.

"I knew that you'd tell the truth once the judge gave you a chance to change your story, without punishment or anything. I mean, if you were unconscious from the time of the car crash until after all the murders, you couldn't very well—"

"Yes," she interrupted him. "I had to say that, didn't I. I had to say that I didn't remember anything, that I didn't see anything, or else they'd have locked me up too, right?"

"Exactly," Schroeder replied, missing her point completely. "Well, you go and have a nice visit with your father, and I'll wait for you right here." He watched her walk through the doors, and then he returned to the sofa and sat down heavily. "Hope she hurries up," he muttered. "I'm too old to do all this driving around in one day."

He looked up again at the clock, and then shut his eyes. Maybe I can catch forty winks while she's in there. Couldn't hurt to give it a try. Probably won't be able to, though. I never have an easy time falling asleep. Probably prone to insomnia.

He was snoring loudly a few minutes later, his hands folded in his lap, his head leaning back against the sofa. An hour passed before he felt himself being gently shaken by Rowena. His eyes snapped open and he looked up at her with momentary confusion, and then he smiled. "Oh! Back so soon?"

She smiled. "I've been in there for nearly an hour, Mr. Schroeder."

"You don't say!" He rose to his feet and yawned, stretching. "I guess I must have drifted off for a while."

Rowena retrieved her belongings from the nurse and then she and Schroeder left the hospital and went to his car in the visitors' parking lot. As they got in and he turned on the engine, he asked, "How's Simon doing?"

"Fine," she replied, "just fine."

"You tell him what the lawyers said?"

"Yes. He was happy to hear it."

"Good. I figured he would be. What else did he have to say?" He began to drive out of the parking lot and onto the boulevard which bordered the hospital.

"Oh, this and that," she replied.

"Such as what?" he asked. "What did you two talk about for an hour?"

She laughed softly. "You really want to know?"

"Sure," he said as he stopped for a red light.

"Okay," she smiled. "He spent a good deal of time talking about predestination and free will, and the problem of

351

reconciling the need to obey a moral code with the doctrine of justification by faith."

"That's nice," Schroeder said, staring up at the traffic light, waiting for it to turn green. Some small part of what she had just said reached his brain and he snapped his head to his right and looked at her. "What? What did you say?"

She laughed again softly. "Daddy's been doing a lot of reading about religion lately, since—well, you know, since everything happened."

"Sure," he nodded. "That makes sense. A lot of people get religion when trouble happens. I mean, he just went through a real bad time."

"Mr. Schroeder, you have no idea," she muttered. She looked out the car window as Schroeder began to drive through the intersection beneath the now green traffic light. "Are you sure you can find the address?"

"Sure, no problem," he replied. "I checked it all out on a Boston street map yesterday, after you called me. We'll be there in a couple of minutes." He paused. "What's at that address, anyway?"

She shook her head. "I have absolutely no idea."

"Huh?"

"It's a long story," she said tiredly. "I'll explain it all to you someday. But for now, I just want to get there and—" She paused for a moment and then said quickly, "Mr. Schroeder, can you pull over for a minute? I want to get something from that store over there."

Schroeder obligingly moved the car toward the curb and came to a stop beside a fire hydrant. "Sure, Row. Whatcha getting?" But she was out of the car before he could finish his question. He watched as she entered a florist shop and emerged a moment later, holding a simple wreath made of roses, violets, and fronds. "What's that for?" he asked.

"I'll explain it to you sometime," she repeated.

"Right," he laughed. "It's a long story, right?"

"Right." She smiled and then turned away to watch the streets of Boston drift by.

Weird kid, Schroeder thought. Spends too much time in that little cemetery up there in Bradford. It isn't healthy. Probably bought those flowers to bring back and put on the graves.

But Rowena had already decorated the graves earlier that day, before Harry Schroeder had picked her up in Bradford and begun the drive to Boston. She had placed flowers on

Jeremy's grave, on the grave of her grandfather, on the grave of Reverend Wilkes, and on the grave where the charred remains of her brother had been placed. The graves would be unmarked for at least another week as the markers were carved and their names and dates emblazoned upon them. It was of no matter. She knew exactly where they lay in the old Bradford grave yard. She knew exactly where each one of them lay.

The bodies of Mark Siegal, Larry Herricks, Tom Mahoney, and Carl Strube had been claimed by their families and had been laid to rest in various places around the country. Someday, Rowena had decided, she would find out where they were buried and would visit their graves and leave wreaths, tokens of regret, acceptances of responsibility on the part of her family, past and present.

Simon had voiced a slight, tentative disapproval of her preoccupation with the graves, but he was understandably reluctant to make an issue of it under the circumstances. He had willingly paid for the funerals and the tombstones for Jeremy and Reverend Wilkes, and of course for Lucas, and had sent a veritable greenhouse of flowers to the funerals of his band members.

But no funeral for Karyn, Rowena thought sadly, no marker and no grave. She knew what had happened to Karyn's body and felt sadly certain that her soul and that of Lucas were in the same place. Rowena shuddered and shook her head. I don't want to think about that, she told herself. It's too horrible. Poor Lukie.

Traffic was heavy on Boylston Street, and nearly an hour passed before Schroeder broke into her reverie by saying, "Here it is, Rowena. Boylston and Francis. Which way now?"

"Left, Mr. Schroeder, up to that hospital in the middle of the block."

As Harry Schroeder turned left and drove up the steep incline of Francis Street he said, "A hospital? This is what you've been trying to find? A hospital?"

"Yes," she said, opening the car door as he pulled over to the curb. "I'll be right back."

"What do you want with—?" But again her speed at climbing out of the car left him without a reply. He shook his head in bemusement as the girl walked toward the entrance-way.

As she walked into the main lobby of Brigham and Women's Hospital, she remembered the difficulty she had had finding the entry in the old record books, the old colonial registries, the crumbling, yellowed volumes housed deep in the basement of the large municipal library in central Boston. But find it she did, after hours of effort: buried amid a hundred thousand other entries in the records of the old colonial constabulary, a notation dated January 5, 1702, to the effect that two women were found hanged to death in a stable. The identities of the women were unknown, but Rowena had known who they were, and she had known why they went into that stable to die.

It had taken her another month of painstaking research to discover precisely where the old potter's field of colonial Boston had been, precisely where the place was where they buried the bodies of the poor, the unknown, the unwanted, back in the early eighteenth century. Her persistence had again been fruitful, and she had at last found the information she needed. The potter's field had been paved over in the early nineteenth century. Homes and other small structures had rested upon it through that century into the next, and today a well-known, ultramodern hospital stood upon the ground into which the bodies of the miserable, the unfed, the unhappy, and the unloved had unceremoniously been cast back in the sixteen- and seventeen-hundreds.

As she stood in the center of the lobby and watched as the doctors and the nurses and the patients went about the business of healing and being healed, she could not but reflect upon the irony of it, that what was once the final abode of the unwanted dead was now a shrine to the enemies of death. Where once was nothing but dust and decay, now the struggle to prolong life was daily being waged. The ground which once held only the remnants of broken dreams and shattered lives, of lost hopes and bitter tears, now rested beneath a medical complex devoted to hope, to life, to dreams. She took another moment to look at the people who were going about their lives all around her, and then turned her attention away from them. It was not the living who had brought her here. Ignoring them, she looked down at the shiny floor of the hospital lobby.

Mary was down there somewhere. Somewhere in the earth beneath the floor of the hospital was the dust which had once been Mary Warren. Somewhere beneath Rowena's feet, beneath the hundreds of thousands of feet which had passed over this ground over the past few centuries, was Mary Warren's nameless, eternally unmarked grave.

Rowena knelt down in the midst of the bustle of people and

gently placed the wreath upon the floor. She stood up and gazed at it for a few moments and then turned and walked away. She knew that someone would in all likelihood kick the wreath out of the way in a short while, and then the custodial staff would surely sweep it up and throw it away; but she did not care. No one had ever placed a wreath on the poor girl's grave before. No one had ever known where she was buried, no one had ever cared where she was buried. But Rowena knew, and Rowena cared, and so Rowena had laid a wreath.

She walked out into the warm sun of the Boston summer, glancing over at the car to see Harry Schroeder watching her with quizzical concern. Then she looked up at the clouds which billowed white in the blue sky. "Rest in peace, Mary," she whispered. Then she walked back to the waiting car to begin the ride home.

ABOUT THE AUTHOR

JEFFREY SACKETT was born in Brooklyn in 1949, and counts himself fortunate to have made it home from the hospital unscathed. After studying briefly for the ministry, he chose to pursue an academic career—this being preferable at the time to his alternative, which was a year in the Mekong Delta as a guest of the government.

He obtained graduate degrees in history from Queens College and New York University, and also studied classical Greek, Latin, and several modern languages. Being thus possessed of a vast fund of fascinating but unmarketable information, he became a teacher of history and English, which he has remained until this day.

He explored other career alternatives at various times. He worked for a while as a bank guard (during which time the bank was robbed) and as a finder of missing persons (most of whom had disappeared by choice, and threatened him with all manner of violent reprisals when he found them). He decided that on the whole, teaching was his safest bet.

Candlemas Eve is his second novel. *Stolen Souls*, also published by Bantam, was his first. He is currently working on a third.

Sackett lives in a ridiculously overpriced house in Tanglewood Hills, New York, with his wife Paulette, an artist; their daughter Victoria Simonetta, an infant; their dog Paddington, a cocker spaniel; and their lizard Horatio, a seven-foot iguana. Theirs is the only house in the neighborhood with a sign saying Beware of Reptile on the fence.

Meet John Skipp and Craig Spector, writers at the crest of a new wave of horror.

"SKIPP AND SPECTOR GIVE YOU THE WORST KIND OF NIGHTMARES."
—George Romero
Director of THE NIGHT OF THE LIVING DEAD.

"THESE GUYS ARE AMONGST THE FORERUNNERS OF MODERN HORROR. SKIPP AND SPECTOR TAKE YOU TO THE LIMITS . . . THEN ONE STEP MORE."
—Clive Barker
Author of INHUMAN CONDITION

"SLAM-BANG NO HOLDS BARRED HORROR FOR THOSE WITH STOUT HEARTS AND STRONG STOMACHS."
—T.E.D. Klein
Author of THE CEREMONIES

☐ THE LIGHT AT THE END
25451-0 $3.95/$4.50 in Canada

It's bizarre graffiti splashed in blood.
Something evil is lurking in the tunnels beneath Manhattan.
Something horrible is hungry for souls.

☐ THE CLEANUP
26056-1 $3.95/$4.95 in Canada

His name is Billy Rowe. Yesterday he was just another talented loser who was chewed up and spat back on the streets. Today he discovered the *Power*. Now he has a mission. Now there is nothing left to fear. Nothing but Billy Rowe.

☐ THE SCREAM
26798-1 $3.95/$4.95 in Canada

Welcome to the heart of the Nightmare!

Look for them at your bookstore or use the coupon below:

- -